Hardscrabble Books — Fiction of New England

G. F. Michelsen, *Hard Bottom*

Anne Whitney Pierce, *Rain Line*

Kit Reed, *J. Eden*

Rowland E. Robinson (David Budbill, ed.), *Danvis Tales: Selected Stories*

Roxana Robinson, *Summer Light*

Rebecca Rule, *The Best Revenge: Short Stories*

R. D. Skillings, *How Many Die*

R. D. Skillings, *Where the Time Goes*

Lynn Stegner, *Pipers at the Gates of Dawn: A Triptych*

Theodore Weesner, *Novemberfest*

W. D. Wetherell, *The Wisest Man in America*

Edith Wharton (Barbara A. White, ed.), *Wharton's New England: Seven Stories and* Ethan Frome

Thomas Williams, *The Hair of Harold Roux*

HOW MANY DIE

R. D. Skillings

University Press of New England

HANOVER AND LONDON

Published by University Press of New England, Hanover, NH 03755
© 2001 by R. D. Skillings
All rights reserved
Printed in the United States of America
5 4 3 2 1
CIP data appear at the end of the book

And grief's hardly

more pitiable than joy.

—AESCHYLUS

Contents

HOW MANY DIE

1

ORIGINS

B Y MIDDLE AGE Edith Pelham dwelt at a discreet remove from her only offspring, Julian, b. November 1969, no less an enigma than his father, Eduardo Esmeralda, a steely interloper her patrician parents had despised at first sight, who had decamped with a few, loose hundred thousand dollars in 1975.

No trace of him remained on the leafy estate in rural Connecticut, where he had idled in restless rancor as the Vietnam War laid waste the brave vista of the self-proclaimed American Century.

Herself an only child of only children, Edith had resumed her maiden name, never mentioned the vanished man, devoted her days to the sun, wintering on chaise longues at a succession of southerly windows, in summer dragging an old aluminum recliner in a more voluptuous arc of sequestered recesses around the outside of the house.

Besides solar balm and solitude she wanted only gothic romances, crossword puzzles, cocktails at dusk and pills, episodes of nearly catatonic anomie being the sole ill effect of her abandonment. She had ample income, providing she rationed extravagance, especially cruises, that inveterate recourse of widows in similar circumstances, which in any case she was generally too languid or sedated to crave. To end alone, she told sympathizers and suitors alike, was not the worst that could befall a woman.

Julian had a docile childhood, but at sixteen began to behave peremptorily and do poorly in school. According to his principal, "He was just too precocious in his imagination."

Never a rude or angry boy, without Edith's cognizance he had grown willful and preoccupied—less sociable even than she was herself, nor did she see many other children to compare him with, nor had she ever had much use for youth.

He grew suddenly, rapidly fat. "I want to see how big I can get," he said. At any hour he might be found in a silk bathrobe eating bowls of carbonara, cartons of cannolis, cans of cashews, cakes, quarts of ice cream, pizza-size omelettes. Once school was out, he had no need ever to leave the precincts, no hindrance to full-time, pensive expansion.

Mrs. Pelham hummed ti-dum, ti-dum, ti-dee about the house, adjusting drapes and windows to sun and breeze, keeping her peace while he made an end of the doe-eyed, slender, darkly beautiful boy, who had never, as all observed, much favored either parent.

After several days of separate lives in their spacious domain, she would be distressed to hear his heavy breath before he waddled through the door. By summer's end his weight at 250 pounds, whose normal was 115. There was no question of his going back to school; the day came and went, unheeded by either.

"This must be dreadful for your heart," she ventured, wincing at his sweat-beaded brow. "What makes you so perverse?"

"Research calls for sacrifice," he said with a dauntless shrug, but by Christmas he was a bit downcast, sunk on the couch, like a dyspeptic sumo idol with an overloaded plate in his lap.

"You know," she mused one day, slyly offhand, "I do believe your looks may be gone for good."

Whereat he ceased to eat, was soon bound for ethereal slimness. "Way stations to nowhere," he said with renewed cockiness.

She shared her vitamins while mulling how to impede this new, more menacing caprice. Impossible to play on his vanity, for his tubercular air was alluring. Transfixed and mute one moment, the next he was taken by tongues, unable to shut up or even slow down, words hurtling headlong, like "souls into hell," she re-membered from some long-ago sermon, his language English of a sort certainly, but peculiar, a garble of intergalactic lore—tita-nium robots with silicon brains, autonomous planets with cities inside, reverse time, curvatures of space, flight from cycles of crunches and bangs—foolishness nonetheless preferable to his juvenile obsession with weight.

He was, after all, just a dreamy kid with a right to his own ideas. She herself could not say what lights in the sky might mean, or how history came about, nor why people did as they did, and she half heard without demur his fantastic depictions of worlds within worlds beyond distance and time.

To her relief and his apparent disgust, his fasting did not last. Appetite won out. He had a few ravening days of gloomy defeat, then in better humor seemed to accede to the constraints of the flesh. Mrs. Pelham was just settling back into their old, by and large satisfactory routine of ignoring each other except in matters of immediate, practical moment, when he interrupted her re-newed pursuit of tranquillity to report that he had been abducted one night she could not by any means recall herself. In this gap of mutually missing time he had been siphoned cell by cell through a beam of light into a translucent, multidimensional space module, and altered in his essence. The memory had just surfaced, but it was not an uncommon experience, merely a preparation already undergone by thousands of humans, perhaps millions, pending enlightenment of the planet by bodiless beings, who roamed the universe at the speed of thought.

After two minutes or so of this, she hummed ti-dummed her end of presence hum, pulled the hem of her skirt further up her shapely thighs to catch the late sun, and picked up her book again. But when he ran on regardless, to the effect that he was no longer a mere earthling but a graft from a vastly advanced civilization, with unimaginable technologies and totally different laws of phys-ics—mind and matter being interchangeable shells of a prior, primitive phenomenon—she deemed it time to intervene.

"Perhaps you ought to do something," she suggested, "since you've given up school."

"Like what?" he wondered with scorn.

"Other people occupy themselves," she said, "I mean besides just thinking."

"Only because they have to," he observed.

"People do all sorts of things," she said. "They find a job they like. They fall in love and get married. They have children . . ."

"What's the point?" he said. "I'd rather wait and see if there's going to be a nuclear war first, because if The New Intelligence takes over in time everything will be so changed that nothing anyone's doing now will make sense."

"Would you like to see a psychiatrist, dear?"

"Cool," he said, brightening.

She took him to Dr. Merckers, who had helped her cope with the absconded Eduardo, the only man she had ever succumbed to. Neither analyst nor office had changed. He looked the same quizzical cherub with prematurely white, unruly hair, wire-rim glasses, manicured hands, and immaculate, tan suit. His walls still offered the eye only the same large photograph of his wife, no less ageless and placid, holding a bouquet of fat peonies.

In the confusion of choosing chairs with Julian, aware of her quickening relinquishment of will, Mrs. Pelham's knees felt a sort of rolling below, like setting out to sea, or perhaps regaining terra firma, she wasn't sure, though by the time she withdrew to the anteroom with its pile of *Travel and Leisure* magazines the doctor's familiar courtesies, so casual and cordial, yet astute, had renewed her hopes that human happiness was attainable, if only one could avoid unhappiness.

Julian himself seemed pleased with his first session and thereafter twice a week drove alone to the village, always returning in voluble excitation, which lasted until he smoked a joint and became withdrawn again.

"Should you smoke so much, dear?" she inquired.

"It's only marijuana," he said. "I quit cigarettes and booze two years ago. It only takes a few tokes to get high, and it's much better for the lungs than tobacco."

"Even so," she murmured. "It must be expensive."

"Not really," he said. "I grow it out behind the barn."

"I never knew that," she said, taken aback at his enterprise.

"I didn't want to worry you," he said.

"Thank you, dear," she said, a bit dryly.

"Dr. Merckers wants me to cut down," he conceded. "I really like it though, it helps me think."

"*That's* what worries me," said she, fearful that morbid states came of introspection, as in her marital mishap, a thing in the long run doubtless a blessing.

TIMOTHY MERCKERS was struck by the boy's steady intensity. He seemed avid for guidance, lacking resentments, not at all fraught with loss, glad in fact to have no father, at least not the vanished one, whom he described as surly and cold. Edgy among his adopted resorts, he shrugged at his claims of special experience, disowned them without ado. Who he was, or rather, what he should become, was the real question.

The doctor himself began to be tried by the eager transference. Julian sat forward on his seat or lolled back in ravishment, absolute in his attentiveness, and very smooth-skinned.

Invariably the top button of his shirt was undone, affording a glimpse or—worse—the intermittent possibility of a glimpse of olive-hued throat and breast. Loath to terminate the face-to-face, Dr. Merckers prolonged the preliminaries, until one night he dreamt of them progressing to the couch together, and heard Mrs. Pelham croon, "Joolian, Joolian," then his own mother's spectral lament, "Johnny, Johnny Boone, they were like twins. Johnny Boone and Timmy. It's so sad Major Boone got posted away, just when they'd made such good friends."

He recalled the commonplaces his mother had helped him write, the pathos of school vacation dates, then the strange signature T I M M Y in bird-track capitals that meant nothing more than Johnny Boone's best friend, and last the stamp's gummy stickum on his tongue.

For a while notes on blue stationery replied in Johnny's hand, with the wistful assurance of his mother's promises of a visit some day soon, and then the blue envelopes came no more.

Timmy had written and waited, written and waited, but his third-grade friend had gone into the void. Now, fifty-five years later, Dr. Merckers could conjure nothing—no face, no voice, not a single moment of their brief idyll—nothing but the radiance of the name Johnny Boone, dormant but undiminished bereavement of his own psyche that never since had felt wholly at one with another human being.

At their next session he told Julian that little could be expected of the therapy, that occasional mismatches occurred, but were injurious only if perpetuated. Dr. Cassandra Edenswald would be just right for him.

Pausing not quite without pity at the thought of vibrant Xandra taking possession of this cupid born to torment her, he saw Julian's face fall.

"You'd prefer a man?" he said, very bland.

"Yeah," Julian said, ill-humored for the first time in his purview.

Timothy Merckers crumpled the leaf from his desk pad, upon which he had written her phone number, and dropped it into the empty, resounding wastebasket.

He wrote another name, folded the square once, thrust it endwise at Julian like a ticket. "Try to attach yourself to reality," he said humbly, "and develop a philosophy of life. Dr. Occifento, now I think again, is the right one for you."

JULIAN TOLD his mother that Dr. Merckers had pronounced him "only a little bonkers," in no need of further tinkering.

That didn't sound quite right to Mrs. Pelham, though she was glad to inter her doubts without autopsy.

Moreover, Julian had stopped smoking pot, looked superbly healthy, if a bit lackadaisical, and was often absent from the end of supper till breakfast next noon, keeping, as he called them, his "vampire hours."

"Did you have a nice time, dear?" she would inquire.

"Not too bad," he would say.

She was so thankful of his approach to normality that she was able to ignore the situation in the barn, a hay-smelling, old behemoth, now filling with household implements—toasters, blenders, colanders, skillets, vacuum cleaners, coffee grinders, juicers, grills, electric can openers, knife sharpeners, bathroom scales, a litany of domestic existence.

Subsequent visits revealed only accretion, nor did she venture its mention, since no matter how bizarre his activities, when asked he always had an explanation equally unsettling .

UPON EXPULSION by Dr. Merckers, Julian had felt the need to build something, but what? On impulse—he could not have rendered motive or rationale—he undertook to weld a grand ziggurat of gadgets to be inset with altars dedicated to gods he had yet to invent.

He got caught red-handed with what were described as "burglarious tools," and his scheme came to a muted end, thanks to the police chief, whose imperishable flame for Mrs. Pelham was fed by her faithful, flirtatious remembrance of his chivalry once many years ago in lugging her groceries to her car in a downpour, then borrowing an umbrella to keep her dress and coiffure dry.

He knew Julian was no kleptomaniac. The boy was affectingly mortified and vague, very vague; gravel-throated Dr. Merckers provided technical explanations and assurances; the *Village Weekly* printed a short, dry report of a sort of extended prank, restitution promised; and with no little difficulty and embarrassment at least some of the loot got returned with apologies, although an unclaimed, untraceable smattering remained, eventually causing Mrs. Pelham to giggle helplessly when she thought of it.

By then it was clear that left to his own devices he might like his sire become an out-and-out idiosyncrat. He brusquely declined further counseling, shied from every ordinariness, seemed to have no life outside the house. Sunk in chagrin he hardly spoke, lived the whole next summer with the iron rule of a monk, baking naked on the roof by day, playing in the basement with his paints between dark and dawn, till he was swart, bleary-eyed, and muttering to himself, which state Mrs. Pelham called "nobody home," and did not hesitate to assign to the same implacable bent for excess.

Still she forbore. The basement was a mess, his daubings deplorably many, vulgar and unseemly, phallic fountains of sperm, cannons on gonad wheels, petal-like whatnots—in garish acrylics —and she made but one clandestine investigation, then suppressed further interest, for if no one else saw them, what harm?

His tan, nearly as deep as hers, was a happier matter, his first unequivocal triumph. His whole sleek person glowed evenly on every inch of skin—armpits, insteps, back of the knees, under his chin—stunning in its absolute, dark dazzle.

The exquisite and exotic eased her acceptance—secretly she was not displeased—of the feminine persona he began to affect. He would appear late at night in a white gown and aura of perfume, nails painted, shining hair piled high, earrings a-glimmer. At first he borrowed her jewelry, but soon acquired his own—whence she refused to ask. His late-night fashion shows became frequent as fall came on; she could not fault his taste, and so long as he did not leave the house thus adorned she did not mind.

Amid the snows of February, as Julian, tan sadly faded, was consoling himself with mukluks and furs, an abominated mole upon the comely slope of his left pectoral muscle, the only visible flaw he possessed, suddenly began to act up. Strangely pigmented, bifurcated like a valentine, it grew larger, keeping its emblematic cast, by the end of March had become sore and rough with tiny, encrusted bumps that oozed, nor would it heal with the help of antiseptics and unguents.

The doctor without waiting for a biopsy ordered it removed. Grave and matter-of-fact, he sketched for the sobered matron and silent son the pathology of melanoma, laid an eternal ban on sunbathing—since childhood Julian's one sure way to rest his mind—at the end of six months pronounced him provisionally cured, but consigned to self-vigilance and shade.

THE SCAR SHRANK to an inch of candle wick, a chasm of fear —the longer the cancer didn't come back, the less likely a recurrence—which vastly intensified Julian's normal narcissism, prolonging his daily dalliance with the mirror. He looked up the word provisional, the first time he had ever used a dictionary: It did not mean problematical, but temporary. He did not know if the doctor knew the difference. Every day, every week, every month that went by, he stood on safer ground, but never again would ever be safe. He told no one of these milestones, his relentless sense of immanence; who was there to tell, except his mother, who had her own bright fear?

He now painted with large, apocalyptic apprehension, finishing with frightening speed every second or third day a horrendous new canvas of an erection in the guise of something else, meanwhile perfecting his female persona.

When his mother observed that he painted nothing but penises he said, "Sex is the least of what I mean."

Pointless paradox could not allay her misgivings when she learned he was planning an exhibition in a new gallery in the village, with intent to preside at the opening himself, doubtless in high attire.

That Julian had tendencies neither doubted. She declined to picture the practice of Greek love, which she had been raised to regard as nothing to speak of, especially if it remained a platonic, English public school sort of prelude to maturity and marriage.

But when Julian began a new series of paintings of moon-like lawn fannies, pairs of bare, spread buttocks with lipsticked anuses, she bethought herself of one Murray Humber, the bearded son of friends of friends, who had moved to Provincetown, Massachusetts to paint, twenty years before, and met and married a poetess there.

By ordinary standards this would have been Julian's high school graduation spring, and it occurred to her now—she broached the notion with trepidation—the place might supply him with a congenial milieu and edifying elders.

To her delight he was not averse, and dropped his show in the village with a shrug. He knew the name Provincetown—if nothing else—but got a vertiginous presentiment when he opened an atlas and found the printed word in tiny letters curving out into the blue sea from the tip of the great, embracing peninsula.

MRS. PELHAM pulled herself together, put off her appointments, packed a trunk for Julian with male clothes only, and at noon, July 11, 1987, took to the road.

Arrived toward the dinner hour, ensconced in the Holiday Inn, they set out to peruse the town in Mama's immense Cadillac, inching the narrow neck of Commercial Street, thronged with the exodus of Tea Dance.

Slowly they rode to the breakwater, then past the sunlit salt marsh, and back along Bradford, till finally by blind, first-timers' good luck they found a parking space, and after only a short wait got a window table at the Lobster Pot.

Mrs. P treated herself to a second double gimlet, courting a pang of appetite, while Julian drank Perrier and sampled the bouillabaisse, glancing from the glassy bay to the nimble waiters swiveling among the packed tables.

Of the town his mother had an impression chiefly of flowers, flowers everywhere, pastel-painted, clapboard houses cluttered with dormers, and hordes of tourists. The place seemed carefree, busy and benign, if rather too fond of sun.

"Don't worry," Julian said. "For me it's Southern pallor and parasols."

Back on the crowded street, after some cold shrimp and black coffee, she found the growing multitudes ingratiating. At the redolent door of the Governor Bradford, with belle's impudence aged to hauteur and heightened by gin, she asked a loiterer, "Where's the art colony?"

The man wore a grimy baseball cap backwards, had a stubble beard, squinted at her, then turned his head slightly to one side and squinted fiercely, as if the low sun had got in his eyes, or he were stumped for an answer.

"Come on," Julian muttered, pulling her arm.

But still she stood, a shortish, plumpish, much made-up dowager, in butterfly glasses, shiny pumps, and yellow dress a bit snug, and obstinately, insinuatingly, put her hands on her hips.

"Which way?" she demanded in pidgin, as if he were dimmer than he pretended.

He turned his unrelenting face toward hers again, and continued to squint, not exactly *at* her, but in some definite, personal vicinity, his mouth working, doubtless rehearsing a comeback.

She smiled implacably, raised an eyebrow, and waited with zest while Julian sidled off a bit and pulled a martyred grimace.

The man's glower and mouthings having merely made Madam's eyebrows climb the higher, he finally asserted his right not to suffer dolts on this side of the bar. Never meeting her gaze, giving only the least hint of a shrug, succeeded by an equally inconspicuous, circular action of one hand left hanging, like turning a faucet on and off, he took a last gander at the crowds, grunted and went back inside to finish his end-of-shift drink.

"Who was that?" asked his companion.

"Who knows? They get crazier every year," said he.

Julian dragged his snorting parent to the car, drove back to the Holiday Inn, settled her, invincibly complacent, before the TV, and hiked back into town.

Amid the mob, he wandered up and down, then sat on the benches in front of Town Hall.

Immediately a young man swerved into the empty place beside him, gripped the bench with both hands, shook his head balefully, said, "Where y'all from?"

"Connecticut," said Julian.

"West Virginia," the young man said. "I've been here a month, I've had five different dishwashing jobs, I couldn't stand any of them. Know some place I could crash?"

"I just got here myself," Julian said.

"Good luck!" the young man said. His eyes darted, his head jerked left and right, he kept his white-knuckled grip on the bench. "One thing I do know. I don't have to follow my dick. I'm not a slave, I'm a free man, I can go without, I can wait, I can wait five years if I have to, but I'm not going to be led around by my dick, I don't care how desperate I get. I'm in control here, not my damn dick."

Julian, nonplussed, plausibly nodded.

"That's why God gave me a brain," the young man said. "Know what I mean? Take my advice."

And he sprang up suddenly, rushed onward, turned back, gave an embarrassed laugh, "If you luck into anything let me know," and went the other way.

Julian marveled at the many, very many homosexuals in view. In fact there were three now, and there were four, and there, just milling along, were too many to count. The females, now he took notice, were likely lesbians, though he had never seen one out before. Everyone seemed to be holding hands. This was going to be gay indeed.

THE NEXT MORNING, finding a vacancy sign on a well-kept, white house on a privet-lined lane north of Back Street, he was shown a small room by a cold-eyed lady with tightly curled, white hair and genteel speech.

Everything was clean, smelled of fresh paint, and the fixtures of the bathroom down the hall shone intimidatingly.

"I hope you're not a messy person," she said. "The previous tenant got sick, he was very quiet, he was here almost three years, he had to go home."

"Oh no, I'm extremely neat," Julian said. "I don't drink or smoke."

Mrs. Gurley nodded, relenting a bit. "You'll find the sun porch very pleasant."

"Thank you," Julian said.

"You could paint in the shed. Our sons used it for a workshop but they've been gone for ages and it's nothing now but waste space for my husband's rubbish, the accouterments of his life so-called," she said with a grim little sneer.

"Great," said Julian, and got moved in by noon.

MAMA PHONED the Humbers, and got an invitation for what she presumed would be cocktails, but proved to be Soave in water glasses, leftover cheese rinds, carrot sticks, and some pungent babaganoush, which Julian gobbled.

Mrs. P hated wine, nevertheless quaffed several alert refills, while Jane and Murray politely nodded at Julian's cascade of opinions and plans. She gazed about, unsure what to think. They were crowded at the kitchen table, the only piece of furniture not dribbled with paint. There was no dining or living room, just the one all-purpose space, rather dusty and dingy, with spider webs in the corners and moths on the screens. Murray's studio looked as jumbled full as a flea market compacted by a snowplow. She could not imagine how he got in, being none too slim. Through another door a bedroom lay, evidently Jane's domain, with a desk made of a door with a cloth-covered typewriter on it. But there was really no room to move about because of the books, cases and cases of them, spilling over, piled in corners, shelved all the way to the ceiling on every wall, and it occurred to her that they must share some fetish, not a bit healthy. Still, who knew what might not make a marriage work? And they themselves were quite nice, and strangely authoritative.

"You seem to have found your theme," Jane said as she and Murray held Julian's slides up to the skylight one by one.

"Sell like hotcakes," Murray grumbled. He was leery of this overwrought naif, and the mother gave him the creeps. What did she want?

All she said the whole time was that she had bought a sixty-pound abalone shell lamp because she always liked to bring home a souvenir from everywhere she went.

At seven the Humbers wished Julian good luck, watched the preposterous pair descend the steep steps, Mama a little precariously, waved the mammoth Cadillac out of sight, went back inside, rolling their eyes.

"This kid's going to get AIDS," Murray said gloomily.

"He's awfully young," Jane said. "Is he gay?"

"I don't know," Murray said. "He's a . . . I really don't know."

"He's certainly strange," Jane said.

"He's flying pretty high," Murray said.

They put the pasta water on and finished the liter of wine.

"I'm *not* going to be father to that boy," Murray roared.

THIS TIME there were lines at every restaurant, night was coming on, the street burgeoning. In the strolling throngs they eddied a little way east, then a little way west of the benches.

At the Crown and Anchor three glittering drag queens raucously hawked the evening's first performance. "It's show time, Ladies and Gentlemen, it's *show* time."

"I think I'll just go back to the motel," she decided. "We may as well say good-bye now. I'll be on the road early in the morning, and you can sleep late."

Julian with constraint bent to kiss her forehead, hesitated, then started west very slowly, glancing back once, twice, at last lurched on, gangly despite his small stature, and was lost in the mob. An awful pathos bit her heart, she could not say just why.

At the motel she couldn't get comfortable. It was humid, hot, dank and chill. She closed and opened windows to no avail. There was nothing she could stand on TV. Too depressed to get undressed and put on her nightgown, she sat thinking of the mauled baby rabbit she had rescued from the cat as a child, nursed for a week and finally let go — hop, hop and stop, hoppety-hop into the deep grass. How sad, how bereft she had felt!

She wished now she had said more than just good-bye, something more . . . more . . . comprehensive! But she couldn't remember his address, nor his landlady's name, nor could she visualize the house, nor how to get there, only the high, bee-bustling privet hedge, and how could she ever find him, lost in the crowds?

In panic she packed and fled the unendurable room, leaving the door open, lights on. At Snail Road, before turning onto Route 6, she swallowed a precious black beauty with a slug of sherry from the silver flask she kept in the glove compartment.

Their instantaneous beneficence cozied her for the long ride. Passing Pilgrim Lake, she decided that the dim silhouette of the dunes looked like a medieval king on his bier, and suddenly her house in Connecticut rose in her mind's eye, without doors or windows, solid and ghostly as a mausoleum beneath a red, sickle moon.

In dread she let up on the accelerator. The perfectly tooled sedan coasted in silence, hardly losing momentum, then she pressed the gas pedal again, till the needle hit 70, and she set the cruise control.

2

THE PASSING WORLD

THE NEXT MORNING Mr. Gurley, popular Jim Gurley of the glad girth, bon vivant and raconteur, despite his haste to quit the house, took time to take his tenant's measure, found the boy preternaturally alert. Even sober Jim loved a good palaver and the chance to tell a tale. His swashbuckler's belly swung as he spun a silken sentence out, elaborate and slow, in a low, effortless rumble that put Julian in a swoon. Marvelous too with what speed and quiet this top-heavy, white-haired reprobate could slip through door and gap in privet hedge at sound of heels on hardwood floor.

Mrs. Gurley gave Julian a cup of coffee with real cream from a silver service, and bemoaned the old days when the train went out on the wharf, where the Boston steamer docked daily. Everything was so romantic then, but now the hordes had come, and all was spoiled. She hoped some day he would paint her a nice picture of beach roses.

Julian promised to try, lauded her antiques, never let on that he was enamored of her husband, always hoping to waylay him at the gilt-lettered door of his desultory practice—James F. Gurley, Esq. —impatient for the magisterial ambulation past the meat rack every evening of the kindly jowls, button-popping belly, and oracular bass, steeped in nostalgia, smoke, and gin.

"Come along, young man," Jim would say. Even underage Julian was more engaging than his own two sons combined had been, who had shied from his flagrant paganism while they still remained at home.

Julian's introduction to old Provincetown came one evening when they chanced upon some elders in Pepe's otherwise empty pub. Hardly a murmur could be heard from the formal dining room, soon to close for the season, where waiters in nautical white fed the last of the elegantsia before they and their remittances took wing for the winter.

Jim Gurley was the youngest, the only native. The others, all born early in the century, by its midpoint had found their separate ways to Land's End.

O'Rooney had followed his wanton wife—as far as he could— but she had given him the slip at last, and had been sleeping now for two decades beneath a headstone incised with the name of her downfall and final flirtation.

O'Rooney lived on alone in their mildewed house, year by year mounting its walls with row on row of Franklin Mint Collectors' Plates. The expense debarred all else, and the commemorative discs themselves no longer gave him pleasure beyond a brief relief, nor dared he sell them off, even his initial, nuptial acquisitions, nor fail punctually to order a new one from each monthly catalogue, lest he die. He smoked a pipe with trembling hand, his face was mottled and splotched, he walked with difficulty on a cane, his bladder was a feeble thing, his pecker leaked and it was an arduous trip to the head for him, whose olden joy had been the Guiness, but who now confined himself to Paddy's, which packed more wallop than he wanted and lacked the nourishment of that rich stout, yet let him sit in peace. Learning Julian's avocation he bent a pleased gaze on him and prophesied in a brocaded brogue, "God bless your art. You'll live a long time here and do a lot of work."

Finn was lanky, dignified, and dry. He had fought in the Spanish Civil War, and lived in aftermath, embittered by the depravation of socialism by the Bolsheviks. Brezhnev's Afghan adventure had brought the ultimate ignominy, forcing him to endorse the Reagan plutocracy's policy of arming the mujahideen, though lately he found hope in Gorbachev's reforms. He and Jim jousted mildly, but had long since discounted each other's casuistries. Unrepentant, the former radical still quipped about the stint he had done in jail in 1965 for income tax evasion. He drank substitutes for absinthe abstemiously and chain-smoked yearly weaker, more tasteless brands of filter cigarettes, fearful of his hoarseness, hating his fear.

Alfred Dale, "entrepreneur extraordinaire," as the *Advocate* persisted in styling him, wished never to see his name in print again. Behind a white beard turning yellowish as beach foam, he had seen his schemes materialize beyond intention or surmise.

His adopted town, spurred by his ideas, had attracted wealth and priced out those he had meant to benefit, and now he set his faltering wits to reverse trends he had pioneered, crestfallen to find all projections dismal. He once had gloried in the power of money, now despaired that pure profit ruled blindly, and forgot the good he had done for the arts.

Ashingham from Idaho, the most pathetic in demeanor, the happiest in fact—a former dandy inhabiting a soiled blue blazer, polyester pants, and sandals—looked like a mad paranoid with wizened squint and cocked head, walking the streets like a crab, his back so bad he had to sidle sideways, peering up through eyebrow thickets. He had outlived three ex-wives, lost track of his thankless progeny, lost his memory, had ceased to care, quit of the manuscript designed to revolutionize all philosophical discourse, upon which he had toiled unremittingly, but never finished, though he had typed it through three hundred drafts.

In youth he had boasted of his coming fame, till mockery silenced him and he sought solace in fancy dress, by mid-life had achieved a modest sartorial distinction, but read and wrote in strict privacy, sustained by his brilliant future. One recent day, skimming here and there with horrified indifference, he found not one line, much less one page, worth printing.

Appalled by the miseries he had inflicted and endured for the sake of this foot-high pile of pages, he bore it to the garbage can, where he was stopped by a young man who castigated him for wasting paper, in disrespect of trees, and demanded he keep his squandered reams and use the back of them.

Ashingham disparaged the nature of the trash, whereupon the baleful youth—pale, unshaven, fierce-eyed behind wire-rim glasses—revealed a tender side, promised to read the manuscript and return it some day, with his impressions, if any, on pages of his own. A writer himself, he would be irresponsible to let it go to oblivion merely because its author was distraught; such works of the spirit, the boy insisted, were all that mattered in the end.

Ashingham acceded with vague thanks, a free man. From time to time he wondered what his first and only reader thought. Mostly though he just forgot and tended his garden, painfully stooping in the sun, bringing the most comely of his vegetables to his friends. He looked deranged, but no riper man ever met with his last days in Provincetown than Ashingham of Idaho.

For Julian they dwelt on bygone days. Nobody had any money of course and paintings served as payment in kind. Not a few tradesmen found themselves well invested when fame came to some late patron or friend. People got through the winters somehow, picking coal from the railway, and the fishermen always helped, the sea teeming then, the town smaller, people closer and kinder. Who in American art had not sooner or later come to Provincetown?

"I met Franz Kline standing in the middle of Commercial Street," said Alfred Dale in the reflective voice that had once effortlessly reached the furthest corners of Town Hall. "It was noon. He was dressed in an absolutely immaculate white suit and a Panama hat, but he had bare feet and he was drunk as a lord. He said, 'This is the hard part, the thinking. Painting's easy.'"

"Myron Stout could spend years on a single shape," O'Rooney said. "He never made two of anything, not like some assembly lines I know."

"Afon," said Finn, "was a Russian White in the Civil War. He had typhus so bad he got put in the morgue by mistake. The Reds captured the town and shot all the sick and wounded soldiers in the hospital where Afon had been. Then the Whites retook the town, and someone noticed he was still alive. He ended up here, painted his native landscape from memory, went mad and had to be institutionalized, but in his last years he was quite calm and everybody loved him.

"He always dressed like a harlequin. I saw him run out of his house, spread his cape, and embrace Edwin Dickinson—these two great artists meeting on the street in the middle of winter, not another soul in sight. God knows what Ed Dick thought, but that's the kind of place it was."

Ashingham recalled the twice exiled Hemmerd, an Alabama scion paid to stay away, who died and was buried without notice, having so decreed. But his relatives nonetheless got wind, and, abominating Provincetown even more than him, had his bones exhumed and brought home to the family plot in Florala.

"People with no roots here just disappear," Jim Gurley sadly said. "In the pink one week, next they've got that zombi shuffle. One day you realize you haven't seen them lately, then some year you can't remember the last time you even thought of them, and this is how they end, so far as you're concerned, a glimpse in the mind, a sensation, not even a name."

"Don't let him scare you," O'Rooney adjured Julian. "You'll have a great career here, and a most memorable wake, I'm sure."

He raised his whiskey in salute, dipped his tongue, and set the glass down again on the marble tabletop with a ring of certitude.

The others gravely joined the toast and Julian chewed the dregs of his third espresso. He felt a guest at a club of relics, sensed they meant to enroll him, but doubted they would like the life he had in view. Meanwhile, touched and exhilarated, he enjoyed their solicitude, envied their ease, their courtly deference, the common ground they stood upon. That this world was not his to inherit he did not rue. Who were they anyway? His greater future blazed beyond their twilight; the brash and bright were what he craved.

"We'll have a nightcap, dear boy, with thanks for your good company," Jim Gurley said, as they were making their slow way home. Hunched at the Town House bar, among middle-aged habitués, he seemed lachrymose, maundering, slurring his words and coughing, coughing, ungainly, unsteady on his feet, portly beyond excuse. By the time they got home Julian felt repelled, but as they parted at the hedge his tainted idol, tiptoeing toward the back door, sang out, with throbbing nonchalance, "Good night, sweet ladies, good night, good night," and won his heart again.

IN THE MORNING, leaving the house, Julian heard Mrs. Gurley's imperious accents soar, "There'll be no drunken slumber here!" and returning late in the afternoon, glimpsed Jim's monumental belly and grey face through the window of the rescue squad van as it eased up the unpaved lane, turned onto Back Street with a brief choke of the siren.

"A stroke," pale Mrs. Gurley told her anxious boarder, when she drove in at nine that night. He was conscious; his left eyelid drooped. He was out of danger but would have to stay in the hospital for a few days. He was comfortable. She looked done in, drank the tea and ate the toast Julian made her, gave heartfelt thanks, and went upstairs.

Each morning she put on her public face, dressed as for an outing, and drove up to Hyannis. She returned after lunch to say Mr. Gurley was convalescing, would soon be coming home. Julian did not ask to go along, and she, unaware they were more than formally acquainted, never thought to invite him.

The patient's progress could be gauged by his wife's reviving irascibility. The shock had put a tremor in her tone, distraction in her eye, but these did not last. Already he was able to receive visits from his "pards," as she called them, and Julian envisaged the elders he had met ringed round their sick friend's bed, scattered like leaves by her wintry arrival.

"If he was going to live like that," she scoffed, "what did he expect? Now a new regime begins." And she threw out his mermaid ashtray in the corner of the sun porch where he read his trashy books, scouted out every last cigarette, and poured the gin in the sink.

She meant to curb him back to health, once she got him home. The doctors had prescribed a Spartan diet, exercise, and calm. Julian trembled for him and felt treacherous when Mrs. Gurley cleaned out the shed, so he could get down to work. "I've been wanting to do this for years," she gloated.

"All of it," she affirmed to the two young men with the pickup truck, and everything went, if not to the dump, at least forever from Jim Gurley's ken. Clothes he never could have fit into again no matter what he ate, hats, boots, shotguns, fishing gear, posters, theatre props, sheet music, mildewed albums, memorabilia of the Kennedys and King, antique tools, billiard cues, umbrellas, canes, boxes and boxes of what not?

All went, the boys in haste lest Mrs. Gurley introduce some discrimination. But she had no second thoughts, and the moment they were gone took a broom to the cobwebs in the windows and a scrub brush to the wonderful workbench that ran the length of one wall.

Julian swallowed with dread, but the space made his heart soar.

"He sends you his best regards," she told Julian the next day with an air of surprise.

Julian winced again at the empty shed, but it was worry wasted, for the dispossessed man died during Mrs. Gurley's next visit.

He had been waiting for her, she felt sure, because the moment she got there he sat up and tried to speak, but only an awful gurgle came. His face was purple, his eyes bulged. She rang the buzzer, ran into the empty corridor, rushed back. His jaw still gaped, but the gurgle had stopped.

"I can't hear you, Jim," she cried.

The CPR team came and worked over him with astounding, bloody savagery, but couldn't bring him back.

In the end she could only kiss his hollow cheek, receive his wedding band, wallet, keys, watch, and change, and drive home. Everybody at the hospital was so nice, she said, and wept at last.

Then the house was all activity. The sons flew in from Duluth and Santa Cruz. Julian, in bitter grief, kept from sight, stayed home from the funeral, loath to intrude, with chagrin read in the *Advocate* that the church had overflowed in tribute to a beloved, native son.

The family departed. Julian set up his studio, gessoed some canvases, but was too disturbed to work. He painted a rose for Mrs. Gurley, but it resembled an anus, and he kept it for himself.

Within the week a Pakistani friend of Mrs. Gurley came for a few days to keep her company, and the visit lengthened out until he seemed a member of the household. He was suave and elegant, with flawless English politesse, and a most enviable wardrobe of loose trousers with long overblouse, which he only and always wore indoors. Once Julian saw him, through the open door of his room, down on his knees, no less unsettling than the tobacco reek that persisted on the porch. Whether he and the widow were lovers Julian could not tell, for their facade was smooth and cool as marble.

The three were discussing the future one warm November afternoon when a slight tremor shook the house.

"A jet," said Mrs. Gurley. "They like to buzz the town."

"America is a mighty military nation," said Ahmed.

Two more tremors rattled china in the pantry and made the hanging ivy swing.

They looked at one another.

Came several more jars, then an accelerating whomp, whomp, whomp, like a wrecking ball at the wrong house. They glanced transfixed from each to each as the phenomenon increased.

Ahmed with stealth went toward the hall, glancing out windows, then entered the bathroom, which occupied an alcove, while the concussions seemed to become a settled feature of the day.

He returned, bowed slightly. "It would seem," he murmured, "that a sodomy is being perpetrated against the kitchen wall."

The ruckus ended with a crescendo of laughter.

"That's all!" cried Mrs. Gurley. "Call a realtor, I'm getting out of here!"

3

FIRST LOVE, FIRST BLOOD

THE HOUSE SOLD the day it went on the market. Mrs.
Gurley's gratification instantly turned to indignance at the
song it had gone for. Coming from away—albeit forty
years ago—she did not mind telling her dismayed neighbors that
things up Cape at least still kept some semblance of sanity. By
year's end she owned a condo in Brewster, the old Gurley house
was under renovation, and Julian was houseboy, with room, board,
studio, and minuscule stipend.

Arthur Dowwer, the buyer, had spent the last eleven years inn-
keeping in Ogunquit. Lately bereaved, his sufferance of winters in
that staid resort was no longer enjoined. His age a provoking mystery, his shoulder-length, grey ringlets and somber visage in re-
pose foretold a larger reticence. He wore a ruby ring, silk blouses,
and now and then an apron, moved with formal matronliness,
took a flinty tone where morals were concerned, and at moments
parodied an arched, lubricious eye. Here he seemed to have con-
summated a final stasis, posed in his ample flesh, hand on hip, gazing out the window at his newly hung sign: The Madam's Maid.

"Providentially you," he told Julian, inspecting him from crown
to sole. "How's your health?" he inquired relentlessly like a refrain.

AIDS had been but a word to Julian. Of current events neither he nor his mother read much beyond *TV Guide*. As a child he had loved the fairy tales she read him, the more macabre the better, but by the time he was ten, art books and intergalactic comic strips totally engrossed him. Gaetan Dugas he would have presumed a misprint, Surgeon General Koop a mad Protestant preacher, Rock Hudson Doris Day's husband. The exodus for the National March on Washington in October barely gave him pause. His ignorance was armored by having never known sex-hatred himself, and his sympathies were rudimentary, retarded by his own untold terror, and his hardening ego, grown ambitious and aloof.

"More funerals than brunches," someone half joked, and indeed Julian's first professional notice came via the squat silver penis with vibrant, red dorsal vein, painted against a blue background, entitled "Space Probe," that he donated to an AIDS auction.

Of his first show, in a small, midtown gallery, a reviewer wrote, "Some may find this set of straining male organs out and out outré. There are limits, after all, even in matters of taste. Esmeralda has gone too far."

Too far was an oxymoron to Julian, and lay enthusiasts agreed. He sold three of thirteen canvases at the opening and then two more. Arthur bought the biggest and best—a golden glans emerging triumphantly from a prepuce of imperial purple—gave it pride of place in the parlor, and began to treat Julian less as help than kin.

His virginity became a social asset. He never lacked an invitation, was blandished everywhere, and behind his back mildly derided by the cynical. Few could boast of more than a rote word from him; all were intrigued. Realists scoffed: abstinent was all he meant, no rare feat these days. Moreover, according to critics, as an artist he was a fraud, though superlatively assaultive none would deny.

Julian by his eighteenth year had experienced only a few disorienting embraces in the dark with all-too-willing girls, whose lack of a handle had left him at a loss. As for boys, shy pride, confused mischance of futile crushes, and the life of rife fantasy he had led on his mother's estate had blocked his entry into manhood, that more and more mythological state, ever receding into the future.

The jaded gibe that sooner or later everybody had everybody offended him. Perforce the mirror remained his most intimate friend. Himself the best man he had ever seen, the young could not compete, and elders were all too timid and too drab.

The first week of November brought him his first real romance —with the legendary female impersonator, the Black Queen, Jessica Jordan. Gaudy remnant of a doomed caste, pushing fifty, on stage he looked a lissome thirty in rhinestones, and gave off sparks when he sang, "Take me, I'm yours."

Julian caught a cameo performance one noon in the Old Colony Tap, an old-time straight bar where he had gone to put up a gallery poster. The regulars were skimming the papers, or methodically shredding their scratch cards into ashtrays already half full of charred filters. In the stale haze the TV was blank, voices subdued, physical movement nil—till the star blazed in wearing a skintight, black and cream cowboy outfit with whipcord jeans, blue boots with spurs, and diamond ear studs. He flicked a fifty off his wad, and ordered top-shelf tequilas and beer chasers all around.

"Wake up, you jerk-offs. What you running here, a morgue?" he ragged the bartender with loud derision. "Come on you jerk-offs, suck those down."

Malcolm with bemusement eyed the unexpected elixirs set down beside his mug of Coke.

"Here's to you," Miz Maud said, cheeks aflame.

"And yawl," said Jessica Jordan, taking his quick as a pill.

"Hear, hear!" hoarse Kimball Tardiff crowed, balancing his glass on top of his head, then drank half of it and had a sip of beer.

"Bottoms up, you jerk-offs," Jessica Jordan railed. "Let's get it on."

A boyish grin broke through Malcolm's grizzled deliberation. He lifted his glass high, bowed consecration, squinted up at it, drained it, grimaced, sustained a spasm that wracked his frail frame, then drank half the beer. "God," he said, tipping his head sideways to grin, "that's good!"

"You too, darlin'," Jessica Jordan said. Julian, whose pleas to be left out had been in vain, stepped up and obeyed. He had not imbibed in three years and the viscid liquid hit the bottom of his stomach like a meteor.

The bartender stood by, holding the bottle, looking out the window.

"How are you, dear?" Miz Maud said, taking little sips.

"Oh, not too bad today," said Jordan in the hollow tones of Cape Cod.

"What'd you do, rob a bank?" grinning Higgins said.

"One thing I ain't *ever* is broke," Jessica Jordan said. Sternly he nodded and six more brimful rounds were poured.

"Drink, you jerk-offs," said he, and downed his.

"I can see it's going to be one of those days," Malcolm said with cheerful resignation, and grinned sideways again at the specter of luck that so often appeared to thwart his intentions.

Miz Maud sluiced hers down, had a coughing fit, whacked her bony sternum till she regained her breath, lit another cigarette, picked up the pack of cheap generics, inspected it critically. "One of these days," she vowed.

"That'll cost you your coffee and booze. Sex too," Kimball said. "It's all or nothing."

"I can do without the sex," Malcolm said, "apparently."

"You jerk-offs don't get laid but once every nine years anyway," Jordan said.

"That sounds about right," Miz Maud allowed. She chortled, sipped, chortled and sipped, her eyes fixed on the lithe ex-Marine with feminine features, flawless complexion.

"Myself," quoth he, "I never spend a night alone. I take my pick."

"You want to watch out," the bartender warned with superior sincerity.

"You the ones got to watch out," Jordan rejoined. "That AIDS a honky disease. The white man invented it, he spread it around, he be lucky if it don't kill him off tirectly."

"Good luck, I say," Malcolm intoned, looking down his long nose, his black, hollow eyes magnified behind his glasses, "to everybody."

After a little pause of accord, Miz Maud asked, "How much longer are you here for?"

"When the snow flies so do I," Jordan said.

The tequila was gone, the chasers sunk to foam; little side chats came and went along the bar while he brooded out the window.

Struck dumb, Julian took him in with the awe, joy, defiance, dread, of meeting fate face to face. He looked like a basketball genius with a piano player's hands and regal gaze, distant and storm-tested.

"One last!" he rallied, and the glasses filled again. He downed his impassively, "Drink up," he said.

Julian, too shy to speak, followed suit; the others toasted their benefactor with polite sips.

"I can't keep up," Miz Maud said with pleasant complacence.

"Nice to see all you jerk-offs." The Queen abruptly tossed another fifty on the bar and turned to Julian. "You take care," he said with exquisite, brief regard.

"Thanks for the cocktails," Miz Maud called after him as he strode loud-jingling into the street.

Julian reeled out in his wake downfallen, determined to dare this paladin's closer acquaintance, but next Friday when he set out early in the evening, intending to get a front seat and take in the Queen's final performances of the season, he found the club closed, having consulted an out-of-date playbill.

THE MAID'S RENOVATIONS being well underway, Arthur Dowwer had got up an inaugural dinner party, late in starting, and now, near midnight, settled by the fireplace with their coffee, liqueurs, and Camel Lights, his guests had still not had their fill of chaffing Julian.

"He may not even *be* a homosexual," Arthur intervened at last with admonishing lack of reproach.

Don Weeming said, "Has she not got style, flair, personality, talent, breeding, and refinement?"

"She aspires," Gil Bright said kindly. "You must give her that."

He and Don had been colleagues in real estate and matrimony for twelve years. The others were single.

Julian hardly listened. Lacking their outward respect, he dreamed of the vindication of his next show, of spring and Jessica Jordan's return, of the Black Queen's entrance at his opening, of strolling about in drag with the outrageous star, of actually being in bed with the man. These mundane, middle-aged friends of Arthur, who twitted him with such persistent fascination and affection, were no more than mere shadows, well-meaning, over-weening, curiosities from the realm beyond his studio shed.

"Love of one's own sex is nothing to be proud of," Arthur chided, "nothing to boast about or flaunt before the less fortunate. It is pure vanity and unpardonably bad form to indulge, much less display, a sense of superiority. It is indisputably not something one has earned, or been rewarded with; it has nothing to do with merit; it is a gift—of God, if you like, or luck, if you prefer—and should never be seen in any light but that of a trust to be treated with grateful humility."

Pensive and dour, Charles Cahill seemed to emanate a faint smile without moving his lips, swirled and sniffed his cognac, sank back among the cushions, swirling and sniffing, warming the glass with both hands.

"I'm serious, I mean it, I really believe that illness comes more from what you think than what you do," Ted Madbury climbed back on his hobby horse, exasperated by having been constantly unseated by the general fixation on Julian. "AIDS is merely a manifestation. Judgment is the disease of the planet, and AIDS has evolved from negative attitudes. To heal AIDS it's necessary to resolve our relations with the earth, our mother. A so-called cure for AIDS won't be discovered until people have cured their thoughts about scarcity, guilt, and competition."

"You are a simpleton," Baxter Perkins said without warmth. His house in the West End was a library surrounded by tulip beds where he spent every moment he could cadge from his PR firm in Boston.

Madbury, a refugee from shoe sales in Cleveland, now a cashier at the A&P, rented a basement apartment from him.

Perkins was an austere, blond mandarin. Implacably diffident, a formalist in every act, he strolled of a summer evening, toes out, hands clasped behind his back, a look of distant rumination upon his face. When he bowed one first through a door—and no one ever thought to defer to him—he would turn slightly toward one, bend from the waist at a 130-degree angle, and stand perfectly still till the esteemed one had passed through. His ninety-year-old parents lived without assistance, but as the last of his line he was a pessimist, wore a stoic face.

"If they hadn't just turned their backs on it!" Nicky Heldahl said. Dubbed the Trust Fund Baby by his friends, once rakish and cute, now balding, pink-faced, and plump, his life in the last few years had become a progress of small, problematical, increasingly costly mishaps, while his eyes shone with flustered consternation.

"If it was their fucking daughters!" Madbury said bitterly.

"Let us not!" Arthur said.

Helping himself to more cognac at the low table where he reclined, Weeming said, "Some people still don't get it. I was showing a house today, the owner insisted on doing all the talking, we got up to the top floor, he says, 'And this is the orgy room.'"

"These two very straight-looking prospects from Mashpee," Gil said.

"Now high-tailing for Montana," said Cahill.

"Some of these guys," Gil said, "once they're out they become complete reactionaries."

"Plus royal," Arthur murmured.

"Our bread and butter, of course," Gil allowed.

"They won their revolution," Weeming said. "They just want to enjoy it in peace."

"While you get rich," said Madbury.

"Well," said Gil. "Not rich."

"Walk a mile in my shoes," Madbury said.

"Too far for me," Weeming said. "And none too straight either."

"I'm non-sexual," Madbury said. "I've got rid of all that."

"Bon chance," said Arthur, "for all concerned."

"Ah, The Good Old Days," Nelson Ryder said. "Who can believe they're gone? I can. I missed it all; I was in a very small, dark closet in Burlington the whole time."

He had been selling prints and rare books, the late Judge his father's estate. He had moved his treasures to Provincetown in 1983, nearly went broke because of the rents, managed to find a fair buyer for his entire stock, acquired the flower shop of a late friend he had nursed, now like an adjunct in the Grand Guignol sold bouquets and wreaths.

"The high point in world history," said Heldahl. "Why not say it?"

"Albeit brief," qualified Baxter Perkins.

"We had it all," Weeming said. " 'Early retirement,' we called it. We were all settled in, all our best friends had moved here, it took years to arrange. Nobody'll ever really know what it was like."

"There'll be nobody left *to* know," said Charles Cahill, who at last count had lost a dozen lovers.

Silent horror sat in the room, convulsive exhaustion, blood-leadening despair, phantasmagoric foreboding.

At last Baxter observed, "It's rather like middle age. Not an experience anyone looks forward to, no way to avoid it."

"KS, PCP, AP, AZT, PWA, HIV, ARC, MAC, CMV, DDI, DDC, PML," Nicky sang in bitter song. "I'm sick of acronyms. I'd like to think about something else for just one minute, I'd like to hear one normal thing."

"Nothing's normal any more," Gil said.

"What about the swimming and boating?" Weeming demanded. "Life goes on."

Heldahl said, "It's bad enough to give up sex. You're not even supposed to stay up late."

"Self-surveillance as lifestyle," said Gil. "What's that cough? Is that a spot?"

Julian, who had never mentioned his melanoma to a soul, now realized that AIDS was all diseases at once, beyond their mere names all very much alike: he differed only by a day from anyone else.

"I've Tested Negative And That's That," Madbury said to himself aloud.

"Did I mention," Heldahl asked after a half-glance at him, "my last visit home? I couldn't understand what my mother was getting at. Finally I figured out she was suggesting I get castrated. She kept saying it was for my own good. When I got back the first thing I did was call my shrinks."

"I'm glad mon ami Dover died when he did," Arthur said decisively. "He went to California and lived like a prince. He used up all his credit cards, sent all his friends very lavish gifts, including that."

The others turned eyes upon what all had noticed at once, but refrained from mentioning, a sort of elaborate wall hanging, raft-like, rather barbaric, feathery, horny, beaded, with shells and tassels and tufts and hollow bones tied to ingenious weavings and pleats of complexly patterned cloth of ferocious colors, odd, to say the least, amid Arthur's tranquil decor.

"What on earth is it?" Baxter wondered.

"A talisman," Arthur said. "What else?"

"I cannot conceive," Baxter said.

"Where'd it come from?" Heldahl said. "A lunatic asylum?"

"The Yucatán," Arthur said. "Where else?"

The best of us are getting wiped out," Heldahl cried, agonized by diversions.

"Of course," Arthur said. "The youngest, the boldest, most beautiful always go first."

"When Parmenter died," Weeming said, "his worst fear was leaving Gerald. It wasn't the dying that bothered him. He'd looked after Gerald all these years."

"I went to the hospital the day Jimmy Woodman died," Gil said. "The nurse was very snippy, she says, 'You can't go in there, he's past wanting visitors, he's been in a coma for the last twelve hours.'

"Well, I walked right in; he'd been very worried. I took his hand, I said I had arranged the funeral, I'd seen to the flowers, the obituary was written just the way he wanted it, with a whole nice tribute to all his friends, everything was going to be absolutely according to his wishes.

"He opened his eyes, he said, 'I feel much better.'

"I had some champagne in a jar. I sat on the edge of the bed, we each had a nip in a plastic pill cup. After a while he said, 'I'm going to go to sleep now, I'm tired.' And I left. I don't think he ever woke up."

"We're all going to die," Heldahl groaned. "We're just ghosts sitting here."

"Goodness gracious!" Nelson expostulated. "This is not . . . ah . . . news." In youth he had developed a stammer, which after his father's death had faded to a hesitation, which he used for emphasis or pause to word his thoughts.

Cahill laughed with eerie mirth, strange jocosity.

"What's funny?" Madbury demanded.

"The truth is always funny," Gil essayed.

"That too," Baxter said.

"So many of us," Cahill said, "spent their youth wrestling their one impossible problem. They never had time for anything else, and then they got out in the sun, and looked around, for the first time really, in what you would call a normal way, and there was the whole beautiful world for them to live their lives in, then suddenly everyone was dying, but nobody was old. It didn't make sense."

"When I think of all the people I know who've died so young," Gil said, "I can only hope their souls are happy somehow, somewhere, on some other level."

Cahill said irritably, "Don't pity dead."

"I don't really believe in heaven," Weeming said. "And I certainly don't believe in hell."

"I mean," Cahill amended, "dead is the best you can realistically imagine for anyone. Try it and see. Nothing you can possibly think of will be preferable. Zero is always best. Best before life. Best after."

"I'm a Shakespearean myself," said Baxter. "I'm perfectly serious," he told Julian. "Shakespeare knew everything about life. It's all in his plays. Each human quality brings its own reward. Though around here," he added, "all people want to read are menus."

"You're all escapists," Madbury railed. "Ideas are stupid. All there is is reality."

"No reality but in ideas," said Cahill. "I'll tell you my worst fear—that one's last moment is the only true eternity. Die in horror, that horror never ends."

"You love the dark," Heldahl said, "you enjoy . . ."

"Therefore," Cahill overrode him, "my ambition is to die laughing."

"I have complete faith in you," Arthur said.

"I think I'd rather die dreaming I'd just turned sixteen," Heldahl said.

Painting, Julian fantasied, himself white-haired, but still robust, the last touch just put to his greatest work, the brush slipping from his fingers, the floor there to stun him.

But Cahill had ceased to attend, wore the look of a man counting his heartbeats.

"This Plague Is Not Going To Get Me," Madbury said, each word distinct.

"Nor Julian either," said Weeming, and all eyes turned upon the silent boy with amusement, pleasure, curiosity, envy, satisfaction.

Julian stared at the floor as if he had not heard.

"Art kills too," Arthur Dowwer murmured. "*Faîtes attention.*"

Julian raised his head slowly.

"Oh, yes, my little cherry," Heldahl said, "watch out for those paint brushes."

"Do keep those bristles out of your . . . ah . . . teeth," said Nelson with rare camp.

"He might at least put condoms on those pricks of his," Weeming said.

"LEAVE EVERYTHING till tomorrow," Arthur commanded when the last guest left, but Julian, intent on getting to work first thing in the morning, kept on like a robot till the cleanup was done, driven by the endless talk about AIDS and by earlier incidents of the day.

He had happened on the heels of stately, bald, dome-headed Otto Jahrling, celebrated luminist of cloud and sea, discoursing to a student at each elbow.

"Acrylic pricks!" snarled the master. "The vulgar vice of our age, the violation of nature. Even his colors revolt each other."

"He's like Georgia O'Keeffe," one boy noted with faint demurral, "but inside out."

"If only he could see what the world looks like," declaimed the votary of light.

To be incognito abraded Julian's thin skin, rubbed raw his status as nonentity, but what irked him most was the resistless admiration he felt for the old man's works.

As the three arbiters of the world strolled on oblivious, a cruising BMW swerved to the curb, and assessed the facade of the Town House Lounge. Two straight couples got out, the boys with a lurch of swagger like college hockey players in sweaters and loafers; the girls were a little dressier, with skirts and long stockings, very pretty and game, all obviously in town for a lark.

"Just time enough for one last Sambuca," said the driver, and led the way. The boys' faces were flushed, regular, rather sweetly pugnacious; the girls trod quickly behind in loud pumps.

Here Julian had spent his last half hour with Jim Gurley. It was a wrinkle bar, evening domicile of older men, who sat in the window, smoking and dishing, but these kids didn't know that, wouldn't care in any case, so sure of their place in the world, so unconscious wherever they went.

What did they expect from life? What was one likely to get? All Julian wanted was fame—fame and Jessica Jordan—and he would have them, wouldn't he? Why not? He would, or die trying.

He finally forced himself to lie down at dawn, albeit fully clothed, but arose without having closed his eyes, took a handful of Arthur's vitamins, drank some cold coffee, and went to his studio muttering, "One last Sambuca!"

THURSDAY WAS *Advocate* day, obituary day. In an issue in which the deaths spread over three pages, Julian was struck by one Eldred Foster, 26, of Akron, Ohio, who "had only wanted to be an ordinary person and live out an ordinary life."

Trying to weigh this little, unfulfilled ambition, Julian realized that Eldred was Eli, the shy clerk in the hardware store, the first person he knew to die of AIDS. He was so amazed he nearly did not register the passing of Jim Gurley's friend, Edvard Finn, 82, of cardiac arrest, concurrence too sad to believe until his eye reached the next name down, the strangely familiar Jasper Gordon, aka Jessica Jordan.

Crossing an eight-lane freeway north of Miami at night, the well-known performer had been hit by several cars, his recklessness imputed to dementia of subacute encephalitis.

Julian painted a blue horizon with a black tombstone spewing stars. He had never told his infatuation to anyone, nor did he now, nor name the painting, nor sign it, but he knew he had met some irrevocable end.

4

JULIAN'S HEROIC PERIOD

ULIAN WENT HOME at Christmas. His mother—stunned by how much older he seemed, how somehow morose like her father in his last years—tried to make everything festive, but he managed only perfunctory efforts to appreciate presents or tree, and kept to the basement, sitting on a stool with some stale cannabis, looking at his old paintings. Intolerably restless, he cut short his visit, impatiently rode poorly connected buses for eight hours, arrived at 9 p.m. on a bleak December 26th, the only passenger on the last leg after Orleans, met not one soul, his breath billowing as he walked the long, strange street of wreaths and purple ribbons to The Maid, and a new *Advocate*, with its dirge of faceless names—and those of their surviving partners.

But who were *they*? Were they sick themselves? Did they know one another?

"You forget," Arthur said, "I've been in town hardly longer than you. We are both newcomers to Utopia. It's a small world, but not that small."

BY FEBRUARY winter had consolidated its grip, like ice talons reaching bone. Those who could had fled for the sun: everything was closed. On the street, reft of the summer multitude, the sick stood out starkly, spectral pairs of slowly moving men, one helping, the other emaciated, muffled up in scarves and overcoat, hollow-eyed, stubble-bearded, inward-gazing.

Charles Cahill began to have sweats and diarrhea, undertook a regimen of AZT, his face now drawn and grey from headaches and nausea, which failed to abate with continuing use of the drug.

Julian kept hearing that someone else had got it, was living with it, was fighting it, was failing, reviving, dying or dead of it.

Don Weeming, who reckoned his lost friends at more than fifty, confided, "For a while there — I came out long ago, I'm perfectly comfortable with my sexual orientation, my whole family is very supportive — I'd break down and cry. I know it's an awful thing to say, but I'd wish I wasn't gay because then I wouldn't have to have so many friends who had to die. Now I guess I'm just re-signed to it. I'm lucky to be alive. The main reason is, to tell the truth, I never cared much for anal intercourse."

Which was what Julian coveted more than anything but fame, feared beyond anything but failure. His deepening bereavement held such trials at bay. He so clearly did not welcome approach that people were put off. Living in the future he half heard, half saw the world outside his shed. It did not occur to him that he had not a single friend his own age. Nor were the avuncular men at The Maid avid to lose him.

WALKING THE BEACH beneath a chill April rain, Julian lifted his eyes to ponder a cluster of skewed pilings, last vestige of miles of wharves, wasted away to twenty-odd barnacled, seaweed-festooned sticks aglow on the north side with green moss.

He went home and painted the scene with a pathos new to his harsh palette, those woeful black bones on the rim of the silver bay.

"Leprosy," Arthur said. "Syphilis."

"Time," said Julian with a certain complacence.

Next he chanced on a book about Stonehenge, and dwelt a while among ruins, painting starlit, tooth-like megaliths seen from afar in the mouth of Salisbury Plain — fifty-ton stones that had come from Wales by sea, then overland on sledges moved on rollers by levies of men five hundred strong.

Grim Wessex gave way to the remnants of antiquity. He read in the library by day, at night composed colossal views—the Hall of a Hundred Columns, overwhelming ranks of white phalluses against empty desert, empty sky; the strewn pillars of Palmyra; the seven massive Dorics at Corinth; the three Tholos Temple columns of Delphi, tear-thrilling amid the crags, bearing, beneath a huge cumulonimbus, a last, vertiginous fragment of architrave.

Void this deep could not be plumbed, only peered into. How could whole epochs simply end, disappear in cataclysm, or slowly pass into oblivion? Even death could not explain. Mutability ruled alone. Once was no more. Gods, tongues, myths and history too, all were gone. His ignorance for the first time humbled him; his ambitions, never gravely measured, now, faced with any epitaph, seemed paltry and presumptuous.

He did a series of Easter Island statues. Eerily tilted every which way upon volcanic slopes, or lying still in their quarry like waking Frankensteins, or from the rocky cliffs gazing out to sea, all waited, alike, stylized, heads elongated, brows smooth and blank, ears stretched, noses concave, chins jutting, lips compressed in cool disdain, interchangeable, yet each unique, depicting the character of some illustrious ancestor, subtle penis-faces, patient and sublime, all brooded out of time, all expressed a single, solitary sense of the mystic, mocking nothingness.

Corrupt these paintings seemed to some. "Is she stuck?" cried Madbury. "Is there nothing else in life but cocks?"

"Lots," said Julian.

He meant minarets and totem poles, steeples, steles, obelisks, bollards, telescopes, standpipes, smokestacks, but mid-May came. Entering his studio one day he heard a peremptory voice inquire, "Would you mind, Miss Maid, getting me some ice!"

WITH BEDS to be made, bathrooms cleaned, guests accommodated, he sat late nights in his studio, communing with his memorials, determined to elude the dooms of history, die only in due time, as one adored, armored with honors.

Shun the Unfortunate was his way. He tried to block his thoughts, did not stop to talk, skirted one and all, like giddy edges that might call. AIDS was no part of him, yet he felt it closing in, suffocating, pervasive. He wore rubber gloves while cleaning, would have added goggles and a particle mask, had not his once limitlessly indulgent employer glanced askance to meet his house-boy so direly clad upon his pleasant premises.

Bundling sheets and damp towels, dumping condoms from ashtrays, scrubbing tubs and toilet bowls, Julian held his breath against the odors in the rooms. Disgust with human things grew in him. He banked his rampant ego against the general ruin, swore he would not go down. Why should he, after all? What real danger was he in?

I am the one and only one I love, he exhorted himself, kept watch on every inch of skin. But still he had a raging need for love, but the one he loved was dead. When he masturbated Jessica Jordan flicked off all rivals, no matter how recently met or vividly recalled. His psyche remained faithful to the Black Queen, whose mummy spun in dream one night, unreeling its skin in strips like electrical tape, till bones showed through, and his cries brought knocks on his wall.

Augustitis set in. The practice of his career now felt burden-some; at midnight, framing his winter's work, he could see noth-ing in it to like, nothing to bolster him. At his opening, angered at flattery and chitchat, the private air of prelude to more important doings, he could hardly abide a single face without Jessica Jordan there to requite him, despised one and all who came, even those he knew would come back another day, and actually submit to the paintings.

IN THE AFTERNOON LULL before cocktail hour, he would take himself down to Spiritus Pizza for a cappuccino and watch the ever-changing crowd, the kaleidoscopic life he once had thought to join.

Alone. Alone. Alone. The hollow word reverberated. In the street he tried not to turn as the beautiful men went by. They gathered and stood, half-dancing, robust in groups, flushed with laughter, inviolable youth, animal brio and grace.

Fantasies crowded out his concentration. Desire was all he was, but his shadow was fear. Love and hate mated, begot insatiable masturbation. No sooner had he spilled one sea than another flooded in. Bed gave no rest. He could hardly sleep for dreams, each aching night of conjured love a loss of actuality, a mockery of his self-regard.

Steeled to resist the excruciating languor, nor envy the sun lovers who spent their days on the beach, then strutted their glows beneath the moon, he himself was very, very wary, mapped every freckle and mole.

The obituaries kept coming—names he'd never heard, names like inklings, then that of Alfred Dale, 88. Commander of a destroyer in the Battle of Leyte Gulf, he had settled in Provincetown for love of the sea. His passing took up three-quarters of a page. His widow, appalled by his final, uncompromising assessment of his life's miscarriage, had insisted on a photo taken in his prime, long before he had grown his eremite's beard, nor did the panegyrics sound a note of his own views.

Julian ran into Murray Humber that Thursday. The painter knew nothing of Julian's show and, wondering what the kid might want, beyond credible backers of his phallic atrocities, kept trying to end the encounter and get on with his day, not a wholly agreeable one, since the Art Association had asked him to donate a painting to its auction for the umpteenth straight year, and he had once again acceded, though with ill grace, and now, while he half-listened to Julian's gluey effusions, he was trying to decide which hard-won work to part with, how to compromise between lost, potential income and gained prestige, if the latter could ever be supposed to accrue to such transactions, and why, at this stage of his life, must he still suffer the indignities of charitable bids, or worse yet, no bid at all?

And what was this about Alfred Dale? Humber had not seen the *Advocate*, and scorned all public figures beneath the national level. Dale had once built some so-called affordable studios, priced well beyond his means, which ballyhooed project at the time had struck him as more boondoggle than benefaction. Even today no one he knew owned one.

Aware of Humber's impatience, Julian jumped subjects like a tin frog on a spring. He only sought some vocal balm, and would have been glad to fabulate the weather, had he known how much isolation and dismay were thus daily dispelled on the street. But he looked shifty and drug-driven, and Humber interjected a terse farewell and fled, feeling guilty. He might have been a little generous, he might have said, "Let's have a cup of coffee," or, "Is your gallery open? Let's go look," or, "Come to dinner tonight."

He forged on through the throng, his cumbersome belly confirming the verities: you can't solve everybody's problems, you can hardly deal with your own. And besides the kid was gay, somebody else's baby.

Julian smarted. He meant nothing of course to this bluff but timid mediocrity who could not even feign interest in someone younger. Though Humber could not have conceived it, the novice beneath notice knew much about him.

For Julian had surveyed the oeuvre of every artist in town, and found to his surprise that almost all by middle age had achieved something convincing, even if derived. Humber it seemed was one of those who had never become quite himself; his squares within squares within squares were curiously touching, plaintive, whimsical; but unmistakably he was an imitator of Kimball Tardiff, who himself cared for nothing and nobody. Nearing sixty Humber appeared to be repeating himself repeating the master, while awaiting the octogenarian's next departure.

Everything Julian saw of life seemed only to reveal pitfalls and futility. Not to end up a P-town artist was certainly a first priority. Though he had just come already he saw the need to leave.

CHARLES CAHILL was dying. Gil Bright in tears on the post office steps told Arthur, who came home and told Julian.

The cynic, who had never harbored the least hope, had wasted with relentless speed, AZT in his case of terrible toxicity. "Smart lad, to slip betimes . . ." Arthur started, but choked and went out on the porch.

Julian's hour for cappuccino arrived; with a shudder he passed by the sunlit crowd at Spiritus, trudged on through town to Garbage Gables, Cahill's apartment house since the renovation that had deprived its name of sense. Come to view the face of death, Julian felt ghoulish, afraid he would affront the dying man or demean himself by some display of faintheartedness.

Weeming sat by the bed, holding a skeletal hand. Cahill was down to toes tenting a sheet, a blade of nose, a parchment skull with sunken eyes that saw or did not see, who could tell?

Weeming, when he rose, lurched with exhaustion. Julian sat down in his place and took up the weightless hand.

"Julian's here!" Weeming cried in a high voice. "Back in a sec," he said sotto voce.

In the depths of Cahill's pupils something seemed to liquify, less than recognition, more than happenstance.

Julian fought a pitiless repugnance. He stood. "Hello, Charles," he called and bent, still holding the papery hand, and kissed the cold brow, and sat down again.

As Weeming returned something else commenced beneath the sheet, some change or strain. They stared transfixed. A transcendent effort clutched Cahill's face, a stiffening rictus, quick jerks at the corners of his mouth, and then a kind of catchy gasping passed his lips in faint gusts. Julian shrank in fright. It was happening; the mystery was underway; nothing could stop it, no science, no prayer could intervene. Here was the dreaded death-rattle. Spellbound he saw, could not help but see, how Cahill's eyes strangely shone for an instant, then muddied out the light. No breath ensued. They waited, hardly breathing themselves.

"I guess you brought him through," Weeming whispered. "We thought he'd last till dark. The nurse just stepped out for a minute, went down to the beach actually, it's such a nice day."

Weeming led the way into the next room, collapsed on a couch and looked out the window, instantly struggled up again. "Here she comes," he cried.

Shoes in hand, she was running, as if she knew she had been gone too long.

Weeming had seen many a death; no matter how peaceful or glad, they never got any easier for him; he couldn't grow used to them; more was always worse—another someone gone, whoever it was, by then a friend—yet this one was eerily abrupt, brief, inviolable somehow. He began to weep with relief.

Julian too suffered a reaction. His heart raced, he felt about to explode, tears rained down his cheeks.

"I'm very upset," he wailed in astonishment.

Weeming regained control. "You go," he said. "I'll deal with this."

When Julian's panicky feet hit the street an elegiac high displaced his fear. He felt bad but he felt good too, but why? The faster he walked the more elated he felt. He delved for the cause. Was it merely that he himself was rushing down the street, alive?

As he passed Spiritus nearly at a run he realized that what he had heard was not the death-rattle. No! Cahill had been laughing.

Reaching The Maid, he began to shout in a voice he did not recognize, "Arthur! Arthur! Arthur!"

5

FALL COMES AGAIN

THE COUNTDOWN till Labor Day began. The workforce reeled numbly toward the final marathon, already nostalgic for summer's pleasures, luxuries they had bestowed on others but barely sampled themselves.

And then in the silence of unpeopled streets and overflowing trash cans they strolled with choral acclamations of amazed triumph and relief: "It's over."

The Maid was empty, except for weekends. Arthur held court from Jim Gurley's chair, a bit in dishabille, jowls sagging, acerbic eyes still quick as finches.

Edward Estes recalled a witty, brilliant man whose first symptom had been an instant of riot in a cocktail lounge. Himself again, the spilled drinks and consternation of his friends foretold his fate, but he escaped further humiliation, dying soon after of sudden renal failure, to the sorrowing consolation of his intimates, who knew with what disdain he could have borne physical destruction, but had dreaded the ruin of his proud intellect.

Paul Pozerycki, manager of The Gnu Gallery, where Julian showed, cited his fellow art major at Oberlin, Jon Cumont. Upon settling in P-town some years past, Paul had found Jon owned a shop here, wintered in Rome, where he rented a studio and painted, one feared, less each year.

Gentle and intelligent, Jon was beloved by women, made many a minor alliance with many a subtle beauty, but never married. Nor did he inhabit the gay world. Maybe once or twice while drinking he gave himself to some exotic traveler, but why surmise? Doubtless he put it out of mind, a meaningless slip. He never admitted he had AIDS, not even to himself, though awful ailments followed one another in the familiar, infernal pattern. He denied it, denied it, denied it, but when he gave up the ghost that's what the 1984 Town Report said: he died of AIDS. And he never painted much either.

Estes eulogized his favorite dancing partner Debra Cobb, who eschewed vaginal sex, or sex with straight men, shared needles, dildos, gay dicks. Sodomized at sixteen by a cousin, she loathed power in all forms, despised restraints, sought all extremes, donned a harness late at parties, became a friend of Bill W, ended a dry drunk. At a certain stage of an evening she would turn savage.

"Did you see her turn? What was it? Was it something I said?" her companions would marvel, for these sea changes differed not a jot from the nightly descents of Jekyll into Hyde of her boozy days, when a single, inevitable sip too many brought her to sudden, mean fury, causing those in the know to disappear till she took sleep.

At the end she spent her strength trying to keep going, tottering around and around her bed until she fell. The only good that could be said of her orphan's death at thirty-five accrued to her senile dog that no one would take in, even for the funeral week, and thus met prompt mercy at the vet's.

A passionate Irishwoman, on St. Patty's Day she paraded about bare-assed in a white miniskirt with a green-dyed bush. Odd was Debra Cobb, but a good soul, Estes said. She too loved Provincetown.

"Grazzy Frazier," said Gil Bright, "had an embolism in Lopes Square on a summer evening on his bicycle and got caught in the chain. When they cut his pants off he had a salami strapped to his thigh."

Madbury began to rant, Madbury the new moralist, Madbury

with no sympathy left at this late stage. "Anyone who gets AIDS now deserves it," he cried.

"Merde!" said Arthur. "Children don't believe in death."

"The Great God O will never die," said Paul with proud resignation.

"You mean Zero," Gil said. "What're you supposed to do, sit around jerking off in front of a mirror with a surgical glove? Right!"

"I was the most beautiful fag in Paris," droned André Evre for the ten thousandth time in his toneless monotone. A natty little man, seventy-four, very severe about people's appearance and manners, nor slow to let them know his opinion, he was wont to jeer. "Everybody wanted me. I had everything in the world. We were young then. You remember that, Arthur? Youth?"

"Let me see," said Arthur. "I do recall something or other."

"Burlington!" said Nelson Ryder, who had grown corpulent since Julian had first met him.

"This crazy town," André said. "I keep telling myself to go live in some normal place like Florida. But every time I go away I realize it's hell out there. We're lucky to have this lunatic asylum to come back to."

Pozerycki said seriously, "Well. When you consider. The blighted lives. The people who were able to bloom here and nowhere else. I owe my life to this town."

Glancing at Gil, Weeming averred, "I was born here. Who says I'm not a native lies."

A little breeze disturbed the talisman, which Arthur had moved to the porch, hoping the sun might fade its intensity. A stronger gust blew and it gave a kind of clacking cackle against the yellow clapboards.

"What is that hideous contraption?" André inquired.

"Gruesome, isn't it?" Arthur smirked. "Mon ami Dover gave it to me just before he died. Such nice gifts he sent everyone else."

"I don't see why," André drawled, "your guests need be afflicted with it."

It cackled softly in the wanton breeze. All shuddered involuntarily.

"I dassen't dispose of it," Arthur admitted. "Inasmuch as it was my last missive from Dover."

"Can't it go in your bedroom closet?" Gil Bright said.

"This is *too* . . . ah . . . depressing," Nelson said.

Mouth ajar, straw hat upon his knee, Julian gazed at the talisman, wondering if there ever had been such a being as this legendary Dover, who went off to die by himself, on a last fling.

A cloud eclipsed the sun; goose pimples rose on bare skins; high overhead the vanguard of diurnal gulls homebound from the Back Shore to Long Point cried out, cried out, cried out, thrice again cried out.

"Thank God!" Arthur groaned. "It's cocktail hour," and all instantly perked up. Julian made half a gallon of martinis, drew a goblet of tepid tapwater, with one small ice cube for André—crabby if his whims were not honored—and served a bowl of marinated mussels and a platter of smoked bluefish and crackers, head down in studied thought slipped away to his studio.

THE PARADISIACAL FALL went on, as if forever. This late October day John Ashingham was hobbling he knew not where beneath a blue sky and white sun. He was trying to remember something, but could not remember what, and kept forgetting at every step that he was trying to think of something or other, though whatever it was kept calling his mind back to its manifest existence, always at a dimmer remove, so that he felt it drifting irretrievably away, bemused but undistressed unless he had left his coffee burning on the stove or hose drowning his garden, lapses he had guarded against by devising ritual precautions to take before leaving his yard, though these too mostly got forgotten.

What with the heat, his unwieldy legs and corkscrew back, he found himself at a loss and blinked several times to still the swarming at his feet—and down he went without sound or sensation, and lay on his back by the edge of Bradford Street like a derelict in thriftshop clothes, with the mammoth sun baking his wide-open eyes.

After a while he resumed the pursuit of what it was he wanted to remember. André Evre stopped in his old, white Karman Ghia.

The fallen man serenely smiled up at him, but did not respond. André slipped his just-dry-cleaned safari jacket out of its plastic wrapper, folded it under Ashingham's head and hastened to a phone.

André knew him only by sight, felt remorse for him, so decrepit and shabby, a darkening skim of dried froth at his lips, his gaze now a glare.

Too late the rescue squad came. André watched the futile thumpings shake the frail corpse, apologetically retrieved his jacket, irreparably smudged with tar, went on home to refrigerate his groceries, resigned to some such of the same.

Judd Ames helped load the body into the van, his eyes stinging. He too had seen Ashingham for years, nor ever given him a thought. Still he felt bereft. These days it seemed he drove more hearse than ambulance, and he always felt terrible when they lost anyone, even an ancient like this.

"Let him go. He won't thank us for bringing him back," Walter the senior had said, and both had straightened up where they knelt, remembering the revival of Bobby Costa, not an old man at the time, who had cursed them when he came to, foreseeing that his damaged heart would torment him for long years before the Good Lord finally saw fit to take him back unto His bosom.

JOHN ASHINGHAM'S OBITUARY was so curt it implied inconsequence. No longer than those of three young PWAs, the week's harvest gave Julian a sense that death now meant so little that it had nearly ceased to exist. Though he had never spoken to the Idahoan after the night at Pepe's, he had seen him once in his garden, fantastically stooped, in perfect stillness, as if he were sleeping on his feet, or peering down at the dirt. What could he have been looking for? Worms?

6

DOOLEY JONES AND BILL WILBAND

DOOLEY JONES was nearly blind. Wasted, bedridden these last five months, he meant to complete the antique abode, compilation of which had beguiled his long dying. All he needed was an end table, a 1920s American sewing cabinet, shaped like a Classic Revival temple minus the dome, with three drawers, and semicircular, septagonal wells on each wing—such a stolid, bourgeois piece as his invalid grandmother had employed in her finger-busy, final years.

At dawn he would climb in her bed and they would roughhouse till headboard thumped and plaster fell, a parent's eye appeared at her cracked door, and she said, "Oh, dear, is it very early?"

When she died her sewing table was relegated to the attic, where he hid in hounded times. The memory of her massive, wrinkled, amused face had sustained him throughout his HIV, and he was determined to fly no matter how briefly the flag of her spirit.

Browsing Androgyny's end of season sale infelicitously near closing time, Julian had been impressed by Estes, now found himself a party to this search, gazing out the window, while Dooley gave advice on where to hunt.

A lull ensued, the sick man's obsession for a moment faded,

and Marzarat, nearly a shut-in himself, said, "Well, what's the dirt?"

Estes told the first thing on his mind: "Chester Glenn died. I had a letter yesterday."

Marzarat waved an angry hand. "I can't keep track," he said, "I don't even want to hear about it."

"I know," Estes said. "I had friends over last night, one of them says, 'That's a nice salt and pepper set, where'd you get that?'

"Well, of course it was Isaac's. I have remembrances from all my late tenants, and people say, 'Ooh, that's nice,' and then I have to say, 'That was Josh and Jack's.' Or whoever's."

"An eclection," said sepulchral-sounding Dooley Jones, whose quips his friends strove to requite with rueful sniggers. Torso closely wound in a sheet, surmounted by his pale, bald head and huge glasses, he looked like a chrysalis leaving its cocoon.

"It's true," Estes said. "No two things go together. But I don't care."

DRIVING TO Moontide Estate Auctions & Sales, Julian's misgivings were confirmed—of them all only he himself was negative.

Estes said, "Maz got sick even before Dooley. I'll live till I die. I guess. Don't worry about it. Everybody's got it. Just when the Cold War's getting over and there's nothing really big left to fear. You were lucky or unlucky, I don't know which, born at the end of history. As we know it."

Moontide buzzed with florescence. Once a garage, it had become a hive of cluttered halls and densely furnished galleries, one filled with bureaus, dressers, armoires, another with tables and chairs or kitchenware, another with desks or mirrors or sofas or bedsteads of every period, style, or finish. Young men, peaked under rigged-up chandeliers, were busy at restoration, and lacquer and shellac fumes piqued the nostrils.

"Rare as virgins in a bathhouse," the dour proprietor advised Estes. "I'll call you if anything like that ever turns up."

"Actually we haven't got a lot of time," said Estes, and explained.

"Well," said the proprietor, pointing to a jumble of high-piled, unsorted furniture, "you can look."

They wedged in among the tangled legs, cramped angles, and hard edges. There were numerous end tables—or what might serve as such—and in truth plenty of genuine sewing tables, frighteningly many in fact, but not the particular type that Dooley Jones had set his heart on.

The cram-packed storage room was close and musty, felt palpably inhabited. Estes sweated a sheen. Julian's scalp prickled. Simultaneously claustrophobic, they withdrew to the main hall where the nostalgic vapors recalled fingernail polish remover.

"Won't some facsimile do?" asked the proprietor.

"I'm afraid our friend Jones is a purist," said Estes.

"Circumstances may dictate a compromise," the delicate dealer said. "Sewing tables may fairly differ."

"I'm sure," said Estes, "Dooley would say his context must decide."

Impatient Julian said, "He can hardly see."

Estes answered sharply, "He can still tell one thing from another."

"Compos mentis," mused the proprietor with qualified regret.

"If we could borrow one somewhere," Estes dreamed.

"Rare as virgins," said the proprietor.

"How much," muttered Julian, who was mad to get back to his studio, "can it matter to him?"

Estes cried, "It's all that does! He's having his whole house photographed, documented, room by room, wall by wall. That's the point. This photo album. It's his posterity, this perfect domicile he started assembling back when he first got sick."

"And who'll live there?" said Julian.

"Well . . ." Estes dwindled into silence. Their eyes met, and together strayed to the proprietor, who folded his hands upon his momentous belly and gazed with dolor back at them.

"Who'll inherit the photos?" Julian wondered.

"Maz, I guess," said Estes.

Julian opened his mouth to ask, then closed it and his eyes both.

Estes nodded acknowledgment.

"In the circumstances," said the proprietor, "some surrogate may not be amiss."

"We'll see," said Estes. "But if I know Dooley!"

Empty-handed and mute they drove home in the immaculate, cerulean afternoon, each keeping faith with his thoughts.

ESTES DROPPED JULIAN at The Maid. Two rescue squad vans were blinking in the driveway.

BILL WILBAND had been staying in #3 since his return from the Bahamas a month previous, much deteriorated, wretched with horrors, never without pain. Something like barnacles had grown on his tongue, baffling his veteran care givers.

He had drunk a pint of brandy and slashed his wrists. Julian stood aside as he was helped down the stairs, blood-smeared and bandaged.

The walls of his room were red with handprints. Arthur had heard him blundering about.

Judd this day was senior, trying for circumspection. Week by week he was getting acclimated to these horrific scenes, and it disturbed him. He was a big man, an ex-athlete always at war with his weight, a husband with two young daughters, who'd built his own house because back in Virginia his grandfather and father had done it, and he'd felt the call himself. He loved guns and good talk late at night over a bottle of bourbon, and the gay world was a mystery to him, though he strove to gain an enlightened view.

To his wife he confessed, "Some of these disease-ridden perverts routinely do things I can't even imagine. How're you supposed to know what to feel? First you worry about them, it really tears you up, then you start to get blasé. We're like a limo service to Hyannis, the same guys sometimes, again and again. Then you start to worry because you don't worry about them enough. Then you realize you've got used to it, maybe you've grown too callous to care. Next thing you begin to wonder about your own humanity."

"I don't know, Judd," she had said. "I don't think you should worry too much about *that*."

Getting Wilband's stats from Arthur, Judd thought of the guy on Vine Street—who knew what *his* troubles were?—who'd shot an ear and cheek away, and then shot himself again, in the other ear, with the other hand, dead this time.

The rescue squad took Bill Wilband to the hospital in Hyannis. Arthur called his mother, who set out for the Cape early next morning by car.

She was still en route when Judd returned to The Maid about noon, to complete his report. Julian led him upstairs to Bill's room, where Paddy Galligan in rubber gloves, having washed the walls, was preparing to paint. He was a bit hair-raised, and the perilous blood was only the most intelligible part of it. He had been in the country less than a month, and everything was strange to him. He had never seen pornographic magazines before and here were stacks of them, men and more men with built bodies, pricks lolling and tall.

In flight from the awful dominance of rogue men, his immediate impetus was his father's black eye got by intervening in a fight between two grounds-keepers, one Catholic, one Protestant, over something that had happened eight hundred years ago. His Pa was a belligerent drinker, an all night disputant, professor of English at Trinity, poet who preferred the Dublin pubs and the rambunctious low life to scholastic gentility, a man ablaze with wild furies and griefs, who demanded Paddy aspire to be, if nothing else, exactly like himself.

The arrival of Jan and Elaine had interrupted his task. They had come to help Arthur pack up Jan's dear friend's few effects, winnowed by illness and chronic travel.

From the bottom bureau drawer Arthur plucked with mild fanfare a Peter Pan outfit of pink taffeta, wand and matching tiara, then leather chaps, hood, and whip.

Said he, "I think perhaps we need not include these."

"Why not?" said Jan, indignant.

"They're his, aren't they?" Elaine said.

"I doubt he'll want them," Arthur demurred, "where he's going."

"Don't say that," Jan said. "He's going to pull through."

"I mean," Arthur said patiently, "in Pittsburgh."

Judd had been eyeing the getups with bemusement. "I have just a few questions," he interjected in his official voice.

"I am devoutly thankful," Arthur sighed, "because I have few answers."

"Yup!" said Judd, in rube-like acknowledgment of mutual humility. He rather admired this indefatigable queen with the pouches under his eyes and the weird resemblance to Benjamin Franklin.

Paddy gave an involuntary shake of the head. He recognized Judd at least as one not apt to introduce surprises, and looked to him for guidance.

The women were in no mood for philosophic rapprochements. Judd to them was an intruder and probable enemy, his stupid questions best kept to himself.

"You can't make a decision like that on your own," said Jan, snubbing Judd with a shoulder. A last nail in the coffin of all wrong, she was lean from working out, wore a well-maintained flat-top, pressed shirt, clean jeans.

"Don't play God," said Elaine, a youthful amazon, who envied Judd the half a head he had on her, the red rescue squad patch on his blue sleeve.

"Darlings!" said Arthur with resigned antipathy.

"What's the deal?" Jan said. "He's out, isn't he?"

"This seventy-three-year-old woman," Arthur said, "does not need instruction in the facts of life."

"Says who?" said Jan. Bill had always disparaged his divorced parents, vowing never to forgive them for his circumcision, but his mother, who had raised him, had always come in for the worst abuse.

"Hey! Let her wise up," said Elaine.

"In the circumstances," Arthur decreed, "I'll give them to you for safekeeping," and he tossed the garments on the bed.

On the wall a framed photo showed Bill partying with friends, all grinning, stripped to their underpants, arms and legs entwined, posed in a kind of mandala; at the center a naked girl with an implacable challenge on her starkly made-up face sat cross-legged like a lewd Buddha, a bottle of champagne foaming in her lap.

Arthur took it down, dusted it, wondering what time and place, what Bill Wilband it depicted. Arthur had never seen his tenant, except in misery. He drew breath to speak, found no words, sighed.

The nude girl filled Paddy with yearning and another, queasy feeling. Those men who had no want of her—it was past grasping that they should prefer one another, and what did she think, behind that hard stare? Did she care only for women? Then why was she with them?

Julian was smitten with delight by the roses in Paddy's cheeks, thinking, *Ireland, rain and green, green, undying green,* thinking, *I must see the world.*

Like Arthur, Elaine knew Bill only as one who came and went unpredictably. Unknown to both, Bill had worked in the same office with Jan ten years before she met Elaine. The naked girl was Nan, Jan's old lover, an alter ego so close their friends called them Janan.

Jan had only sketched her earlier life for Elaine, a list of casual liaisons, a frivolous youth, prior to joining AA, the past nullified by her conversion to politics and ideology, the source and sap of their relationship.

To Elaine the nude in the picture was a mascot of shame, all men being depraved, cursed with a penis, and even gay men, despite their sporadic alliance with women, shared in that same, irreducible sin.

She felt that Bill's mother should not be made complicit in the degradation of gender by her own grinning son. "We'll take that," she said, and laid it with the costumes, thinking to please Jan, who wore an iron visage.

Judd fiddled with his clipboard, waiting to try his questions again, feeling a bit disdained, by heterosexual wellness excluded from significance for the infected elite.

Paddy, not to ogle Nan's breasts, flipped open the next magazine in the stack he had been perusing with stupefaction. Forgetting everything, he yelped in a cracking voice, "What's this?" and held up a full page, glossy picture apparently of two men, or parts of two men, taken close up, showing one pair of buttocks and a wrist ended therein.

All eyes took in the picture, then dwelt upon Paddy, who stretched the magazine wide with both hands, like a placard or shield.

The silence lengthened out, as after some unexpungeable faux pas. With a kind of entreaty he gripped the binding firmly with one hand, turned it, tilted it, craned his neck to see. "If that's an

elbow," he reasoned with pointing finger, "that must be a forearm . . ." He swallowed, glimpsing purgatory.

Arthur Dowwer had favored young Paddy with a day's work, in
deference to Julian's fear of blood. Infatuate of maps and topo-
graphical romance, out of funds in this lovely, cockeyed, money-
devouring town, where nothing made sense, he now saw his hope
of a place gone a-glimmering. How to restore his proper invisibility, he knew not, and he glanced for help at Judd, who, capping
and uncapping his pen, glanced away.

Judd himself did not know what to think, and kept still, wincing at his last mishap. He and a paramedic named Fred had gone
on a call. The subject had a headache, a terrible, ineradicable headache, had taken every pill, all medication for all ailments, had
emptied the medicine cabinet, and was not feeling a bit well, sitting in the doorway, a female at first glance, when they got out of
the van.

The patient and his housemate, who had dialed 911, proved to
be transsexuals, in progressive stages of their hormonal and ana-
tomical reconstruction.

Fred did the preliminary survey, and trying to be especially
polite kept formally addressing the patient as Mr. Marino.

The other one kept saying, "It's Miss."

But try as he would Fred kept calling her him.

The friend got furious finally and insisted that Judd take over
the interview. But after navigating several shoals, he too got the
pronoun wrong.

"Please!" said the friend. "How many times must you be
asked?"

Lost in a gathering fog, Judd picked up the patient's wrist
again. "I don't know. This guy's got quite a pulse," he ruminated
to Fred, who blanched.

"She's not a he, she's a she," roared the friend, his voice as yet
unraised. "She's very sensitive about it. So am I, and I'm *pre*-op."

Judd bent his fractured concentration to the task but his tongue
tripped him again.

"I wish I'd never called you," the outraged one gave in to
disgust, "I knew this would happen," and he flounced into the
house.

Judd and Fred gaped at each other and wilted, soundless whistles deflating their lungs.

"Never mind," said Miss Marino, tactfully testing her temples with long, red fingernails, "I think my headache's gone. All I needed was some professional attention."

The paramedics took thankful leave, clambered into the van, held on till they turned the corner, then burst into forced whoops and howls of rivalrous incredulity.

Judd felt guilty now, seeing Paddy's lonely distress. The boy couldn't seem to put the magazine down, nor take his eyes off it for more than a moment.

Elaine grimaced. Though she despised men's mad rage to fill holes, she secretly wished to be omnipotent herself, by sheer charisma vanquishing everyone she met, male and female alike, visiting irresistible orgasms upon them against their will, playing all their organs, converting them to slaves.

"Shall we?" said Arthur decisively to Judd, and led the way downstairs.

"Don't take it to heart," Judd said over his shoulder to Paddy with rueful jocularity.

WHEN JUDD DEPARTED, Arthur left Julian in charge and repaired to his suite to brood upon Mrs. Wilband's sharp intonations. She had sounded eerily like his own mother, whom he never thought of without resentful remorse, and a kind of foreboding grew in him as he lay on his bed, hands folded on his soft belly, a light breeze wafting through the lace curtains with the voices of schoolchildren coming home.

AT CAPE COD HOSPITAL, Bill Wilband woke from nothingness to see his mother's aging face, for the first time in memory devoid of censure. Touched beyond tears, he made an immense effort to smile, stunned to realize his flight was over, his independence at an end.

JAN HAD GONE for her daily run on the beach. Elaine was rearranging their Rogue's Gallery, making room in the middle for the picture of Bill and his friends, wondering how long it would take Jan to notice.

Deep in thought, Jan slowed to a walk, stopped at the wrack line to ponder a dead skate's empty eye sockets. She and Nan had succumbed to jealousy of each other's every minute out of sight, and had to break up. After a year of anguish, Jan had called her. It seemed that ecstatic night as if no time had passed, nothing changed. They moved back in together, the same frenzy, the same end ensued, and Jan had not seen her since, nor ceased to pine, nor at each corner feel hope and dread collide, for Nan must surely turn up some day in P-town.

HAVING FINISHED REPAINTING Bill Wilband's room, Paddy was being fed lunch by Julian in the kitchen, wondering, *Is this guy gay too?* thinking, *He seems like a nice guy,* saying, "Sure, and you'd like Dublin, though it's a bit grey, a bit drab, to my taste, I admit."

JUDD WAS dead tired. He had been on the road much of the night before, having got up at three to make a second run to Hyannis, this call a simple case of angina, the worst of it the old lady's distress at not having a clean dress to wear. He closed the bedroom door on his wife and daughters, pulled the shades, lay down and tried to sleep, but his eyes wouldn't stay shut.

DOOLEY JONES was waning fast, draining Marzarat's frail energies, keeping Estes on the road. The elusive sewing cabinet had become a ghastly joke, tribute to Dooley's will to live till his perfect habitat was complete, photographed, mounted, bound, and bequeathed to some suitable repository. He cared not if no one ever lived in it, which irked the servants of his final days, who nonetheless kept up their hopeless hunt.

The documentation was nearly done. Rudy Radiccio and his assistants had overrun the house with archaic-looking apparatuses on tripods, and prints were being produced and passed upon. All that remained were a shot or two of the northwest corner of his parlor, where empty space defeated Dooley's memorial intent, known to none but himself.

Emaciated as a fossil, he slept except when wakened to consult with Rudy or sign checks. The mortgage was unpaid, unopened bills accrued. Rudy required regular remuneration, and Estes and

Julian were obliged to sneak choice pieces from the second floor down the back stairs and sell them cheap for cash, theatrically tiptoeing about, fighting off facetiousness.

In desperation Estes bought a certain sewing table—plain, austere, more in keeping with Dooley's high style than the dowdy item he demanded—and set it in the empty place.

"He'll have to adjust himself to reality," haggard Marzarat agreed.

But in Dooley's body's wreck ruled a mighty will, still like to kill them all. For two days they were at wits' end how to reconcile him to the wrong table, without finding the courage to confess what they had done. Each secretly relied on some last-moment miracle, some answered prayer of their advertisements, some sign of relinquishment on Dooley's part. But the helpless man was too far gone to moderate, humor, or defy.

This—September 17, 1988—was the day all had agreed to cry in joyful chorus that the long-sought table had been found, brought in while Dooley napped, and placed where it belonged, bringing to fullness the project of his life—then pray he would be deceived.

At noon, while Julian dreamed out the window at the yellowing, sun-drenched garden, while Marzarat was upstairs resting for the coming ordeal, while Estes was folding sheets in the laundry room, Dooley Jones became no more, sitting erect, eyes wide open, awaiting yesterday's prints.

Resuming his vigil, Julian realized at once that the end had come and gone without notice, motion, or sound, perhaps without portent to the deceased, the corpse still sitting there of the late Dooley Jones.

It felt seismic—ancient, humbling, beyond sense or sentiment. A smell pervaded the room, shockingly sweet, then faded, like a dreamt thought.

Julian's gaze strayed back into the garden, so untended, so mysteriously unchanged. A catbird on the rim of the marble bath took wing.

It seemed nothing, this second, easy death he'd witnessed. So far he had himself been spared, had lost no one yet he loved, except his childish love, Jessica Jordan, though some future day might bring the end of someone truly dear to him, if such there ever were.

Consoled by his apprehensions, he sat till Estes came in with an armload of laundry. He too at a glance knew Dooley was gone; wordless, both were loath to wake Marzarat. Estes sat down with the toppled sheets beside his chair and the three went on waiting in formal silence, till they heard Maz's halting step upon the stairs.

Estes eased up and went to meet him. Maz at first refused to believe—but Dooley had no pulse, was cold—and then he sobbed to have missed the moment he had braced for, napping at the pinnacle of need, and Estes clutched his head to see; then together all three tried to close Dooley's eyes and fell to laughing shakily, unitedly, with vain vindictiveness, as the stubborn lids kept sliding up. Finally they stretched out his weightless form decorously beneath a sheet up to its chin on the bed in the guest room where Dooley had spent his last three months.

The town nurse came without delay, signed the Pronouncement of Death, and departed. The wheels of the hearse crunched quietly into the vacated driveway; and at the very moment Dooley was being zipped into the maroon body pouch, his thin blue nose and still-slitted eyes vanishing, as beneath the surface of a muddy pond, Rudy arrived with the prints.

"There are just those few last shots," Estes said.

Rudy, having never seen a death before, marked how quickly a person could disappear. Disinclined to work this day, not at least until some sure succession could be confirmed, his eye sought a place to leave his latest bill; but then, having increased esteem for the deceased and sensing that absent his redoubtable drive nothing further would be wanted here, he decided to forgo the final outlay. Uttering heartfelt condolences, backing toward the door like an oriental go-between, he departed and went for a walk in the dunes with no camera.

The survivors were left alone. Marzarat hung upon some last pike of strength like a scarecrow that had seen a ghost. He had hardly been home in months, having given himself wholly to Dooley's care. His raison d'être was gone. The dead man's resplendent residence, pillaged upstairs, steeped him in silent immobility; photographs of its every niche looked out of the dining room; in the garden where the lambent fountain plashed unfamiliar shadows spread.

Estes went about, shutting windows, thinking that Marzarat was next, and then some day himself. But for the moment they were free. "Let's go," he said. "There's nothing we can do here till tomorrow."

His cohorts gladly nodded, without asking what he meant. They locked the doors for the first time. Julian helped Marzarat into Estes' car, waited till they drove from sight, then walked slowly along Commercial Street for six blocks and came upon O'Rooney, leaning on his cane under a chestnut tree, looking up into the sparse foliage, a newspaper under one arm and two cans of tuna fish in a plastic sack twirled to his wrist.

Julian approached unheard and stood silent, fearing to startle him, so old and frail he seemed. He smelt too, of whiskey and urine, and his eyes when they mildly descended to Julian were watery, red-rimmed and dim, and then they cleared and a smile of recognition, of delight, of love suffused his face. "I was just taking a bit of respite from the sun," he said.

"It's very hot," Julian agreed.

"Tell me all about yourself," O'Rooney said. "I trust you're flourishing."

Julian squeezed back tears. "Which way are you going?" he said, taking the newspaper. "I'll walk you home."

And back they went the other way, slowly, painfully, past Dooley's grand facade and white shell driveway.

O'Rooney lived up sandy Atkins-Mayo Road, deep in the oaken shade. Julian waited on his mossy porch till he got his door opened, then handed him the paper. "Thank you, thank you," O'Rooney said.

Too stricken to speak, Julian stood gazing at the pallid, pink-veined, unlately shaven face, not knowing how to turn and leave.

"Here now, give me a kiss, lad," said the old man, reading him aright.

Julian gratefully bent to kiss his cheek but O'Rooney met his lips in a rough, wet smooch. Julian stumbled back down the road, tears streaming. There had been nothing carnal in the kiss but only valediction, and he resisted the impulse to wipe his mouth.

Back on Front Street, he rushed along, his heart crying, *I must paint something great.* Meeting a fan of his, who stopped to chat —there being no one else in sight—he hurried brusquely past, increasing his reputation for snooty arrogance.

On the next block he halted under O'Rooney's tree and peered up. What was the elder looking for, birds? The mottled leaves were withered, the topmost branches barkless. Apparently the cause was not only autumn but some sort of blight. The few trees in town seemed each a transcendental presence, and by the time Julian got home his tragic exultation had sunk to dismal dread.

7

REUNION

ON OCTOBER 5TH two new guests were due to register at
The Maid, one Gustave Royal, from San Francisco, and
Selwyn Royale, of Portsmouth, New Hampshire.

The coincidence of names, with their romantic cast, lent anticipation to their arrival—Gustave on the morning plane, Selwyn by car in the early afternoon.

Specters both they looked, exhausted by their trips, not very communicative, seeking rest above all else, nor did they meet until the cocktail hour, when they appeared simultaneously at opposite doors of the long, glassed-in porch.

Midway between, from the capacious chair Charles Cahill had called the Throne, Arthur arose to introduce them. But their locked and dream-like stares as they converged obviated words.

"Gus?" said Selwyn Royale.

"Selly!" Gustave Royal said.

Slack-jawed, tremulous, they clutched each other by the elbows; in profile their widows' peaks and eagle noses proved them kin.

Arthur and Julian effaced themselves in shuttle between porch and pantry with herbal brews and hors d'oeuvres, and finally served a light supper that kept them at table long past their soul-racked guests' customary bedtimes.

Half brothers, born in Indianapolis in 1948 and 1953, they had not seen each other since '68, when Gus had fled west and dropped from sight. Five years later Sel had gone east, ending finally in Wilmington, Delaware. Neither had ever gone back, nor after a few years kept track of their mother Amanda, a frenetic businesswoman, grandiose, mercurial, and cold.

Gustave's father, who had been in pharmaceuticals, died in 1952. Amanda dropped his hyphenated Saxon surname, too high-falutin for her raw milieu, and reverted to her own, Royal—worse in its way—which she fastened on both boys.

Her liaison with Selwyn's father, whom she never lived with en famille, dissolved before their son was one year old, leaving the dadless lads to the care of a spinster nanny named Jane, who flagellated them with her single, dire bit of wisdom: that they could never know how lucky they were, never to endure the supreme pain of childbirth.

They laughed now to recall her twitching eyebrows when she succumbed to her fixation, this otherwise sane and kindly soul.

Amanda herself hardly acknowledged her sons' existence, acquired and lost bankrupt businesses with epic consistency, already displaying rages and fugues, wild swings of confidence and fear, in retrospect probably first signs of Alzheimer's.

Eventually she slid into destitution, died on the street in a blizzard, was buried by estranged relatives before either son heard of her undoing.

Selwyn, after a trip to Quebec, had added an e to Royal, to assert the proper stress of his true identity. The brothers had not known each other's sexual destiny until this very day, which revealed another, less ambiguous truth: both had AIDS.

Gustave pulled up his shirt. "I look like a Dalmation," he said.

Alfred had been spared KS, but not much else.

Over the next few days they traced their finally intersecting trajectories. Most pathos-laden was the fact that they had not met till now, for both had frequented P-town at various seasons and perhaps missed each other by moments on the street, at the beach, or in the bars. But the greatest wonder was that their riven beginnings and dense divergencies had led to this one end, this simultaneous farewell visit to their mutually favorite place on earth, virtual farewell to the joys of life itself. At the unbelievable moment though both were feeling revived, too full of sympathetic delight to give up and lie down to die in any immediate future. There was simply too much untold, unheard.

Upon leaving home, Gustave had cast off disguise and lived the brute life of the Gay Revolution, adopted every fad, joined every orgiastic joy or folly, broken every taboo. He had walked in the candlelight march to city hall to protest the murder of Milk and Moscone, stoned police in the White Night Riot that ensued when the homophobic assassin got off with six years. He had marched in every pride parade, and exulted to see a free, new world emerging.

Monogamy was the main barrier to human happiness, as the married world so grotesquely illustrated. The limits of feeling imposed were worse than death in life because the natural need for intimacy and the lack of real restraint rent the soul unendingly.

The answer of course was to uncouple lust from love: the pair were partial opposites, and all too often adversaries, not that they never amicably occupied the same household. But familiar affection was no aphrodisiac. The highest pleasure, as everyone knew but public ethics denied, arose from adventure with strangers, who names were never learned, whose virgin delights could never fade.

Therefore he had inhabited the bathhouses, imbibing the pungence of poppers and hashish, the buzz and sway of cocaine and Quaaludes. He had sex with as many men as he could; it was never enough, but there was always tomorrow. Deriding the Puritanical warnings of his well-intentioned but prudish doctor, dupe of those who would suppress gay liberty, he braved the wave of diseases that battered his body—shigellosis, hepatitis B, herpes, constant gonorrhea—paying his dues, as he called his medical bills. The canceled checks were his Purple Hearts.

By 1985 infection was everywhere. The bathhouses and clubs were closed. Health food stores multiplied with meditation and mysticism, trips to Mexico for unapproved drugs, flights to Lourdes for miracles. Rumor spread that the CIA had loosed the virus in the gay community; right-wing zealots were demanding universal testing and detention of the ill. The blood supply was tainted.

He awoke one morning depressed by his usual hangover to reflect that he was a gay man living on a picturesque hill on the second floor of a well-kept Victorian on Hartford Street, near the center of things lively yet residential, a scene perfectly idyllic and bourgeois, thirty-seven years old, and alone.

What had he to show for his fucking? He had no one even to reminisce with. He padded about the kitchen, dandling his cock, then called in sick, masturbated, showered, felt worse. Should he spend the day cruising dim bars, terrorizing himself with the risk each fresh drink brought?

He walked the day away. His image in a shop window was no more distinct than any of the countless guys he had dallied with, among whom he had lost his identity. Who was he? What did he want from the rest of his life?

He dined by himself, without even a newspaper for company, skipped the movie he had planned to see, went home and without bothering to flip on the lights or try the TV, sprawled in his swivel chair, rotated toward the window, and stared at the clear constellations.

Had he been wrong all along? Perhaps it was not too late. Had he strength to change, the discipline to hold fast? A fierce excitement seized him. This empty sensuality, this unseemly fever need not be. Love. Of course. Love was the answer to incurable loneliness. Every philosopher, every poet of every age had affirmed it. Love was the music of time, the flute to beguile meaningless death, the golden rule of life.

To have someone to talk to, make plans with, rely on, share joy and sorrow, live and build a future with—what an ineffable blessing that would be, sweet fidelity! And how unexpectedly horny the prospect made him!

He shuddered like a besmeared child; one more bite of chocolate and he would puke.

A new Gustave was born. The thought of sex repelled him. The booze, the drugs he little missed. Hardest to renounce were the cigarettes with their sudden numbing of the lungs, their use as worry beads or social connection. He even started to work out, drudgery he hated until he got in the shower, went readily to bed at ten, relished his sleep, woke glad at dawn.

But his quest for lasting love was not successful. Sober chastity stripped mercy from his judgments. He hardly met a soul he could endure; worse yet, the men he liked best were apt to be fathers with children.

The eligible men he met seemed shallow or dull or self-involved, and somehow the younger, the handsomer, the less character they seemed to have. The clone modality ruled within as well as without, and none could please him.

Celibacy was becoming painful, his fears intense, when fate came to his rescue in the form of William P. Manion, D.D.

Two years later, looking back, Gustave knew he should have sensed at once that something was drastically wrong.

He had accompanied friends to a social mixer, a discussion group at a gay Bahai House of Worship. Standing in an animated circle with a cup of punch in his hand, enjoying the mildly profane repartee about what qualities the next Prophet would need in the new world, his face suddenly felt hit with a bale of air, and glancing up he had a burning sensation in his forehead, realized he was the object of intent scrutiny by an extraordinary personage diametrically opposite, an older man, deeply tanned, so oddly dark he seemed dusk-hued, with a gently rueful, wise, artfully lined countenance. Upon being observed he smiled, and his eyes and teeth glimmered.

Mellifluous, charming, with a massive head, beautiful, silvery grey hair and an aura of distinguished authority, he proved to be most interested in Gustave, and the flattered layman invited him home for a cup of tea.

Will, as he was called, was a Presbyterian minister, but impatient with unimaginative and unbending elders and congregations alike, he had sometime since put by the cloth. He was divorced; his two daughters lived with their remarried mother on Telegraph Hill; he was not apparently much in touch with them any more, and had moved around a lot in the last few years, though without ever leaving the Bay Area.

Amid this fluent chronicle he paused, leaned his head back, for a moment reposed, then with a languid air swept his hand across his crown and down the nape of his neck, as if he had long tresses. "I just love my hair," he said with grand flamboyance. And then, with no more transition than before, resumed his grave discourse.

Gustave took the gesture for encouragement, and presently told his own tale, expressing his aspirations in such heartfelt terms that tears blurred his eyes and he began to understand the full import of his conversion to the pursuit of a life informed by love.

At midnight, at the door, when Gustave tried to give him a farewell kiss, Will restrained him gently, held him in a steely grip, for a long moment kept their faces so near, so far, that their breaths mingled, but their lips never touched.

Gustave awoke the next morning and knew he was enchanted. His instinct was to draw back a little, but immediately his sworn resolve put down his misgivings. Wasn't this exactly what he sought? So quick was his heart's leap of Yes, it gave him pause again, and again he fought off a vague unease.

Then nothing happened. Days went by. He had a sinking sense of loss one moment, joyful expectation the next. Intuition told him he must be patient, that whatever was going to transpire between them was out of his control, and he prepared himself to wait, though not he hoped till doomsday.

For every once in a while the disregarded shadow edged the sky. One day soon he must get tested. Meanwhile he felt strong as a lion. Since his meeting with William P. Manion, D.D., he felt his whole constitution infused with fire, was almost convinced of his own providence. He had somehow got through. He had been careful now for several years. All would be well, he told himself, and if not, then not.

Two weeks later, when the episode had begun to seem an unreal dream, he came home from work to find Will's initials and phone number chalked on his stoop, and went upstairs and with a happy sense of rightness dialed.

They drank coffee beneath the dingy awnings of a neighborhood café neither had ever noticed before and Gustave, feeling boyish and out of his depth, threw himself into the maw of romance with never a look back.

Manion was a most sensual man, as well as most sensitive; he had many talents and exuded a contained energy, was withal so kind and responsive, unerring in his grasp of things unsaid, so appreciative of every subtlety, that Gustave luxuriated in just such companionship as he had fantasized.

They met again; and went to bed; and thus it began.

Several idyllic dates they had, ate in obscure restaurants, strolled away the evenings, made love late into the night; Gustave had never been so happy, saw, to his amazement, that his dream was coming true.

And Will, after an initial reserve, little by little opened up to the younger man's idealism, and one night spoke about himself, his origins and wellsprings, in a way both shocking and pitiful. For he had been a victimized child. Horrified to hear how harmed he had been, Gustave felt flooded with unbearable tenderness.

Will, outwardly the masterful, the invulnerable, the intimidatingly suave, wept to tell of the fled father, the mother that had slipped a finger up his anus and stretched his penis, the shark-faced uncle who raped him while she was at work.

For the first time Will stayed all night; until then he had always gone home before dawn, back to his apartment, where Gustave had never been, nor been invited. But this night they clung to each other in sleep, shared breakfast pastries on the street, drank a second cup of coffee on a bench beneath some acacia trees, and Gustave the punctual got to work late, giddily grinning, bore with good humor his cohorts' raunchy speculations.

Home from work he called and called and waited by the phone till long past the dinner hour, then rushed out, snatched a bite and came back to try again, but no Will. Several days passed. Gustave assessed the situation, wondering how fragile the erstwhile minister really was, and if he might not be having second thoughts after his burst of self-revelation.

Finally Gustave went to check out Will's address, only ten blocks away, the bottom floor of a rundown house with untended lawn, tall yuccas gone to seed, all the downstairs shades drawn, a torn screen door and no life to be seen. Will had said he did counseling of all kinds—loss and grief, family, marital, gender, and old age—and served a steady clientele, but there was no sign, not even a name on the battered mailbox, and Gustave got the creeps, could not help imagining the Samaritan lying murdered within.

On the seventh day, about dinner time, Will appeared looking grim. He looked like it had been a bad day. His manner was not intimate. Gustave could see he had something to say.

They sat at the kitchen table and talked at random guardedly, till finally, quietly, with evident difficulty, Will brought out:

"I must tell you something. I'm a multiple."

"Oh," Gustave said. At first he thought it meant a triplet or more, but then he recognized it as a technical term. He had read something somewhere; they were in the news.

"But I have been through extensive therapy and am well integrated," Will added with precise enunciation.

"How many of you are there?" Gustave asked blithely.

"Fourteen," said Will.

"Well!" said Gustave."Can I meet them?"

"They don't manifest," Will said, but described several. One was a cellist, who hated the color orange, one a promiscuous girl of fourteen, another an organizer. One was like each of his parents, though he had long ago set both free.

But the upshot was that they probably ought to break up now before their affections became entangled. He was a freak, not in fact good for Gustave, or anyone. He left at once, with formal, somber dignity, as if to let Gustave think it over.

At midnight he came back looking distraught, broke down in tears, made a clean breast of his true state. He had been a captured chaplain in Vietnam—he too had had his idealistic fling, pro Deo et Patria in his case—and had paid dearly for it.

He had gone mad after a betrayal of his battalion by Viet Minh disguised as ARVN, and in revenge had killed three monks of the village that had harbored them and stuck their heads on pikes.

Caught by the Communists, he had been dragged by night from camp to camp with a rope around his neck, tortured and left for dead in the jungle.

This and the disassociative disorder stemming from his cataclysmic childhood accounted for his plight. He was in deep suffering and needed Gustave's love more than he had ever needed anything in his life.

He wept until he seemed to dissolve—not bitter tears, just

pure grief—and Gustave held him, stunned and appalled at the story, whether fanciful or true.

Then, calming, relieved and detached, his old impressive self again, Will proceeded, with noble zest and sympathy, to delineate some of his other personalities. One was a world historian, a professorial type, a trifle remote, who favored corduroy, one was a stone apparently, one a kid who lived in a tree, whose legs were entwined somehow with its roots. One was a discontented housewife.

He spent the night and they fell asleep in one another's arms without making love, though in the morning they nearly consumed each other's rectums, their cries applauded with crescendos of broom thumps on the ceiling below.

When they parted, Gustave pressed his key upon Will, in case he needed sanctuary at any hour of day or night, and Will received it with thanks humble and grave.

They had made no plans; when Will did not appear for two days or call or answer his phone Gustave did not worry overmuch, but held himself in readiness.

In the evening of the third day Will showed up in a peach polyester suit, not his usual jeans, white shirt, and sneakers, which sent a chill down Gustave's spine, till Will reassured him that he merely felt free to dress variably. He hoped Gustave did not mind. That was the first thing therapy had taught him, to have the courage of his true moods.

They drank a bottle of wine. He was in fine form and ranged with light irony over his lifelong struggle to master his demons. His therapist, of course, had fallen in love with him. "I always get what I want, whether I want it or not," he said, "and then I must die and be born all over again."

But that unhappy epoch was ended, his therapy complete. His whole history was one of chagrin. It was not something one cared to bruit about; he was passing, in short.

"In the past, people like me were burned at the stake," he remarked with a laugh.

And he had been looking, always looking, he realized now, really looking all his life for someone to confide in, someone brave enough systematically to tear down all human barriers, someone to merge with, someone equal to his reality.

But what was that? Gustave almost didn't want to know. He was always amazed however, reassured in a way, by Will's earnest, penitent tone, moved that a man so rare, handsome and accomplished, should find him a worthy comrade.

And whatever Will's mental state, Gustave could hardly wait to get him into bed at night, where the minister's voluptuous avidity in the dark and shyness of his own nudity that invariably appeared with daylight seemed the wondrous poles of their paradise.

Will always got up first, and rushed into his clothes as if in a panic, while Gustave, propped on one elbow in bed, wholly charmed, watched him through the door, hopping about in the living room, struggling to get his socks on.

They were becoming inseparable. No day went by without at least a long phone call, during one of which Gustave mentioned that he'd related Will's psychic trials to someone at work, who said he had known such a person.

Dead silence ensued. It was a casual conversation, the unwitting betrayer pled; he had not meant to slight Will's privacy; his name had not been spoken, at least not his last name; nothing would be remembered, nothing passed on. It was a mere acquaintance; they never met outside of work; they moved in different circles.

But from that day—really from that moment—Gustave noticed a certain wariness in Will's demeanor. Nonetheless one evening soon after, with an air of special occasion, Will arrived unannounced in slacks and a spectacular red sweater and took Gustave out to an expensive restaurant and evening of barhopping in the straight scene, where they hardly glanced at a soul, except to make risible observations of the women, and where, at a climax of feeling, when they could hardly restrain themselves from open displays of mutual ravishment, Will told him that yesterday all his selves had held a kind of formal confab and agreed that Gustave was the best lover he'd ever had.

"I should have dropped the relationship right there," Gustave said.

"Love," said Arthur with acid.

"Sex," said Selwyn.

"With all fourteen?" Julian asked.

Yes, yes, even amid the blitz of booze and heated blood, Gustave had recognized it as a most disturbing utterance, but he never delved, not even the next day. Things were going too well, and after all it was flattering, comforting, even quite relieving, to think that Will's familiars approved of him, for the fear that Will would suddenly change into someone new and strange never wholly left him, yet he was happy as he had never been, happier than he had thought possible.

Doubtless inevitably, their main subject of interest was Will's personalities, his alters, his other sides, as he variously called them. He was not unfond of them. They could no longer take him over, as they once had done, and now he merely eavesdropped or spied on their respective misadventures, or rather, relived them from the past, and indeed at times, though fleetingly, with an alien gesture or look, he almost seemed to Gustave to trace their psychic signatures.

These days the girl was being very bad; she was maturing into a jezebel; he was worried about her; she thought she knew the world, she thought she was shrewd and hard, but she had no idea how black it was at the bottom of the stairs.

Will himself sometimes seemed distracted and distraught; and then he would hug Gustave for relief with his strangely strong, steely arms and solid shoulders, so odd in one of his sedentary mode of life. Nor were clothes a guide to his inner weather. Much of the time he acted as if he wished to be invisible, but all the while he talked and talked, if not always precisely or exclusively to Gustave, or so Gustave began to surmise.

Once—at an exclamation of remorse rather de trop amid their pleasant debate of dinner plans—Gustave expressed bewilderment. Will answered dismissively, "Oh, that's just Dondo."

"Dondo?" said Gustave.

"Dondo Lazar," Will said with weary derision. "Mr. Indecision, Mr. Coward Conscience, Mr. Traitor Himself. He's always got a hundred reasons and none of them agree. With him everything is right at the same time everything is wrong."

As a rule these characters were not overt, or did not clash openly, and it was hard for Gustave to keep them separate in his mind. Dondo remained dim, but he formed quite a clear picture of the historian—an aging, resentful scholar, often pompous. The man called out each word, as if he lived at a lectern in some huge, empty hall. He was winding the thread that held the world together. Of course the man was a buffoon and bitterly, bitterly knew it half the time, stumbling on the stone that nothing repeats, everything is unique. And worst of all he was losing his memory.

Gustave felt privileged to catch glimpses of these inner denizens, and filled with pity for their long-suffering host. He had only his instincts to go on—an uncharacteristic swivel of Will's pelvis while dancing, an ebullient apostrophe in a casual monologue, a fleeting change of mien—for the besieged man never volunteered an explanation for anything or threw open the doors to his bedlam.

But Will could be outwardly mercurial too, charming to an audience or group, afterward belittling their insipidity, their insufferable, middle-class ideas, their complacent good will. Then the shape of a sort of bigotry seemed to emerge, but when confronted, no matter how gently, he would deny or modify, rationalize or simply obfuscate with dizzying double-talk, like glossolalia, or he would take off on flights of theory, disclaiming his own view as limited to a single locale on the circumference of the infinite ways of looking at anything from a purely human standpoint.

"Do you believe in God as much as you did when you were ordained?" Gustave wondered.

"That's a difference to defer," Will snapped. Apparently the subject did not attract him at present, or he was not yet ready to reveal his ultimate beliefs. He could have an air one moment of cavalier calculation, the next of being absolutely at wits' end. He spoke ever more candidly of his psychotic ordeals. One doctor, a noted analyst, had been convinced he was merely a severe manic-depressive; another had branded him garden-variety schizophrenic; and indeed, he almost seemed to boast, by exemplifying one or another symptom of his fundamental disorder, he had mimicked various classic pathologies so faithfully that many a specialist had been misled.

He was still in therapy, it came out casually, though of a higher level, and on an equal footing, more a consulting consortium of two, the Dire Dyad, as he called it, his colleague not the aforementioned therapist who had fallen in love with him and whose treatment had perforce been terminated, but another, much older man, with whom, for the nonce, Will was exclusively engaged in an exploration of his relation to his own practice and patients.

Gustave began to feel slightly rocked and confused. He was troubled by the careless relinquishment of the lie or semi-lie that Will had finished with therapy. No doubt he was integrated to some degree, but a whole, sound soul he clearly was not; though, on second thought, that he was still getting professional help was surely something to applaud.

The more intimate they grew the more guarded Will was one moment, the more abandoned the next, and Gustave, fearing who or what might be in store, grew haunted by a vision of the blind facade of Will's house, with its overgrown lawn and shades drawn. Inside dwelt the fourteen, bound within one skull, one soul, one heart, Will's, not to mention Will's patients, of whom Gustave naturally heard more and more, meanwhile wondering if Will might not be internalizing them as well, adding endlessly to what must be an infernal congregation. Gustave felt overwhelmed at times and had to smile, in spite of himself, at the thought of some therapist, no matter how agile and sage, trying to harmonize this swarm.

"I'm a lecher really. I'm a playboy," Will said one night in bed.

"No, you're not," Gustave said firmly.

"No, I'm not," Will agreed with resigned relief.

But too often now he would say horrid things, then take them back or introduce mitigations. He brooked no argument, never admitted to being wrong, took refuge in decorum, or declared that what he had meant was not what he had just said, till Gustave realized there was no telling how much was invented, how many the inventors, nor what was real, what mere distortion.

His worst enemy, Will said, was the anguish he felt at attracting wounded souls to his practice and wreaking havoc on them, as he knew he surely would, though of course—it went without saying —in the process he did them immeasurable good. He could not help himself. He was a master manipulator—it was his true gift and métier—and lately he had even begun to charm his aged mentor, who now seemed inclined to indulge him in certain little irregularities.

What these might be Gustave didn't ask. He had become adept

at accepting his lover's extremities, and prized him more each day, for always came the night and the delirium of bed. Sleep refreshed them both and they smiled with thrilled gratitude into one another's eyes for long intervals over their morning coffee.

THEY WENT one evening to the Bahai House where they had met, to the opening of an AIDS art exhibit. Will had contributed a piece, a mirror framed with barbed wire, symbol of oppression, he explained. Going around the basement room, viewing the various works, he lingered in front of his own, then burst into histrionic sobs, engaging the whole assembly, which one by one or in little groups sought to comfort him.

His ex-wife and two daughters were there, though he did not tell Gustave. The girls had stayed in the next room, the older fanatically banging chords on the piano, the younger screaming gibberish.

Lost on Gustave at the time, the scene might never have come back to mind, were it not for Will's puppets. One night he brought over his latest creation, a papier-mâché doll like a crazed Martha Washington with a sagging bosom like mammoth teardrops and eight god-awful little ogres hung from her skirts.

Gustave's inklings resolved themselves finally into a flash of Will briefly facing a florid woman with strained face and lank, grey hair, who must have been the wife. The ogres Gustave ventured to identify as Will's daughters, with four personalities apiece.

PROFOUND THOUGH he obviously was, Will could be simple as a child, one moment enfant terrible in the lead of a play, the next touchingly eager to please the director. While others lived in fear, he took a blithe attitude toward his health. Gustave gathered that he believed multiples were less susceptible to disease than single psyches, because there were more of them to fight it off, or because the sick might simply abdicate or be abandoned. He and Will practiced safe sex of course; both assumed both were negative; yet no one knew for sure absent a test, an undertaking that seemed more daunting as time went by, which subject, with all its perils, they rose above broaching.

At about the eighth month of their affair a kind of delusional resentment beset the beleaguered minister-actor-artist, almost overnight it seemed, and in recounting the onslaught Gustave could only call it paranoid, for he had never meant Will any harm.

"I'm waiting for when he tries to kill you," said Selwyn with dread.

"This cannot have a happy outcome," Arthur conceded.

"About that I'm of two minds," Gustave said, and described his consternation at Will's hostility. What it consisted of essentially, he had concluded after pained reflection, was Will's fear that others were much like himself, likewise dissembling many sides, especially perhaps Gustave.

Hence Will's penchant for secrecy and mystification. His wife had never been told the true import of his psychiatric sessions, had thought them devoted solely to his marital discontents, his narcissism and need for male companionship.

"You'll never figure me out, I'm beyond logic," he told Gustave morosely. "There's nothing that can't be picked apart psychologically, but the final tally is always zero."

Gustave understood that here was his life's challenge, the crucible in which he was to be tested, if he were to win happiness, and he was brave, braver by the day, but he trembled a bit, all the same, when he stopped to think about it.

Their sexual life meanwhile luxuriated, obliterated unresolved differences, misunderstandings, moments of cold alienation. But even in bed, so deep in one another's bowels they felt they must have crossed some boundary of human solitude, disconcerting things occurred. Once it seemed as if Will had forgotten how to make love. Gustave wondered who it was—this dark, angry face and pain-begetting prick—though in the morning Will had never been more himself, more masterfully charming, gravely dear.

Vortex WAS HIS favorite word; he used it in every context. "You are my vortex," he told Gustave, who answered, "And you are mine," but only Gustave was willing to drown, though it sometimes seemed that Will sank straight to the bottom of some awful, metaphysical despair and lay there crushed and buried in the mud, unrousable.

It began to get exhausting. Would Will come, not come? Would he call? He did not open his door the one time Gustave got up a desperate courage and knocked, a nerve-racking gamble never revealed or repeated. Unseen pressures enough on Will already widened the fault lines of his fragile psyche. Abysses gaped, down which whole continents of time vanished, as into amnesia. His increasing conflation of people and place, his zigzag past and inclination to revise, led rapidly now to the dissolution of Gustave's sense of reality. Finally he had to admit that he did not know one single thing for sure about his lover.

He concluded there was no William P. Manion, D.D.

For the first time he frankly questioned the ultimate wisdom of the relation and considered the complications and agonies of ending it.

One night after Gustave had waited for him in vain, then dined alone on leftovers, Will appeared and announced with an air of finality that he must leave San Francisco at once, within the month probably.

The time had simply come, he said. He hoped to persuade Gustave to accompany or join him later, once he was established in Sante Fe, which haven he had chosen for its purity, its deserts, mountains, and mesas, its Indians and folk art, its fantastic colors and dry, invisible air, but equal was his need to escape the sea with its unstable influences, its petty, imported cults, its murky mists and smells of rot. San Francisco was just too tame, too cosmopolitan for him; he wanted more heat, more cold, more adventure, solitude, renewal, and change.

He was quite excited, grew more so as he revealed his plans, and their possible new future together. Gustave, despite doubts, got caught up in his enthusiasm. His reckless mother having caused him to live frugally and save money, he was positioned to resist the misgivings of a leap in the dark. Nor need he burn bridges; he could sublet his apartment, take a leave of absence from work, return and resume if Santa Fe didn't pan out.

But Will was determined to get rid of his own place, cut all ties; he might have to move in with Gustave for a few days, but he would rent a van and get his books and art supplies to Santa Fe promptly and begin hunting for a suitable house for them and means of employment. He hankered to preach again.

Whether Gustave could arrange his affairs quickly enough to come at the outset Will professed to doubt. Perhaps it would be best if Gustave waited till Will was ready for him. He would hate to depart alone; on the other hand it would be nice for Gustave to come and find a home all made, their new life underway.

Will had not much furniture, but Gustave's would go a long way toward getting them set up. And they discussed logistics—vans and rental contracts, prices, sizes, mileage—but Gustave, feeling guilty, said nothing of his plan to sublet his apartment, leave work on terms of accrued vacation.

"The plot thickens," said Arthur.

"This guy's a basket case," Selwyn warned. "He's a leech. If you're not careful you'll be stuck with him for life."

"Hardly," said Gustave. "The worst part hasn't begun."

"I don't want to hear any more," Selwyn declared, as if to undo the done.

"But hear we must," said Arthur. "But first you both must take a little nourishment," and with a flourish, like an entrechat of wrist and fingers, he bade Julian decant some of his best Madeira into glasses standing on a silver tray nearby.

"Don't we wish!" Selwyn and Gustave sighed with rue.

"A touch," said Arthur, "will fortify you both," and nodded firmly at his hesitating maid, who then poured meager measures, which the brothers sipped with obvious relief.

Julian also got a goblet of tap water with a small ice cube in it for André Evre, who had unobtrusively entered, distributed token bows, and settled himself without interrupting Gustave's narrative.

"This would make a marvelous novel," he now made bold to interject.

Gustave shot him a look of horror, and Selwyn one of indignation. André raised an eyebrow, but forbore, old enough to attend without undue dismay, to see all go wrong, all dreams fail, to give art equal rank with life, but not insist that others see it so.

Gustave told on. Plans and expanded plans, revisions of revisions, preoccupied him and Will for days on end—no closer had they ever felt, reversing their recent plunge into detachment and doubt—their talk spiced by speculation and information gathering about life in Santa Fe.

Yet nothing came to pass. Each day brought some new delay or reason to reconsider which was the wisest course.

"I'm flexible," Gustave always said. "Whether you go first or we go together, either is fine with me, only let's agree on a timetable."

And Will would gravely nod. One day though he suggested he take a week and reconnoiter their prospective home of choice, in case its virtues should prove illusory. His old Honda was a temperamental wreck, however, sure to blow a bald tire or burst a gasket in the unaccustomed stress and heat, and so they exchanged cars—Gustave had a used but nicely kept Volvo—and thus one morning, after prolonged embraces, Will set forth on this first, exploratory phase of their common pilgrimage.

When several days went by with no word from Will, Gustave was not surprised, though he could hardly help but worry. It was 1,200 miles to Santa Fe, and Will lately had begun to seem ever more fragile, flaky and unsure behind his magisterial facade.

One week to the day of Will's departure Gustave glanced out his window and saw the Volvo pull up outside. He practically danced down the stairs with amazed joy at Will's unheralded return, and found his lover in a state of pathetic disintegration, obliged to admit he'd never left town. He'd turned back for a forgotten map and had never been able to cross his threshold again, nor answer the phone, which rang and rang and rang with God knows what desperate appeals for help, which all went unanswered, for every moment he was on the verge of getting back into the car, and finally once had actually done so, but then only driven around and around the Bay Area, unable to persuade himself that going to Santa Fe alone was not a fatal step.

He looked exhausted beyond remonstrance, and Gustave let him drive home at once in his Honda—which had developed a loud knock—to rest and recuperate, where, Gustave realized the instant he was out of sight, the would-be trailblazer had spent the whole week past in paralyzed torment.

Next he remembered Dondo Lazar, and then the boy in the tree, invisible in the leaves, whose legs grew into the ground like roots, who never came down and shot at adults with his bow and arrow.

So many questions flew into his mind that he called and kept calling Will's house, once letting it ring for an hour, of course without result, so that finally he felt quite frightened and despairing, faced with the truth that he didn't dare go to Will's house again, for fear of who or what he might find.

It was well after midnight, Gustave had sunk into a dead sleep, when Will let himself in with the key—which he had never used before—and made frenetic love to Gustave, then sat on the end of the bed, wrapped in a blanket, and said he had decided not to leave San Francisco after all.

He had not seemed so self-possessed in ages, as if in surviving the ordeal of his nontrip to Santa Fe he had been exalted—reborn really—and Gustave felt suddenly so optimistic that he urged Will to move in with him.

"Don't do it!" Selwyn cried.

Rueful, Gustave shrugged. Will had hugged him for a long while, rocking and rocking him, evidently deeply moved, then said he'd like to think about it, because he was not at all sure they should not break up now, having already experienced at full intensity everything life could offer any two human beings, especially men, and whatever followed must inevitably be diminishment and decline.

"Good riddance!" cried Selwyn.

"I can't imagine what I was hoping for," Gustave mused.

"Nothing's easy," André allowed.

"What a . . . what a!" said Julian.

"Nothing like mon ami Dover," Arthur murmured, "in his own way the worst of men."

"Well. I finally got angry!" Gustave said. "For the first time really. I grew icy cold. I said it was entirely up to him what became of us. He was quite surprised. I think he was offended. As if I had been mean to him. He put his clothes on and went home."

Several days passed and then Will appeared in his usual way unannounced. Gustave listened without comment to what amounted to a philosophical monologue on the relative merits of breaking up at once or waiting for the day when nature would take its course, no matter their efforts or intentions to the contrary.

And if and/or when they *did* diverge how should it be done—cold turkey or gradually, with, say, weekly dinners to keep in touch, or monthly phone calls, in hopes of maintaining their friendship; and how should the issue of sexual jealousy be resolved, and the ultimate problem of taking new lovers, and sparing *them* pain?

To his groaning auditors, Gustave admitted that he had been drawn into consideration of these questions, which anyway seemed unreal, so much talk having diluted the awful possibility that their love was truly moribund—for now to Gustave at moments it blazed more brightly than ever, and he renewed his vows, tried squarely to face the ordeal he must undergo in keeping faith with his exorbitant, dream partner.

Will went home that night in an aura of warm feeling. Gustave had simply insisted on his own flexibility, reiterating that he would prefer them to share as much of their lives as they could, and not be too grim about the future. After all they were free to choose, and choose one another, if they so chose.

Eyes shining, Will had nodded gratefully, and gone home, leaving Gustave to a hopeful sleep, came back the next night to declare that the one sure way to bind themselves together was to adopt a child, preferably a boy.

This unconsidered option led to mental activity compared to which the Santa Fe move had been tranquillity itself. The child ought to be a member of some minority, oughtn't it? About age ten? Or seven? Asian? Or Guatemalan? Or Afro. Haitian perhaps.

Whatever the particulars Will was anxious to proceed, as if the impulse, not acted on instantly, must fade. He was overwrought and irritable at objections Gustave raised, not least that Will already had two children.

"Daughters," he retorted with disdain. "Not ours."

And in some measure Gustave too saw adoption as an answer to the disadvantages of gay love, the lack of family and stability, of a future beyond their own span, of natural purpose in their lives, and the awful problem of finding responsible fulfillment in each other alone.

Curiously, touchingly, Will seemed to feel he was the nurturant one, the most apt for the female role, but Gustave, sold on flexibility, deemed such nebulosities not of great import, at least not yet.

He was willing, eager even, to give the idea a hearing—full

time, full speed ahead, with full attention—so that they might reach agreement, a marriage of minds.

And thus they vowed, that very night, with formal kisses like Arab potentates, to try to blend their lives, adopt and socialize a boy, in a manner befitting their common view of human propriety; and once more, but never so powerfully, Gustave felt the tidal promise of the voyage they were now finally embarking on, after so many and such tentative wadings out and timid retreats to shore.

Will returned the second evening thence with a familiar air of distraction, which soon devolved into one of cool and rational despair. In short, he feared the boy's upbringing might cause a rift between them. When Gustave tried to reassure him that such concerns were premature and could be negotiated in due time, Will allowed that his real sense of the problem was that it would be best if their adopted son and heir were mentally stellar no doubt, but not, definitely not, physically attractive, perhaps best be crippled or ugly, as there were no prohibitive blood ties among the three sides of this most treacherous of triangles.

Gustave was stunned. He knew that something else was up— so much at least he'd learned—that this caveat, though earnest, was bound to be merely a decoy or disguise or leader, and sure enough, in another moment, Will confessed in a panicked voice that disaster had struck his ménage, and now he looked genuinely distraught, and sighed and shook his head and groaned.

Marni was pregnant. Gustave gathered—though he had never heard her name before—that she was the brash adolescent who had caused Will so much anxiety in the past. Worst of all Will, feared that he was in some way the father, if not in material fact, at least morally, was even at some spiritual level the genetic progenitor. He had to go right home to help in her travail.

There was nothing in this that could be effectively protested, at least in Gustave's view at the time, and his hearers merely gaped at him, and said nothing, not even André.

Will stayed away for several days and never called. Gustave didn't bother to dial, for the phone had never yet been answered, but he did belatedly start to wonder how Will's patients got in touch with him. And then he fell to wondering how many of Will's patients might be figments. The whole thing began to seem sinister, menacing in some new way he could not encompass. It was like walking in the mist at night, this loving Will, for each next step might bring him face to face with whom or what?

And then Will appeared late one night, sharply dressed, eyes a-shine, exhilarated, triumphant, ready for a drink and a well-earned rest, "Some R&R," as he put it.

Gustave opened a bottle of Fumé Blanc and made supper while he reported on his salvaged domestic situation. Marni, bless her normal hormones, was now eager for motherhood; she had chosen life and sacrifice over abortion or renunciation of the infant at birth. It had been the most arduous counseling task he had ever undertaken, and he was deeply gratified and proud.

Gustave had managed to congratulate him. He admitted to his incredulous audience that he had been so disappointed and demoralized, had for so long invested such hopes in his love, that he had simply forced himself to see these fantasies as headed for a happy ending, and led Will to bed at the first pause in his torrent of talk.

Their plans, solid by day, melted overnight, or got postponed or were supplanted by complications—next by Marni's problematical pregnancy.

So difficult, so uncomfortable, so ultimately unresolved a question was it still for the unfortunate young woman that Will himself began to show the strains of her burgeoning ambiguity, and took to his bed at last, a crisis so severe that he made use of the phone to apprise Gustave of at least the outlines of its development.

Marni had changed her mind. A titanic test of wills was underway, one of enormous delicacy and import too, for both of them. Naturally he did not wish to act the tyrant, for the final decision must be hers, yet to dither and delay was to refuse either to deny or ratify the choice nature had already made.

Gustave begged to come to his aid, to bring him something to eat and drink at least, but Will was so firm, sounding withal on the brink of hysteria, that Gustave dared not disobey his oft-repeated injunction to keep away from his house unless expressly summoned. And again Gustave was obliged to recognize how huge was his fear of Will's secret life, and he had to despise himself, for courage was the touchstone of his pride.

The weather grew dank and depressing, and Will's next visit, late at night, lasted but moments. He would not take his raincoat off, looked bloated, as if he himself were somehow the womb of this ghostly child. He would not embrace, would not allow Gustave even a peck at his cheek, seemed frightened and flighty and fled at once, without explanation, and did not call nor appear again for three days when—a sunny Saturday noon—he knocked and entered and stood faintly breathing there, sallow, unshaven, in a soiled white shirt with sleeves rolled up, the very picture of defiance and defeat.

The whole story poured out. Marni had at first suppressed the ugly truth, that her fetus was almost certainly the product of rape, and rape by a cousin she abominated.

Will, not two hours since, at the last possible moment, had performed an abortion. He scrupled to provide details, but apparently a crash reading course and common sense had taught him how to fashion a curette from a kitchen implement, scrape the uterus, and keep all sterilized.

It had been a gory chore, and a deeply conflicted one, as Will had no way to know she was not lying about the parentage of the hardly humanoid, little knot of bloody tissue he had flushed down the toilet. Marni would recover; she was young and resilient, but he—here he choked upon dry sobs—felt damned by a second shadow that only death could rid him of.

Gustave strove to feel inured. He urged Will to look on the bright side. Just as well perhaps, he said, not to have brought into the world yet another character to join Will's hapless cast, especially an innocent baby.

This half-intended sally seemed to stiffen the slumping surgeon, revive his stoic stance. He looked now a tragic figure, standing by the table, vodka glass in hand. He downed it, poured another. "I'm an evil man," he said.

"No, you're not," Gustave said, plaintive and irritated both.

But Will wouldn't hear of exoneration. Marni was a naive kid for whom he was responsible. He was guilty as sin, a loathsome scum, for all his many parts in the debacle of his own life, and for the invariable betrayal of everyone who had ever relied on him.

"You can't take the blame for everything bad that happens," Gustave cried.

"No?" Will inquired between a sneer and a smirk.

"No!" said Gustave, then rued his imprudence.

For Will's self-pity unindulged turned instantly to surliness. He affected now to be a man misunderstood, wounded in his pride, derided, belittled in the hour of his extremity, and nothing Gustave said the rest of that night could quite put them back on an even keel. Their every word seemed after a moment to reveal an edge, jibes in the guise of polite obliquity.

And the possibility occurred to Gustave, as he went to bed alone, that Will was actually contriving day by day, week by week, a conscious policy of outright, calculated lies, was taking pleasure in the bestowal of pain, enjoying the creation of chaos. For the first time Gustave had to admit to himself that he was losing the battle for Will's heart and soul.

The unthinkable once thought made Gustave as wary as Will, and their sex life ended. Gustave began to notice and attend, to check every detail of what Will said against the pattern and texture of the known past, assess every flicker of eye or intonation, every hesitation or haste of speech, every smile or furtive stare; and Will seemed to welcome the change in him, to approve, even with a kind of cold avidity to bare himself to meet the challenge.

At inappropriate moments, in an objective tone, as if in answer to all perplexities, Will would say, "I love you."

But Gustave wondered what role he was playing, which of his personae were ruling him, or taking the stage at his behest. More and more he suspected Will had no conscience, or rather that it consisted of pure intellect, feeble and unalloyed, without the least sentience or feeling, and might, at a change of breeze, rebel or be subverted by his alters. Gustave had to speculate upon the awful temptations, the struggles his actor-lover must undergo to keep from expanding his repertoire until it embraced his whole known world of personalities, and even those but dreamt.

"You're dishonest," he said straight out to him one Sunday brunch over shots of tequila at their dingy café where they never saw a soul they knew.

"Of course," Will said. "I've never told the truth about any-thing in my life."

"You've just been jerking me around," Gustave said. "Lately anyway."

Will laughed, proud and lonely in his knowledge. "I wish I could get back to being the person I was when we first met," he conceded gently, "the day you gave me your key. Remember?"

"Why can't you?" Gustave pled.

Will smiled his weary smile. "In the first place," he said, "we're not standing in the same river. And to return to the original ques-tion, the truth does not exist. There's never been any such thing, and never will be. Truth itself is a lie."

"Why are you always trying to mind-control me?" Gustave asked. "You don't have to do that to fuck me. You never did."

Honest words, such as he might not have risked before, but Will merely smiled with narrowed eyes and looked away, as if he were waiting for something, listening, testing the day, and for an instant his face seemed to darken the deserted café and a smell arose from the cement floor like emanations of an ancient sewer. The moment was almost palpable and Gustave shivered for their sanity.

Will was both there and not there. Speaking passionately, but also oddly by rote, he went over the familiar ground of his social past, how fragile he was, how desperately depressed when alone, how impossible he had always found it to sustain relationships, his lack of trust being due to what he had been taught about love as a child, and his adolescent discovery of what love really was. He was needy, needy, but it made him hate himself.

"You probably don't know yourself what the truth is," Gustave essayed.

Will laughed delightedly, unfazable at his own game. "You know what Nietzsche says," he said. " 'What does not kill me makes me stronger.' "

"Well," Gustave said. "I like *that*."

"It's just another lie," Will cried. "The truth is, what does not kill me maims me."

"According to your system," Gustave said lightly, "that too must be a lie."

"Of course," Will said with a fleeting expression diabolical, fiendish, at the same time featureless and empty.

Gustave felt another chill and asked himself if he had any real existence for his lover, or were merely another of his apparitions. And what did they think of Gustave, now they had got to know him better? Did they all still agree he was the right one for Will? And for that matter, how did they feel about Will, not to mention each other? And poor Will, always trying to find his way back to the happy man he had become upon meeting Gustave, and then so quickly, strangely lost.

It was all a morass, all a mirage.

"I have to tell you," Will said, and frowned at the littered table and the round of tequilas, newly arrived. He paused long enough for Gustave's dread to explode in the realization that Will was purposely prolonging the suspense, demanding concession of his total dominance, before he pronounced:

"I'm leaving."

"Town?" said Gustave blankly. He felt not a thing.

Will nodded slowly, pursing his lips. Yes, he was going elsewhere, a destination he had already chosen but would not divulge, though not Santa Fe, and he must go alone.

"Why the secrecy? I'm not going to pursue you," Gustave said, though he felt with horror that he well might follow him through the grave to the fiery center of the earth.

"It will be better if no one knows," Will said. "I need a new life, and this is the only way I can get it."

"Bon voyage!" said Gustave.

Will evidently welcomed such sangfroid and began zestfully worrying his perpetual conundrum, whether they should break up at once or diverge more casually. But the more he talked the more lachrymose he grew, until tears filled Gustave's eyes too.

Another round arrived. They were on their way to quite a day. Now that things were settled the retrospects came thick and fast, and Will was moved to acknowledge that Gustave had nearly saved him, *had* in fact saved him for a brief, golden while. But eventually they had escaped TONTB.

"TONTB?" said Gustave.

"The obsolete need to breed," Will explained.

"Well, raise, at least," said Gustave, "for which there is a real need. That you won't deny."

"Same-same," Will said gloomily. "I'll let you know."

"Know what?"

"When I'm leaving. So we can say good-bye."

"Let's go home," Gustave said, "and go back to bed. We don't have to ruin this day."

They paid the bill, and at the bar Will downed another shot in one swallow. He was driving the Honda, jumped clutch, screeched tires and careened the short distance to Gustave's house, with Gustave shouting at him to slow down, but he didn't pull up at the curb, but stopped mid-street and raced the engine.

"I've got to get home," he said. "I've got things to do, and promises to keep."

Gustave knew better than to argue, or ask for explanation. "Bye," he said with cold sarcasm. He had never seen Will so drunk.

Will crossed his hands on the top of the steering wheel, yelled, "Wheee!" like a boy, and screeched off in swerves.

Gustave stumbled up his stairs past caring, relieved at his numb acceptance that the end had finally come. He could hardly be surprised, after all.

"Not the end," said Arthur.

"Should have been," said Gustave.

"This affair is nothing *but* ends," said André.

"This guy's a disease," Selwyn said with grim animosity.

What Will was up to was not clear; meanwhile he kept away, making phone calls every few days, leaving gnomic messages on Gustave's answering machine, as always never answering his own.

When he did deign to communicate with Gustave it was even more torturous, because Gustave had to spend the whole time trying to identify which of Will's alters was talking, then determine whether Will was aware of it.

In Will's tone was always that taint of angry malice, as if Gustave had injured him. At times too Gustave thought he could feel Will's inward struggle to meet his love honestly, but it felt like a tide running the wrong way, though Gustave still could not help hoping it might turn in time.

Will called one night to make plans, as if nothing had happened. Gustave would love the small, lakeside city he had chosen, with four distinct seasons, quite unspoiled. He wanted Gustave to sign on before he revealed its name—a sort of test, Gustave surmised. But he couldn't bring himself to say yes unequivocally, and Will grew lugubrious, mourning their lost happiness and trust. "I'll always love you," he said, as he hung up.

The next night's phone tape—when Gustave got home from work—commenced in a vindictive voice, "I know you've just been on pins and needles." Then it switched to an evasive babble about remorse and the endurance of love, ending with the simple pronouncement: They were through. Their relationship had run its course. Will would not be coming or calling again. Farewell.

Gustave interpreted this to mean that Will had foundered, and was beset with helpless grief for him, and yet he wondered with a kind of hope if it had all been planned.

Indeed, after an awful week in which Gustave was nearly unhinged by anguish, Will called, sounding brisk and businesslike, and suggested they mediate their differences with a view to getting together for dinner some evening.

Gustave could not speak. In the silence he pictured Will awaiting his response, crouched like a panther at a mole hole, and the terrible thought seized him: This Man Hates Me.

Finally he said, "Will, I can't stand any more of this craziness."

"I agree," Will said. "We can turn this thing around; we can work it out; we have too much to lose. We just have to remember we are two absolutely different people."

"Are you saying you think you're me?" Gustave said as coldly as he could, but began to wonder, in spite of himself, how *that* might play out.

"No, no, no, no, no," Will chuckled with a huckster's voice Gustave had never heard before. "But our points of view might be aligned. We might consider doing a retreat."

"For the love of God!" Gustave cried, "who's this?"

"Oh," Will said, audibly abashed, "Mr. Busybuddy. He keeps an eye out. He's Mr. Last Resort. I could never get by without him."

"Great!" said Gustave, and hung up, another first.

"About time," André droned.

"But not yet the end," Arthur said.

Julian tried to pour more Madeira, but Selwyn and Gustave declined with quick, distracted shakes of the head. Arthur shrugged accord. André had yet to taste his water though the ice cube was long gone.

"I disintegrated," Gustave resumed. "I loved this madman, and sometimes I even believed he loved me."

He couldn't keep his resolve to forget his demonic lover. His ear waited for the phone. He could not bring himself to turn off his answering machine, not that Will left any more messages. His thoughts never strayed from the anguish of loss. He became immersed in reconstruction of their affair, remembered events unevaluated at the time, began to feel he had been voyaging along the edges of a parallel universe. He felt eerie. His native rationalism began to fail. How had he gone from Heaven to Hell with no door between?

He remembered his strange, initial impression of Will—so soon overlaid by his sophisticate's veneer—of Will's physical uncanniness, the odd swarthiness of his face compared to the rest of his luminous, pale body. He remembered, on their second or third date, Will's casual mention of psychic powers, never alluded to again and hardly distinguishable from subsequent remarks about therapy and psychoanalysis, and his remark about people like himself having been burned at the stake.

A palpable sense of evil beset Gustave. When the phone rang—though it was never Will—he picked it up with trepidation, lest some sort of mental transferences enthrall him. He recalled Will's burning eyes, first felt across the circle at the Bahai Temple, and then the gleaming teeth and eyes, and realized he had been looking directly into what?

Gustave had never credited anything occult, rejected all religions, disbelieved in the supernatural, but now suddenly he had no doubt of other worlds, other realities, ghosts of the dead, satanic spirits, malign telepathy. He could feel Will conjuring him.

Science could not explain evil, but it was an active force, not mere misfortune, but human, evolved, purposive, just beyond our power to glimpse. History hid it in cause and effect, but now Gustave felt it, the unacknowledged demiurge of destruction.

He walked the streets, and, as if a veil had lifted from his under-standing, all the faces he met looked vicious. He was afraid of everyone and everything, but most of all he dreaded seeing Will again and never seeing him again, terrified equally of both.

In the mirror he saw a haunted starer. Sleep abandoned him. He weighed suicide, who once had scorned such dodges. One night he drank desperately at the kitchen table, each beat the phone did not ring a glowing rivet pounded into his heart. At bottle's end he staggered to bed and fell asleep.

He was dreaming of the key, a clear constellation above his soul's boat, and woke to Will, pants down and priapic, groaning his name, pushing and hauling at his waist.

Gustave let himself be rolled on his front. Will was very drunk himself, implacable in his want. Having got Gustave mounted face-down over a bunched pillow, he started working Gustave's stiffening penis with one lube-slathered hand while he delightfully resisted penetrating his anus more than glans deep.

Gustave was on the edge of a most tantalizing orgasm, one with-out the slightest personal involvement, when Will's prick reamed into him all the way like a thunderbolt that hurt worse each thrust, till he began to shriek, and Will came in silence and withdrew, sat back on haunches and heels, fell back on his elbows, coughing and coughing his cigarette cough.

Gustave turned on the light, and felt himself. His hand came away red. The cock ring Will was wearing was no ordinary affair, but a pink and green gold band worked with a pattern of inter-twined roses.

"Now we're really married," he said. "That's our wedding band."

Gustave stretched a disbelieving finger to touch the thing where it lay around Will's shrinking member.

"My crown of thorns," Will said complacently. "I wore it for you."

"You're mad!" Gustave said.

Will smiled his most understanding, sweetest smile, and even his face seemed to lighten.

Gustave seized a corner of sheet and blotted himself, then held it out to Will. "Look," he said. "Is this what you meant?"

Will swallowed and turned away. "You should shower," he said.

"Get out, get out, get out!" Gustave screamed and kept screaming while Will pulled his pants up and fled, covering his ears.

"The end," said André.

"Amen," Arthur echoed.

"Oh, no," said Gustave, smiling wanly at them.

"I hope you took a good revenge," said Selwyn. "I'm not a vindictive person, but I actually hope you killed him."

"I should have maimed him at least," Gustave said. "I guess life already did that though."

"Small consolation," Arthur murmured.

The next day Gustave changed his lock. The day after that he took a week off from work, then found he was too depleted even to leave town for a respite, much less go back to work when the week was up. He took another month; it was his firm's slow season. He hardly left the house, hardly got off his couch, felt his tendons atrophy. And he wished, wished, wished Will would come back and knock, and he would let him in and they would talk at last with complete confidence and honesty. And he knew this for a fantasy, yet did not know for sure.

He wandered out one evening like a convalescent and let his feet take him where they would, past their favorite café and beyond. A friend stopped in a car and whirled him off to a party like a zombi, eyes fixed straight ahead. He did not know the host; he did not know the guests; he did not care; he had no reason to be there or anywhere.

Looking resplendent, Will appeared. He was overjoyed to see Gustave. He introduced him proudly to one and all, arm around his shoulder, repeating, "I want you to meet my better half."

The guests gazed upon Gustave with envy. Gustave's heart swelled with hideous joy. He thought, *Can this be happening?*

Will met his frontal stare with wet-eyed tenderness, traced the sunken contour of his cheek with gentle fingertips. Gustave downed his drink at a gulp, and Will made gentle haste to replenish his glass. In crossing the room he seemed for a moment to slouch, to become simian, shorter, furtive, no one Gustave knew.

In horror he thought to save himself. Will, on his way back, drink in each hand, had stopped by an armchair, to listen, head inclined, to an older man, who was visibly charmed. Will looked like a senator, gracious, grave, attentive to a favored constituent.

Gustave backed out the door, stumbled, regained his footing and ran two blocks, caught a bus and hid himself in the depths of a disco, where he shivered with cold sweats till alcohol calmed and warmed him, and he was able to give thanks for his escape.

He awoke at dawn with a deathly hangover to the ringing phone. It did not occur to him that it might be Will.

"We've got to meet and settle this, once and for all," said a perfect stranger.

"Who's this we?" Gustave shouted.

"I mean you and I," Will said.

Gustave listened. Will sounded as if, face to face, the past could be redeemed with a word.

Gustave agreed to meet once more with Will on one condition —that it be at Will's house. Will refused. Both were categorical, and their goodbyes collided.

Gustave lowered his head, sat silent.

"That's it?" Julian said aghast.

"That's it," Gustave said, not looking up.

"No mayhem," said André. "How outré."

"That's my one regret," Gustave conceded, "that I didn't just go over there and kick the door down. I was just too afraid of the place. I'll always wonder what it was like."

"It wouldn't have been worth it," André said. "There was nothing there, a few parts of puppets, a half gallon of Scotch under the sink, bare floor."

"How do you know that?" Gustave cried.

"How does one know anything?" André shrugged.

"And that's it?" Julian said.

"That's it," Gustave said. "Just about."

"Ah, of course, there's more," Arthur mused.

Gustave went back to work, but couldn't focus and made mistakes, then took more time off. His health broke, fatigue and thrush came on. Ready for one agony to cancel another, he got tested. The positive verdict scarcely discomposed him. He had a bad few weeks of facing the unfaceable, then took it more or less in stride. What could be said, after all, about his getting AIDS? That it was inevitable?

Bad as AIDS was, falling in love with Will was still the worst thing that had ever happened to him. The good side was all false hopes and fears had vanished, and he felt complete, at ease with himself, able to endure whatever might come, and happy, in a strange way happier than he had ever been, thanks to this reunion with Selwyn. And so maybe Nietzsche was right; he wanted to think so.

"And that's it?" Julian cried, ever more incredulous.

"I saw him one more time, "Gustave confessed. "Months later. At another damn cocktail party. I went out on the porch—it was on the second floor—and saw him on a patio down below, where some other guys were having a party too.

"He was learning to two-step. He had an arm around these two young guys. He looked absolutely terrific, like he was having the time of his life. I just put my drink down and went home. I never saw him again."

"The End," said Arthur.

"Zilch," Julian muttered. "Zero."

"Enough for me," Gustave said.

8

SELWYN

NTIL RECENT TIMES Selwyn's life had entailed an almost total constriction, a drab invisibility, broken by uncontainable indiscretions like a recurrent, incurable rash. Dreading exposure more than death, he had learned the ways of artful guile, lived for weekend trips, knew the thrill of flight, of legerdemain and track covering, in public places stifled an impulse to jump up on a chair, and shout, "I'm gay."

"You never?" said Julian.

"Never," said Selwyn.

He had moved and moved. The moment his closet cracked he fled. He took risks and afterward berated himself. For the past few years he had avoided big cities with their anonymous temptations and would, in other circumstances, have gone yet further north, up the coast, to Blue Hill, Maine, or Eastport, or even St. Andrews in New Brunswick. He longed for the joyful life of seasons and weather with the younger man he had forsworn immediately upon testing positive.

Till then his life had been vain discontent. Nothing had satisfied him. His mode had been perfectionism. Every job, apartment, street, suburb, town, and state had its spoiling element, yet he had been dogged by the conviction that exactly what he wanted existed somewhere. And the right man too. But in each painfully sought-out possibility of a mate he found some defect—this one smoked and drank to excess, that one was too old or too conventional, or too tall or small or bald, or had a certain mole, this one belonged to a crazy church that knew God's plan for history, another was apt to lapse into languor or break out into defiant camp at fatal moments. He had hoped to live in marital obscurity, two bachelors sharing a house in oblivion. The gay life was anathema to him.

"I didn't want to be found out," he said, "even by myself."

Bent on improvement, he gave up all vices, starting with cigarettes, alcohol, and drugs, then meat, poultry, fish, coffee, tea, sugar, salt, finally even sweets, the Achilles' heel of his reductive character, his last pleasure in life. He was an expert on desserts, and after making his meager supper would saunter to some French or Italian or Greek emporium and sample tortes, éclairs, Napoleons, flans, canolis. It was ludicrous, he knew, but he loved the luxuries of taste, and the more he loved them, the more determined he grew to rid himself of this last weakness. He fought many doubly lost battles, slinking out at midnight to get a soft ice cream sundae in some fast food joint, long after the elegant establishments had closed.

He grew sanctimonious and got angry at those who went on enjoying life. He felt like a fool now when he looked back on himself.

By the time he moved to gentrified Portsmouth he had reached a point where he did not expect much, and everything seemed a surrogate. He was like a spy on people's impression of him. If asked they might have called him a courteous man good at his job, who minded his own business, whom no one disliked or knew very well —profile of the mass murderer about to run amuck.

Then—he now granted what he would have denied at the time —the inevitable happened: he met someone. He actually met someone and fell in love.

He was getting his new apartment in order, reconnoitering the neighborhood. There were no end of gays, more than he had expected—a thing both good and bad in his personal economy of promise and pitfall.

Directly across the street, in a lavishly restored, red brick, Federal-style mansion fronting the sidewalk behind a wrought-iron fence, a familiar tragedy was being played out. Seldom could human silhouette be seen through the tall lace curtains, and at night the monumental chandelier glimmered goldenly in the empty drawing room like a vestige of noblesse oblige. A grey Jaguar reposed before the door, but in back, at the end of a feldspar driveway, beyond the badminton net and perfectly kept croquet lawn, amid an old oak grove, a spacious carriage house sheltered a sleek, black Maserati and a battered, blue Land Rover.

There, at 1075 York Street, resided Gregory Gibbons and Rick Kendrick. Selwyn would see them, if the day were warm, taking a drive in the Jaguar, with a robe around Rick's knees. Sometimes a third man drove them like a chauffeur, though he seemed more friend than employee. This was Miles, their all-purpose, live-in man.

Rick looked like Gregory's decrepit father, leaning on his arm when they came down the granite steps, though they were the same age. Ravaged and gaunt, the sick man looked to be on his last legs, but handsome Gregory was the picture of robust health, besides being rich as Croesus, having inherited not one, nor two, but three small family fortunes, preserved by abnegating aunts.

Selwyn grew acquainted with the household through Miles, whom he kept meeting in a nearby grocery store. If Gregory was commandingly handsome and good-humored, Miles was simply beautiful, a happy god gifted with perfect self-assurance.

Quite a couple they might make in due course, Selwyn thought with a morbid twinge. Miles stirred in him admiration, envy, and gratitude. Fifteen years younger, Miles belonged to an incomparably later generation, took his sex for granted, and without the slightest effort or hesitation caused others to accept it too. It had never occurred to him that he was in the wrong and he never doubted his right to a place in the world. His manly charm won everyone over at once, though he could, if balked, look quite intractable and grave.

"I'm afraid I don't know your last name," Selwyn said one day, as they were walking back together from the store.

"Enelen," said Miles with his smile that melted Selwyn.

He puzzled for a few steps. "How do you spell that?" he said at last. "You look sort of . . . Scandinavian?"

"NLN," said Miles, and the smile, like wine, subtly elaborated, inspired all his features with a complex of nuances, unfamiliar and unique. "No Last Name," he explained.

"Just Miles?" said Selwyn.

"Yes," said Miles, his nod somehow belying Selwyn's assumption of the ease of his attainments, and the smile, with kind eyes dominating, now seemed to infuse his whole person with a chaste but sexual charge.

That was the end of Selwyn's search for an adequate object of love.

Miles had several times promised to present Selwyn to the inhabitants of 1075. They were dear people, he said, with more troubles than they deserved. On that improbable irony, he seemed both reticent and alarmed.

Attentive only to Miles, Selwyn little wondered what he meant. AIDS hardly seemed to admit of proportional degrees of woe, warranted or not, and who deserved anything, birth and death included?

As the days went by Miles appeared ever more thankful to see Selwyn when they met on the street, as both contrived to make happen at least once a day, their front doors now opening together almost by prearrangement, their faces instantly aglow.

"Let's go for a little walk," Miles would say. "I had to get out of there for a minute. There's just nothing I can do."

"What is it, for God's sake?" Selwyn finally entreated.

"Love," said Miles with uncharacteristic grimness, "is a terrible thing."

Selwyn looked askance. This was decidedly not what he desired to hear.

They walked in silence for a block, till Miles suddenly skipped himself into step with Selwyn and said, "Why don't you come by about noon Sunday. That'll give me time to prepare. They're most eager to meet you, after all I've told them. And they could use a little diversion. They hardly see anyone any more. Though sometimes I feel I'm the one who's trapped," he added with a rueful laugh. "If they're not up to it I'll give you a ring."

And Miles went on to depict his employers—Rick the sensitive, who had drunk away his life and manifest talents, for a long time now a recluse, who spent himself at home in the study of shipwrecks, and Gregory the indulgent, the imperturbable trustee of prestigious, nonprofit charities, who seemed hardly to have noticed his lover's wasted chances and nightly oblivion.

There had always been plenty of money; Gregory had bought Rick whatever he wanted, closets full of clothes he never wore, kitchen gadgets, trips to exclusive resorts. They had been together for twenty years, and now, in an excess of caprice, Rick wanted to leave.

"Leave?" Selwyn said.

"Oh," Miles said with a kind of helpless vexation, "he's out of love with Gregory, who's always looked after him like a baby, and in with someone else."

"Else?" said Selwyn.

"Oh, God, I don't even want to talk about it," Miles said. "I feel disloyal too. It's very hard on Gregory. He never had an inkling this might happen. Bad enough, you see, that Rick's dying."

Selwyn shook his head. All he registered was the fact that Miles cared enough to have been talking about him. When they parted he steeled himself to wait, fearful of some hindrance.

But the days passed without mishap, he caught no glimpse of Miles, nor of the ill-starred couple, Sunday dawned, he dressed at last with anxious care, noon came, he crossed the street with bumping heart and knocked at the white door numbered 1075, once, twice, thrice with the ponderous brass knocker.

Frankly blushing, Miles ushered him into the living room, made the introductions and served a pale consommé with homemade bread and salad on little folding tables. Who Rick had once been no one could have discerned but for the framed photographs of him and Gregory in their green years adorning walls and mantelpiece as if to prove their life had not always been so dire.

Gregory seemed not to have aged from even the earliest of these scenes, but Rick had gone from a tall, willowy, dreamy, intense aesthete to a grizzled, emaciated, and bent decrepitude, unable to rise from his chair unaided, once up barely able to shuffle to the bathroom by himself. Only his voice had not failed.

Gregory was a gracious host and discoursed about the house and history of Portsmouth, spiced with wry views of his eccentric forbears, alternately putting discreet, personal questions to Selwyn, who could not help directing his answers to Miles.

Rick listened with vague politesse, faintly breathing through parted lips, constantly wetting his front teeth with his tongue. At moments he seemed to forsake them for the realms of reverie. Then an intent and preoccupied look, almost of anticipation, dominated his gaunt countenance, giving him an air both ready and resolute, with frequent wince-like tics that fluttered his eyelids and made him grimace, especially when, as it seemed—and regardless of the innocuous sentiment expressed—Gregory's voice, alone of the trio, intruded into his consciousness.

Selwyn, so full of fresh delight, nothing at first disturbed. A kindly sheen lay upon all things. The consommé was divine, the salad a bouquet of flavors; Miles was obviously an artful cook; the Sunday sunlight flooding in felt like true beatitude; his hosts, notwithstanding their extremity, made an impressive couple; Miles' brilliant beauty blazed, and seemed to blaze for him.

Coffee done, the little lacquered tables nested out of sight, each now settled in his corner of the cozy square of armchairs, ankles crossed, fingertips touching antimacassars, all eyes fixed upon some central spot, mute expectancy too long drawn out, a social shadow fell.

Then Gregory started a conversation, but everything he said sounded bizarrely cheerful, out of the blue—like a whistled bar of Haydn in a gun-run neighborhood—and though Miles did his best to second him, he sounded nearly as inane. Rick, looking grim and corpse-like, ignored them.

Selwyn was paying small heed. Enjoying Miles' proximity, he must have missed its beginnings, but at some point he became aware that a tiff was underway.

Rick seemed revitalized, at least in tongue, though not another muscle moved, not even his eyes—and whatever Gregory said, no matter how kind his tone, Rick mocked it or made derisive asides.

Gregory appeared either zealously inobservant or impervious, or perhaps—Selwyn theorized—he was so inured to his stricken lover's irascibility that his laudable mode of coping was simply to endure all without ado.

"He's a complete fool, he doesn't understand anything, he doesn't want to understand, it wouldn't suit him," Rick without warning oratorically railed at poor Selwyn, into whose mind leapt the awful suspicion that this was dementia—little wonder then that Gregory tried to humor or quarantine him.

"Well, Rick does exaggerate just a bit sometimes," Gregory said with a fond, slightly sheepish grin. "I do know a few little things, however, and in a moment I'm going to think of one. Miles, we might have a fire. I think a fire might be nice at this stage."

And Miles, looking relieved to quit immobility, knelt at the hearth, lighting half a dozen little blazes beneath the perfectly-piled trihedron of birch logs, then remained engrossed, watching the flames uncrumple the balled newsprint, involve the crackling kindling.

"There's nothing like a fire," Gregory said. "Ever changing. Only the ocean can equal it."

An obdurate saint he began to seem, full of fustian, but unfailingly generous and good-tempered, magnanimous even, though he did have a habit, understandable given the circumstances, of referring to Rick in the third person, especially in directing Miles to his every need and comfort.

In no time the fire became a roaring conflagration.

"Thanks, Gregory!" Rick said with heavy sarcasm, then confided to Selwyn, "First he roasts me till I sweat, next he'll let me freeze to death."

"You might move his chair back *just* a tad," said Gregory.

Miles with dignified dispatch sprang to; the chair, tilted back, rolled easily on rubber casters, despite which Rick's frail frame got jostled and jarred.

"He might have a glass of juice now too, I think," Gregory said with a glance at his watch and Miles, casually graceful, arose again and went to the kitchen.

"It's very hard on him, not being able to drink," Gregory explained to Selwyn.

"I'm glad not to drink," Rick snapped. "I like being sober. It's a revelation. Let me tell you!"

Selwyn felt it was time to go, and he sat forward a little in his chair, alert for a moment to take leave, but by now relations between his hosts were at such odds, so caustic and scornful on Rick's part, so impeccably pleasant, withal so unremitting, on Gregory's, that no exit offered, short of obvious flight.

Apparently daunted only by silence, Gregory began to talk about next winter—it was raw April now—and their plans to revisit Rio, Rick's favorite place on earth.

To Selwyn's eye the sick man looked unlikely to leave his environs.

Rick confirmed Selwyn's prognosis with quick asperity, "You'll be going by yourself. I won't be here."

"You'll be here," Gregory said, calm and assured, "you'll be here for a long time to come."

"I may be here, but I won't be *here*," said Rick with baleful emphasis.

"I predict we'll be having Christmas dinner in Rio," Gregory scoffed soothingly. "At midnight. Just as we did three years ago. At exactly that same place we liked so much."

"That sounds very romantic," said Selwyn, trying to do his part.

Rick gave an aggravated crow. "It's Gregory who loves Rio. The streets are full of boys, all these little brown cherubs, everywhere you go after dark. They're homeless, they're starving, they'd cut your throat for a dime. We came out of the restaurant, Gregory says, 'Aren't they cute! Of course, it's way past their bedtime, but what a relaxed society they have to grow up in. It's wonderful the streets are so safe.' Meanwhile every night the cops are killing them like vermin and throwing their bodies in the rubbish."

"Sometimes he gets a little down," Gregory confided with a slightly embarrassed glance at Selwyn, who found himself queasily nodding, trying to placate them both.

"Did you ever see such a pollyanna?" Rick demanded of the ceiling and laughed aloud, freely, delightedly, for the first time of the day, as if sprung from dolor by an old, unassuageable amazement, then broke into a ghastly coughing fit, that kept starting up again, eliciting much solicitude from Gregory, who leaned intently forward in his chair, ready to help were he able or needed, while Miles administered sips of cranberry juice.

The spasm abated, Rick slumped with stark face and terrified eye, mouth wide, breath rasping.

Miles, seated once again, assumed an air of ease, but he shot Selwyn a glance that said, *Hang on to your hat!*

"Being ill is not much fun," Gregory at length allowed, "but there are certain positive aspects to it. They don't compensate of course, but at least one can take advantage. One gets waited on, as never since childhood, not since infancy really, and one has uninterrupted stretches of time to put one's thoughts in order, catch up on current events, fit them into the overall pattern of one's impression of history, take general stock and so on."

Miles had to squint, though Rick was too depleted to respond, and Selwyn realized with a shock that, negative or not, Gregory was the more demented one.

"Well," he interjected, in a panic jumping up, "I guess I'd best be getting back."

"Don't go!" they all cried with such involuntary vehemence, such strange coincidence, that he sat down again, stupefied.

Sheer joy, of course, that Miles wanted him to stay, but what could Gregory and Rick care? They must be lonely, desperately bored, at wits' end, cooped up with their despair, nor equal sharers of their misery either, one to die, the other to go on. Perhaps they needed him to separate or entertain them, or be party to their plight—God only knew—or perhaps they had some plan to make the afternoon pass memorably. After all, he reflected, they had only time to kill.

Gregory, expatiating on the position of the sun and the timeliness of "more substantive refreshment," himself got up in haste, and fussily, clumsily, precariously stopping and starting like a man on a tightrope, comedically groaning at each near upset, brought four teetering glasses on a tray, got them safely distributed, then hiked back to the pantry, whence after long delay came low, discomfited laughter.

Rick sighed and rolled long-suffering eyes at Miles, who went to see what he could do.

Presently the two returned, Miles in the lead with a nicely iced bottle of Pouilly-Fuissé and one of acqua minerale, with which he did the honors first for Rick, Gregory dithering nearby, in his outstretched palm mangled fragments of cork.

"I have never yet," he confessed with grinning chagrin, "acquired the knack of getting a bottle of wine open without some sort of catastrophe. Rick at least doesn't have to put up with a lot of corkage."

He tossed the debris in the fire and brushed his hands. "I do apologize," he bowed to Selwyn, who, picking specks off his tongue with a fingertip, shook his head sincerely.

The wine was very cold and very good and down it went like beer and Miles poured his glass full again, as well as his own.

Since meeting Miles, Selwyn almost without noticing had resumed eating salt, sugar, coffee, meat, and now—vino! Why not? Life was beautiful, or at least it should be; he saw no reason to deny himself anything.

And Miles too was drinking away, a little harrowed, no doubt, a little frazzled, no more conscious of his thirst than Selwyn, and the bottle emptied with astounding speed, though Gregory sipped most moderately and Rick never touched his water.

"What's the point?" he said and withdrew into vacancy, his eyelids starting.

Everything was once again quite delightful. Gregory fetched a second bottle and contrary to Rick's acerbic predictions got it open promptly without mishap and poured Selwyn and Miles another brimming glassful.

They were getting potted, happily chatting with no one but each other. It was next thing to a tête-à-tête, and their hosts, without impinging, seemed benignly to be enjoying it as much as them, partaking of their ecstasy, their own concord restored.

Selwyn later recalled thinking proudly that even the sight of love could not help but have a good effect on the beholder.

At the door three muffled thuds resounded. Miles jumped to his feet with a look of belated dismay, glanced at Gregory, who cocked his head quizzically, then at Rick, who sat bolt upright with a spot of color blooming in each cheek, last at Selwyn with hapless, vast remorse, then careened sidelong toward the foyer, caught himself, corrected course and strode from sight with stoic nonchalance.

Voices, the opening and closing of the hall closet could be heard, and after another suspenseful interlude of voices Miles returned, looking nowhere in particular, and stood aside, by Selwyn's chair.

A tall, emaciated young man entered, went at once to Rick, kissed him, knelt by his chair, and a fervent murmuring ensued, while Gregory almost tiptoed to the pantry for another glass and Miles drew up a chair beside Rick, on the edge of which the apparition without ceremony sat.

Now Selwyn remembered having seen him in a car parked just down the street. No doubt poor Miles had somehow been dragooned into effecting Rick's trysts—and betraying Gregory's trust—but which of the inmates of 1075 had expected this visit was not so clear. Miles certainly looked no less nonplussed than Gregory.

The newcomer's fierce face was alight, as was Rick's, and Selwyn now regretted not having left when he intended.

Miles apprehended him and, laying a light hand on his shoulder, squeezed gently, which, notwithstanding Selwyn's aversion to psychodrama, made him glad he'd stayed.

Gavin Daly was Gregory's unlikely rival's name. For he looked even further gone than Rick, though still nimble, still strangely filled with stern purport. His long, concave skull, hair so short, so raggedly shorn it must in rage have been self-hacked, his rawly shaven cheeks, flecked with dried blood, green wool trousers and red and black checked shirt, old brogans, and gloomy air of righteousness, all marked him as indigenous.

He took Selwyn in with one grim glance, as if calculating whose ally he might prove to be, then spent no more regard on him, nor conceded the least gesture of civility to Miles, nor Gregory either, but kept bent upon his sole end.

Selwyn refused to be offended personally, but felt a chill for the household.

Miles did not sit down again, but retrieved his glass and took up a standing position a little behind and halfway between Selwyn's and Gregory's chairs, so that the three made an awkward party of their own, while Rick and Gavin lost themselves in each other.

"Gavin is a very dear friend of Rick's," Gregory confided to Selwyn in a plausible voice. "Albeit quite new," he added to the floor.

"He's a Mainer," Miles said gamely. "From Kittery, right across the river. He went to the Bangor Theological Seminary for a while. Well, some time ago."

"But didn't, I believe," said Gregory, "take his degree."

"Ah," said Miles, "I didn't know that," and fell silent, gazing out the window. "Well . . ." he said rather decisively at last, as if some sail of sequel had appeared on the horizon, but once again words failed him and a new silence propagated itself, during which all three seemed to breathe in unison.

"I've always thought a study of the ultimate questions would repay the effort, if not provide answers," Gregory essayed eventually with a sort of gelatinous enthusiasm.

Selwyn finished his glass of Pouille-Fuissé in one swallow. Even Gregory's glass was empty, and Miles unobtrusively refilled them both, as well as his own, then escaped to try to pour more acqua minerale for Gavin, who glanced up with incredulous dudgeon, waved him away like a fly, and resumed his monologue, to which Rick listened with glowing eyes and parted lips, incessantly licking his top front teeth.

Miles returned to his post in the deadly triangle, picked up his glass, sip-sipped, then drank half of it, narrowed his eyes, shook his head, and then, with a relieved expression of perplexities dismissed, drained the rest.

"Sunday afternoons have always seemed to me perfectly suited to socializing," Gregory opined after another exhausting interregnum.

Miles could not help smiling, nor could Selwyn not smile to see it, making Miles smile the more, till their faces warped out of control. Both had turned to mush. Selwyn was in a sort of delirium at Miles' vulnerability, his kindness and goodwill, his anguish at his own role in this awful imbroglio, now apparently reaching a crunch. Selwyn almost felt, if only they were alone, he could melt into Miles, blending them into one voluptuous soul beyond folly or pain, and appalled though he was at what might be about to transpire amongst the three principle sufferers of 1075 it hardly dimmed his happiness, perhaps even added to it as night displays the stars.

For a moment—perhaps because of the wine—he had a humble sense of the strange and tragic grandeur of life. How blind, how unworthy and timid he had always been, how absurdly wistful his every dodge and disguise, how little his doubts weighed in any true balance! *Get living!* he exhorted himself, and with exultation promised, *I will!*

The afternoon light was dying back toward winter, the hearth seemed to darken the windows, its bed of coals redly, hypnotically pulsating. An inevitable contraction was underway. Almost like reverse mitosis the two parties without warning, in one irresistible moment, met and merged without effort or duress, thanks to a sudden nudge from Gregory's solicitude.

"How have things been going for you?" he inquired, catching Gavin's eye.

"My preference," replied the specter, "is to drop the worms on the table and let them squirm."

"Why, yes, I think that's a sensible policy," said Gregory.

I should leave right now, Selwyn advised himself.

"Rick's going to move in with me," Gavin said. "It's what he wants. It's what I want. What remains is logistics. We're counting on Miles to give us a hand."

"I won't need much," said Rick. "The wheelchair."

"Well," Gregory said, "I don't know. This may not be the best idea in the world, certainly not the most practicable. What I was hoping—as I've hinted before—was that Gavin might move in with *us.*"

"But he doesn't *want* to move in with us," Rick minced, mimicking Gregory's ingratiating tone. "*I* don't want him to move in with us. *I* want to move in with *him.* While I still can."

"Well," Gregory said. "But it doesn't make a lot of sense to maintain two residences. This wants to be thought through rather thoroughly."

He turned to Selwyn, and with frequent looks of appeal to Miles, who answered with discomforted nods, he outlined the advantages for all concerned. It would be wonderful for Rick to have someone he liked to converse with close at hand. Gavin's apartment was cold and small—a bit bleak in all candor—and at this point a superfluous expense, given the ample space here at 1075, which it would give Gregory the utmost pleasure to dispose to such good purpose, and of course Gavin would share in the boon of Miles' incomparable ministrations.

"I just want to get *out* of here," Rick said savagely. "I just want to get away from *you*."

"Wellll, yes," said Gregory in his most sympathetic croon, "we all tire of one another once in a while. We weary of our surroundings, whatever they are. Every element has its onerous gravity, so to speak."

His was the nature of a wall, Selwyn inferred, perfectly smooth, without a foothold, unclimbable, unflankable, impenetrable, and yet, all things considered, how could he be blamed or expected to change or submit? And poor Rick, so lately awakened, now tormented by his life's waste, a prisoner at death's door, and in love, no less, marvel of marvels, madly in love — the dying enamored of the dying — and who was this guy anyway, this rube, this fanatical interloper, and what did he want? Not a pleasant fellow, it would seem.

"Let's do it," Gavin said, and got up. His face lost its harsh cast as he gazed down at Rick. "Are you ready?" he said, and his voice too was tender.

"If Miles will bring my wheelchair," Rick said.

Miles stood motionless, sober and grave.

"I'm afraid I can't allow this," Gregory said. "This is much too precipitant. And ultimately I'm responsible for Rick. This needs to be talked over in quite a serious way. This is not something to be done in haste."

"How long do you think I've got?" Rick cried.

"I'm the one that can't wait," Gavin said gloomily.

"You've both got a long and very rewarding period ahead of you, two whole lifetimes in a sense, providing you act prudently, get plenty of rest, and don't expose yourselves to unnecessary stress," Gregory assured them in his bedside voice.

"I have a right to leave if I want to," Rick said.

"Of course," Gregory said. "Of course you do. We all want what's best for you. The only question is how to achieve it."

"I Just Want Out Of Here," Rick measured out on the edge of a scream.

Pent desperation at last spurred Selwyn to spring up and say, "I too must be on my way. Thank you so much for a lovely lunch."

"I'll see you home," quick Miles said, vouchsafing token bows like tiny chops to the others. "If I may be excused."

"Yes indeed, I think at this point we could all use a little break," Gregory said more soothingly than ever.

"JAY-ZEUS!" Selwyn breathed as they reached the sidewalk.

"Amen!" said Miles.

The whole world beyond the doors of 1075 seemed a sanctuary. For the first block though, leaning together, arms tightly linked, heads bent, they trudged in silence like old men leaving a wake, till the raw wind off the Piscataqua stung their somber faces and reminded them that they were free.

"My poor baby!" Selwyn wailed, "how do you stand it?"

Miles sighed and shook his head. "How *they* stand it, is the real question."

"What's with Gregory?" Selwyn asked. "Is he some kind of velvet czar or is he missing a dimension or . . . or . . ?"

"Oh, he's a wonderful man," Miles said. "But he always gets his own way. About everything. Even in the most minor matters. And he's so isolated."

Selwyn blinked. "He is? I thought he was the one who got out and about, the one who had the life."

Miles smiled a little. "It's true," he said. "But his real passion is the history of warfare. He's an expert. He knows every general from Miltiades to Napoleon, but he has nobody to talk to. People take umbrage when he tries, particularly Rick. So he talks to me. He expounds, I listen. That's one of my unspoken duties. You'd be amazed how much I've learned about tactics and strategy."

Selwyn said wryly, "And Rick and his shipwrecks?"

"He has no one to talk to either, since he never leaves the house," Miles said. "Nobody but me, that is. He tells me about Gavin, he can talk about him all day long and never say enough. I'm just a pair of ears."

"You're living in an asylum," Selwyn observed.

"Actually I admire them both," Miles said. "Separately they're great. They weren't at their best today. It was *not* nice of Rick to invite Gavin and neglect to tell Gregory. No, really, they're very dear friends. Both."

They reached a busy cross-street and turned back, arm-in-arm. "All the same," he continued, "I can't wait to escape that house. I'm like a slave there. And yet I can't even wish for my deliverance."

Their eyes locked in consternation for a moment, then glanced apart with shame. They pulled each other closer and walked on more slowly, their breaths billowing in the chill dusk.

"Best," Miles said, "would be for them to be reconciled somehow. Rick says he hates Gregory, he says Gregory's ruined his life, and Gregory simply refuses to take him seriously. It's all a disaster."

"They were never happy?" Selwyn asked. "Ever?"

"I've only known them six months," Miles said. "Rick says they haven't had sex in years. Gregory goes to the bars, he's very discreet, but he has a lot of friends. He gets around a good bit. Whereas Rick—who's hardly left the house alone in ten years, at least to hear him tell it—he's the one who got the virus."

"Not from Gregory apparently," said Selwyn. "Where'd Rick get it? Gavin?"

"Rick says he hopes so," Miles said.

"Who is this guy anyway? He seems a little sinister."

"Oh, he's all right," Miles said. "He's an interesting character."

"I'll say!" Selwyn said.

"Rick's determined to spend his every last minute with him, but Gavin's in a hurry to die. That's all he really wants. Out! And quick!"

"From the looks of him he'll get his wish soon enough," Selwyn said.

"Actually they're both transfigured," Miles amended. "I mean, Gavin really loves Rick, but I guess you could say he loves death more. I don't think Gregory knows that side of it."

Selwyn shook his head, said nothing.

"Oh, it's awful, really!" Miles said. "It's like a tug-of-war over Rick, with me as referee. And they both give me contradictory -orders, all three sometimes, never mind that it's Gregory who pays my salary. I have to collude with them all, so I'm torn to pieces half the time. I don't know what I'd do if I hadn't got you to talk to!"

Which made Selwyn's heart sing, the situation seem not without exalting features. And they walked on past Gavin's parked car, marveling with glad amazement at how powerful their own love was.

"And," Miles conceded at length, "half the time they get along wonderfully. They can be great when they're not paying attention. They hardly have to talk. They only sort of begin sentences or end them, and do a lot of nodding in between."

"Then," Selwyn mused, "what's wrong with a ménage? If Gregory's willing. I should think that was a compromise they could all live with, all gain by. What's to lose for any of them?"

"Ah, you are a reasonable man," Miles said fondly. "I'm sure we would never be able to disagree about anything. What a boring couple we would make!"

At which Selwyn's heart soared to heights till then undared. Such prognostications! What a fantastic future lay in store for them at least, if not for the damned souls of 1075!

"But really," he pursued, "what's the obstacle? Why shouldn't love have its way, when there's so little time left? It'll only give Gregory more to regret if Rick spends his last days pining in vain and raging at him."

"Gavin's a strange fellow," Miles replied rather grimly. "In his way he's as single-minded as Gregory. Ease is something he simply does not accept. Money and comfort are anathema to him."

"I guess," said Selwyn, "he'll just have to make the sacrifice, spend his last days in the lap of luxury. Tended, dear heart, by you. I should think that would console him for lost pride."

"If there's one thing about Gavin, it's that he's unbending," Miles said. "And unfortunately Rick follows him in everything, including his desire to die."

"I see," said Selwyn.

"How could you?" said Miles.

"What d'you mean?" said Selwyn warily. Reaching an end of the sidewalk, they turned again as one, and started back the other way.

"Gavin wants a clean break," Miles said.

"You're joking," Selwyn cried. "That's crazy! Gavin's even crazier than Gregory!"

"It's a toss-up," Miles demurred. "Gavin's a kind of nihilist. You ought to hear him talk! It's not that I don't sympathize! God knows, I sympathize with them all."

With answering emotion Selwyn tightened, then had to relax his grip, having held Miles' arm so fast his biceps were cramped.

Miles explained, "When Gavin lost his faith he turned against every convention. He's been a barfly ever since. To him the whole world is corrupt, and always has been. I mean from Eden on. Everything's a pack of lies to him except sex and death. He's an ascetic of debauchery. He also has a certain swagger. He once said— he was gloating—he had sixteen different strains of AIDS. And now Rick says he wants them all."

"Great!" said Selwyn.

"Of course, Rick's become quite derisory on the subject of Gregory's indestructible health."

"He really *isn't* fair, is he?" Selwyn said with dismay sharpened by a first pang of Gavin's steely appeal, and another sense, equally unwitting but less welcome yet, of his own resemblance to Rick, as if their predicaments were somehow the same—no matter their outward differences—and stemmed from similar temperaments.

"Well," Miles allowed, "that's the one thing Gregory can't rationalize, that disloyalty, after so many years. Simply to be left. He can't quite digest it."

"The gentle jailor jilted," said Selwyn. "But he oughtn't to be so surprised."

"I'm not sure how clearly he reads Gavin either," Miles said unhappily. "Rick hasn't told him a thing, and neither have I. It doesn't seem my place to be forever interpreting each to the other. Gregory always sees the best in people, he's a great truster of motives. In his view bad things can happen. Maybe. But not because anyone wanted them to."

"And you think this Gavin might be a bad person?" Selwyn said, taking alarm.

"Well, you know," Miles shrugged, "everybody's got their case. Gavin's a predator. He wants to die. But he wants more."

"More?"

"He doesn't want to do it alone."

"It?"

"Die."

"I see."

"I'm not sure I see myself," Miles said. "But." He shook his head and sighed heavily.

As they were just passing Selwyn's apartment across the street, he suggested Miles come in for a moment, but Miles was too keyed up about developments at 1075, and soon would have to start dinner—though he dreaded it—so on they went in perfect step while the unearthly, peach-colored street-lights intensified.

"I guess we've lost our buzz," Selwyn said.

"I could have gone on drinking all night," Miles said.

"Damn that Gavin!" Selwyn said.

"Damn all!" said Miles.

They laughed and made some petty jokes, felt better at once, reached the cross-street, turned back once more, passed 1075, passed Selwyn's door on the other side, and wholly engrossed in each other, looking neither left nor right, nor even straight ahead, eventually found they'd gone so far toward Gavin's parked car— where all three of their erstwhile companions were gathered— that it was too late to turn back with any credible show of obliviousness, and so, with mutual glances askance, onward they strode with intrepid smiles, as if glad not to have missed the chance to bid Gavin adieu, but what was Rick doing out in the cold, why was Gregory helping him into the front seat?

As they approached, Gregory closed the door and straightened up, looking a bit sheepish, not pleased, but not fazed either.

At a loss Selwyn went round to the driver's side, where Gavin was revving the engine, and mouthed through the shut window, "Nice to meet you."

Gavin gave an oblique grin without turning his eyes or head, and away crept the wreck of a car, clattering jerkily, Rick's head helplessly bucking, till Gavin got control of the clutch.

The three started miserably back toward 1075. It had grown cold and the sidewalk, slick with black ice, glittered with diamond-like lights that vanished as they advanced.

Gregory had come out without a coat, and strode ahead, hands in pockets, explaining over his shoulder to Miles and Selwyn, who half-ran to keep up:

"This is just a trial. Rick says he'll never come back, but of course once the realities begin to set in I feel confident he'll be more open to a reasonable assessment of the situation, and at that point we'll all be in a better position to explore the possibilities of what ought to be worked out for the benefit of all concerned. I'm sure something mutually agreeable will suggest ooops . . ."

His feet started out from under him; he managed to extract his hands from his pockets, flail his arms and by dint of a desperate wrench reverse his backward trajectory, but then plunged head-long to all fours, tearing his pants and skinning one knee.

He leapt up like a kid and rushed on, disdaining help or even sympathy, instantly resuming his monologue in the same tone of steadfast unction, but as he limped and talked he slapped at the bloody knee to stop it from hurting each time that foot hit the pavement.

They reached the house. They climbed the steps. "I'll just put a little merthiolate on this, and be down in a jiffy," he said, limping about, turning on lights in every dark corner. "Then it will defi-nitely be time I believe to sit down to a bite—don't you think, Miles?—though perhaps only in the kitchen. Selwyn, I feel sure you've worked up quite an appetite after all that wine. I haven't the slightest doubt that each of our respective stomachs would welcome some solid sustenance."

Selwyn would have preferred to go home and collapse, Miles notwithstanding, but somehow it never seemed possible to resist Gregory, whose voice, whose whole demeanor, never left room for choice.

Miles smiled his smile and without fuss put out some bottles of Black Horse Ale, a platter of cold chicken and a baguette, and made a watercress salad, with endive, Roquefort, and toasted wal-nuts in a walnut oil and shallot vinaigrette, by which time, one bottle down, Selwyn felt quite revived. Gregory returned in fresh pants, beaming and rubbing his hands, and they sat down and fell to.

Raspberry ice cream bonbons and cups of black coffee with splashes of grappa left them at disconsolate reality. Miles brought an ashtray and Gregory with a small gold lighter ignited his after-dinner cigarette, his never-exceeded, never-foregone, one and only mentholated Sherman of the day.

Selwyn, declining to renew that perilous habit, began to admire all over again this strange, stoical despot, whom nothing could dishearten or deflect.

"This is all for the best," said he at last, blowing a fine stream of smoke to one side. "It will give Rick a chance to try his wings, in a manner of speaking. After which, I dare say, he'll be ready to fly home again."

Still he sounded a bit stricken and Miles was quick to say, "I'll go over first thing in the morning and see how he's doing."

"I think one night may well be enough," Gregory said, regaining his affable ease. "I'm sure he'll be glad to see you."

"Well, yes," said Miles, also brightening. "Gavin's place *is* rather unimproved," he added to Selwyn. "There are rats in the alley."

"You've been there?" Selwyn made bold to ask.

"I've heard," Miles said curtly.

"He's the sort of man who keeps a tomato in his refrigerator and nothing else. He doesn't even have a phone. He lives on pizza, or so *I've* heard," said Gregory. "Well, from you," he conceded to Miles. "In any case, I don't think the accommodations are exactly commodious."

"What worries me though," said Miles, and Selwyn could see him rousing his courage, "what disturbs me most about Gavin— though I like him a great deal, that is, I respect him—is his obsession with suicide."

"I suspect," said Gregory, "that it's essentially just talk, an expression of justifiable outrage, at least at this stage. At a certain point of course it becomes a perfectly viable option, but I thought he was looking quite well today."

Miles cast a despairing glance at Selwyn. "I'm afraid he wants Rick to help him do it."

"When the time comes," said Gregory, "that will be something we will all have to face. I think he will be much less extreme in his views once he gets comfortably settled in here."

On that hopeful note, Selwyn rose to make his good-byes, suddenly so exhausted he bumped into the doorjamb going out. He practically reeled across the street, with difficulty fumbled his key into the lock, barely bothered to get undressed, overslept the next morning and was late for work, an unheard-of lapse of self-command, reminding him of the deleterious effects of alcohol.

Home again at 5 p.m., he called Miles—so grown their intimacy that it only seemed natural—before he had even taken off his coat.

"You must visit," said the beloved voice, rather low, "the new zoo. Come on over. The more the merrier."

"Would that be all right?" Selwyn asked.

"Oh, yes. Gregory's very insistent. He's been waiting for you. Mr. Buffer Yourself. Come and have a drink. Help me make dinner."

"Nothing I'd like better," said Selwyn, full of joy. "But what's up?"

"You'll see," said Miles. "Never mind, my dear. Nothing for *you* to worry about."

"Oh, my poor baby," said Selwyn, changed his shirt, danced across the street and was admitted by a wry-smiling Miles, who ushered him into the living room where Rick, looking ghost-like but smug, was bundled up before a sedate blaze, with a cup of mulled cider.

Gavin, minus any amenities, sat on a hassock close by, as much a bumpkin as ever, no less sullen, but with an added air of brooding disgruntlement.

Gregory greeted Selwyn with earnest effusions, Rick rolled his eyes, though not without welcome, and even Gavin proffered a thin and fleeting grin, which Selwyn realized with relief wasn't malice at all. The sick man simply wasn't interested in anybody but Rick, had not a moment to spare for anything but his own predicament.

Presently Selwyn adjourned to the kitchen with Miles, who made him a perfect Manhattan, and began to brief him, while fixing two menus—curried chicken for three; green algae, seaweed, and brown rice for the invalids.

Selwyn gathered that Gavin's heatless house had frozen Rick half to death. Also—big surprise—it happened that the cooking gas had run out for nonpayment, suspension of electricity impended, and eviction proceedings were underway, no rent having been paid since last June.

Thus had Gavin yielded to what Gregory called *force majeure*, and allowed himself—on Rick's account—to be moved to 1075, where all was now well, more or less, except that somehow, overnight, the world was turned upside down.

Rick, long so pacific and meek, lately such a shrew, had become a towering tyrant, while Gregory, despite the triumph of his will, had dwindled to inconsequence, which only increased Rick's contempt and fury.

"He's a vengeance volcano," Miles said, "spewing spite. It's appalling. I mean for me. Gregory doesn't mind *that* at all; what he can't grasp is that Rick would leave him if he could."

"Evidence to the contrary," Selwyn said.

"Right," said Miles. "Their whole past life is a little like Pompeii. With Gregory digging around in the ashes. God knows what it looks like to him. Serenity, I suppose."

Selwyn groaned at his own recent excavations.

"And I go on reassuring him," Miles said. "He depends on it, and I don't know how to stop."

"And now you've got a new ward," Selwyn observed.

"Ward is hardly the word," Miles said. "He's not even here in some way. He's a man plotting his own redemption. He likes misery. It's the only thing that's real to him, or rather the only thing that exalts his moral sense. Everything else is hollow. Except sex apparently."

"Please!" said Selwyn.

Miles laughed cheerfully. "Life goes on," he said.

THE DINNER CONVERSATION was quite unbuttoned, though not unenjoyable for Selwyn, mellowed by another bottle of Louis Jadot, delighted by the emergence of an unsuspected side of Miles, a puckish irreverence, issue no doubt of his untenable position.

By the time the table was cleared and Gregory had lighted his Sherman, a sated jocularity reigned over a shambles of general contention, toward the end of which Rick had even ventured to take Gregory's part against Gavin, with whom Selwyn strangely found himself aligned, the subject, having started at suicide, come round at last to religion.

"I never thought the existence or nonexistence of a Supreme Being mattered one way or another," Selwyn admitted. "At least what one *believes* affects nothing, except of course oneself."

"The only question left," said Gavin impatiently, "is the nature of the universe, whether it's finite, and whether there's intelligent life elsewhere. Statistics about the trillons of stars, and the probable distribution of oxygen and the so-called building blocks, argue there must be. I doubt. There's no reason similar evolutions should proceed from similar possibilities—who knows what monsters may be out there, what loathsome mentalities—and anyway it might take our telescopes longer than our sun will last to locate some hunk of rock no less wretched than ours. If the human race itself isn't extinct by the year three thousand. So. No more metaphysics. Ethics, yes!"

"Get rid of these religions!" Miles said with unwonted vehemence. "At least the Big Three, spawned in the desert. No wonder they're so sold on misery. Monotheism equals war."

"But then, what would be left?" Selwyn wondered.

"Curiosity," said Gavin, with a quick grimace. "That's the worst of the human condition, the certainty of death without answers. The more science tells us, the less we know that matters."

"It can't all be just an accident, can it?" Selwyn asked.

"You'd have to live to a zillion," Gavin said, "if you want to know *that*."

"You'd get fed up," Rick said.

"I don't think I would," Gregory said. "I could be happy forever just to know I exist."

"Right! The brain is more interesting than the rest of the universe, at least what we know of it," said Gavin, less intent, less strident. "It's the only really interesting phenomenon there is, the only known blight in the universe, the only freedom, the only unpredictable element, apparently the only evil."

"I agree," Miles said gloomily. "If this is the best evolution can do!"

"I'm afraid we'll have to wait and see," Gregory said lightly.

"Meanwhile would you mind passing the wine?" said Miles.

"I have no choice, nor can I wait," Rick apologized, trying to push back his chair. "Though in my case it's only water."

"Divorce at Cana," said Gregory with a lunge at levity, looking for a moment at home in his own house.

Miles, with prolonged blink and half-nod of acknowledgment,

rose and helped Rick to his feet, went a little way with him on his slow shuffle toward the bathroom off the hall, sat down again, poured Selwyn's glass full, then his own, finally conceded, in Gregory's direction, a single choke-like chortle through his nose with mouth closed.

Gavin waited impassively. "You're a Christian?" he said to Gregory, once Rick's urine stream sounded from the left-open door.

"I manage to get to church about once a month," Gregory said. "Ever since childhood actually. I sit in my great-grandfather's pew, when it's unoccupied. Universalist-Unitarian it is now. Belief in God is not required. It's quite a liberal faith, too liberal I'm afraid for some people." He smiled with rueful goodwill, pleading indulgence.

"And Rick?" Gavin said.

"He stopped going years ago. He was raised a Catholic, and then for quite a while he went with me. We both used to derive actually quite a lot of comfort from it."

"Then you believe in a benevolent or purposeful world?" Gavin pursued. "I mean behind appearances."

"Yes," Gregory admitted. "Essentially. Not in the particulars, of course. The whole is unknowable obviously."

"What's obvious?" said Rick, getting sat down again, waving off any help.

"That God, if He exists, is evil," Gavin said. "That we have no reason to love Him. One look at history disposes of that bêtise. Is civilization advancing? Hardly! Only science and the prolongation of suffering. Be honest. Given a choice, would you chance being born again, if you couldn't say when, where, or to whom? What percentage of all lives in history do you think you would be willing to undergo? Even today. AIDS is a drop in that bucket. From the human point of view it makes more sense to hate than love God. It's a simple fact that the most godlike act we can conceive is human forgiveness of divinity in all its deadly manifestations."

Though Selwyn's beliefs were vague, blasphemy always gave him qualms.

But Gavin was in his element. "To Nietzsche I'd say that God is not dead, just unborn, and to Dostoyevsky, that he got it backward, that *because* God does not exist *nothing* is permitted."

"Why so?" said Rick, grinning, and Selwyn could see one aspect of what Rick—and for that matter he himself—found so intriguing in Gavin, his startling incongruity of crude manner and glib intellect, dourness and pizzazz.

By now Miles was crookedly grinning too, and Gregory wore a look of pleased bemusement.

"Equally obvious," Gavin said, a little blandished by so much favor. "If God exists there's no problem. Sooner or later He'll make everything right. It's out of our hands. If you're a prick you'll get roasted in hell or be reincarnated as a wildebeest on the Serengeti, galloping back and forth in a panic of dust, or He'll cast you into the outer darkness and make His face never to shine upon you, and vice versa, bliss everlasting, if you're good; but nothing, no act, not the smallest thought, ever goes untallied, and even if He's merely indifferent or pityingly powerless to rule what He once created, albeit maybe by mistake—with that bang we still hear the echoes of, and have such reason to regret—at least the resulting spectacle has an Audience equal to the play and the unspeakable script, but if God does *not* exist—ah, horrors upon horrors unending, everything matters absolutely, every instant, every single thing you do is final beyond all possible futures or past, for then the world has no redress, no redemption but personally, through you and your actions in the here and now."

"Wellll, but there's others besides oneself," Gregory protested. "It's rather a bit of a burden to lay the whole world on each one."

Out of breath, purple-faced, inward-staring, Gavin half shrugged and said nothing.

"And if people don't accept their role in your scheme?" Rick inquired.

"Then they don't," Gavin whispered. "And things go wrong proportionately."

"I guess I'm not going to worry about my little role in this mess," Rick said.

"Just so long as you play it," Gavin said, his old grim tone resurgent.

"Whatever it is," Rick said with contrary gaiety, "I'm with you."

"And I'm with you too, Gavin," Gregory said at his most resonant.

Miles raised his empty glass, mimed a sip.

"And I am with you all," said Selwyn, seizing the moment. "But I must get up in the morning. It has been fun."

He made his good-byes with an odd nostalgia. It was like the end of a late-night bull session in the Student Union, except it was only eight-thirty, the years had gone, and youthful wonder with them, the questions new then, now hoary indeed, if not dead, unrelated to anything real in any of their lives, mere winged words, flight of the selfless mind at play, a pleasure lost and forgotten, well met here again tonight. He felt close to them all somehow, veterans of a larger world.

Miles saw him to the door. "That *was* fun," he agreed. "Thanks to you. Even Gregory got through all right. I guess he'll survive, I guess we'll all survive."

Selwyn's face darkened to remember. Everyone for a moment had seemed transported, everything changed. "I completely forgot," he said with shame, "all that."

"We have a right to forget it once in a while," Miles said gently.

"Do we?" Selwyn said.

"Of course," Miles said, and his face seemed to blaze from within. "If we had to see the world as it really is for even a second we'd go mad. One's own life is enough. That's God's mercy, our unbearable solitude. We just don't know how lucky we are."

It was true, Selwyn reflected. One hiked along in the dark until one tumbled into the grave alone. Meanwhile though, Thank God for Miles, Thank God, Thank God. And suddenly he would have liked to talk all night, try to learn what he really thought.

All the same he was glad the evening was over, glad of the fresh air, glad to stretch his legs. Before going in, he stood for a moment on his stoop, listening to the silence, then, drawing breath, bent back to look at the stars. His neck cracked and he reeled, reached for the railings and held on, while overhead the heavens swarmed. He stumbled in at last to lie down gratefully in his own bed, without remorse or fear, trusting Miles to mediate and master the troubles of 1075.

HE WOKE ON the morrow, dragged himself through the weary day, resolved to go easy on the wine, left work early, longing for a quiet evening at home, with a few minutes with Miles on the phone before bed. But his heart hollowed when he saw the ambulance at the far end of the driveway, the police cars in front of the great brick house.

He parked and ran across. The door was ajar. No one was in the foyer, no one in the hall, nor in the living room. The parlor, never used, was empty as ever; no one was in the library; nor in the dining room; everything gleamed and glowed in its place; he did not dare to shout, but a trail of slush and gravel led through the pantry to the huge, old-fashioned kitchen, which seemed crowded with blue uniforms.

Through the windows more men could be seen—some in civvies—standing around the garage, all three doors rolled up. Inside were the Land Rover and the Maserti, its doors wide open. The ambulance suddenly, slowly began to move, and Miles, who must have been talking to the driver, stepped back.

"Gregory Gibbons?" said one of the cops with an impassive face.

"No," Selwyn said. "A neighbor."

The cop nodded, said no more. The others merely looked at him with lips compressed.

"What's happened?" he said, and went out to meet Miles, who was walking white-faced toward the house between two men in overcoats and hats, both hunched, heads bowed. Miles appeared to have his eyes closed against a strong wind.

Selwyn had always shied from authority, especially the police, but this day without exception they seemed kindly, humble, truly grieved, even the state troopers.

He dreaded to see them leave, for while they stayed they staved off the onset of comprehension, but once the last of them had gone he and Miles were left to brace for Gregory's return.

He had driven to Boston right after breakfast, should have been back long ago. Miles had done the grocery shopping about ten, and when he came in again Rick and Gavin were gone. It was the warmest day yet of the year, and he was glad to have the house to himself.

God knows when they would have been found had he not wandered out to look at the crocuses near the garage and heard the car engine.

They had run a vacuum cleaner hose from the exhaust pipe through the back window and sealed the gap with duct tape. Gavin sat in the driver's seat. They had drunk some of a bottle of Gregory's best champagne from red, picnic cups. In Rick's lap lay a pen and notebook with only a few jagged marks on the first page, as if to get the ink flowing. They had been dead several hours when the medics arrived.

Miles, ripped between guilt and rage, wept and raved.

"It's not your fault," Selwyn kept saying helplessly.

"I could kill them both," Miles said. "What right did they have? Gavin, that coward, he couldn't do it alone, he never did anything alone in his life. He only looked like a loner, but he always had somebody."

"Everybody was so happy last night," Selwyn wailed.

"God, yes," Miles said. "Talk!"

The phone rang. They stared at each other. It rang again. Miles rose and walked into the hall, paused at the phone nook beneath the stairs, while it rang twice more, thought better of it, and went on to the wall phone in the pantry, whence Selwyn heard only a murmur.

Miles returned, sat down again, explained with a tinge of his normal dryness. "He's having a bite in Newburyport in one of his favorite haunts with some old friend he ran into. I didn't tell him. What's the use? He'll know soon enough."

Selwyn let out his breath with undisguised relief and looked at his watch. It was already eight o'clock.

"Go home," Miles said. "You don't need to be here."

"I'll stay a while," Selwyn said with gratitude, "till nine anyway. He can't be back before then."

"I'd rather you went now," Miles said sharply. "I need to get myself together." He straightened to his full height like an apologetic host.

Selwyn trembled for him, but very definitely did not want to be present when Gregory got home.

LONG PAST MIDNIGHT Selwyn lay awake with dread, trying to share, in spirit at least, the ordeal next door. How far short his imagination fell he learned the next day upon return from work, when Miles came out to meet him, and arm in arm they paced up and down the sidewalk, with brooks of snowmelt sluicing in the gutter, loud-splashing in the drains.

Miles had tried to forge a farewell note from Rick to Gregory, praying the handwriting would be attributed to haste, travail, champagne. Hard though to find the right words, harder yet to hear Rick's voice in them, so snide had he grown of late.

And what could explain or excuse or mitigate? Miles used up one notebook and started another, keeping only his best efforts, spread out on the table, all glaringly bogus to his guilty eye. The wastebasket overflowed with crumpled rejects. He ransacked the house for examples to follow, but in fact Rick had a flowing, flamboyant script, idiosyncratic, inimitable. At last, he thought just to write, *I love you, Gregory.*

But Gregory arrived unheard, and light-footed with anxiety slipped in the kitchen door and caught Miles, elbows amid the scattered pages, clutching his head.

It had been a terrible night. In the morning Gregory had called Rick's father, a bankrupt oilman in Midland, Texas, and was ordered by a peremptory voice he had never heard before to have the body shipped, C.O.D.

There was no question of commiseration, ceremony, or future contact, not even a willingness to hear the circumstances or learn whom the caller might be. The man had grimly cut him off.

And Gregory, bedeviled by the complications, confessed he would not have known how to explain, what to clarify, what to leave unsaid.

For Rick had not been home since his mother's death ten years ago. Only males remained in his family. He was virtually an orphan, never phoned, never confirmed his suspected infamy to any relative or friend in Midland, had always said he was dead to them anyway, naturally had never divulged his HIV.

Thus ended Richard Kendrick's unlamented exile in Portsmouth, New Hampshire. A memorial gathering would be held at 1075 at a later date.

Gavin was the only child of an older man, late-married; his much younger mother lived in Denver, address unknown. Other relatives were scattered, remote, unattached.

Three days hence a graveside service took place in a balmy, noontide calm on a hill near South Berwick, Maine, with buds bursting from the ancient maples that ringed the original cemetery. Head-cocking robins hopped and stopped, listening for worms in the grass. Cows cropped assiduously in the vale below. Faint crows cawed in a distant dead elm.

Mr. Daly was pitifully bereaved. A retired ship fitter, he had not seen his son in more than a year, understood nothing of his illness, had been stunned by the thinness of his face at the mortuary.

None of Gavin's other friends had come. Who even knew who they were? Barflies, transients, street-people without cars, casual or out of touch.

The minister had a face creased and burnished as an old baseball mitt. An unfelt breeze riffled the pages of the Bible while he read brief passages. The murmured amens were barely audible. He closed the book, bowed for a moment as if adding a personal prayer, raised his head, gave a slight nod.

The grave diggers approached and with painstaking gentleness lowered the coffin into the muddy puddle at the bottom of the hole, then stepped back again and looked aside. The minister stiffly stooped and cast a sprinkle of dirt on the coffin, then the father, then Gregory, Miles, and Selwyn.

Then they hesitated, staring at the peaceful scene. At length, the common battle with lack of more to be said or done decisively lost, the minister broke the spell with a vigorous sniff and clearing of throat, then led the way back toward the cars. One by one the rest straggled after, Mr. Daly last. Halfway down the hill they heard the first spade load of earth hit the coffin's lid, then an irregular, quickening reiteration.

The minister with handshake and grave words to the father departed. The hearse had already gone. The four mourners rejoined at a diner five miles down the road.

They sat in a booth and drank beer. Mr. Daly was pathetically grateful, proud that his son had such well-dressed, well-spoken, such worldly, well-to-do friends.

To them it appeared he was unaware they might share his son's sexual bent, perhaps had never fully understood what it meant. Apologetic, weighed down with rue, he asked no questions about

Rick; they said nothing to perturb, and only tried to assuage his loss.

"It was books that led him off," he said. "He always had a book with him, I hated to see it."

"He was a very, very intelligent person," Gregory said.

"Too smart for his own good," Mr. Daly said. "Too smart for seminary he was, too smart for his teachers, too smart for the Bible. When he left Bangor he lost his way, learning things God didn't intend."

"He had a brilliant mind," Gregory said. "And an eloquent tongue."

"He always got all A's," Mr. Daly conceded. "He could talk all right. He'd rather talk than eat. He could have had his own church by now."

"He would have made a wonderful preacher," Gregory said. "I think everyone would agree on that."

"Oh, absolutely," Miles said.

"A most extraordinary person, really," Selwyn said.

"He taught school for a while," Mr. Daly said. "But he got fired. He was always getting fired. Everything he ever did."

"Situations can be very difficult," Gregory said, "for people whose superior abilities set them apart."

"However it was," Mr. Daly said, "the wages was death, and I guess finally he just had to face up to it."

Gregory, Miles, and Selwyn knit their brows and looked at the table, fiddled with their glasses, lifted them almost with one motion, took sips, set them down, slid them to and fro, twirled them a little in the rings of wet.

Mr. Daly too drank, set his glass down in exactly the same spot it came from. "I'm thankful there was a place for him in my father's lot," he said with a kinder tone. "I don't know where they'll fit me in. Drop me in the drink, I guess."

"That was your family plot?" Gregory said.

"Ayuhp," Mr. Daly affirmed. "My people farmed hereabouts. The house I grew up in don't exist any more. When I got out of the army I moved to Kittery to work in the shipyard. Gavin's Ma, soon's he left, she took off too. All's I had to show for it was a garage full of books."

They waited politely, inquiringly.

"Oh, he come back and sold them finally, years later. Had a sale on the lawn. Then the rest he drove somewhere, four or five carloads, he and some friend. You never saw so many books. He didn't get much though, nothing to what he put in."

"Books depreciate pretty quickly," Gregory said, and fell mute.

"I guess," Mr. Daly said. "Unless you keep them long enough. Then they go back up. You got to live forever though."

"Eventually they turn into antiques," Miles said, glad of any words at all.

"Everybody admired," Gregory said, "everybody respected him."

"There was nothing he didn't know all about," Mr. Daly admitted. "He knew where Timbuktu was. Africa. I remember the time. Somebody claimed it was only a fairy-tale place."

"He had a very wide-ranging knowledge," Gregory said. "He traveled widely in his reading."

"Ruined his life," Mr. Daly said. He shot them a sharp look. "You're not readers, are you?"

"Just history," Gregory said with prompt authority.

Mr. Daly looked grateful to be allayed. "The Bible was always book enough for me," he said. "Too much sometimes. I could never keep track. Too many begats."

"But there are passages," Gregory said, "those sublime passages that have comforted so many people down the ages."

"He maketh me to lie down," Mr. Daly said, and two tears swelled, hesitated, and ran down his cheeks. "I hope he's at peace," he said.

"He is, he is," Gregory said. "He was a good man and God . . ." He stared at Mr. Daly, who nodded dumbly, with thanks.

The waitress came. Gregory paid for the two rounds of beer. Mr. Daly insisted on leaving the tip. He put down a quarter very quietly. When he had gone out the door Selwyn slipped back in and left a dollar beside it, and the waitress smiled at him.

The Jag soon overtook Mr. Daly's old Mercury on the winding road to the Maine Turnpike. They waved, he waved, and then, disappearing around a curve, the bitter spirit of Gavin Daly was forever behind them, the empty house at 1075 ahead.

THEN DAYS WENT BY without event, as if their lives too had ended. Miles spent most of his time with Gregory, or half-heartedly looking for another job, and a place of his own. Gregory wanted him to stay—indefinitely—and of course it was a tempting offer, with little work, generous recompense. And he liked Gregory, and felt an obligation to support him whom misfortune had never visited before. Nor was it proving easy, for Gregory could believe no lies but his own, and nothing Miles could say could allay his remorse and despair.

"I tell him," Miles told Selwyn, "that he was the one least responsible, but that doesn't matter to him."

"You always seem to be in the middle," Selwyn said cautiously, "trying to absolve everybody of everything."

"Not forever. Not if I can help it," Miles said, resolute. "I hate to even bring this up. But . . ."

"What?" Selwyn demanded in dread. "What? What?"

"He wants you to move in with him. With us," Miles said. "He asked me to ask you."

Selwyn gaped at him, aghast.

"He's lonely," Miles said. "It's a very big house. He hates to see it going to waste."

"I can't do that," Selwyn said with cold dismay.

"I know," Miles said. "I can't either. I've got to get out of there myself."

Selwyn breathed again with relief. "Thank God," he said. "I was afraid . . ."

"Of what?" said Miles. "What, what?" he mimicked when Selwyn seemed to hesitate.

"Oh, that you and Gregory . . ."

Bemusement briefly silenced Miles. "How could you ever think such a thing?" he said at last, then grinned outright. "Not my type," he said.

"SO," SELWYN SIGHED, interrupting his account, "that put an end to my worst fears."

"Aren't there any happy gay lives?" Julian demanded.

"Of course there are," Arthur said. "As many as anyone else."

"Arthur sounds just like Gregory," André said.

"Sometimes it doesn't seem like it, does it?" Gustave said. "These days."

"Who was ever happy anyway?" André droned.

"Selwyn and Miles," said Arthur readily. "For a while."

"For a while," Selwyn echoed with empty voice. "And even that was tainted."

NIGHT AFTER NIGHT all three had sat up late in Gregory's kitchen, one single hallucination it seemed, veering between post mortems and diversionary fantasies of summer in Provence, Crete, Capri. Military inroads were made in Gregory's distinguished wine cellar. After dinner he smoked a dozen Shermans and developed a cough. On weekends he didn't shave, some days he never left the house, missed appointments without notice. In the midst of some commonplace utterance, all too often melioration of the awful—*Mr. Silver Lining* Rick had called him—his voice hoarsened, and he bowed his head.

They were all beginning to feel a bit run down. "We might try meth," said Miles one evening after Gregory had breakfasted on brandy, eaten nothing all day, started to sup on gin. "Not to mention Percodan," he added, and jumped his eyebrows at Selwyn.

"Oh, I don't think we'll go *that* far," Gregory said with a wan smile.

But he was more and more immobilized. He hardly ate, his face was taut, and a terrible, unspoken fear took hold of Miles and Selwyn, that Gregory harbored HIV after all, and grief would bring it forth.

Selwyn suffered from so much sleeplessness and wine, then got the flu, which flattened him for a week. He thought it was over, but soon began to have dizzy spells and feel weak. A series of sinus headaches forced him to take four days off from work, and when he went back he felt no better.

Gregory's doctor sent Selwyn to the hospital for some tests, and wrote prescriptions, to no avail. His sinuses gave him no rest, and he had another battery of tests and a CAT scan, which showed nothing.

He seemed to have been assailed by four or five different viruses, doubtless a result of the flu, and now his vision blurred with the pounding in his head.

He went to an ear, nose, and throat specialist, by which time he had already spent $2,500. He no longer drank any wine, and while he was sorry to lose that pleasure, it was nice to be looked after a little by Miles and by a very concerned Gregory, who now seemed suddenly to have become his old self, and one evening, in his most domineering, take-no-prisoners way, renewed his appeal cum advice to Selwyn, to move into 1075 with them.

He and Miles shrank from glancing at each other. They were pledged to other plans. But Selwyn looked thin and did not feel well. The specialist imposed a regimen of rest and massive doses of antibiotics. "We'll see," he said.

The fear that once attached to Gregory now moved to Selwyn. Miles hid his worry, but Selwyn could see Gregory gladly girding for battle as he revived and summer came on.

"I'm going to get tested," Selwyn decided. "Then at least we won't have *that* to worry about."

"Well, I will too," said Miles. "I know I'm negative, but we ought to do it anyway."

"We're both clean," said Selwyn, "and we both know it," but doubt was born. He had given AIDS little thought, or rather, he had dismissed the possibility, having had so little sex at such long intervals and mostly protected, it had all amounted to nearly nothing, at least compared to everyone else.

After two weeks of dread only Miles' results came on schedule, and they drove home from the clinic in worse apprehension, unable to rejoice by halves.

The next week Selwyn went alone.

Then was blank horror. Selwyn couldn't believe it. Why should he? The odds were with him, astronomically against the virus, and fairness too was on his side. By this time he had regained his health, his sinuses were clear, his headaches and vertigo gone. The doctor had pronounced him well.

He repeated the test in Boston—fearful of gossip—and got the same result, with a T-cell count down 200 in the interim.

"That was the end," Selwyn said. "We never had any really carefree time together. I was starting to get sick, disaster was always just back of us. And we'd waited so long to begin with. We kept getting disrupted, until Gregory's crisis was over, till things settled down, till we could take a little trip to Monhegan, till God knows what ghosts were laid to rest!

"Once I knew I was positive I just didn't want to go on. I'd been alone for so long, I went back to blaming myself. I couldn't do this to him. He's only twenty-five. He had his life to live. I didn't want him spending his best years nursing me. I couldn't even stand the thought of him having to see it."

They all looked at Selwyn, appalled and mute.

"He didn't believe me at first," Selwyn said. "Then he got furious. I'd never seen him mad. And Gregory kept saying I had many good years ahead. But. Once I make up my mind. I guess this is the kind of choice I was born for. Who knows why? I didn't have the heart to put him through it all over again. I never loved anyone before. All I cared about was him."

All nodded almost imperceptibly, each to himself.

"He just wouldn't accept it," Selwyn said. "He said I was crazy. Maybe I am. I sort of flew the coop. I didn't tell anyone. I went to Maine. By myself. It's a big state. I didn't go up the coast where I always dreamed of living. I went up in the middle where there's nothing but woods, in case he came looking for me. It's the loneliest place I ever saw. I drove and drove, and then I'd look at the map and see I'd hardly gotten anywhere. I was trying to bury myself, and my health was fine."

"And Miles?" André ventured.

"Gone!" Selwyn cried. "When I got back he'd gone! Nobody knows where! And I moved in with Gregory."

A silence followed.

"The funny thing is," Selwyn finished in a distant voice, "I think everything would have worked out for me after all if it weren't for AIDS."

9

MELOPSITTACUS

O N O C T O B E R 25th Baxter gave a send-off for Selly and
Gus, who were going to Portsmouth to stay with Gregory. Having arrived at The Maid in darkest duress, the
half brothers, through sheer familial discovery, seemed to have
stabilized each other's vitality and were moving on in monumental wonder akin to joy, their impending deaths suspended.

Baxter's Halloween theme required his guests to come in pairs
with exchanged identities. The half-brothers must play one another; that was a given. André with Arthur, Madbury with Heldahl, Weeming with Gil Bright, must transmutate. Nelson came
alone, as Estes was not feeling well, leaving Julian and Baxter to
be mutual surrogates.

Julian, painting without cease, missed the preparations, the
gleeful intimations and thrills of fond trepidation. In P-town's
casual climate his contrarian nature had jettisoned all interest in
theatrics. His old life at home, screened by green trees, had faded
in the light of Commercial Street. When the hour came, he
cleaned up his studio meticulously, donned a tuxedo jacket Nicky
and Nelson had found for him at Ruthie's Thrift Shop, and tagged
along with the others, ravenous as always for hors d'oeuvres to
tide him over cocktails till dinner.

Large, stately Arthur and small, dapper André were effortlessly droll. Arthur had draped himself in a tan sari covered with ribbons, like Hermann Goering in a wig, sat upright and still, droning unfavorable pronouncements upon the sartorial efforts of the others.

André wore a ferocious red robe, distinctly had not shaved, otherwise evinced no interest in the proceedings. Arthur, who observed a morning and an evening ritual of the razor, was always so clean shaven no one was sure he *had* whiskers.

Weeming and Gil Bright had simply traded clothes and looked vaguely at sea. They took digs at each other that no one got the gist of, grew testy as the evening progressed, bobbing at each other like pigeons at the same pebble.

Madbury played a dither, plunging into thickets of disconnected phrases, gaping about with desperation, while Heldahl at moments mastered his mirrored fluster, adopted a peremptory tone of officious indignation. "Twitch off their tweddies!" he demanded. "Ram up their rectums!"

Baxter appeared not to have honored his own rule, though amid the banter he would become unresponsive, or irrelevant in rejoinder, then blurt blank half thoughts from what mental life only Arthur had tried in any concerted way to fathom, apostrophes reminiscent no doubt of Julian's arrival in Provincetown, a time so distant it almost seemed to belong to someone else and did not so much discombobulate as give Julian to further abstraction. He would not have come at all were it not for Selwyn and Gustave.

Estes being sick vexed as well as sorrowed Nelson. Having practiced his elegant friend's irrepressible condescension toward women and arrayed himself in silk finery, every stitch from Androgyny, he had thought at first to drop his costume and come as his own portliness magnified, but finding those last-minute tryouts dispiriting had decided to go on with his planned, more affectionate impersonation.

"Actually, you know, darling," he remarked to André, "that shade of puce is really your most flattering color because it so exactly matches the varicose veins in your nose."

"You're a bigger you every day, like a matroyshka," André observed. "No gain on your head, though."

Nelson fought off the urge to verify with mournful palm his unfamiliar, bare pate. Three years in Provincetown had left him plump as a porpoise and equally bald. He minded the mirror less than the suppressed amazement of those who had not seen him recently.

Absent Estes reminded Gil that Charles Cahill was not there either, would never be met again. In oblivious formality, he tilted his glass to their late compatriot, whom he had not so discreetly adored, and drank deep, shook his head with lips compressed, then nodded and nodded, sunk in loss.

Weeming revolved his own head in a slow circle, wrong reflection in a dim pond, waited for his partner's reaction; Gil, breaking from reverie, merely gazed unblinking, like a wall, back at him. Weeming had never cared for Cahill's nihilism, liked Gil's susceptibility even less.

Gustave and Selwyn did not join in, sharing too few ideas of each other, nor could either have guessed if or when the other had switched identities. Side by side they watched the general high jinks, holding private converse, looking first more, then less like each other.

"I was the most beautiful fag in Eastham," Arthur droned. "They queued up for me all the way to Wellfleet."

"Truro, wasn't it, dear?" said Weeming.

"North Truro, actually," said Gil.

"All reverently kneeling, I'm sure," Madbury sneered.

"That mean amigo Rover always came first," André said.

"Never!" said Arthur with quick disdain. "That was Rover's one virtue—you could whistle all day and all night too but he wouldn't come."

"Couldn't," André sniffed. "He needed a leash."

"No collar on *that* cur," Arthur drawled. "My ice cube won't melt properly in this glass of unparalleled inferiority."

"Convict his prick and snip it!" yelled Heldahl, and catching the eye of the departing local lady, who had brought a large, cold fish on a pewter platter, coughed into his palm, then inspected it studiously.

Initial inspirations and inanities diffused by cocktails and dinner, the party lingered at table over coffee and liqueurs.

Baxter, as he did at this stage of an evening, opened the door of his parakeet's cage. It flew out with a flutter and circled the room, coming to roost on Baxter's head, where it strutted about.

"Mellow," Baxter crooned, "Mell-lloww." He put up a finger, but it climbed down the side of his face instead, pecking his ear stud, while he squinted. His guests gazed mesmerized at the spectacular bird's green breast, yellow mask and cap, dark zebra stripes on the back of its head, and luminous, blue throat spots

"Can he talk?" Selwyn asked.

"Squawk!" Madbury scoffed. "Can he shut up?"

"Squark!" said the bird.

"He is eloquence personified," said Baxter.

"He's a spoiled brat," Madbury asserted with baleful sincerity. To the tilted head with its single, black, unblinking eye fixed upon him he said, "Squark yourself!"

The bird took flight, twice circled the table, partially clipped wings menacing the chandelier, alighted upon Heldahl's head, whence it flew up at his involuntary swipe of hand, went round again amid marveling merriment, and settled at last among Arthur's curls.

"Comfy now?" said the veteran guest.

"Meh-low," Baxter doted, "Melll-owww."

"Ucking fock kukker," said the bird.

All smiled complacently except Selwyn and Gustave, who looked stunned, whereupon the others snickered.

"You'd be surprised," Madbury told them, "how much one can hate a bird."

"Chicklet," said Mellow. "Pipsiss."

Baxter's apologetic air assented to credit for his prodigy.

"Mirror time," Madbury said. "Go fool yourself."

"If that bird has balls," Heldahl said, "we should mate it with a hatchet."

"He is in fact a cock," said Baxter. "Cocks talk more than hens —which are quite spiteful and hard to train."

"Isn't that the truth!" Madbury said.

Baxter told a story about two lesbians who'd moved next door to Lars Langbehn with a Shih Tzu named Brandy, which they walked past his deck day in, day out, but Lars was bad at names and kept calling it Boozer.

The women were in AA and thought he was mocking them, being usually stinko himself. He could never figure out why they always glowered, and the more they glowered the more he tried to mollify them by baby-talking the dog—Boozer-this and Boozer-that—dwelling on the pleasant sobriquet. For a long time he thought they just hated men.

The neglected bird fluttered up, landed on Weeming's head, began to walk about. He hunched and said, "One of our neighbors rented his condo to a guy, perfectly nice guy, but pretty soon he stopped speaking to us. It was almost rude the way he'd go by. Half the time he'd snub us, the other half he'd be all smiles. We couldn't figure out if he was gay. Then he died—we didn't even know he was sick—and we were told he'd had these terrible rages, he was going to come over and kill us, because he thought our garden was breeding rats and they were invading his cellar."

"He didn't even *have* a cellar," Gil said.

"Well!" said Weems, "*We* didn't have a garden."

"Nobody knows the first thing about anybody!" Heldahl wailed.

"Fortunately!" Arthur said.

"When I was a kid," Heldahl said, "my sister told people I'd been planted among them by aliens."

Julian laughed immoderately.

"What's funny?" Madbury demanded. To him Julian was the alien, his every silence and utterance equally cryptic, designed somehow to mock or mislead, always redolent of a sense of superiority, of utter indifference.

"People *believed* her," Heldahl explained.

The bird gave a flitter and hop and landed on André's white head.

He said without friendliness, "I hope this is just a flying visit because . . ."

"Tghost!" the parakeet interrupted.

Selwyn and Gustave were entranced. How could something so smart and beautiful be happy in captivity?

"It's a stupid, garish pest," Madbury said. "Like one of Julian's paintings."

Julian looked at him and laughed, thinking of a tubular bird of his own with fantastic markings.

"Melopsittacus," said the bird.

"Shoo!" André flicked a hand. "I am not impressed by pedigrees."

Mellow made two buffeting circuits of the room, like a fan with a power surge, finally subsided on Baxter's head. He put up a finger, brought the affronted bird down, and scratched the back of its neck.

Gil said, "I went past Adam's house the other day. He was carrying something in a blanket, all wrapped up. He never carried anything in his life, not even a bag of groceries. Chad always did everything in *that* house. I couldn't figure out what he had in the blanket. I sort of peeped in, it was Chad, like a little bird nestled in there, completely wasted away. It was the most horrible thing I've ever seen."

"What's horrible? He's doing extremely well," Nelson protested.

Madbury snorted, "He's going to set the Guiness World Record for recoveries. Last I heard, he had a catheter infection."

"That's what killed Lionel," Gil said.

"Strange character, Lionel," Weeming said. "He threw everyone away like trash. There was nobody at the funeral."

"Sooner or later he got rid of everyone," Gil said. "Every lover, every friend he ever had."

"This crazy town," André droned.

Weeming said, "That kind of vindictiveness I can't understand. He treated his best friends like dirt. They'd be amazed at the things he did to others, then they'd talk revenge on him like a voodoo doll, but when he was present no one spoke. No one ever thought he'd get around to them."

"Quite a statement," Madbury said.

"What statement?" Arthur said, indignant.

Gil only wished Charles were there. He laughed but no one heard, Mellow flitted up and landed on his head, and he hunched his shoulders and sat still.

"Anyway, Chad beat it, it's gone," Nelson insisted. "He's fine. Never better. Lately."

Mellow flit-hopped back to Baxter's head, and walked in a circle, then, edging sideways down the bridge of his nose, uttered a shrill whistle.

"Quiet!" said Baxter, snatched his pet, scratched the back of its head. "I have a theory," he said. "Since unconscious processes organize mental life and limit free will . . ."

"Buncha knee jerks! Nobody to blame for anything!" Madbury broke in. "You're all such a bunch of old auntie-duddy liberals!"

"Auntie-duddy liberals," Arthur murmured wonderingly.

"Arthur," André droned, "do you remember when life was expected to wound, not heal, as people these days seem to believe. You'd think everyone was a recovering fetus."

"I greatly doubt it can be done," said Arthur.

"Coincidence," Baxter interposed, caressing his bird, "is merely a term for relations we don't understand. Properly speaking, they don't even exist. My theory is"—he put Mellow back on his head, where it stood on one foot—"the world is nothing *but* coincidence, infinitely many, simultaneous and incessant. It's what we mean by context, but human brains are so weak we have only an equally infinitesimally sketchy picture. Once in a while some egregious conjunction impinges on us, and we notice it, but nonetheless we go on as before."

Julian remembered Gavin Daly saying the human brain was the most important thing in the universe.

Gustave smiled at Selwyn, who shook his head very slightly and said in an undertone: "If you could would you trade lives with me? I mean our pasts, of course. Since our futures looks to be identical."

"Why not?" Gustave said. "Past is past. What's to prefer?"

"Do you think I did wrong?" Selwyn said. "It haunts me, leaving Miles like that. More like making *him* leave, really."

"I don't like to regret anything," Gustave said. "I wonder though, if I hadn't mentioned Will's problems to a friend at work . . . That was the start of our troubles."

Selwyn looked at him curiously. "I always regretted everything," he said. The only thing I don't regret any more is being gay. I used to have all these phobias. Not anymore. I hate to say anything good about AIDS. You'll think Gregory's won me over."

"And the other thing that bothers me," Gustave nodded, "is that I wasn't quite honest with Will. I was secretly leaving myself an out if things went bad. He may have sensed that, he had such a propensity for paranoia, he had great antennae . . ."

Selwyn suddenly said, "Do you think we might have done better as each other?"

"Well, we're both Amanda's sons," Gustave shrugged, and noting Julian's half-attendance added, "Different fathers, different . . ."

"Mine," said Julian, "took a powder when I was six. Best thing that ever happened to me."

The half-brothers looked at him with kindly skepticism.

"Fathers are useless," Julian said grumpily. "Mothers interfere."

"That," said Madbury, "is the understatement of all time."

"So much for theories," Weeming was saying. "Chad's still going. And the end is neither yet nor changed."

I wish Charles were here, Gil thought, but didn't say it. Then he tried to laugh, but all he got was a loud sigh.

"Some people refuse to die," Nelson said. "There are things I could never have dreamed . . ."

"Ars Moriendi and Ars Vivendi are one these days," Baxter murmured.

"Love!" said Gustave.

"A burnt match skating in a urinal," quoth Baxter. "Harte Crane."

"But true love," said Arthur at the other end of the table "is a durable fire, in the mind ever burning, never sick, never old, never dead, from itself never turning."

"Says who?" said Madbury.

"Raleigh."

"Raleigh who?"

"Nobody *you'd* know," said Arthur.

"Just because you went to college," Madbury sniffed.

"Actually," Arthur said, "it was one of mon ami Dover's favorite sayings."

"I wonder if I would still paint if I knew I was dying," Julian said to no one.

Baxter said, "Medical knowledge is the curse of the modern world."

"You were born dying," André droned. He had come to Provincetown in 1948, for a weekend of love, had stayed on a few days by himself, got cajoled into a job by the smitten owner of a scrimshaw shop, stayed all winter.

Though he hadn't guessed it at the time, his amours for practical purposes were over. His fastidious arrogance, his love of alcohol, a deep vein of quietism, his fast-fading looks and his contempt for imperfection, settled him in derisive nostalgia. He at first seldom, eventually never, set foot in the wilderness beyond Provincetown—to his unmitigable exasperation, season after season, year on year, the place ever more certain to be his drab, incredible, thoroughly fortunate destiny. "Arthur, you remember sex, don't you?" he said.

Arthur had touched no one since meeting Dover, never would again, if he could help it. "Dimly," he said. "Days of 1926. I can't remember a thing about them."

"All this talk about sex," Heldahl said. "None of us ever get any. That's why we're here."

Gil and Weems glanced at each other, and chuckled inscrutably.

"Except Estes," said Nelson firmly.

"Another glutton," Madbury said.

And Charles, thought Gil Bright, unable to speak.

Arthur, reading Gil's vivid stare, raised his glass six inches and said, "To absent friends."

They drank, and the silence grew long.

"And to that family man in the White House," Heldahl finally broke in with choked scorn. "Mr. Denial."

"Just say no," Madbury said. "He's got a point."

"Right!" Gil said. "And wear a hat when you go out."

Julian with apprehensive fingertip rubbed the end of his nose like Aladdin's lamp.

"It's those bad trees that cause that acid rain," Weeming said.

"Deforestation!" said Selwyn. "What a beautiful choice!"

"Bane of the ozone," Gustave said, "those cows and their methane!"

"You've all heard, I'm sure," Arthur said gravely, "when they went out to dinner the other night? Nancy says, 'I'll have the lamb with mint jelly.' The waiter says, 'And the vegetable?' and she says, 'He'll have the same.'"

"Catsup!" said Gustave.

"What I don't understand," Nelson said. "Didn't he have any gay friends after all those years in Hollywood?"

"Politicians don't need friends," André droned, "only votes."

Caustic Weeming cried, "It's morning in America," then crowed in falsetto like a rooster, "Dukakis! Dukakis! Dukakis!"

The startled bird stretched itself from lethargy, rocked to and fro, cocked its head and screeched, "Dukakis!"

"Shush," said Baxter. "It's Bush."

"Never!" Nelson said.

"Bush," said the bird.

"I don't care. It doesn't matter here," Madbury said. "We're a world unto ourselves. What happens here is up to us. It's all up to us!" he shouted.

"Off with our heads," Heldahl murmured.

"You should have seen the two young guys who were here last weekend," Weeming said. "They hardly had any money, so we let them stay with us. They were sweet kids, but a little . . ."

"Militant," said Gil.

"They haven't even graduated high school yet," Weems said. "They were scary. They make ACT UP look meek. They compete to be gayest. I mean every minute. They never stop. And they're loud, like they own the world. They don't admit any authority of any sort whatsoever. They wear dresses and yell at people who gawk at them. They were furious because none of the bars would serve them, they're only seventeen, they're absolute cherubs, but they're just . . . mutants, they're like South African or Palestinian kids. They're not going to take it any more."

"I love it!" Nelson said.

"So I bought them some vodka," Weems said." I figured it would keep them out of jail. They did the whole bottle in about ten minutes. And then they went right out, they said they were going to suck each other off in the middle of Commercial Street."

Julian shivered with leery admiration.

"If you wouldn't do it at home, don't do it here," Madbury said. "That kind of behavior is no help."

"I wasn't sorry to see them go," Weeming admitted. "Cute though."

"Both," said Gil.

"Ah, youth!" André said. "Remember youth, Arthur?"

"Dimly," Arthur said. "Eighteen fifty or so."

Heldahl said, "Times really *have* changed. A friend of mine's grandfather gave himself a ninety-fifth birthday party. He was a great patriarch. When he spoke, everyone obeyed. So the whole clan gathered. There was a huge tent, and after the feast he summoned them all around him and raised his glass and said, 'I should like to live to a hundred and celebrate it with you all here, but as that will not occur I hope only that you will remember me on this day for the next five years. This is all I ask,' and he drank and looked each one of them right in the eye, and then quite consciously died."

"I presume he invited a mortician," André said.

"No, but isn't that amazing!" Heldahl cried, "I mean, really!"

Baxter said irritably, "If you want a family, you could adopt a whole litter, and fill your mother's castle. I'm sure she'd love it."

"No, but really!" Heldahl said. "Who's going to remember *us*?"

"No one, I trust," Baxter said. He plucked Mellow from his head, with a quick flick of the wrist slung it down the table where, after a single flitter and glide, it alighted on Julian's gleaming head, and began to tread about, as if on sentry duty.

It was an odd sensation, those sharp little feet on Julian's scalp. All enjoyed the slow dumb show, which he tried to follow with uprolled eyes, till Baxter whistled Mellow back to his hand, arose, conveyed the bird to the highboy, where a little black-shrouded alter stood. He parted the curtains upon the mirror within and transferred the ready bird to a perch below, then returned to the table, but stayed on his feet, leaning slightly against his chair.

Arthur led a last toast, made mostly with dry glasses, directing fortune to grant Selwyn and Gustave many happy returns to Provincetown and many more such evenings in present company.

The parakeet was bobbing and pecking at the mirror, preening left and right, quietly chittering and chattering.

"Happy bird," Baxter said.

"Can that be?" Gustave wondered.

"Yes and no," Selwyn said with solemn certainty.

Julian passed his fingers over his hair, found it speckled with minuscule pellets, yelped, "He shat on me!"

"That's good luck, m'dear," Arthur said. "The luck of talent born."

All but bald Nelson and Madbury, whom Mellow had not ventured near, felt their heads, and each—to Madbury's sanctified schadenfreude—found himself blessed with a few tiny, dry droppings, even Gustave and Selwyn.

"Still no hope for you, I guess," Baxter commiserated mildly with his employee.

"Quark," said the bird to itself.

They went laughing into the night. Last to leave, Julian watched Madbury start to clear the table, while Baxter sat down again gingerly, bent chin on hand, and gazed grey-faced into his library.

Julian ran to catch up with Arthur, who, majestic in his ludicrous costume, seemed to sail along between the shrunken guests of honor, who lagged slightly behind, like escorts of a tall ship making for harbor.

10

NELSON RYDER

BY MID-MORNING Selwyn and Gustave were gone.

Back at his easel, Julian's face felt petrified by an intimation of time. He loved the world, and would be true to it if he could, but when it came to putting brush to canvas, his hand drew only pricks, with an occasional anus, to be sure, one as eye, sprightly in its way, a sort of grand observatory betwixt a pair of shining buttocks, the image marked for him in Aristophanes by Baxter, and a second, a dim, funnel-like, all-swallowing blue hole with a black maw—but these were stopgaps.

Maddened, he undertook a series of candle flames, figures more nebulous and subtle than anything he had yet tried, but finally no less fixed—"like Peroni's disease," Don Weeming noted—followed in utter exhaustion by group portraits of screaming busts, with tongues spitting gism.

"Isn't it time for a move," Weeming cried, "to a nicer neighborhood? Or at least a different one."

"He's like Thoreau," Gil said kindly. "He travels widely at home."

"The Maid is his Harvard and Yale," said Baxter.

Madbury snorted. "You and *Arthur*?"

However variously Julian worked, he invariably repeated his insatiable theme, and suffered the taunt that he was a freak with a single gimmick. And though he swore to find new ways, in the studio he followed his muse, wanting not only fame, but the rewards, the solace, of all-obliterating love itself, and love not only in its glorious, fleshly forms, but the moral affections, the respect, the company of great men, men such as he had never met, never even heard of, the greatest of his age, men finished, strong and wise.

While hand and eye spawned their own ambitions, the world beyond reach made him want to weep. A leaf indeed might make him weep, a mundane bar of sun, a glimpse of glassy bay, a cloud, and yet he must paint pricks. He told himself, when his first phase was done he would paint everything else.

He kept ever more strictly to his studio, only occasionally appeared on the street, empty-eyed, slouched. He began to use oils —though they were slower, trickier—found it hard to begin, hard to finish anything, where once he had worked steadily with confident anticipation of results invariably prideful, more or less easily obtained.

A kind of pallor began to underlie his bronze cheek, dark circles grew under his eyes. "You're so thin!" a familiar woman said. "Are you all right?"

"Never better," he said. Who was she, where did he know her from? Drugstore, post office, A&P? She seemed to know him.

If he could paint one masterpiece he might achieve some ease. Only the future could measure the present. His growing bereavement set him further apart, more and more deeply drawn in dreams down the road to fame, European tours, his works sought by museums, even, if fortune smiled, a place in art history; but empty of all but paint, the decades before his rewards could be had stretched ahead, in the end perhaps only a heap of ashes in an old man's lap, all his friends dead, knowing no more of him than they did now. "Only a fool," Heldahl had said, "paints for the past, or posterity either."

IN NOVEMBER David Marzarat's obituary appeared. Among the bare facts, saddest were the two brothers and a sister, in vastly scattered domiciles—Florida, Oregon, Vermont—whom Julian had never heard of.

Later the same week he saw Estes unlocking his shop, and slowed his steps. Beautifully clothed as always, Estes looked smaller by the day. Julian knew he should say hello, but feared a prophetic glare, feared loss of focus, loss of time, and, as usual now, the moment he left The Maid, he was seized by panic to get back to his studio. Some days he knew his melanoma would recur soon; some days he knew it never would. Possibilities between seemed not real. He felt safe only when he was at work, hoped only to live to finish his painting in progress, hoped anew at the start of the next, tried always to have many canvases going at one time.

In blind flight he bumped into a lumbering Murray Humber, who, though it was but midmorning, had a drop or two taken and, having built up a vexed exaltation and huffy head of steam, without amenities commandeered Julian's ear to inveigh against the trials of the artist life.

"Just don't get married," he said, too lazy to adapt his rant. "Single is best. Alone is the only true freedom. Wife is a tyrant, husband a slave."

Julian twitched while Humber expanded a gargantuan scorn for the disrupted, the domestically contented.

"You have to be a bastard," he said. "What great artist wasn't? Weeping women are an essential ingredient of art." He laughed a rueful, defiant laugh. "At least I never had kids," he said, "I never made that fatal mistake."

"No Humber the Younger?" Julian said.

The veteran shuddered majestically like a schooner meeting a cross-sea. "Too much competition already," he acknowledged with sharpened glance, "from what I call the Manqués. You know the sort I mean," he rolled on, borne by long indignation, "legion their names, quaint their scenes—false tints, hackneyed nostalgia, slabs of color, narrow streets, sand dunes at sunset, flats at low tide, beached dories—worse than the tawdriest modernists! Why do they do it? The blind buy, that's why!"

Despite his aversion to the whole project and its obvious derivation from a mode once tried by Kimball Tardiff—the master had never made another—Julian managed to speak well of the least

cluttered—and first—of Humber's series of twenty obscurely ti-
tled, numbered glass boxes filled with floating, found debris in
geometric webs of thread, a postseason exhibition, the meticulously constructed but hardly distinguishable pieces of which had
come down the day before largely unseen, unsung, none having
sold.

"Glad *somebody* liked them," Humber grumbled. With belch
and bow, he hulked onward, his day redeemed, his opinion of the
boy much gone up.

JULIAN FOUND Nelson Ryder on the porch with Arthur. No
day went by now without a visit from the florist, whose entire life
had been preempted by HIV.

He had just come from his morning sit with Tony Gompertz;
and, as usual these days, he absentmindedly plucked from a bulg-
ing pocket and ate with astonishing speed a succession of small
peppermint patties, betweenwhiles assiduously balling the tinfoil
wrappers into pellets, which he slipped into a second pocket.

Julian, despite his haste unable to go to his studio before hearing the latest, no matter how grim, had begun to suspect the
Samaritan of saving them for some obscure purpose.

Nelson looked bigger and more distressed. He had grown up
in the shadow of his renowned father, the silver-tongued judge, a
mountain-climbing paragon of rectitude, the chaste and courtly
possessor of innumerable women's esteem.

Nelson Jr. kept apart, shunning all strife. He had hated the cen-
sorious old man, whom he had made gloomy by his ill-omened
lack of ambition and constant social discomfiture.

Junior—as he had been known at home—still regretted the
pure joy of freedom his father's sudden death had brought him. In
not quite unconscious celebration he had consoled himself with a
large, peppermint patty. His mother, when he met with humiliation at school, habitually had cheered him up with one or two little ones, a nickel apiece. While the last deliciousness melted on his
tongue he would toss the tinfoil ball at some target of easy distance and size, rock or tree or street sign, symbolizing his tor-
menter, which, if hit, or, in aggravated instances, nearly hit, would
be annihilated, never to trouble him again, secret avenger, escaped

without trace, still pursued, still uncaught in his imagination that night, thrilling with shivers in bed before the sheets warmed him to sleep.

In later years, when he felt beleaguered, he bought himself a peppermint patty, still tossed the tinfoil—randomly, at nothing— for who could be blamed now for anything but his own foibles or life itself?

Now, faced with the triple catastrophe of Tony Gompertz, Dom Ponoma, and Chris Whitman, he found himself a ridiculous addict, chocolate-covered peppermints his only relief. The balled wrappers he dropped into the first trash can on his way home, bile brimming his throat.

"You've taken on too much," Arthur observed.

"But I'm not *doing* anything," Nelson maintained. "That's the problem. I just sit there."

"You give comfort. You perform small chores. You are perfectly indispensable for your four hours, I am sure. How many days a week? Six? What more can you do? You are certainly most generous with your roses."

Nelson hunched his shoulders. He supplied every AIDS organization in town with fresh flowers, as well as brightening the houses of the sick with bouquets no longer salable, or, lacking lost merchandise, whatever was on hand.

The flower business too—to his surprise—scourged him. He was privy to things he would have preferred not to know, inscribing cards with phone-dictated words that revolted or tore his heart. Grown a familiar of the funeral home, arranging floral tributes, adorning caskets, he thought half in jest, *I am becoming a necrophile.*

The ruddy, young undertaker, a born-again Christian in three-piece suit, with a Balinese wife like a porcelain doll, was building a mansion on a dune in sight of both ocean and bay, and was always in a hurry, washing his hands, rushing out the door, rushing in, washing his hands, rushing out again.

The exchange of formaldehyde for blood had always troubled Nelson, and one day he ventured, "I suppose this line of work must make one a bit, well, strange, I mean it probably gives one a slightly . . . different . . . ah . . . take on life, that is, being so intimately involved with . . . ah . . . remains . . . and their . . . er . . . disposition . . ."

"Oh, no," Jay Marden said with brisk decisiveness. "No. No. Oh, no. No, no, no. No, no. Oh, no. No, no, no, no, no. Not at all."

On another occasion, passing the family meditation room, which the cleaning lady had just finished vacuuming, he noticed a coffin, rolled into a far corner, with a sheet over it.

"There's nobody in there," he inquired, "is there?"

She gave him a forthright eye. "His wake's this afternoon," she said. "It's still open. I told Mr. Marden, I don't want any stiffs watching *me* while I'm working."

Such experiences were as strange to Nelson as his new girth and baldness. *I must cope*, he thought. But what was it he must cope with? Himself apparently.

"I shall go mad," he told Arthur. "That's what I'm really afraid of."

Julian asked, "How did you get to have three?"

"There was a crisis," Nelson explained. "They kept calling up, I kept saying yes. It's only four hours a day. You'd think I could manage that."

"Drop one," Julian said. "Drop two."

"I can't," Nelson said.

"Why not?" Julian said. "You're a volunteer. There're others, aren't there?"

"Oh, yes," Nelson said. "And the crisis is over. A lot of people died, so at the moment there's plenty of help. But once you've started I don't think you can stop. At least not until . . . I don't think I could stand to just . . . desert."

"My dear boy," Arthur said. "Something has got to give here. Otherwise you are going to turn into a peppermint patty."

"I know," Nelson confessed. "You can't imagine how embarrassing it is. Clerks see me coming and get out another box." He shook his head, went on in distress, "AIDS is like quicksand, it's as if you're on dry land and can't reach them, no matter how they thrash. And Tony's difficult anyway. He takes it personally."

Arthur sighed, caught himself, raised his chin, sucked air, sighed again.

"He thinks the virus singled him out, he thinks it has a will," Nelson said. "Never mind about everybody else. He's furious, he wants revenge."

"Good luck to him," said Arthur. "On AIDS in general, or just his own?"

"Good question," Nelson said, absentmindedly rolling a wrapper. "He says, 'I never did anything to deserve this.'

"And I say, 'Of course you didn't.'

"And then he says, 'Oh, yes, I did. I did plenty of horrible things. I should be dead already.'" Nelson shook his head. "He goes from one extreme to another. I'm just a foil."

"At least you have a function," Arthur said.

"He keeps talking about Stickybuns. He says, 'How can this guy still have his health? Everybody he was ever in the same room with is dead,'" Nelson marveled. "Do you know a Stickybuns?"

Arthur and Julian exchanged looks.

"There are so many men in this crazy town," Arthur droned like André.

"The worst of it," said Nelson, "is Tony's fear of dementia. Sometimes he says things that don't make sense, and then he sees my face, and gets terribly frightened."

"How old is he?" Arthur said.

Nelson said, "Forty-two."

Muteness lengthened out. Of such ages eventually, inevitably voiced, nothing could ever be said. Julian could feel time, like roots around a rock, growing in the pit of his stomach.

"He sees things coming out of the TV," Nelson resumed. "He doesn't even dare to turn it on anymore. It used to be his one distraction, and now he *dreams* he's watching TV, and horrors *still* come out at him."

"Maybe this disease *does* hate people," Julian said. "It's like a genius of torture."

Nelson said, "He sleeps with his eyes open. I used to be thankful when he dozed but now I can hardly keep myself from making him stay awake. *I've* started to dream about those eyes. Now *I'm* scared to go to sleep."

"Your conscience," Arthur said, "is working overtime. You have absolutely nothing to fear and nothing to repent."

"I wish I believed that," Nelson said and shook his head with certainty. "The last thing today, he woke up, he was very lucid, he started talking about Bob Savage. I didn't know what to do. You're not supposed to intervene.

"Finally I said, 'Bob's dead. You went to his funeral. Last summer. Remember?'

"He just closed his eyes. I didn't know what to say. What possible difference can it make whether Bob Savage is dead or not? Or any of us, for that matter! And then my relief came, and I felt worse than ever. Tony despises him, I don't know why, just some spontaneous aversion, and of course the guy doesn't know it. He's just trying to help. Amos is very sweet actually—some of these people are saints, you know—and he's very, very beautiful. How can anyone hate someone as beautiful as that?"

With empty finger fidgets, Nelson sat oblivious, feeling the sun on his face, while one by one whole moments passed. Finally he bent forward, gripped the arms of his chair, drew breath to rise, said, "Well . . . ah . . ."

"Num-num-num, allll gone," Arthur trilled, startling Julian. Looking bruised in the eyes, Nelson too gaped at his host and friend.

"Remember one thing," Arthur said. "You didn't make the world."

"I certainly didn't," Nelson said. He departed ponderously, dismayed by the bouncing steps. He paused at the shaming trash can, glanced around, emptied his pocket, and plodded on to his shop.

Two guys sailed by on bicycles, faces bright in the wind. The front one called over his shoulder, "After this we'll go home and play a long, slow game of strip Scrabble."

Too shaky to be bitter, Nelson forged onward, preceded by the appalling abdomen that overhung his melancholy cock, in which he felt an amputee's faraway ache. Sex was for others, he knew, not him. Who would want him anyway? Of course things might have been different had he developed a stronger character or had he been born with a more robust nature, but in that case he might also be dead.

He thought, *Maybe I'll grow a mustache or a beard or even one of*

*those neat little goatees. It might balance my bald head, make me
look scholarly. I am, after all.*

Then he felt dreadfully guilty and wanted to turn back and
comfort Tony Gompertz, make him see how wrong it was to hate
Amos, sweet Amos, but he didn't, he couldn't, he had too much
to do.

HE HAD JUST addressed his neglected paperwork, under the
eyes of his employee, Priscilla, whom he feared thought him lazy,
when a small, dapper man in cowboy hat, string tie, pointed boots,
emerald pants with knife-edge press, swinging a thin briefcase between two fingers, jauntily entered, shot out his right hand:

"I'm from the National Small Businessmen's Lobby Group. I'd
like to talk to you about our new office in Washington, D.C. Sub-
scription is cheap at only $200, in return for which we . . ."

"Oh, I'm afraid," Nelson interjected, "I'm not interested."

"Oh, but you are," sang the man. "It will only take me four
minutes to prove you can't afford . . ."

"I really don't have time," Nelson said apologetically.

"Four minutes," said the man. "That's all it takes."

"We're terribly busy," said Nelson, aware that the shop was
empty, that he was merely standing befuddled there, that Priscilla
too appeared unoccupied, leaning against the freezer with her
wrinkled impassivity, breath audible through her open mouth, at
moments approaching a whistle.

"Nobody can be too busy for this," said the man. "Everybody's
got four minutes. I know when you hear . . ."

"Please," Nelson begged.

". . . my proposition . . ." said the man.

"I really can't . . ." Nelson tried.

". . . you'll see . . ." said the man.

"Unfortunately . . ." Nelson insisted.

". . . why I'm 100% sure you'll sign on," concluded the man with
a bob of his head.

Loath to be rude, more loath to lose a test of wills, Nelson
squeezed around the counter, unsure what he intended. "I am
terribly sorry," he said. "I just don't have time for . . . ah . . . this
. . . ah . . . this . . ."

"Shit," Priscilla wheezed cheerfully. Ten years a widow, she came with the business, shared with a slow-witted son her late husband's old homestead, had lost a lung to her youth of housebound chain-smoking, now lived for her five grandchildren.

The man cast her a look of scorn. "Two hundred and forty seconds. Let's get real!" he said to Nelson man to man. "For people like ourselves there are only two possible futures—do you know what they are?"

"Life or death," Nelson admitted with unblinking eye.

"Right!" said the man. "Growth or strangulation. I'm talking taxes. I'm talking red tape. I'm talking clout. I'm talking vision here."

He flashed a grin and started to unzip his briefcase as Nelson's deplorable bulk loomed gravely close, then closer, nudging, crowding the salesman toward the door, his sepulchral voice repeating, with accelerating zest of new pleasures, "I'm sorry, you'll have to go now. I'm sorry, you really must go. I'm sorry. We're busy. Good-bye."

"Have a nice day," the man sneered from the sidewalk.

"I'm glad you did that," Priscilla said hoarsely and loosed a pent-up cough.

Nelson, flattered by the stranger in himself, felt forgiven.

11

A FUNERAL

ATOP DOOLEY'S END TABLE Julian's plate-glass palette blazed with a circle of paint squeezings like tiny, ossified bonfires. Estes had insisted he have something from the house. It had been the only piece left both useable and without monetary value.

This day he could not recall Dooley's face, his mind's eye defiantly supplying only a fin of sundial slipping beneath the surface of an upside down valentine of tar.

Feeling ominously disoriented, he went out without touching a brush, found nowhere to go but the meat rack, nothing to do but sit and squirm in the claustrophobia of land's end and ocean void.

No one was in sight. The shops opposite were closed for the season, display windows papered over. Between the buildings a heavy mist was billowing in off the beach, everything growing muffled and dim. The street in both directions seemed to end in a white cocoon.

He breathed slowly, purposefully, trying to relax, closed his eyes, saw a prick as compass needle, a black arrow atremble amid greenish flares, lost in a vast opalescence, heard enter his trance a tap, tap, tap, tap, tap, and reluctantly, hands gripping knees with the stress of concentration, turned to see a mechanical dummy with a cane, or an impersonation of some sort, a holdover from Halloween perhaps.

He suppressed an exasperated laugh at the apparition, which kept coming, taking tiny steps, tap-tapping the metal-tipped cane, making progress undeniable but excruciatingly slow, forever passing his bench, atomizing his vision.

It was a very old woman evidently, quite sober, about four feet tall, very erect, in an antiquated, black dress, long grey stockings only a little fallen, high buttonhook shoes, a black hat set squarely on her head of sparse white curls, a visage wrinkled but alert, and an immense red smear of lipstick.

Julian stared, not wanting to be made a fool of.

She stopped and looked back at him with steady eyes. "Do you know what time it is?" she piped.

"About ten, I think," he said.

"I can never tell any more," she said.

Julian nodded, still suspicious.

"I am ninety-two years old," she said.

"Good for you," Julian said, somehow put out.

She turned and started tapping onward.

"Congratulations!" he called, to belie his air of disparagement.

She stopped again, turned herself with meticulous taps and confided with an ingenuous lilt, "I've had a good life. It hasn't always been easy. But when things get hard I ask God for a little help and He always gives it to me. He's never failed me. Not once."

Julian nodded, speechless.

"The next time things get bad for you if you call on Him He'll answer," she said. "You'll see."

"I'll try it," Julian lied.

She turned, tapped onward again, like a mechanical dummy.

Clutching his knees with the effort to envisage the quivering compass needle, Julian closed his eyes again, while her cane taps faded.

When he glanced again she was gone. He hurried after her on his way home, but saw no one.

"I think I just met a ghost," he said to Arthur as he came in.

Arthur opened and closed his mouth—his suffocating fish—

said, a bit sourly, "Then you'd better get to the A&P, lest we become immaterial ourselves."

So ended the disrupted day. Julian finished his chores, sat on the porch with *The Waning of the Middle Ages*, ex libris Baxter Perkins, and read:

> To the world when it was half a thousand years younger, the outlines of all things seemed more clearly marked than to us. The contrast between suffering and joy, between adversity and happiness, appeared more striking. All experience had yet to the minds of men the directness and absoluteness of the pleasure and pain of child-life.

Julian let the book down upon his lap, and simply sat. Afternoon mellowed into dusk. Maple leaves kept tumbling. A touch of chill made everything cozy. He rejoiced suddenly to be alive and lonely, lonely, himself and no one else. The moment was almost too wonderful, the future too tantalizing to bear.

He supped in the kitchen with Arthur on a dish of cod baked with sautéed mushrooms, onions and artichoke hearts, risotto, and salad, then drank a sludge of coffee, and sat up late skimming Huizinga, so that he was hardly awake before Nelson came in from his morning sit with Dom Ponoma.

"He's Mr. Serenity," Nelson said. "I'll say that for him."

"You're complaining?" Arthur inquired.

"I'm just afraid it can't last," Nelson said.

"You're afraid of everything," Arthur said. "Even things you should be thankful for."

"I'm Guilt and Fear personified," Nelson admitted. "I'm mostly afraid of what he'll say next. He reminisces the whole time, *he* never sleeps. He tells me these . . . intimacies."

"Tune him out," Julian said, impatient to get to work.

"I'm not a radio," Nelson said mildly.

"Where are your peppermint patties?" Arthur interrupted.

Nelson's bite tightened. "I've given them up," he said. "I think I've been fooling myself that nobody noticed but whoever I bought them from. I doubt I ever shall have another," he added with an undertone of loss.

"I am glad to hear it," Arthur said dryly.

"Today," said Nelson, one hand slipping into his pocket, clenching there, "Dom had to tell me all about his first job after college, his . . . ah . . . misbegotten career as a high school math teacher.

"Well . . . ah . . . he fell in love with one of his freshman students, this very beautiful, sensitive boy with long lashes . . ."

"Aren't they always!" Arthur sighed.

"Not in *my* school," Julian said.

"That's because *you* were the one with the lashes, m'dear," said Arthur. "Besides, you didn't go to school."

Nelson went on: "It was a village in New York State, up near the Canadian border, a very straitlaced place, with one bar, where the teachers dared not set foot. If they wanted to drink in public they had to drive forty miles to the next town."

"And why, pray tell . . ." Arthur wondered.

"Ohhh," Nelson said, "it was a way to beat the Vietnam draft."

"You see your luck in being born so young," Arthur said to Julian, to whom wars were ancient history.

Nelson said, "It was pure anguish. The boy was very bright, he would stay after school for extra assignments, they would talk about his other classes, his family, his future. And Dom was in a quiver the whole time. Of course he never dared to touch him. And weekends were the worst, just drinking and waiting for Monday in this strange town where he knew not one soul.

"He *had* made one friend, another new teacher, named Trudy, and they got very close, except he didn't tell her about his infatuation, or about his indifference to women. She kept begging him to sleep with her, and finally he did, just out of desperation, and of course it wasn't terribly great for him, and she was miserable and couldn't understand why he wouldn't do it again.

"Meanwhile the thing with his student had gone over the brink. As soon as the boy left school, Dom would go to the bar and sit in a back booth and get blotto. He wouldn't come out until dark, hoping no one would see him. Some days he would go to school unshaven because his hand shook.

"He was also was making Trudy wretched. He depended on her company. She'd nursed him when he got sick, covered up for him when he skipped out on teachers' meetings. And he was terrified of losing contact with . . . ah . . . Jason, the kid's name was."

"This," said Arthur, "is the oldest plot in the book. Man meets cock-tease, steps over line, and it's lynch time. N'est-ce pas?"

"Dom never knew if he understood or not," Nelson said. "The end of school was coming, he finally got up the courage and asked the kid to meet him down by the river, for a walk, you know, at noon the day after school closed. And the kid said he would, he seemed eager even.

"By this time Dom was a wreck, his whole life hinged on this romance he may have . . . ah . . . spun out of nothing, and . . . ah . . . the kid never showed up. Dom waited till the sun went down, he went back the next day and the next. *And* the next.

"It was a nice spot. There was a bench with names carved in it under some trees. He sat there, smoking cigarettes, tossing the butts in the water, watching everything go by. Then he started to bring a bottle with him. He thought of drowning himself but it was just a lazy little stream and he was a good swimmer. He didn't dare call the kid's house, he didn't dare drive by except at night, he never saw him again, and he never found out why he didn't come."

"Painful," Arthur said. "But hardly unprecedented."

Nelson said, "He was soon made to understand if he didn't resign he'd be fired. He had to tell Trudy the whole business. She was so sympathetic they wound up sleeping together for a week or two, consoling each other.

"After which he went to Tangier and hung around the Casbah. He wore a jellaba and lived on kif and majoun, he was mixing opium *and* amphetamines, until he tried to stab a friend of his to save him from hell, and wound up in a madhouse with a shaved head, sort of like ah . . . as he said, a cockroach hiding from the electroshock machine. Finally—they never said a word, why should they? he was an infidel—they took him to the airport in a straitjacket and put him on a plane for New York."

"Another bel époque bites the dust," Arthur murmured. "I trust at least he got his fill of boys."

"I daresay," Nelson said. "I was up in Burlington the whole time myself."

"You should have traveled," Arthur said, "when you were less encumbered."

"I was too timid," Nelson said. "I was trying to be somebody else anyway."

"Who?" Julian said.

"I forget," Nelson said. "But what ails me is how he gloats at his own squalor. He likes to lay out all his worst debasements. He's talking about someone he has nothing but contempt for. It hurts to hear him. He has no pity on who he was. It's deliberate cruelty. And it's false, indecent, it seems to me. That's hardly how he felt at the time.

"And one doesn't want to partake of these . . . ah . . . A little reticence, please! Why should he rub my face in his dirt? But it's the nasty *way* he speaks of his life that's so disturbing. He takes pleasure in it. You wouldn't want to hear your worst enemy reviled that way. And of course I keep expecting him to catch a glimpse of himself. As he is now."

"He sounds the ideal client," Arthur said.

"Actually, he is," Nelson said. "He says he's completely content. So long as he stays out of pain. He says he's already lived longer than he ever imagined he would. *And* had more sex than Priapus. Did I mention his phenomenal memory? He has total recall of every contact he ever had, male *and* female, the particulars of which he delights to inflict on me."

"This is really most amusing," Arthur observed.

"I guess," Nelson allowed. "Or would be if it weren't the real thing. I don't know whether to hope he comes to his senses or not."

"What's the dif?" Julian demanded.

"Well!" said Nelson, derogatorily, decisively, as if the answer were too obvious, too large for circumscription.

"Why should you care anyway?" Julian said. "What's it to you?"

"Well . . ." Nelson said. "I . . . ah . . . suppose it matters."

"More Henry James," Arthur murmured.

"Who's this Henry James?" Julian said.

"What hope," Arthur cried, "*is* there for you?"

"Indeed!" said Nelson.

"Another writer," Julian concluded a little warily.

"My dear boy," Arthur said. "I shall give you some things to read."

"Great!" Julian said, brightening.

"But I," said Nelson, hoisting himself, "must be on my way. I'm going to Arnie Rosen's memorial service. Care to join me?"

"I didn't know him," Arthur said curtly. He did not attend funerals, no matter whose; it was an ironclad practice, an abstention, in the circumstances, more and more curious. To protests or queries he only answered, "I don't indulge."

"Everybody knew Arnie," Nelson objected. "Everybody will be there. There'll be something to eat after, I happen to know," he added guiltily. "*And* drink."

"I don't eat lunch, as you well know," Arthur said. "Lest I lose my svelte figure. Julian, however, has the metabolism of a colt. He will accompany you."

Julian hadn't known that Arnie had died, nor even that he was sick. He had had only a glimpse of the popular restaurateur, having once sat late with friends at his bar.

Elfin in a white t-shirt and stained white apron, Arnie stood beside the bartender, occasionally swirling a cognac, in a soft voice bantering with his patrons and waiters, smiling and smiling, very bright-eyed, quick, delicate, frail—unceasingly smiling but bone weary, Julian now realized, remembering how at length he had set the untasted snifter in the sink, with movements deliberate and slow hung up his apron, donned a shirt, and departed with a rueful half-laugh, saying, "Well, it's on to another hot date with my pillow."

"You're going?" everyone wailed. "You're going?"

Some liveliness went from the evening with him, some element of good spirits, kindly warmth, and well-being. The waiters downed their drinks and left. The others paid up and drifted away. When last call came the place was empty.

"Well, then!" said Nelson. "Shall we?"

Julian ran upstairs, put on clean clothes, and the two stepped into the dappled noon, so weirdly warm and windless a dense swarm of insects like a solid block with wings a-blur held still in the air, till the whole formation, unchanging in shape, with the instantaneity of a TV space ship, suddenly moved ten yards, perhaps to a grander shaft of sun. They passed by with drawn breath, eye-brows and shoulders raised. By the time they reached the church Nelson was grunting, and Julian wished he had not come. What was he doing there, when he should be home painting?

First to arrive, they sat by an aisle in the next to last row of pews. Nelson went forward to inspect Priscilla's floral arrange-ments, and Julian, alone in the nave except for some whispering ushers behind him, felt an interloper, at the same time vaguely anxious, as if he might be called upon to say something. He would have to say, *I didn't know him. I shouldn't be here.*

While he fretted the church filled up. He had envisaged a for-lorn little gathering, with himself somehow at the center of things. Now his ego shrank.

It was a distinguished-looking throng. Though he could not place them, many, many faces were familiar, but how different they all seemed dressed for death, how dignified and impressive, how substantial! He began to feel buoyed up; he began to feel a certain pride.

Two young women with flutes played sonatas by Telemann and Loeillet. The music made Julian's heart swell; his eyes swam, and he lived a vivid flash of Arnold Rosen's ceaseless smile, had a rush of hope that Arnie's soul somehow survived there still, somehow witnessed, somehow heard.

More and more people crowded in and stood around the back and sides of the church. The deceased seemed to have a large fam-ily, with numerous siblings and their offspring. His parents were there, still alive, still young. White-haired elders filled the pew be-hind. All exuded a self-possessed, attentive air.

The music ended. Coughing commenced, subsided. Stillness came.

The dead man's sister took the pulpit and recited the Kaddish.

Then a pale young man with a luxuriant mustache read a poem named "To Another Friend," comparing death now to having tea, demystified and lovely, like forsythia cut in March, stuck in a glass brick, budding yellow, tricked into spring, illusory and immortal with hope. His voice rang on the last word—Arnold—which res-onated with accent rising, like a question.

After an uncertain pause a woman in a grey suit strode down

the aisle and stumbled in her high heels. She threw back her head and arms, cried with extravagant asperity, "Thanks, Arnie!" and the whole assembly laughed. "You always get the last word," she added, and more snickers rippled away.

The powerfully perfumed woman crushed in on Julian's left kept craning forward, asking, "What did she say? What did she say?"

On his right Nelson was perspiring, blinking steadily, lips moving synchronously.

To ever less restrained laughter the woman in grey narrated a series of anecdotes, fondly illustrative of Arnie's foibles, notably his lack of embarrassment at contradicting himself.

"When did he die?" Julian suddenly thought to ask.

"Some time ago," Nelson said. "Several months. I forget."

Julian shrank a bit, ever the fool of excess.

Down the aisle came what looked like a Hell's Angel, a big biker in worn leather jacket with armadas of studs, torn jeans, and black boots. Tangle-haired and bearded, he was massively muscled and looked ominously about to explode out of his clothes.

He said in a grating voice, "Arnie was my best friend in grade school. We used to hide in the closet and dress up in girl's clothes together. He was always nice to me when no on else would be. Well, he went his way, I went mine, but I never forgot him. Last year I ran into him in Boston. He invited me down. He was just the same. He always had a cheerful word, he made you glad to be alive, he made you feel welcome, even if you didn't really belong. He was an extraordinary man, I never doubted that. He's dead, but he was never defeated. I don't think we can ever be defeated. I don't want to think so, and I won't today. We're going to come through this."

He walked hulking back, sat down, and a troubled pause ensued. At last, with a rustle and a moving of knees, another sister, large and middle-aged, assured of countenance, arose and made her way to the pulpit.

"We always knew Arnie would be somebody," she said, nodding with dour emphasis. "He always had all the answers, even as a child. He was born bossy, he was always right, he was unerring, but he wasn't as nice or as patient as you all knew him here.

"He was a little Napoleon. We were all afraid of him. We stood in awe, he was so commanding. We made fun behind his back, but we had to respect him. We simply did what he told us to do. His conscience was so strong. And he was never mean. And he was never wrong, that was what was so exasperating about him. He had a lot of failures, but they never discouraged him. I'm sorry most of you never saw him then. You would understand what made him so beloved in later life, and why he loved all of you so much."

She sat down in a suddenly wet-eyed silence.

In front an elderly gentleman eventually stood up, braced one hand on the pew, turned to the back and called, "We may now retire to the Lobster Pot for some refreshments. You are all invited."

Nelson was the first out of the church, Julian second.

12

FESTIVITIES

ELD BY MOROSE reflections, high-piled books steadied
with down-thrust chin, Arthur bent before his shelf of
Henry James. Having missed his own mother's sump-
tuous obsequies, since which egregious dereliction an implacable
and impenitent remorse had never ceased to jar his moral qui-
etude, he had simply never attended another funeral.

At the time, his father had been dead for half a dozen years.
The eldest son, Arthur had contained with difficulty a rising rebel-
lion at his destined role as head of the family. After all, he had
three brothers and two sisters, each of whom was better fitted,
would indeed in his place have fought with unquestioning ferocity
to keep that rich, prestigious eminence.

But Arthur was just coming into his own true estate, had grown
unpredictably and giddily by turns operatic, feisty, flighty, tart,
lethargic or insolently effete, modes little esteemed by their red,
white, and blue neighbors—dairymen, and livestock and grain
brokers. Nor did he aspire to bide among them forever.

At his father's deathbed, Arthur had been unable to avoid promising the agonized, cancer-doomed patriarch, who had thought

to live for many years yet, that he would look after his mother and steward the family fortunes.

So, with deep misgivings, he had intended to do, at least for a decent while.

But Adelaide (Addy) Jackson Dowwer, a leather-faced, large-jawed horsewoman from Arkansas, who had seldom set foot in her husband's office, neither needed nor brooked help of any sort, immediately succeeded to all his authorities in every aspect and domain, but rode no more, grew imperious at home.

At first this did not crimp Arthur, who, increasingly epicene and aloof, sailed insouciant and oblivious through the liberated house, staying out late at night, consorting with friends mentioned but never brought home, from noon till dusk lounging in a favorite nook with Huysmans, Firbank and Gide, Proust, Pater, Verlaine and Wilde, the only event of his daylight hours the mail delivery of graduate school catalogues from East and West Coasts.

That of all her brood Addy loved him best—perhaps nostalgic for the joys of this first, brightest, most poignant child—did not stint her goadings. Just the reverse. There had always been a man inside her, waiting to get out, and now in widowhood she became insatiably demanding of her lackadaisical, odd, obstinate, eldest one, unconcerned with the others, so clearly hewn to be steadfast pillars of county, town, and state.

"Isn't one degree enough?" she said. "How many books do you need to read? You're a feckless thing."

Arthur didn't think so; anyhow he hated physicality, the hallowed pleasures of the homely smell of sweat and manure, the joggle of saddle sitting most of all; he stared back at her in mute consideration, across an impassable divide; the world was what he had; life was what he wanted. Nor did he feel the slightest need to conquer Joplin. In his room at night he compared plans, maddened by the proximity of escape from tedium and constraint.

His father's charge, so fairly dismissed by irrelevance, resumed its awful force one Sunday afternoon, while Arthur was still debating whither to seek his freedom.

Friends of the Dowwers—a couple their age who had joined them on hunting trips to Alaska—ran for the sheer zest of it in nearby Duenweg a private airstrip, rented Piper Cubs, and gave flying lessons, lately to Addy herself.

Upon landing from a jaunt to Table Rock Lake a gust of wind tipped one wing to the ground, and the plane cartwheeled, spared the pilot, killed his wife, crushed their pupil.

Bedridden, she languished, white-haired and querulous, so bored she lived on the edge of a scream. The friend, withered with grief, sold the airstrip, came every day to the house, hat in hand, with flowers, but Addy's only relief, only consolation, only hope was Arthur, who could not bear to be in the same room with her, so piteous and needful was she now.

Despite an ominous sense of future retribution, he packed his car one day and left, ostensibly for a brief visit to friends in Kansas City, went thence to New Orleans and stayed, found a place in an auction house, fell in love with Dover at mutual first sight, pled business responsibilities, and seldom came home thereafter.

The last time he saw his mother he could never forget. At the end of three days he was almost prostrate with hysterical depression, and knew he had to go. He dreaded the leave-taking, for he was expected, had steeled himself, to stay for a week at the least—she had grown desolate beyond speech in his absence, and both sisters had begged him to come and cheer her up.

Sleepless that last night, he had nearly succumbed to an impulse to get dressed, slip past her always open door, and be on the road for hours before anyone knew he was gone.

The next morning, glad at least not to have added to his growing sack of shame, he went in to announce his wretched departure. She was thunderstruck, and kept blinking at him with disbelief.

"I'll be back soon," he wildly lied, "as soon as I can, maybe next week," and bent to kiss her cheek, felt her chilly fingers clutch his wrist. With panicky persistence he undid her grip and stood back from the bed, tried to smile, stretched his mouth in a terrible rictus, but no more mitigations came, and finally he could only gape.

She closed her eyes against his consternation. Then with brave revival of her old panache, her immemorial good nights to Arthur's pipe-smoking, bourbon-sipping father, who had always turned in last, she said, "You'll know where to find me," and added, to herself, with a ghastly whisper, "I doubt I'll be going anywhere."

He turned for the door, feeling her eyes on his neck, got halfway down the stairs, light-footed and abject, then realized he had forgotten his car keys.

Numbly he tiptoed upstairs again, with one long stride got by her door without glancing in, but on return could not avert his eyes and glimpsed on the pillow her pink skull in its white nimbus turned to the wall and one thin shoulder shaking.

"Y'all come, y'all come," his youngest sister sang with droll dolor as he drove down the dusty drive, "y'all come back and see us when you can."

Adelaide Dowwer died in the spring.

By the time Arthur got himself to Joplin the family was gathered. There was blessedly nothing for him to do. On the eve of the funeral he ate to excess and finished a bottle of bourbon on the porch with an affable uncle from St. Louis, a ne'er-do-well, who lived no one knew quite how, an unassuming, graceful man with eyebrows independent of each other, always somehow sympatico, who never expressed a hint of vehemence about anything, except, perhaps, in a veiled way, a distaste for hypocrisy, and whom everyone in the family liked personally, though in company all felt bound to join in his general censure.

Possessed of an invitation to visit St. Louis, Arthur was slow to appear the next morning, slow to dress, slow to set out for the church alone, last to leave the house.

When he got there, the cars lining both sides of the street for blocks around, the fact that he was already a minute late, and would be later yet once he found a place to park, the irritating sight of some young women stragglers hastening up the walk in their black finery, the implacable sun, his hammering head and churning guts, persuaded him it was best to skip the service, use the respite for coffee and self-repair, in good time return and join the procession to the cemetery, for his mother in her coffin would not care.

He drank a beer at the counter of a new restaurant in the late-morning lull, felt better, ordered another, skimmed an abandoned newspaper, feeling an alien in his native place, kept reluctant watch on the inching clock, then hurriedly, with a sense of incumbency, tried to focus on his mother, to recall some warm moment, rouse in himself some sentiment of accord, anything to make her seem dear beyond mere pity.

She had never, he reflected, been in need until the end, when he had failed her, and now he was failing her again, the more iniquitously because public. A rage of resentment clogged his throat and brought back a fragment of childhood.

He might have been ten. She was driving, he in the back seat, the ashtray mounded full of butts and ashes. He asked her if he could blow into it.

"Certainly not," she said.

He importuned.

"Do not," she said.

His wish, sprung from a seed of intuition, had burgeoned with curiosity. He begged, he wheedled, he whined, and she kept saying Do Not, while his will to do it grew.

"You'd better not," she warned, engrossed in the stop-and-go traffic.

"*Why* not?" he attacked the new ambiguity. He would not disobey her, never had, never would, and she knew it, which exasperated him.

She did not answer, her massive back between him and all things desirable.

"Why *not?*" he demanded. He had a right to a reason, but she deigned to give none, and he began to want, more than anything, to see the result of blowing into the ashtray. He knew it would be so much fun it would balk her. Why couldn't she be fair?

He pestered till she said, with a lack of concern he had never heard before, "If I were you I wouldn't."

Ambiguities multiplied, punishment neither promised nor specified. He hesitated. "Why not?" he appealed.

She said in an absent voice, "I wouldn't."

What could that mean? She was her; he was him. His sense of risk lost to hope of high fun, he drew a huge breath, opened his eyes wide, not to miss the spectacle, and blew with all his might.

Sitting at the counter in his black suit, Arthur relived his blind wails, his mother's amazing lack of sympathy when they got home and she took off her hat and hung her jacket up before flushing his eyes at the kitchen sink. Shocking too the bitter malice he felt now toward her cool remove from him that day. Perverse, vindictive to fixate on so small a transgression, while her remaining time above ground flew.

A bit drunk, he found he had miscalculated. The cars were gone from the church. His hangover too was gone. It was a glorious day; the dogwood was in bloom; outside the city the air was sultry and sweet with the scents of spring. He had seldom been to the cemetery, and having searched distractedly for some time conceded he had taken a wrong turn.

It was a beautiful road and he was loath to turn around. For a while he kept expecting to meet a crossroads that would take him back, then drove defiantly on and on, engulfed in the luxuriant countryside. He got home long after dark, his absence unremarked.

THE PHONE BROKE Arthur's reverie. The stacked books buckled, cascaded to the floor. He answered crossly. It was Mrs. Wilband, to say that Bill had died two days ago, peacefully, with dignity, in her arms, at home.

Arthur condoled with heavy heart, lied that Bill would be greatly missed—in fact he had been a surly recluse during his stays in Provincetown—thankful as he hung up that no funeral had been mentioned.

He repiled the jumbled books, toted them downstairs, and stood them by his chair. As he sat down they toppled again. Ankle deep in splayed bindings and bent pages, he sat warily staring at the artifact from the Yucatán, its barbaric reds undimmed by a summer in the sun.

"Dover, you're not missing a thing!" he muttered, summoned his will, arose and made two piles instead of one, sat down again to wait for Julian's return, while woeful ruminations flooded in.

TO AVOID BEING first at the Lobster Pot, Nelson had led Julian out on the wharf. A dragger rounded Long Point, turned straight toward them, its silhouette shrinking to a tiny, black V with white curls at the base and a minuscule cube on top, then remained perfectly still in the distance.

With growing impatience they glanced elsewhere and back, while it stayed exactly the same size, no closer, no larger. Then a vertical hair materialized above the cube, from which, after another exasperating while of changelessness, seemed to stream a faint plume of gnats.

Nelson, suddenly apprehensive, said, "I don't suppose we want to be . . . ah . . . rudely late either."

He strolled away, not quite slowly. Julian cast a last glance at the harbor and followed, having wanted to see the fishermen.

Behind them, on a brief wave of sound, a diesel hammered.

Not an instant too soon they found themselves in the crush at the top of the stairs in the Lobster Pot. The second floor, reserved for the funeral party, was already packed, and still more people pressed in behind. Up on his toes, Julian peered over the crowded heads toward the wharf. Nelson ogled the food.

Of which there was a plenty, many restaurants in town having supplied a specialty dish, creating a feast worthy of the late chef and of the multitude of his mourners.

Pink shrimp and cherrystone clams on beds of ice, mussels steamed in garlic and wine, crabmeat salads, antipastos, caponata, calamari, patés, cheeses, chowders, a vat of kale soup, chicken wings, curries, Newburgs, meatballs, melon balls, tiers of triangular little sandwiches trimmed of crusts, sundry tidbits on toothpicks, carrot sticks, celery sticks, dips, and rich desserts were being devoured on close-held plates, amid a convivial din.

"I say, this is jolly. Sad day, what?" said a bald man with small, round glasses, English accent, and great black beard, whose vaster girth seemed to disparage Nelson's.

"Do you . . . ah . . . know Julian . . . ah . . . Esmeralda?" Nelson said. "Coughlan Dice."

"Coffee," said the man deprecatingly to Julian.

"How's your book?" said Nelson.

Coughlan rumbled, chuckled, grumbled into his beard, finally was heard to say, "Too many different endings, none can I abide."

"I suppose you'll have to . . . ah . . . choose," said Nelson. "We're all waiting."

The would-be first-novelist bent upon Julian a kindly, pained regard. "I applaud your bold paintings," he said.

"What do you paint?" said the little wraith of an old woman at Coughlan's elbow.

"Beach roses," Julian said, adding flatly, "also phalluses. Mostly phalluses."

"I think that's a *very* nice proportion," she said with sincere accord.

"Haven't you seen his shows?" Coughlan protested. "He's the toast of Provincetown."

"Maria Nore," Nelson said to Julian. "Our mystic. How nice to see you, Maria!"

"I just don't happen to believe that this is all there is," she demurred to Julian, tracing a finger with slow particularity around the crowded room. "If that makes me a mystic."

The two corpulent atheists eyed her with fond forbearance.

In one corner Baxter Perkins, a thin slice of radish pinched between thumb and first finger arrested before unparted lips, gazed upon the scene, still as a suit of armor on a pedestal.

At a nearby table, in profile, Weeming and Bright picked at the debris on a ravaged tray.

Out in the middle, alone, distraught, revolving his head like one about to go down for the third time, Heldahl seemed on the verge of a scream.

Julian's heart yawed. Neither sorrow nor remembrance was to be seen or heard.

Pressed close to a table with replenished platters, Dice piled his plate and began filling his mouth with meatballs, dribbling sauce into his beard, beaming about at one and all. Nelson plucked one small morsel at a time, chewed, swallowed, sucked his tongue guiltily for three seconds, plucked another. Julian ate some shrimp and felt dissolute, resolved that tomorrow he would do two days' work, today mourn mortality, eat, and try to socialize.

"Maria," said Dice, regaining control of himself, "let me make you up a plate. What would you like? Fish, fowl, flesh?"

"Oh, no thank you," she said. "That's all too rich for me. And of course it's nowhere near my dinner time either."

"You've got to eat," said Nelson decisively. "What do you normally eat? Those mussels look most nourishing."

"Oh, once in a while I eat a nut," she said, her blue, ingenuous eyes unblinking. "I'd rather not have to eat at all. Especially any-thing that ever lived. I think we should evolve to draw our suste-nance from the sun, like plants."

Julian couldn't tell if she were joking, but his inner eye pro-duced an infinity of gold and silver pricks of light shooting through the blue empyrean toward ruby lips and black holes.

"Wouldn't that be a sort of abortion," jocosely interjected Hig-gins, who had eddied near with a beer in one hand, plate in the other, "eating a nut?"

"I'm afraid you're right," Maria said. "Eating is the universal tragedy of humankind. Of course I never could face it until now, but now I have no need for food I understand completely."

"Don't be perverse, Maria," said Nelson. "How much do you weigh?"

"I used to weigh 99 pounds exactly," she said, very demure. "I was always terribly proud of keeping below 100. One of these days I shall manage to weigh nothing at all. I look forward to giv-ing gravity the slip."

"You'll have to be patient," said Higgins. "The skeleton lasts forever. Just about."

"I should like to be made into fertilizer," Maria said, not to be swayed by frivolous caveats.

Higgins grinned more and more widely, projecting energy, joie de vivre, contagious good will. "How are you?" he cried to Julian familiarly.

"Fine," said Julian, taken aback. "Good. Great."

"Glad to hear it," said Higgins, and seeing his bafflement added, "You came in the O.C. one day."

Julian flushed miserably, could only nod, and wonder if Hig-gins knew that Jessica Jordan was dead, unable to ask, *Did you know him? What was he like?*

Higgins went on grinning at him with good-natured consider-ation, kindly lines radiating from his benignant squint. Julian was speechless. Higgins was a type he was always drawn to, brimming with pleasures and confidence, practically panting with love of life, like an ecstatic black lab on a winter beach.

Higgins turned from Julian without a word. "Reef!" he cried with quizzical delight.

"Sir!" with military alacrity answered a sallow young man, cere-
moniously raising a Budweiser in each hand, bowing between. His
shift finished, he had come up for his customary quenching of
thirst, only to find his bar wholly taken over.

"Lotta people," he said a little askance. "I didn't even know
him."

"No, no, he was a nice man," Higgins affirmed. "I just felt like
going." He grinned. "I didn't expect this dividend."

The party was in full swing. Nelson had got himself a second
glass of white and was eating freely, licking his fingers with zeal.
Coughlan, quaffing a third glass of red, flashed a regal gaze. Higgins finished his beer, came back with two more, offered one to
Julian, who declined, embarrassing himself with thanks too heartfelt and profuse.

Everyone was having a good time but him, everyone was at ease.
He was tempted to drink and try to join them. But what he craved
was tequila, and his tenacious bereavement sharpened again.

"How's your book, Coffee?" said Reef.

Julian saw the twice-ambushed, fat man wince, briefly gained
admittance to his eyes, a-shine with public haplessness.

"I tend to think of it as being in a state of hibernation, otherwise my only predator. You have strayed among the damned," he
adjured Julian. "Men of the pen. In more ways than one."

"No, no," Higgins disclaimed Julian's involuntary glance. "Just
doggerel. I inherited my father's knack. Actually I'm a well-known
menace," he confessed with diffidence. "Some people can't help
rhyming; it's an incurable affliction."

"He's a devilishly clever fellow," Coughlan told Julian, "a true
scholar if not a gentleman."

"I've seen your pricks around," Higgins said. "Are you gay?"

Julian nodded with shock.

Higgins said, "I figured. Just thought I'd ask."

All went on assiduously eating and drinking, except Maria, who
stood unmoving with hands folded at her navel in an attitude of
casual prayer, though she was only trying to keep them out of
the way.

A tidal wave of relief rocked Julian on numb legs. He thought
with astonishment, *I could be friends with these people, Higgins es-*

pecially, but Coughlan too, and even fierce, unsmiling, scrawny Reef with those black, implacable eyes. What's with him?

Without thinking, he put a hand lightly on Higgin's elbow, and said, "Thanks."

Higgins glanced down uncomprehending at first—the hand was quickly withdrawn—then up at Julian's constrained face, but didn't grin. "Of course," he said. "Of course. That's why we're here." He put his head back, drank the last of the second beer, started for the bar, stopped sideways and said, "I grew up in Topeka. I did five years on the Chicago Stock Exchange. I saw millions of dollars change hands every day, I was doing pretty well myself. What kind of a life was that?" He shook his head, turned again and squeezed into the crowd toward the bar.

"How's that manuscript you saved?" said Coughlan to Reef. "Last I heard you hadn't been able to get past the first page. Not seldom the fate of philosophy in this heedless age."

"Well, I finished it," said Reef with a glare. "Finally. It was an act of will. I read every word. Sixteen hundred and six pages."

"You are a noble soul," Coughlan rumbled.

With asperity Reef tilted his chin up an inch, then snapped it back down so hard his roof of black hair bounced.

"Well?" said Coughlan.

"It's a disaster," said Reef, "I couldn't even get the gist. It was all so hedged and convoluted. And complicated. And sprawled. And boring."

"Oh, dear," said Maria with sincerely placid mien.

"And then," said Reef, "I had to read it all over again. Because I didn't have the heart to take it back and tell him it was worthless. I had to find *something* good to say. It was so obviously *written*, there were no lapses in *that* prose, absolutely polished and incomprehensible, page after page. And then I began to wonder whether a thing could have some perfection of its own, and still be no good."

Higgins returned with two more beers and gave Reef one.

"Haven't you finished with that manuscript yet?" he said. "It's going to take you over."

"Has!" said Reef, who, unable to sell his collection of stories, had spent the last, infuriated year, at the behest of his agent, trying to splice them into a novel. "Has! But I'm beginning to see the light. I think. At least a glimmer."

"So?" said Coughlan.

"I don't know," Reef said, a little dogged. "I'm not sure yet. I can't tell if it's an intentional puzzle, or he simply doesn't know his own mind. It's sort of like a refutation of everything that's ever been thought. It might be a joke."

"You might consult the . . . ah . . . author himself," Nelson said.

"I'm getting up the nerve," said Reef. "I'm ashamed because it's been so long and I still don't know what to think. In a way it's like he's saying the same thing over and over."

"Which is what?" Coughlan demanded.

"I'm not sure yet," Reef said. "Exactly."

"But you still think it's no good," Nelson persisted.

"I'm not sure of that either," said Reef. "Anymore. When I read at random it almost makes sense. At a certain point it begins to sound sublime. That's when I want to throw the whole thing in the fire."

"So who is this guy?" Coughlan said. "This master of murk."

"I don't know his name," Reef said. "And it's not murk either exactly."

"How are you going to find him?" Nelson wondered.

"I'll go knock on his door," Reef said. "I know where he lives. Down a little shell driveway across from Kendall Lane."

Higgins started. "What's he look like?"

"He's an old geezer," Reef said. "I told you. All bent over. I only saw him the once."

"Did he sort of talk through clenched teeth?" Higgins asked.

"Yeah, that's right," said Reef excitedly. "Do you know him?"

"That was Ashingham," Higgins said. "I never knew he wrote."

"Was?" Reef said.

"He died," Higgins said.

"Died!" Reef said. "When?"

"I don't know. I don't remember," Higgins said. "A year ago?"

Reef compressed his lips and breathed in and out quietly while they all gaped at him.

"I'm sorry," Higgins said at last in a contrite voice. "I wish I'd known. I could have spared you."

"Spared me? Spared me what?" Reef nearly cried. "I've still . . . I'd still have this freaking manuscript."

"May one look?" asked Coughlan after a decent interval.

"Sure," Reef said, inward gazing. "Be my guest."

"After you," said Higgins firmly.

Nelson said, "Well, I suppose you'd better sign me up too. Though I don't know where I'll find the time."

"I should certainly like to *try* and read it," Maria said.

"After you, my dear. *I'm* in no hurry," said Nelson, then blanched, quickly turned to Reef. "At least you can get back to your own work now and let this . . . ah . . . settle somewhat."

But Reef went on staring, a little slouched, his usual pallor gone yellow-grey.

Behind Julian someone said, "I heard Touhy's dying."

A second voice said, "I'm not going to worry about *him*. He'll come back as crabgrass."

"Maria, how nice to see you!" cried a stylishly dressed woman with shining black hair in a chignon and starkly formal makeup, like a Japanese mask.

"Jane Jacoby!" cried Maria, instantly wet-eyed. The two embraced delicately at a distance, fingertips on arms, breath of lips on cheeks, then held animated talk, while Higgins and Reef obliquely attended, awaiting introductions, and Dice and Nelson fell to chatting, withal intent on conveying selected tidbits from table to mouth.

Julian, left out, unwillingly for once, tried to think of something to say to Higgins about Jessica Jordan, but what?

Jane it seemed had left town some time ago. She and Maria had not seen each other for—could it be four years? Was it five? Six! No! Yes! They shook their heads at each other in rueful awe.

Maria had not changed a bit! She looked younger than ever!

But she did not *feel* younger. Oh, no! Every bone ached, and her mind! Well, she shouldn't mention that. But Jane, Jane looked marvelous, a new person really!

Well, it was true; she had a divorce and a fancy new job. The children were so grown up; she hadn't made them go to the funeral, but she would bring them to see Maria tomorrow. Was she living in the same place?

Of course! Where else?

Jane was afraid she might have moved, or left town, or . . . Everything changed so fast these days! She was glad, she was overjoyed really, to see Maria, but never expected to find her here.

"Coffee brought me," Maria explained.

Coughlan presented his girth and bowed, calling forth names all around.

Julian saw his chance irretrievably gone. Lost to the chase, Higgins was all gallantries and wit, inquiries about Jane's past in Provincetown, regrets they had never met, rapid-fire recall of the names, fortunes and present whereabouts of fellow sojourners both might have known during their common era, Vietnam and its aftermath, so recent, yet so remote, so unimaginably different.

"Crazy time," Jane conceded. "Who's left? Nobody remembers."

Maria looked pleased beyond words. Washashores of a later wave, Nelson and Coughlan listened with reserve. Reef, who predated even Higgins, appeared to have forgotten Ashingham, and though his features retained their usual, taut stringency, his black eyes shone unwontedly clement and wry, and never, no matter who spoke, for an instant left the enchantress, herself spurred to frank laughter and glad half-turns in her black, sueded-silk skirt, which wafted among them a warmth of female musk and perfume.

Julian was aware that while she responded to them her grave glance strayed to him. With a bitter shiver he conceded that she was unlikely to have HIV, nor, he quickly chastised himself, much manhood either.

He said, "I've got to go."

"What for? This is just getting underway," Nelson said with reproach.

Indeed, things were reaching a cheerful roar. Higgins looked so inspired it hurt Julian to see, and he rudely shook his head and turned away, muttering about work.

Warm farewells applauded his flight. Wherever he was, whatever the situation, when he wanted to go he went, often without a word. No sooner had he set foot on the street though than he chided himself for lack of grace, but grace took time, and time was life. *Life!* he exhorted himself. *Life is art.*

He had gone but a block when puffing Nelson caught him up. "You're right," he said. "I'd just have another forty drinks and eat myself silly. I envy your discipline."

Julian did not demystify.

At the top of the A-House Alley steps they parted, Nelson going east, Julian west.

"AND WERE YOU edified?" Arthur inquired, Olympian amid his realm of books.

"I guess so," Julian said unhappily.

Arthur put off mention of Bill Wilband, thinking Julian might have had enough death for one day.

"Here," said he, "are some things for you to read."

With gratitude Julian received the worn volume, marked with slips of paper, glad to forget his social ineptitude. It did not occur to him that Arthur would have loved to hear about Coughlan and Maria and Jane Jacoby and Reef and the orphan manuscript.

The sun porch was shut against the dusk and he hunched within, reading "The Madonna of the Future," till Arthur called him to sup.

Julian cleaned his plate in a trice and started to make dessert of the rest of the baguette.

Dismissing his half-hearted protests, Arthur concocted a second omelette, sat morosely watching him eat, got up again to pour him more milk, sat down again. The day and its merciless memories had harrowed him. His Uncle Noddy, the nice uncle from St. Louis, whom he'd talked to as an adult only once, on the occasion of his mother's death—and though invited, to his everlasting regret, had never visited—Noddy, whose haunting smile Arthur would have preferred never to catch another glimpse of, Noddy, now become almost a mythical Noddy—Noddy had been stabbed twenty-seven times, and thrown from a third floor roof.

Twenty-five years had only darkened the horror, deepened the abyss. Who could have harmed such a man? Why? And what was Noddy the urbane, Noddy the self-contained, Noddy the subtle and discreet, doing up on a roof miles from his own neighborhood? Lured? Coerced? It was all unthinkable, unspeakable, not to be borne, never outlived, nor laid to rest.

Oppressed and lonely, Arthur gave in and said, "Bill Wilband died."

Bent over his plate, Julian turned stricken eyes up, his fork stopped in midair.

Arthur bowed with shame. "His mother called," he explained.

Julian resumed a difficult swallowing. Arthur edged about the kitchen, putting things away very quietly.

Finished, Julian carried his plate and glass to the sink, turned on the water.

"I'll clean up. You may continue," Arthur directed, and cast eyes toward the thick anthology splayed in the chair in the cozy corner illumined by the sweet, green lamp.

Julian had never seen Arthur do a dish—dishes were Dover's department—and his double take declared it.

With his severest air, the innkeeper uplifted forearm, wrist, first finger, then chin, and pointed. "Never," he said, "leave a book sprawled out like a trollop."

Julian was glad to reimmerse himself in the tale of Theobald, the American acolyte in Florence, whose passionate vision of the Madonna, his masterpiece to be, is ever deferred in preparation and study, the blank canvas of his whole life cracking, discoloring in his studio, while his model imperceptibly ages and his hand fails.

The lesson, neither lost on Julian, nor needed, soothed his anxieties, blandished his confidence. No procrastinator, his own oeuvre would surely prove large and various—within its limits— marred more by the follies of precipitate action, for no sooner had he found a theme than he gave it substance in paint. Erring instincts, recklessness, bold ignorance were the proclivities he dreaded, not Theobald's deluded diffidence.

Arthur had gone to bed. Julian plunged into "The Beast in the Jungle," at the outset disconcerted by the notion "of those who knew too much and . . . those who knew nothing."

He understood at once that he belonged to the latter. He forged on through the labyrinthine language. What beast could lurk in such a genteel jungle?

At the end, when Marcher flings himself face down on the tomb of the love he had missed through his cold egoism, it seemed to Julian prophetic, and he took to his bed like an invalid and lay wide-eyed. He had no one to save him, no hope, nothing but a void where love should be, a dead man and the fear of AIDS. For in this world, as was well known, one could not love and not die.

13

CHRIS WHITMAN

JULIAN GOT UP late the next morning. As he blearily surveyed the dark, gusty day, Nelson Ryder's ponderous tread reverberated on the porch, and soon the smell of fresh coffee promised to spread its homely patina of ordinariness and distance over whatever gruesome news the visit might bring. In truth, Arthur and Julian dreaded more word from the bedsides of the doomed.

But no! Not at all! Not at all! Nelson was elated. He had not dared mention it till now, but Chris Whitman was better, was actually making a marvelous recovery, had gone in three weeks from death's door to sitting up and eating solid food, to wheelchair, to walker, to dispensing first with diapers, then bedside commode, could now make his own way to the bathroom, though he kept falling down and getting horrible bruises, because his feet were numb and hard to manage. But still! Still! It was a miracle!

Most heartening of all, Chris's true self was starting to appear, and partly perhaps because of him, or so he liked to think.

Chris had been no one but a name that first day Nelson gently pressed his unresponding hand, a virtual cipher to his care-givers, to whom he seemed remote if not comatose most of the time. In light of his evident extremity, the volunteer sitters were already being penciled in for other cases.

But Nelson's advent—or something uncanny—had wrought a strange reversal. As Chris revived, his temperament came more clearly into ken. He must have been, he still was, quite handsome, a vessel of high intelligence, irony, and dry self-deprecation. Even the hard-bitten rejoiced, unable to deny themselves the hope enshrined in the adage: *There's Always A First Time For Everything.* Sooner or later, could there be any doubt, someone must finally cheat the disease of its victory, at the very least survive until a cure was found, for how much longer, after all, could *that* be?

According to researchers—for practical purposes—forever.

Nonetheless, spared a merciful call to wish Chris a quick escape, Nelson now looked forward intently to his greater acquaintance. Chris was indeed somebody—trenchant, funny, well traveled, even a trifle eccentric, though not much enamored of small talk, mundane, silence-filling observations, nor optimism of any kind, even predictions of a mild winter.

Lately he had begun, on occasion, to wave a hand in front of his face like a windshield wiper, a sort of elective tic, a gesture of derision or rebuttal the others smiled at or ignored. From its first instance, however, Nelson, though enthralled, sensed that his client's special sufferance of him hung upon his divining its meaning, or holding his tongue until he did.

Presently, Chris confided a few biographical facts, all beyond Nelson's range of experience. Chris had been a trader; that is, he bought and sold companies, with the aim of getting rich, free from all encumbrances. He was forty and had never lived with anyone, never sought formal relations—a perfect paradox to Nelson, for there was nothing backward or shy or broken about the man, nothing plaintive, repulsive, or lonely. For him everything seemed a question of choice.

"Freedom," Nelson ventured. "From what?"

"Gravity," said the trader. "For starters."

Nelson winced. Still, this was carrying human aspiration pretty far. "Freedom for what?" he pursued after a pause.

The prostrate man pulled a sardonic face and the windshield

wiper went back and forth, back and forth between them, like a wand or pendulum.

Worthless freedom, freedom for nothing, as things had turned out. Seven years ago—Chris suddenly explained, with an air of telling all—he had been staying on the top floor of a small hotel deep in the labyrinth of crowded, narrow streets of the old town in Corfu.

It was Greek Easter, the great holiday of those parts, and after Saturday's solemn procession with the relics of St. Spiridon everything was closed and still.

His window looked down upon a short length of alley, and he pushed open the blinds. He had waked up late, having drunk too much retsina the night before with an austere and elegant youth caught between his family's dictates and his own dislike of commerce.

Nicolas Athanassopoulis wanted to go to art school in London, anathema to his fierce father, who vowed if he left Greece to transfer every drachma of his inheritance to his brother, already in charge of the firm's branch in Salonika.

Chris kept insisting, "London! London!" as the harsh, refreshing wine went down. "All will be well if you follow your heart's desire," he cried.

The Greek, hardly more than a boy, ended by sneering at Chris's naiveté, ordered another liter, demanded that Chris match him glass for glass. When Chris became too drunk to go on to another café, the boy mocked him for a Turk, and left him sitting there, trying to blink still the blurred, whirling world, not puke till he had steered himself to the stinking urinal. How he got back to his hotel he knew not.

Standing at the window in his underpants, still smarting from a contempt not wholly undeserved, he saw that a lamb was tethered by a red sash to a ring in a wall below.

A boy and a girl, eight or ten years old, dressed in their Easter best, were patting it most dotingly. A man with curly black hair strode around the corner in a clean white shirt with sleeves rolled up, sharply pressed slacks, bright-shining shoes, and a long, curving knife.

At a sign from him both children embraced the lamb, then

stepped back and side by side with open mouths watched as he fastidiously seized a dark ear and cut the stretched throat, keeping his distance till its legs buckled and the gush of blood subsided. Plucking up his cuffs, he spread his feet, squatted agilely and loosed the sash, letting the head too flop down, raising a puff of fine dust, which glazed one wide, liquid eye.

He cleaned the knife on the lamb's belly, without a word strode back the way he'd come. The children approached timidly, looked down for a moment, together scootched and with tentative finger-tips stroked the unstained haunch, then straightened up, looked down again, turned as one, and ran after the man.

Wishing he had missed this scene, which, notwithstanding his queasiness, was taking place at hundreds of thousands of house-holds all across the old Byzantine world, Chris closed the blinds and lay back down, depressed to be so affected.

There was no escape from his angst, nothing to look forward to but darkness, some medicinal beer, and a solitary dinner, if he could find an open taverna, and so he waited, perusing his *Blue Guide* between dream-haunted dozes, till midafternoon, when, wandering at random, still shaken, he climbed a rise and came upon the British Cemetery—mouldering, eerie, and dank—beneath a rampant canopy of cypress, fig, and citrus trees.

His first day in Corfu he had met with two of this once imperial people, from whom his own forbears had sprung, on both sides, ten or twelve generations past.

He had gone into a crowded, outdoor patio at lunchtime. A retired British major sat drinking port with two elderly ladies who looked to be his wife and her sister. He was in full regalia, rather woolly and brown for the weather, with beribboned breast and intricate harness of belts and straps and brass buckles and buttons, well shined. Raw, red face bursting with choler, white mustaches and mutton chops meticulously maintained, he was puffing and blowing and railing at the undisciplined Corfiots in a public voice as if this were still the raj. The pallid ladies listened with all eyes, from time to time sipping inscrutably.

He was doubtless a dear old thing in some ways, an ornament and familiar of the place, and this show of indignant flag a daily ritual, for waiters and patrons carried on volubly around the outlandish trio, evidently unoffended, but Chris, the only other obvious English speaker there, felt implicated, and fled, realizing he had never quite believed the type really existed.

He wound his way through the dark warren to the sun-blanched Esplanade, squinted up at the statue of Marshal Schulenburg, Saxon soldier of fortune, savior of the town in the siege of 1716, which marked the Turks' last effort of conquest in Christendom.

He became aware of a presence not quite at his elbow, discreetly, hardly breathing. Lowering his dimmed gaze Chris beheld a wraith with thinning, long, blond hair, dressed in threadbare garb of no definite color or mode—though somehow redolent of pajamas—and sandals worn nearly to paper and string.

"I beg your pardon," he said in public school accents apologetic and pure, "but would you by any chance happen to have a spare cigarette?"

"I don't smoke," Chris said, brusque with surprise.

The man bowed very slightly, gave an angelic smile of approval, and unobtrusively began to back away, preparatory to turning about and departing.

Chris was strangely pained. This was a sweet, a distinguished, a sympathetic beggar. "I'm sorry," he cried, and his voice rang beyond the moment.

"Oh, please don't be sorry," said the man with kind concern. "There's no need. Really. But thank you."

Chris felt awful. He might have bought the man a pack of cigarettes, he might have offered to converse—who knew what might have been learned of sufficiency—but the man's decorum had closed all doors, and then he simply faded away, like an apparition in the fearful light.

All the way back to the hotel, feeling dizzy, Chris had worried the man's plight. What would become of him? Antediluvian hippie or common derelict, he could hardly venture to importune the major, much less any of the remote-faced, olive-skinned strollers, who all seemed to carry a pack of Winstons in one hand, Bic lighter in the other, and in the cafés smoked with such dedicated panache, downing their multitudes of mucky, black coffees.

The next day his eyes felt full of finely ground diamonds, after which he never stepped outdoors without dark glasses, the sun revealed as prime circumstance of the Mediterranean, all life at its beck and call—work at dawn, siesta after lunch, dinner at ten or eleven, roses, arcades, whitewash.

But the English cemetery was so untended, overgrown, and dim he could hardly pick his way among the memorials even without sunglasses. Everywhere in the uncut grass orchids peeped through—some marked with sticks—strange, simian, little faces that peered back at him, making the place weirder by the moment.

At Napoleon's fall the island had come under British protection, a forty-nine-year rule daily deeper in the past, recorded only on a few scattered pages, themselves hardly less perishable than the crumbling tomb he sat on now.

He wandered about, feeling ghost-like. Here was a matrix far older, richer, more tragic than any his New World psyche had traced. If, as sages say, happy peoples have no history, here was only famous woe, its ancient name blood-chilling—Corcyra.

Colony of Sparta's ally, Corinth, it grew powerful, planted colonies of its own, and threatened its mother city, which sent its fleet against its unfilial daughter, which appealed to Athens, leading to the Peloponnesian War between oligarch and democrat that wrecked the first civilization of the West.

Age on age of will to rule steeped the island in gore. Greeks, Romans, Byzantines, Normans, Venetians, Genoese, then Venetians once again held sway, then Epirus, then the Angevins of Naples, then Venice yet again from 1386 till the expulsion of the gentle, last Doge by the ranting Bonaparte, then Czar and Sultan in concert, then Britain, and finally Fascist and Nazi dictated its fate.

Thought of Hitler's death camps with their auxiliary victims—gypsies, the unfit for existence, the non-Nordic, persons like himself—closed his heart, called him to join the shadows, sink down into the mold, enter without protest or regret the orchid world.

Hugging himself against the chill, bending to inspect the dark earth, he wondered why, when he had come to exult, he had led himself upon this morbid detour. Better have gone straight to Athens, and at once, even before finding a room, like a humble pilgrim, have climbed the steep, rock-strewn way to the Acropolis, stood among the cracked columns of the Parthenon, and surveyed the modern vista of jumbled rooves of the smoke-wreathed city below, marveled with true measure.

As he brooded in the greenish gloom he heard voices and beheld two youths in hiking boots and faded khaki shirts and shorts, each with a light pack. At first he took them for twins, but they turned out to be Israeli honeymooners on brief leave from their kibbutz, which Chris gathered was often shelled, though they bore it lightly.

They were friendly, frank, worldly-wise, the most comely people he had ever met in the flesh. Their skin glowed, their eyes glittered, they were quick-witted and spoke better English, he immediately heard, than he did himself. Both exuded such vigor and decisiveness he could only imagine their matings as something sublime, their future offspring godlike.

Companionably the three meandered in the twilight among the tilting stones of young fever victims. What forlorn fates, what brave solace their families must have sought to take in patriotic sacrifice! But it was all obscured, lost, forgotten. Only the trees flourished in this place; the air beneath their thick canopy seemed to drip like dim England itself.

"Cricket and ginger beer," said the girl. "That's what's left."

"There are worse legacies," Chris demurred mildly.

But they were not concerned with the near past. Building Israel was their only care. Of this they spoke with casual rigor, all the hours of the days of their lives consecrated. These were not the exotic exiles of shtetl or ghetto—thralls of The Book—but sabras, a new, bronze breed, soldiers by blood. Splendid in their single-minded simplicity and passionate idealism, they were pleased to speak of their triumphs and tribulations, of the promise of Eretz Israel, ancient prophecies to be fulfilled, and for a moment Chris rued his own lack of purpose beyond acquisition of leisure for philosophical pursuits.

They received his wishes for their national weal with a certain complacence, piquing him to voice what he supposed was the unexceptional caveat that if there were ever to be peace between Arab and Jew, sooner or later the Palestinians would have to be conciliated, and what a pity meanwhile that the refugee camps could not be run humanely!

Instant, implacable hostility transformed his new friends, girl no less than boy. Palestine was Jewish. Every inch.

But surely they must recognize . . .

They did not.

"Torture!" Chris said. "That's what I can't understand. Why torture? Aren't you afraid you'll become like your enemies."

They gaped at him with incredulity.

But what could the outcome be? Chris pled.

The Arabs must go.

And if not, what?

Kill them. Every one.

Chris wanted to lie down and cry. "This seems to me the road," he finally managed, "of endless war."

"How does it feel to belong to a decadent race?" the girl asked after a pause, curiously.

"I'm American," he said in surprise.

"We know," she said, looking down as if embarrassed for him, after which the conversation lapsed and then resumed with inconsequential subjects. He realized they despised him, perhaps despised all who did not recognize God's ruthless providence. They were terrifying, and terribly attractive.

He was lonely, sorely wanted dinner company, tried to broach an invitation, but they had fruit and cheese in their packs and no more time to waste. They were going to look for a place to swim, and left him abruptly with formal, cool farewells.

THE NEXT DAY, instead of going on to Igoumenitsa, he reembarked for Brindisi, retraced his route to Rome, where he felt at home, retrieved by unheard-of good luck his favorite garret room in his favorite hotel run by two elderly ladies, from the lone window of which he could see the dome of the Pantheon, whence, after a miserable week of bleak rain, hounded by a racking cough, he fled to Paris and tested positive for HIV.

He came home to Rhode Island immediately, prepared to fight the disease, and live to the fullest, but how? For seven horrid years, during which he was hardly able to hold a thought in his mind for half a minute, he rushed about in a frenzied nadir of medical resorts, bore in secret his death sentence, revolted by the hysteria, malice, and indifference that attended the gathering catastrophe.

By the time he was visibly ill he could not stand another word on the subject from the media, did not want to talk to anyone, did not even want to be in the same galaxy with anyone who did not have HIV. Wellness to him seemed not quite human.

"Even me?" Nelson had risked.

"I don't know about you," Chris said.

"I'm negative," Nelson confessed.

"I'm glad," Chris said, and the windshield wiper went once, twice, then petered out with a short, fading flourish, like a question mark.

Three years ago, he explained, having liquidated his affairs and moved to Provincetown, he had seen the ancient wisdom of Best Never Born.

Appalled, Nelson had entreated him to soften a bit this hardest of reckonings, permit the lesser judgment that in the circumstances he Christopher Whitman personally might just as well not have been born, though this proposition, unnerving enough—Nelson inwardly had to confess—might equally apply to very nearly everyone.

In any case, at the brink of extinction, the sick man's system—as if it were someone else's—had fought a last-ditch stand and won; and for the moment Chris was glad, in spirit rejuvenated, though such respite would be short-lived.

The last thing he had said was, "It's hard to die."

Arthur said, "I take it he does not entirely share your hopes he'll recover."

"I don't suppose he can," Nelson admitted.

Julian said, "If you wish you'd never been born, does that mean you want to die?"

"Why should it?" Arthur snapped. "In either case it's merely a question of worse coming to worst."

"All my life," Nelson mused, "virtually every minute of every day—maybe it comes from my damn father—I've been bothered by the question: Am I doing what I should be doing? At least I don't have *that* worry any more."

"Somewhere," Arthur said, "Yeats has it that life is a preparation for something that never happens."

"Who's Yeats?" Julian said.

14

THANKSGIVING

A SHARP FROST laid low Arthur's herb garden, all but the hardy little patch of parsley, which only glowed greener, and Nelson's visits ceased. Then, on Thanksgiving Eve, he phoned to beg off on the morrow's festivities.

Upon hanging up, the baleful host in apron went on with his preparations, divulged only, "He's going to have a *tra-dish-un-al* dinner. Not with *us*, however!"

Arthur had bought a most beautiful loin of pork. "Turkey!" he uttered. For weeks he had vilified his long-suffering submission to the Thanksgiving fowl, and broadcast his intention to defy its annual tyranny, at least once in his life.

He kept shaking his head, but said no more, and Julian refrained from questions.

It did sound a forlorn note though, since André couldn't come either. He had been kept in the hospital for more tests. He had felt weak for some time, and following the onset of jaundice the doctor had insisted on a thorough examination. He had hoped to be out by now, had phoned his regrets, made a few unwontedly mild observations on hospital life, and promised to drop by The Maid as soon as he got home.

"I'm afraid it's cirrhosis," said Baxter, the first to arrive at three o'clock. He had driven up to see André at noon, had spent an hour with him; he looked frail, though quite himself.

Weeming and Gil Bright arrived next, received the news with their cocktails.

By the time Madbury came the atmosphere was dolorous.

"Well, what can you say?" he said. "He's seventy-five."

"That's young," said Baxter. "These days."

André had spent a recent evening sitting cross-legged on the floor. At leave-taking Julian started forward to help him up. But André merely put the tips of his fingers down on the rug and rose like a boy.

Madbury said, "People get what they deserve."

"Nonsense," Arthur said.

"He was a lush," Madbury insisted.

"He hasn't had a drink in twenty years," Baxter said.

Weeming and Bright glowered, then in unison took sips of their Scotches.

"He had quite the high old time," Madbury said. "From what I heard."

"That was a long time ago," Baxter said.

"Not long enough," Madbury said.

"Doesn't seem fair, does it!" Weeming said.

"What's not fair?" Madbury said.

Arthur started to rise, but Baxter said, "I'm going up again to-morrow. He could use a little company, I'm sure. Though his room is a perfect madhouse."

"What *do* you *mean*?" Arthur exclaimed with genuine distress.

"He's got three roommates," Baxter said. "And *they* all have visitors. And the nurses are *very* flirtatious."

Said Gil, "Poor André."

"Poor his roommates!" Madbury said.

Baxter said, "They seem nice enough. Though two of them mostly just lie there groaning. One had a hernia operation, the other had his gallbladder out."

"Shall we take bets," Madbury said, "on how many days it will take André to get put in solitary?"

"*And*," Baxter went on, "they filled the empty bed with a man who was *about* to have a heart attack. His wife knew the signs. Very cheerful fellow, I must say."

"About what?" said Julian.

"Nitroglycerine, I suppose," said Baxter.

"*Shall* we sit?" Arthur said, forging up. "Bring your drinks. If you must. There's wine."

Julian went to the kitchen and got two fine bottles of Reisling. The host conveyed the platter of pork to the table, his guests its many accompaniments, and all sat down.

"Grace, anyone?" said Arthur, glancing about. Finding no volunteers he folded his hands, bowed, cast up wary eyes, closed them, intoned, "Dear Gods of the Universe, we are not exclusive here. To One and All we offer thanks for what we've got. Each other. Amen."

Echoes abounded. Napkins were shaken out. Arthur arose to carve the roast. Dishes started round. Once all were faced with full plates, Baxter raised his glass and said, "To André! May he soon be back among us!"

"Is that possible?" Madbury muttered aside to Weeming. "I thought cirrhosis was irreversible."

"And absent friends!" Arthur added from the head of the table.

With token flourishes all sipped again. As always, Gil Bright felt small when he thought of Cahill, haunted that he had not been at the deathbed, jealous of Weems who had. But why must he always be seized by such petty feelings? Why did the dead always seem somehow better, aggrandized beyond failure or flaw?

"Where's Nelson?" Weeming suddenly, worriedly wondered.

"Ah, Nelson!" Arthur sighed.

They all looked at him; it occurred to them no place setting remained empty.

"Nelson is having turkey," Arthur said primly. "At Franco's."

His guests tried to interpret this.

"You're joking," Gil said.

"I invited him," Arthur said piously.

"We *thought* he was coming," Julian said.

Wearied of his mystery, Arthur said, "He has a date."

They gaped. None of them had had a date in the last two centuries, and Julian had never had one, at least with a man. The word had gone out with the dodo.

"With whom?" Baxter inquired.

"Amos," Arthur said. "I invited them both, but they had their hearts set on a tra-dish-un-al dinner."

"Well!" said Baxter. "Good for them! Who's this Amos?"

Arthur said, "He's on the shift after Nelson with Tony Gompertz. And very young. We are told."

"They'd better get tested," Madbury said direly.

"Well, here's to them!" said Baxter, and another, happier toast was drunk.

After coffee they went to Julian's studio to see his new painting, done over the last two days, between holiday duties. Thirty by seventy-two it was gorgeous, far better than he had thought, having not seen it for several hours. It shimmered, it glimmered, it pulsed and throbbed and glowed. The pale, black, horizontal bar trembled amid mingled blues and greens, light-laced, with an unearthly arc of aurora borealis shooting up in the background like peacock feathers to blur and swirl among moonbeams through mist in a sort of celestial estuary, the whole composition abstract and exact, strangely mesmerizing. Julian gazed amazed as anyone.

"What's it called?" Baxter finally asked.

"The Old Lady's Cane," said Julian.

Arthur said, "Don't be quaint."

"Coming from you!" Madbury said.

"Actually it's a compass needle," Julian said. "It doesn't know which way to turn."

They went back inside for more liqueurs. Everyone made predictions of a great future for Julian. It was a triumphal moment for all. Julian had never felt happier, his powers gathering, merging, his many minds becoming one.

About six Heldahl came in. He had gone home, to his mother's stone castle in Magnolia, but one bite of dessert—was she trying to kill him?—and he was back on the road to P-town.

"She wants me to move somewhere else," he said. "She thinks it's like a leper colony down here."

"When in fact it's merely a cesspool," Madbury said.

"Back to Magnolia?" Gil asked.

"She's not *that* crazy," Heldahl said, his sparse, curly hair standing like a corkscrew. "Where's our florist?"

"Ah, Nelson!" said Arthur. "That devotee of turkey!"

Distracted for a moment from his own frazzles, Heldahl heard the news of Nelson's date, of André's cirrhosis, of Julian's latest extravaganza.

At the general insistence, Julian took him to his studio. He was stunned, undone, awed, elated, disconsolate, a-squirm with self-deprecation.

"God, how I envy you!" he groaned. "You don't know how lucky you are! To have a gift like this! It must be wonderful to know who you are, never to have to doubt what you were born for, always to have the joys of your own genius. Most people don't have any reason to get up in the morning, except they have to eat. Or," he allowed with disfavor, "go find somebody to suck or fuck."

Julian said nothing. He took his life for granted, could envisage no different course. How others lived he could not guess. The laity seemed unreal to him, depthless, lacking a dimension, prizing possessions, happiness, and ease.

"I don't care about anything," Heldahl said. "One thing is exactly like another to me."

Julian gazed at him, embarrassed and remote.

"Sometimes I wish I had AIDS," Nicky said. "At least I'd have some point."

"Anyone can get it," Julian said.

"I wouldn't have the courage," he said miserably.

Everyone went home early but Baxter. In profile, he and Arthur brooded out the dark window, speaking occasionally, personal, parallel musings, without need of answer. Julian began the cleanup, mad to resume the gloating study of his new painting.

15

AT THE HOSPITAL

THE NEXT DAY, when Baxter stopped by to get a piece of pie for André, Julian went along, lest André like Jim Gurley vanish—lacking what Julian could not quite say—perhaps only his own last respects. The swirling flurries of the year's first snow made him glad to be on the road.

Compared to the white clapboard of Julian's village medical facility, Cape Cod Hospital seemed a brick labyrinth. Up elevators, down corridors, around corners, past doors open and doors closed, past schools of white-gowned medicos they strode without a word, till Baxter found the room, and Julian with dread followed him in.

André's bed was cranked up. He did not look absolutely awful, only washed out, diminished by his white johnnie, wrist band, and IV pole. The grinning man beside him was also cranked up. The other two, across the way, lay on their elbows, facing each other. Cheery nurses came and went.

After greetings almost aloof, André testily told them he would be out soon, that in fact the disease had been stealing his strength for some time, but could be arrested and controlled. He already felt much better. Baxter and Julian were to stop looking constipated, as if they were stuck on his obituary.

He felt quite humble after his scare. He realized how precious life was, how many and simple, how splendid the commonplace joys he had taken for granted, but now would savor to the full, each day live as if his last.

Meanwhile he directed Baxter to quarter the immense piece of pie for future distribution, and introduced his compatriots.

His gregarious neighbor was Mr. Burrell, the one warding off the heart attack. The horizontal pair were Mr. Crobaugh, of the hernia, and Mr. Trafton, of the late gallbladder. They too grinned, though pallidly, and spoke at intervals, to spare their incisions.

André to them was Mr. Every, which he endured without umbrage. They tweaked him about having to drink water from now on.

"His hell-raising days are over," Mr. Crobaugh confided to Julian and Baxter.

A nurse went round with a fresh pitcher of ginger ale.

"That'll get him in practice," whispered Mr. Trafton. Full voice he avoided; laughter made him groan.

Mr. Crobaugh raised himself a bit to sip from the flexible straw. "When I get home the first thing I'm going to do is fix myself a big whiskey, and dedicate it to you," he said, tilting his cup toward André, "and the second is, I'm going to do it again. *Somebody's* gotta keep your end up."

"It's *getting* it up that's the problem," whispered Mr. Trafton with a wink at Julian, who smiled faintly, wishing he would wink back.

"Mr. Every's a happy bachelor. He's got a different babe every night," Mr. Crobaugh conceded. "No problem for him."

André submitted to their ragging with complacence, seemed to enjoy it. They had no more idea of him than of the man in the moon, Julian realized, but they were obviously fond of him, and he admired Baxter's grave, insouciant gaze that seemed to grasp everything and yet see nothing.

"Think," said Mr. Burrell, "all you'll save on aspirin and Alka Seltzer! Not to mention bent fenders. I'm an ex myself, ex-drinker, ex-everything."

"He's had more lives than the rest of us together," André told Baxter and Julian.

"And never missed a one," said Mr. Burrell grandly. "Ex newspaperman, ex taxi dispatcher, ex state cop—believe it or not—ex clam digger, ex pimp. Oh, I didn't tell you that one! Back in my younger days. But I always got bored and moved on. I ruined my first marriage, I ruined my second. I lost my car, I lost two houses, my whole life's a list of losses. But I'm happy-go-lucky, that's what my mother always said. God damned fool was what she meant. I'm sixty-three years old, and look at me!" He displayed his rugged grin; lines like crisscrossed arroyos gouged his mottled face.

"You're one lucky son of a gun," Mr. Crobaugh said.

"I am," said Mr. Burrell. "I admit it." He wore flamboyant pajamas, the only one with no IV pole.

"My wife—my *third*," he addressed Julian, "she got me off the sauce. She put me to rights finally. I just do what she tells me, I haven't made a decision of my own in the past ten years."

"You wouldn't even *be* here," whispered Mr. Trafton.

"She drug me in," Mr. Burrell told Julian. "I didn't want to come."

In the doorway appeared a little, white-haired man in a bathrobe, rolling an IV pole and dangling a urine bag.

"Mr. Chance!" cried Mr. Burrell. "How are you today, sir?"

"All right, I guess," said he. "No worse, anyway. I'm just going down to the lounge for a smoke."

"Wish I could join you," said Mr. Crobaugh soulfully.

"Me too," declared Mr. Trafton with volume.

"Mr. Chance has been here for six months now," André told Julian and Baxter.

"In and out," Mr. Chance said. "Mostly in. I guess when you get old it's just one damn thing after another."

"This hotel is not cheap either," said Mr. Burrell with baleful commiseration.

"I had to sell my house." Mr.Chance admitted and lifted deprecating eyes to Julian and Baxter. "I don't know where I'm going to live."

Baxter shook his head almost imperceptibly, Julian his.

"It makes me mad," Mr. Burrell grated.

Mr. Chance shook his head in resignation, said to the deprived, "You'll both be back in good shape soon, and we'll all go down together."

He walked slowly from sight, followed by farewells of empathetic envy.

"Not only his house," said Mr. Burrell. "All his savings too."

Mr. Crobaugh gave a groan and let his head fall back. He blew a few loud breaths through pursed lips.

Mr. Trafton watched fiercely. "I wish I could do something for you," he said.

"Nobody can do a man's suffer for him," Mr. Crobaugh said with a gasp.

André said excitedly, "This is his third hernia. They took a polyp out of his intestine at the same time. He didn't even know it was there."

"When I get home," Mr. Crobaugh vowed, "I'm going to cook myself some ribs."

"He's from Culpeper, Virginia," André explained.

"Culpeper," said Mr. Crobaugh with accent pungent and proud. "We'll have a reunion," he said. "A year from the day the last one of us gets out of here. At my house. I'll put on a feed. All you can eat and drink. We'll have a time."

"Now you're talking!" cried Mr. Burrell. "We'll exchange addresses. Last one out lets us all know."

"One year to the day," vowed Mr. Crobaugh. "You're invited too," he said to Julian and Baxter. "And your wives," he said to Mr. Burrell and Mr. Trafton. And yours," he added to Julian and Baxter."

"They're bachelors," André droned with a disparaging sniff. "Confirmed."

"Smart fellas," whispered Mr. Trafton. "They're too young for the harness. In my day . . ."

"Y'all hurry up and mend," gasped Mr. Crobaugh.

"Yawl!" cried Mr. Burrell delightedly. "I'll supply the booze. Top shelf! That's the nearest I'll get!"

BAXTER AND JULIAN drove back to Provincetown greatly relieved, André so cheerful, the prognosis benign, the room so clubby, the sun so warm, as if fall had come again, no flake of snow remaining.

Thereafter Baxter drove up every day, and stopped by The

Maid to report. André was still frail, but most impatient to get home. Mr. Burrell had been released, his bed taken by a Mr. Desmond, a card shark apparently, an irrepressible performer, inflicter of tricks, another loser of his gallbladder.

At the cash register in the A&P, Madbury said, "They ought to remove André's, and his spleen too, while they're at it, fix his disposition."

Julian half nodded. Madbury noted a hostile nuance in Julian's usually remote demeanor, but could find no precise reason for it.

ON ANDRÉ'S TENTH DAY in the hospital, Julian accompanied Baxter once more. He did not look well, appeared to be weaker, not dispirited exactly, but withdrawn and slow of speech; and Mr. Crobaugh and Mr. Trafton, in a race to see which would be released first, treated him with the deference due an elder, all jocularity gone.

He might be the last one out, they conceded, but he wouldn't be far behind.

But something besides cirrhosis was going on. His doctors had prescribed a battery of new tests. André himself seemed unalarmed.

"Name a card, any card," Mr. Desmond kept insisting like a child, fanning his deck, shuffling, cutting it with one hand, plucking aces from nowhere, making them disappear. Malice moved in his cynic's eye, which alighted with insolent speculation on Julian and Baxter.

While his old roommates fended off the interloper, André, roused to pride, in a weak voice related their immediate adversities.

Mr. Trafton's wife had kept the books for his trucking firm, but she was getting vague. Sometimes she forgot she'd had her cocktail. His sons must now begin to take responsibility, but both had jobs, and houses of their own. Neither had ever wanted to work for him. The younger had no interest in the business; the elder wanted him to merge with a wholesaler of dubious repute. Both were preoccupied, the elder getting divorced, the younger about to marry a floozie with three kids from two previous marriages.

"They're almost thirty and they're still just kids," Mr. Trafton put in gloomily. "Nowadays nobody grows up until they're middle-aged. Present company excepted," he amended with a courteous nod to Julian. "The closer I am to retirement the further away it seems to get."

Mr. Crobaugh gave a snort of sympathy.

After silent head-shaking between the two sires, André alluded to Mr. Crobaugh's troubles.

"I druther stay here and have more surgery," said he.

His neighbor, a rich widow, had died, leaving her estate to her grandson, only child of her youngest son, Waldo.

The will skipped both Waldo and his brother, the playboy bachelor, Chauncy.

Not a penny would ever go to either son. An old family friend, Vincent V. Topham, was named executor, with total discretion, until the legatee reached his majority.

Chauncy was contesting the will, on grounds that an illicit relation existed between his mother and Topham, who had deceitfully played his father's best friend, while alienating her affections to gain control of the sons' inheritance.

Chauncy wanted Mr. Crobaugh to testify that Topham had long been his mother's gigolo.

Waldo, who abhorred his brother's profligate life, refused to join the suit, since his son would inherit everything eventually.

Public airing must bring good to none, harm to all. Having been subpoenaed, Mr. Crobaugh must become complicit.

"When mud is thrown," Mr. Trafton allowed, "it sticks. People prefer to believe the worst."

"Even to have knowledge of this mess," declared Mr. Crobaugh, "is to *appear* unsavory. The father couldn't have imagined a scandal like this. Nor his wife either, for that matter.

"I doubt his pal Topham ever cuckolded him, at least not while he lived. Topham loved him too much, loved him better than his wife really, and loved the boy too, and there's the nub . . ."

"Aha!" cried Mr. Trafton. "Truth will out!"

"He really served as the boy's uncle for years, but he had . . . a quite particular fondness for children, you might call it," said Mr. Crobaugh unhappily.

"Wouldn't you know!" sighed Mr. Trafton with profound shakes of the head. "There's always something, just lurking."

Mr. Crobaugh said, "I doubt he ever did a single wrong thing.

He was just very affectionate, very demonstrative. Doting. With the boy, at least. You never would have guessed he was anything more than their mother's chauffeur."

"Ugh!" said Mr. Trafton. "Why should such things be delved into?"

"Spice of life!" said Mr. Desmond, leering broadly.

Julian glanced at Baxter, who looked somber. These days he hardly spoke, except to pronounce commonplaces. In the car coming up, he had mentioned some books Julian should read, spoke not another word.

Mr. Trafton said with vehemence to Mr. Crobaugh, "But you've got a fine son to leave the world!"

"There's no such thing as a fine son," interjected Mr. Desmond.

A glance of queasy acknowledgment passed between Mr. Trafton and Mr. Crobaugh, then both eyed Mr. Desmond with distaste.

"Love is the root of all evil," he said.

"Not what they teach anyway," said Mr. Trafton equably.

"Well," said Mr. Desmond, "when *I* get out of here *my* little pinch is to console the son of a friend of mine."

All eyes gravitated grudgingly to the card shark, who seemed to have forgotten his deck, which lay in disarray by his idle hand.

"He got himself a mistress," said Mr. Desmond. "He had a lovely wife. My daughter, as it happens."

He grinned back at them with stony glee. "They found each other out," he said. "All of them."

"And?" said Mr. Trafton, lifting his chin.

"Kid played his hand like a first-class mark," said Mr. Desmond. "Said to himself, *I love my wife, my wife loves me. I love my honey, she loves me. What's the problem?*

"So he got them together in his kitchen over a bottle of Scotch, and the ladies made friends all right. They gave him the business. And he went in the bedroom with a knife and cut his cock off."

"Solved *that* problem," André wheezed.

Mr. Desmond chortled without mirth. "They grabbed his cock and raced him to the hospital, the doctors were just trying to sew it back on, he grabbed it and gobbled it down."

"Solved *that* problem," André droned.

"I never liked him much anyway," Mr. Desmond concurred. "I

would've stopped the wedding if I could. His father was my poker shill. He don't play anymore. He don't do anything anymore. My daughter and the other girl, they both feel to blame. So he got what he wanted, he got them both."

"And they got *him*," said André with his first real zest of the day.

DRIVING BACK, Baxter and Julian worried about André and wondered about Mr. Desmond. The scalpel seemed not to have subdued him at all. In convalescence he was ahead of Mr. Trafton and Mr. Crobaugh both, yet his surgery postdated theirs. Where was the justice?

"He looks," Julian suddenly realized, "a little like Madbury."

"Bane of my life!" Baxter muttered. In answer to Julian's glance, he added, "He's my tenant, you know. He does my shopping these days, and various other little chores. My garden has gotten out of hand, the lawn, the house, everything. I have to depend on him. I've retired, more or less."

He sounded weary and sore. Julian was surprised that anyone, no matter how obnoxious, could get under Baxter's tight-fitting skin, or that he would ever admit it. Why didn't he simply evict Madbury and get someone else? Someone more . . . more . . . more like himself. For a guilty moment Julian weighed the possibility of escaping The Maid's hectic summers in Baxter's lesser employ, then pictured Arthur's distress, and dropped the thought.

16

LETITIA

THE NEXT DAY Julian started two new paintings. Baxter went up by himself and didn't come back until dark. André was no better. Baxter had cornered his doctor, who with quick apologetics said nothing construable, pled urgency, hurried off.

The worst was, André was alone; all his roommates had gone; he felt bereft, he said; he even missed Mr. Desmond, card tricks and all. Mr. Chance dropped in to chat on his way to and from the smoking lounge; otherwise it was as if André had been disconnected and left nowhere.

Madbury drove Baxter up again next day. They came by The Maid on their way home about dusk.

"It's cancer," Baxter said. "Of the lung. Very advanced. There's nothing to be done. He hardly has any time at all. They told him. He demanded to know."

Arthur breathed audibly in and out.

"He's very weak," Baxter said. "He cried when they told him."

Madbury said angrily, "Nobody to blame but himself."

Baxter eyed him with exhaustion.

Arthur said sharply, "Don't be stupid."

"He smoked like a fish," Madbury said. "Gauloise. He told me himself. He said he loved smoking more than anything in the world. Except drinking. He can hardly complain now."

"He hasn't smoked in fifteen years," Baxter said. "*Or* drunk."

"The wheels grind slow," said Madbury. "But fine."

Arthur said, "Keep your benighted creeds to yourself or leave my house, please."

"I'm sorry, too," Madbury said, aggrieved. "I *like* André."

"It's really dreadful," Baxter said. "Now he regrets he spent his life alone. He said if he had it to do over he'd try to make a go of it with somebody."

Madbury jeered, "Can you imagine André getting along with anyone for five minutes? He would have just ended up dying of AIDS. Years ago. In that first wave. It's a miracle he lived this long."

Baxter got unsteadily to his feet. "Time to go home," he said.

"I mean, he's such a sourpuss," Madbury said.

"Goodbye," said Arthur.

After a moment Madbury rose. "I don't mean to sound callous," he said. "I'm sorry, too. I'm as sorry as anybody."

"Then shut up," Arthur said.

"In the end," Madbury tried to conciliate, "nobody gets away with anything."

"Shut UP!" shouted Baxter and Arthur together.

ON THE MORROW, with Madbury driving Baxter's old blue Volvo, they all went up to see André. He was frightfully far gone. They bent around the crib-like bed. A nurse stopped in the doorway, met their raised eyes and withdrew. No word exceeded utility —a plumped pillow, sips of water, concern with bedsores, catheter and IV bruises, promise of future visits. After an hour they left him dozing, and rode home in silence.

Gripped by high feeling, Julian kept to his studio, finished one painting, started another, then another, conceived a fourth. One day Baxter said, "If you want to see him again you'd better come."

Arthur, who had gone the day before, closed his eyes and shook his head.

"Tomorrow," Julian vowed. But the next day Baxter woke with

a bad stomach, felt too sick to go, and they did not set out until nine o'clock the following morning.

André had been dead since dawn. The room was made up and empty, except for Mr. Burrell, who had dropped by to see his favorite nurse and any remaining old roomies.

He kept running his hand through his thin hair. How could his pal André have died? He couldn't believe it. Everything had been going so well, for all of them.

"He was a chimney fish," Madbury cried out with exasperation.

Mr. Burrell snapped back with bitter vehemence, "I don't care what anybody does so long as they don't die."

He wrote down Baxter's address. "We'll have that reunion," he said, "a year from today . . . part memorial, I guess," and he wiped his eyes. "December 10th. I'll tell Mr. Crobaugh and Mr. Trafton. There's two calls I hate to make."

As they drove back it began to snow. "I hate this fucking shit," Madbury said.

"It's winter," Baxter said.

Julian, alone in the back seat, wondered at Baxter's newly scrofulous neck. Illness and death were everywhere. He tried to count his losses, but stopped at Jessica Jordan. After him they were all the same, one lengthening shadow. It was like being in a war—except there was no enemy—like being snatched by invisible aliens, one by one.

As the days went by, Baxter shrank with the ignominy of abandoning André's relics to the state. Despite Arthur's evident lack of enthusiasm, he finally marshaled the strength to take on the frustrating disentanglement of red tape about a deceased without spouse or kin, in due course acquired custody of André's ashes, and lodged them on his dining room mantlepiece in a fantastic urn like the Taj Mahal, to await inspiration.

"Mellow loves to perch on it," Baxter said with obscure sentiment.

"Shit on it, you mean," Madbury said.

"We must come and pay our respects," said Arthur.

"I say," Madbury said, "just dump them in the gutter and be done with it."

On Front Street once at dusk, Julian had come up on three men with a coffee can. They were drunk, raucous, and stumbling along the edge of the sidewalk, spilling the contents as they went.

As he passed them, they huddled and quieted, then behind him their plangent clamor broke out again. He laughed aloud at the riddle now solved.

Madbury eyed him. "What's funny?" he said.

"Never send to know," said Baxter. "And I very much doubt André would appreciate the gutter."

"Why not?" said Madbury. "That's where he lived most of his life."

"His early years," Nelson observed. "In Paris."

"That's all he talked about, "Madbury said. "Bored everybody silly."

"He lived a long time here," Arthur said. "We're all newcomers compared to him. We've lost our memory."

"That world is gone. Good riddance, and best forgot!" said Madbury.

Baxter said, "Things hard to believe now. No same-sex dancing. At least for men. The police would break it up. He always said the two great signs of change came when Commercial Street got so built up there was no place you could still see the bay and no more unfenced nooks to take a piss in after the bars closed."

"Gone forever," Madbury said. "Gone with the breeders."

"*And* the fish," Weeming said.

"*And* the fishermen," Gil said.

"Gone," Madbury said. "All of it. History starts with us. The past is them. The future is us."

"I don't think André would subscribe to that," Baxter said. "He loved the old town. He always said he liked the intrigue of not knowing who was what."

"All he ever did was criticize gays," Madbury said. "Once he even called me on my deportment. I haven't heard that word since my mother died."

"Both, I fear," said Arthur, "died in vain."

"André did not discriminate," Baxter said. "Everybody came in for his—or her—fair share."

"From the gutter he came," Madbury sniffed, "to the gutter he should go."

Baxter cocked his head, gave an eighth of a shrug. "Maybe we should take him to Paris. Monmartre. He loved it there."

"Some of him. A modicum," said Arthur. "He loved it here best. He's ours."

It was a strangely soothing line of talk.

"We could just flush him," Madbury said. "Or throw him off the Monument, pollute the atmosphere. I never would have let him in the house."

Baxter and Arthur closed their eyes at each other.

"I don't care," Madbury said. "I never liked him anyway."

Julian decided to tell Arthur if he died to scatter his ashes on the highest hill in the cemetery, on a hot summer's day.

NELSON, to his own dismay, took André's death in stride. He felt dreadfully sad, but André had had his life, notwithstanding belated regrets. Its end seemed merely to merge with all the others, recent and soon to come. And he was in love, twice over—maybe that was why he felt so impervious—having never known real love before.

"Twice?" said Arthur. "Amos is twins?"

"And Chris Whitman," Nelson confessed.

"How convenient," Arthur said. "Not to say perverse."

Baxter gazed out the window expressionlessly, and Julian again sensed something untoward.

"I've never really been happy before," Nelson said. "Now I'm too happy. Everything looks beautiful to me. Even ghastly things have a kind of light in them. Nothing bad really bothers me, and then I notice some little detail of the world I always took for granted and now it seems absolutely dear. I know this is the way it's supposed to be, but it's completely out of place. I can't just sit around people's deathbeds grinning like an idiot."

"Love's idiocy is the one thing everybody forgives," Arthur said.

"Or love forgives idiocy," Nelson said. "It's all a bit unsettling. Especially Tony Gompertz. He hates Amos, who can't even imagine such a thing. The nastier Tony gets, the nicer Amos treats him."

NELSON DIDN'T COME again for a week, then appeared, looking no less upwrought, but astoundingly thinner. "I've stopped eating," he said. "I don't have time."

Arthur and Julian took in his sallow face and slack clothes. His eyes glistened and popped.

"I hardly ever sleep," he said. "Everybody's dying."

He had been with Tony Gompertz for the last fifteen hours. It had all come out in a rush, his appalling guilt and rage . . .

"You must eat something," Arthur interrupted, "and then go home and sleep. Julian will drive you."

Nelson shrugged them off; he needed to unburden, to make known how Tony had repented—having long misprized and finally lost the man he loved most—had resolved to reform and live wisely, but HIV had intervened and made him a murderer. The shock, the injustice, the sheer randomness of it, made small all he had wanted to believe in. Bitter vindictiveness possessed him. If he had the virus, why should anyone not?

For several years his health had held, but only brute sex could quell his tumult. At midnight he haunted the shadows at Flyer's Boatyard, by day calmed or bullied partners out of condoms, lived the frenzies of a serial killer. His victims vanished into summer mob or winter vacancy, and he enjoyed a day of respite, of innocence reborn.

Then worse and worse torments came, whetted by envy of the healthy, and he would resume his orbit of death, his "gyroscope," he called it, always afraid he would spin out of control.

Nelson seemed beside himself, though not so far gone that he missed Arthur's dismay.

"If you saw him you would pity him," he said in exculpation.

"He does not know that he ever infected anyone," said Arthur, disparaging and cold.

"He *thinks* he did," Nelson said. "He believes he knows at least two, maybe three."

"Has he told *them*?" Arthur said.

"What's the point?" Nelson said. "He doesn't know where *his* came from."

"You are becoming infected yourself," Arthur declared.

"It's very confusing," Nelson confessed. "Once you get into it deep enough nothing makes sense."

"Then get out!" said Arthur.

"I don't even wish I could any more," Nelson said humbly. "I don't know which is worse, Tony before HIV or Tony after. Those are really two different people, with two completely separate lives, and he can't fit them into the same skin. They're totally at odds now. He's not so much dying as his halves are killing each other."

"You see!" Arthur snarled at a startled Julian. "The conscience is not to be trifled with."

"Talk about revenge on the universe!" Nelson said bleakly. "And now he wants me to help him commit suicide, before he goes into dementia. It's the thing he fears most."

"Making you his ultimate victim, I suppose," Arthur said.

"I don't know," Nelson said. "I don't even know how to think about it. I don't have time."

"It is time for you to eat something and sleep," Arthur said.

Nelson said, "I can't. I've got to go see Dom Ponoma. He's in bad shape."

"Mr. Serenity?" Arthur said.

"He was," Nelson said. "Till Letitia came."

"Ah, Letitia! And who might she be?" Arthur inquired, casting eyes toward the kitchen and lifting his chin.

Julian brought a plate of cold leftovers and a glass of Chianti.

Glaring absentmindedly, Nelson stuffed his mouth with ham and washed it down with half the wine.

"Something terrible happened," he said.

Arthur and Julian merely gazed at him with bludgeoned disbelief.

Nelson chewed another stuffed mouthful, swallowed urgently, said, "Letitia is an estranged friend of Dom's from the dim past. Somehow she heard he was dying and came to make amends. Unannounced I might add. She just showed up. They hadn't spoken in years. They lived together when he first got back from Tangier, they played the cozy, betrothed couple to their families and employers, they cruised together, they came out together, and eventually she stole his boyfriend and went straight.

"Which lasted two months and then the guy dumped her and went back to men.

"She became an addict and a drunk and all her relationships after that went smash for years and years and then she joined AA and stayed single and taught school in Marlborough—had a perfectly ordinary life, rather gray, I should say.

"She was like a little, mousey packrat with this huge bundle of festered ferment. She wanted to talk everything out. All these years she's regretted their rift, but this boyfriend of Dom's that she ran off with who dumped her turned out to have been the love of her life, so she had that to gnaw too. I mean, she was wrong, but she was right, but neither did they cancel each other out.

"None of this meant anything to Dom. The last thing he wants is retrospects. He kept saying, 'It's all right, everything's cool.'

"She went into histrionics, claimed she'd wrecked both their lives, destroyed both their capacities for love and trust. So they both ended up unfulfilled.

"She couldn't forgive herself and he couldn't console her. You'd have thought she was the one dying."

"And how long is this visit to last?" Arthur asked. "Does she intend to nurse him to the end?"

"Ah . . . she's gone," said Nelson.

"Well!" Arthur said. "Much ado!"

"Actually she's dead," Nelson said.

"Dead?" Arthur said.

"Well," Nelson said. "She started to drink again. Dom has a lot of liquor. Nobody noticed at first because she was boozing in the bars at night and just nipping by day, but then we found some needles in her room."

"I've never seen a needle in my life," Arthur said. "I've never even *known* anyone who used heroin."

Julian was loath to admit it, but neither had he. He wondered what sort of prick he might paint as hydraulic apparatus.

"Could you get me one?" he begged.

Dumfounded, Nelson said, "Don't be macabre! They've got blood in them. We threw them away."

Julian was filled with excitement; he could see the red smear in the transparent chamber, a swollen, globular droplet sagging at the needle's tip.

"Actually," Nelson said, "I . . . ah . . . killed her."

"In the circumstances only hyperbole would do, I am sure," Arthur drawled, but his eyes were wary.

Julian refilled Nelson's glass, which he quaffed heedlessly, spilling wine down his chin, wiping it with the back of his hand, quaffing again.

"She became absolutely crazed," he said. "It turned into a dreadful quarrel. I've never seen Dom so upset. He kept saying, 'All right, all right, so you betrayed me, so what?'

"She says, 'You can't forgive me if you don't understand.'

"He says, 'I don't care.'

"She says, 'If you don't come to terms with me you can't forgive yourself.'

"He says, 'I have nothing to forgive anybody. Especially myself.'

"'Well, I do,' she says, 'I've got everybody, starting with you.'

"It got quite bizarre. And then she took a bottle of his five-star cognac out of her bag and began to guzzle it.

"I says, 'Go! You've got to go.'

"It was nine o'clock at night, pouring rain. Dom says, 'Oh, she's all right. I don't mind.'

"'Well,' I says, 'I mind. I'm responsible here.' And I called the Holiday Inn . . ."

"We *do* appreciate *that*," Arthur said.

"I went upstairs and stuffed her suitcase. I got her in the car by brute force—I've never laid hands on another human being in my life—and went back in the house and locked the door. I turned out all the lights and sat in the dark until she drove off.

"About midnight I was listening to talk radio, horrible, ranting crazies. A bulletin comes on, one-car crash, high speed, on a straight, downhill stretch. The car planed on the water, sailed right over the guardrail on an overpass, hit a big square of cinder blocks on a construction site down below. I knew it was her . . . I still haven't told Dom."

Arthur stared and said nothing.

Julian poured more wine.

Nelson said, "People mean well, I guess, but it's all just too much and one had better be prepared for a certain amount of discord and willful selfishness. I should go."

"Home," said Arthur. "To bed."

"What's the use?" Nelson said. "I drank a whole pot of coffee in the last couple of hours watching Dom sleep. I never took my eyes off him. The radio was on in the kitchen—every half hour the same bulletin, same words. Finally about dawn they said it was a single fatality, a female, name pending notification of kin.

"I'm not sure Dom isn't the nearest thing to kin she has. She came all the way down here to see him. I kicked her out and she lost her life."

"A long time ago, according to her own testimony, and her own fault too!" Arthur cried. "Forget it! Tell no one. Go home and go to bed. Neither you nor Dom are involved at all. At all! Do you hear?"

"I hear," Nelson said, looking nowhere. "All night long I could feel her presence in the house. She was there twelve, fourteen hours ago, and now she's . . . ah . . . jelly."

He poured another half-glass of wine, drank half of it, hung his head, stood up, said to his toes, "I feel worse about her than I do about all the others."

"Gluttony," Arthur said, irascible and cold.

"I guess," Nelson said meekly. "She really is mine though."

But home he could not go. He walked slowly toward the shop, wondering why the more people he knew the more unrelated he felt. He was fit only to be a recluse, and for the first time in his life he felt sympathy for his father, whose whole soul had been a zeal for public affairs, who had loved the world of rule and felt of use in it.

He could tell Priscilla nothing; one word would loose a flood, and where it would it go, where stop?

The instant he stepped through the door the bewildering blend of perfumes engulfed and exhilarated him, then faded before that strange human failure of smell after only a moment in a flower shop, and then a sickening tinge of rot pervaded everything.

He went about sniffing. Priscilla gave a good cough of accord. "You smell it too? I can't find it. For a while I thought it was in the freezer."

He opened the door, went in and let it thump shut behind him. It was like a little grotto, beautiful and cool, but he could smell nothing at all. He resisted an urge to lie down on the duckboard and go to sleep.

He stood a minute, trying to envisage Letitia's rusted, green Honda airborne, herself rigid with attention, hands gripping the wheel, eyes glaring through the windshield down the white trajectory of the headlights, the wipers whacking back and forth, the square of cinder blocks rising to meet her, nothing in her face, not even incomprehension.

When he came out Priscilla looked questioningly at him but he held his tongue. All he had to say was, *I shouldn't have let her have her car keys.*

Eventually they found the lost bouquet, fallen behind a shelf of hanging ivy. He parted the green cascade and brought it forth, overwhelmed by the stench at close range, carried it at arm's length and threw it in the trash, vase and all, making a tremendous commotion.

Priscilla eyed him, startled.

"I had a long night," he apologized.

She raised her eyebrows at him.

"Somebody died," he improvised.

"Mary have mercy!" she said. "One of yours?"

Nelson nodded.

"I'm sorry," she said. "Who was it?"

I don't know," he said distractedly. "I mix them up."

She looked at him with concern.

"It's all right," Nelson said, pulling himself together. "He went very peacefully. He wasn't actually mine. Just somebody I knew."

He took the trash out, went into the shed and began breaking up cardboard boxes.

Priscilla put her head around the corner.

He straightened up and gaped at her.

"I'm so sorry, dear," she said.

He shook his head horribly and bowed.

17

BAXTER

ARTHUR WAS IN a foul temper, balefully sailing about, stopping at each window, glaring out.

"A certain amount!" he bit off.

Julian glanced up from his armchair under the green lamp. About his intellectual development he was perfectly docile and promptly read whatever Arthur and Baxter assigned; no page failed to please. Books were alike to him in their fantastic distraction; they were such fun to read they must, he opined, be fun to write, which gave Arthur a look Julian knew well, that said, *You are still a dunce.*

"From closet to charnel house in one step," Arthur said. "That's the fate of your generation."

Julian made an attentive face.

"Nelson," said Arthur, "has lived an infinitely sheltered life."

So had Arthur, it seemed to Julian, and himself as well, but he kept still.

The phone rang. "Yes?" said Arthur, exasperation still sharp in his voice. "Hello!" he cried with delight, then, "Uhm!" in a stoic tone, then, "Uhhmm!" again, like a long sigh, and turned away from Julian, knotting the cord's coils.

"Uhm," he said. "Uhm-uhm."

Julian held his breath with foreboding, but couldn't guess who it might be, or what portend. A consequent wedge of relief slid in, upon which each baneless moment beat, letting him breathe again.

"Dear God!" Arthur said. "This is truly . . . uhm. Uhm uhn. Well. Angels *will* fly in, won't they?"

He listened for a long time. "Of course," he said finally in a conciliatory tone. "He made it. That's enough. For you both. For all three."

He hung up and stood for a moment, looking down at the phone. "That was Selwyn. Gustave died."

Tears burst from Julian's eyes; a huge weight of emptiness crushed his chest; he sat staring, mouth wide open and dry.

"Dear boy," Arthur said with unwonted tenderness. He sat down in the chair opposite. "It appears . . ." he said slowly as one entering a swamp, "Gustave was terribly sick. Selwyn agreed to help him commit suicide. One day when Gregory was out, they drank—a certain amount, I have no doubt—and Selwyn got Gustave into a warm bath and tried to cut his wrists with a mat knife he found in the basement. They were both rather feeble, I gather.

"Anyway he didn't do it deep enough. Or couldn't bring himself to do it. And Gustave simply couldn't. This was two weeks ago. They tried, both of them, they drew some blood. A certain amount, no doubt! Selwyn said the water was all quite horribly red, and then Gregory came back sooner than expected, and called the hospital, which patched him up and kept him going, till last night he finally slipped away."

"What's Selwyn going to do now?" Julian asked.

"Stay at Gregory's, I guess," Arthur said. "Live with his irresolution. Die."

Julian's face showed shock.

"If he can get Gregory's leave!" Arthur's cold rage grew colder. "The NRA is right. Everyone should have a gun, and be required by law to learn how to use it. Suck muzzle, pull trigger."

Stunned, marveling that he had never thought of this most obvious icon of the times, Julian guiltily tried to conceal his rapture in a vision of a long barrel's blue sheen, bullet emergent, a dumdum maybe, the slug flattening, spreading flower-like, splash-like, moon-like as it went! Where? And what a hallucinatory verge of blue! This awful news for him was provident.

"Too messy, I suppose," Arthur went on, "for the fastidious. But it would cure a certain amount of the human element. Or disarm it in others. Poor Gregory. Too late for Rick, too soon for Gustave.

"Selwyn said he'd call in a couple of days—once they've got through the formalities. I suppose he'd like us to come up. And meet the Lord of the Manor."

To Julian, Arthur seemed unduly harsh. After all it wasn't him who had to cope. Nor was he even sick. Or so Julian suddenly, fervently hoped—was absolutely sure, wasn't he? But what *had* Dover died of?

Arthur was watching Julian's inward stare. The boy was simply not always there. He was a sensitive soul. Too sensitive! Well, what else should he be?

"Life is hospice," Arthur said with self-distaste, repenting his spite. Nelson was doing his best. Bless him! What did his bathos matter?

Julian went on staring narrow-eyed, as if to find reply, but said nothing. Lost in his involuntary production of forms, he hardly belonged to himself at all.

Abandoned, Arthur turned to his faithful dolor. Amid disposable lives, what feelings were warranted? Existence was less absurd than repulsive.

Nobody who lived after the French Revolution would ever know how sweet and gentle life could be, according to Talleyrand. How much more grim then the age after Nagasaki?

And after the Plague? There might *be* no after. What would become of love itself, that sole defense against despair?

Julian arose almost furtively, eyed Arthur with unconscious circumspection, as if he feared to be caged, bumbled an apology, and headed for his studio, lest his visions fade.

Arthur was affronted. The boy was a complete egotist, lacked the elemental decencies, along with all worldly knowledge. For all his blunderings, he was extraordinarily cool and detached—virtues in an artist, no doubt—at which Arthur gave way to grief for Gustave, remorse for Selwyn, and even sympathy for the imponderable Gregory.

Presently he picked up the phone and called Baxter. To his annoyance, Madbury answered.

"Ask him to call me," Arthur said.

TWO DAYS WENT BY and Baxter did not call. Perhaps he had gone to Boston, or perhaps Madbury had neglected to tell him, and anyway what was that infernal twerp doing in Baxter's house all the time?

An unpleasant taste touched Arthur's gorge. Noxious though Madbury was, he was not bad looking.

The weather had turned cloudy and cold, with sand-laden gusts that stung faces and pitted windshields. Arthur never left the house. No visitors came. Julian kept to his studio. Nelson did not appear. Baxter did not call, Arthur was loath to dial again and get Madbury's bumptious voice, and there was really no one else he could bear to tell, as Weeming and Bright had suddenly gone to Antigua.

In the third day of Arthur's desolation Baxter dropped by in person, blessedly alone. Arthur was so glad to see him he could hardly keep from bustling.

"Isn't this vile weather! Would you like a little something? I have sad news. Not unexpected, but sad, dreadfully sad."

Baxter looked at him blankly. "Scotch," he said.

Arthur complied and sat down nearby, bursting to bring him up to date on Nelson's ordeal as well.

"Where's Julian?" Baxter said, looking about.

"In his studio," Arthur said proudly. "He's working very hard these days. I've hardly seen him since . . ."

"Good," said Baxter with grim calm. "Because I have something to tell you. In confidence."

Arthur stared with sinking heart.

"No one knows," Baxter said.

Arthur held his breath.

"No one must know. I shall rely on you."

"Ugh," said Arthur. "Of course."

"I've got it," Baxter said.

Eyes veering, Arthur tried to think what else might possibly be meant.

"I've had it forever," Baxter said.

Arthur met his eyes. "Are you sure?"

"Yes, yes!" Baxter said tartly. "I have practically a regiment of doctors in Boston. But now it's beginning to manifest itself. In unmentionable ways, I must say. Charming indeed!"

All Arthur's breath went out of him and he sagged, then lifted his chin, his eye caught on the hated talisman.

"I do not care, just yet," Baxter said, "to have Ted find out. And he will be around, perforce, more and more. I shall need him."

"Replace him," Arthur said.

Baxter shook his head.

Arthur dropped his eyes.

Nelson's step was heard, and then he appeared deferential in the doorway.

"Baxter!" he mouthed, his visage alight. "How are you?"

"And you?" Baxter said. "You're looking fit."

"Ah . . ." said Nelson.

"It quite becomes you," said Baxter, lifting his glass not quite to his lips, letting it down.

"I could use some of that," Nelson murmured to himself.

Arthur made a deliberate way to the pantry, returned with the bottle and two glasses.

"We must combat this weather," he said.

Nelson nodded, drained his down, reached for the bottle. "Well, I . . . ah . . . ah . . . ahhm . . ." he began.

"How," Arthur demanded with swimming head, "did you resolve the unfortunate business with Letitia?"

"I never did," Nelson said. "But it doesn't matter. I've just seen off two of my little family," he explained, and his voice fell. "Dom died two days ago, Tony this morning."

Baxter cocked his head with quizzical interest.

Arthur closed and opened his eyes. "Too much," he said.

Nelson downed another shot without grimace. "I'm so tired. I hate to lose them."

Baxter and Arthur attended with vast, still detachment.

"Dom just . . . went to sleep," Nelson said. "His breathing got like surf. We'd been expecting it, but I was there all alone. I got in a panic. I thought of Keats saying, 'Don't be frightened. Be firm, and thank God it has come!' And then the phlegm 'boiling in his throat.'

"That phrase has haunted me since I was a child. My father read me that damn letter from Severn. Can you imagine?

"I kept praying someone would come. I didn't dare touch him. He just stopped, and then I heard myself panting and realized I'd been trying to breathe for him."

Julian appeared in the doorway ravenous, having just finished his third painting in three days.

Eyes fastened on him. He saw the bottle, the glass in Arthur's hand, but Arthur only drank at dinner. The atmosphere was stark, as if secrets were being bartered. He glanced from one to another, then sat down unhappily, wishing they would come to his studio, be ravished and bathe him with praise, avid also to slip off to the kitchen for a snack and glass of milk, since Arthur's usual, nice lunch looked not in the offing.

Arthur told Julian, "Dom Ponoma and Tony Gompertz died."

Julian contained his disappointment that there would be no studio visits today. He did not know either of the deceased; both had been bedridden before he ever heard their names.

Baxter lifted his glass ceremonially and sipped.

"Well, I did it," Nelson said. "Anyway."

Arthur's eyes snapped to, his lips mimed a silent, *Did what?*

"Who was I to say him nay?" Nelson said.

They all looked at him.

"Do I understand . . . ?" Arthur said.

"He was so ah . . . in such dire . . . straits," Nelson said. "I couldn't refuse."

"Who?" Julian said. "What?"

"Tony," Nelson said sharply. "Gompertz."

"I thought he died," Julian said.

"He did," Nelson said. "I mean I . . . ah . . . killed him. Which seems to be my mission in life these days."

"Don't be depraved!" Arthur cried. "Letitia did herself, and Tony—you merely stood aside, I take it."

"Though I shouldn't bruit it much about," Baxter warned.

Arthur closed his eyes and bowed in benediction.

Nelson saw that Arthur, and perhaps inscrutable Baxter too, if not Julian, who for some reason seemed nervous as a mouse, would all prefer the subject be dropped and never brought up again; but he felt he had to tell someone how Tony Gompertz died, and other than these friends was only Priscilla, and her an ardent Catholic.

"He was so sick!" Nelson said. "If you'd seen him you'd understand."

"I do not need to see," Arthur said testily, "to know."

Nelson's eyebrows jumped. Over the last weeks he could hardly recognize Tony, so wasted, disfigured, reduced to unmitigable throes physical and mental both. To watch its ceaselessness was almost to adore death. What purpose Nelson sought to serve was no longer clear, and he felt upon some new, precarious edge with life itself.

"I told Amos not to come, I said I'd do a double shift, but he's such a sweetheart, he came anyway, to keep me company. He still has no idea Tony hates . . . hated him."

"He wouldn't have interfered, surely?" Arthur said.

"He would have been horrified," Nelson admitted. "We don't discuss such things. He gets upset. He wants everyone to live forever. Maybe that's what Tony hated. He didn't mind being tended by me, or anyone else for that matter. But Amos was a sort of rebuke, he has those rosy cheeks . . ."

"But you succeeded," Baxter said firmly. "That's the main thing, I suppose . . ."

Nelson said, "He got some vodka down and then about twenty sleeping pills, and when he started to get drowsy, which was right away, he said, maybe he was joking, 'This feels like the best sleep I ever had,' and he lifted up his head and helped me get the plastic bag on, and then I taped it tight around his neck.

"It was thick, industrial plastic. I could see him in there, sort of blurry, with his eyes shut. I don't know if I was more terrified that he would change his mind or that he wouldn't, or what I would do if he did or someone came.

"I couldn't watch. I flushed the rest of the pills and poured the vodka out and buried the bottle in the bottom of the trash, I put the duct tape back in the drawer. I kept looking at the clock. I couldn't tell if he was breathing or not . . .

"And then I saw Amos coming. I almost began to hate him myself.

"I became very calm, like someone else entirely. I was counting the seconds before Amos got there. I ran to the door, I probably sounded pretty crazy, I yelled, 'A dog just ran off with the *Globe*, see if you can get it back.'

"Amos says, 'What dog?'

" 'Oh,' I says, 'it was an Irish setter, a real prancer, a big red goofus with a big grin. Around back,' I says. 'Go!' "

"Amos says, 'Tony doesn't need the newspaper.'

"I says, '*I* need the newspaper.'

"He says, 'I'm afraid of dogs.'

" 'This is a very friendly dog,' I says. 'Go!' I felt like God talking to Adam and Eve.

"So off he went, and I ran back in and gathered up the *Globe* and pulled the bag off Tony's head and stuffed it all in the trash. I couldn't tell if Tony was breathing or not. I put the pillow on his face and held it down hard till I heard Amos on the porch. I put it back under his head and ran out and said Tony was asleep so we could sit out in the living room where it didn't smell so sick.

"I talked nonstop about a dog I had. He would go up to kids so they could pat him, and then he would snatch the ice cream right off their cones.

"Somebody stole him. Can you imagine that? It was the saddest thing that ever happened to me."

"You're completely punchy," Baxter said.

"I guess," Nelson said. "Finally Amos says, 'We better check on Tony.'

"And there he was, like an ancient mummy. There was nothing left of him, all of a sudden there was much less, just bones with skin dried on. Amos was quite upset. He says, 'Why are you taking out the trash at a time like this?'

"I couldn't say a word. I had to leave. I had to get out the minute the undertaker started to put Tony in that bag. I've seen too many of those bags. I helped Dom into his two days ago."

Nelson poured and drank another inch of Scotch, absently crunched and swallowed an ice cube, set the glass down and sat staring.

"You should go home now," Arthur said, "and get some rest."

Nelson nodded and nodded, but went on staring. He was too tired to sleep, too fragile to face Priscilla's staunch sympathies, too death-ridden to go home to his empty abode with its one chair by the window, its stale smell and laundry-strewn shambles of his lone life. All he wanted was Chris, but he dreaded to go near him. Everywhere he went he brought death.

Baxter arose, made his condolences to Nelson. Arthur followed him to the door, where their eyes met, Arthur's weighed with the untold news of Gustave's death.

Baxter said, "I do not want there to be any celebrations of my life. If you know what I mean."

"I do," said Arthur.

"You may get together and have a drink or two," Baxter said.

Arthur said firmly, "We will drink to the bottom, I am sure."

"As you like," Baxter allowed. "It should be at my house, in my study if few enough come. One piece of music. Beethoven's string quartet in C minor, opus 131, the fifth movement, about five minutes . . . I will leave it out for you."

Arthur shook his head in ignorance.

"Exultant gaiety, pure joy, spontaneous delight, transcendent humor," Baxter said. "That will kick up their heels, if not mine. Then if anyone wants to say anything they may. Briefly. After which I trust you will take them to your house and give them a nice lunch."

"I will," said Arthur.

"No celebrations," Baxter said.

Arthur bowed him out, shut the door, bent his head against it, remained leaning there, one hand still upon the knob, the other in a fist supporting his forehead.

"Ah . . ." eventually behind him sounded Nelson's apologetic hesitancies, "I'm . . . ah . . . off . . . ahhh . . . myself."

Arthur opened the door and let him out with mute respect, Gustave's death forgotten. "Keep the faith," he muttered to his back.

"I would try," Nelson said without turning, "if I knew what it was."

"You've got it," Arthur said. "Have no doubt."

He returned to the living room. Julian had already cleaned up and was standing plaintively in the kitchen in front of the open refrigerator.

Arthur went past the door with a tremor of fury, mounted the stairs with heavy tread, couched himself on one elbow amid cushions and pillows, and gazed out his dormer at the grey winter, feeling hoary and gravid with monsters.

NELSON TRUDGED to the East End, found Chris asleep, lay down on a couch to wait, fell asleep, slept through the next shift, woke heartsick, bone weary, numb in the silvery dusk of late afternoon.

And was told that Chris had had a bad day, had not ten minutes ago swallowed a spoonful of Jell-o, and gone back to sleep. Two weeks ago Nelson had thought Chris had an indefinite while of good life yet—time enough for them to sit in his sunlit window, look out at the spangled bay.

Nothing had slowed Nelson's growing dependence upon Chris to absolve his guilt, assuage his doubts, solace his losses.

"The one thing that no one could have done or not done was to remain unborn," Chris had said in their last coherent conversation.

"Or die," Nelson had added the obvious, involuntarily.

"But," Chris had said, "that at least can be resisted."

Nelson had seized upon this as Chris's conscious intent to last as long as he could, long enough to see Nelson through of the valley of the shadow where the dying had led him.

But Nelson had barely begun on Letitia. Chris, even that day too weak to listen for more than a moment, had merely traced a ghost of his wave with one crooked finger, like a broken Pope.

Today it was clear he could give no help, that after all Nelson still inhabited his life like a hermit, and might as well go home and sit with himself.

THE PHONE RANG as he opened his door. Though he had told no one, he had been thinking of selling the flower shop. He had meant to ask the trader's advice, but in the turmoil of the week no chance had come, and now, the prospective buyer being in urgent haste to fulfill a lifelong ambition and possessing the requisite cash, Nelson agreed to sell.

That the new owner, Sean Costello, was a novice gave neither pause. Nelson had known nothing about flowers when he started, would be nearby to consult, and anyhow Priscilla had worked there for years, and nodded and coughed amenably when they broached the sale to her.

What could daunt one with full-blown AIDS? With will intact, even after two awful sojourns at Beth Israel in Boston, Sean Costello was back on his feet while it lasted. This was what he had always dreamt of, and on the morrow took possession of the premises, at end of day stood amazed amid his bower of misted, mysteriously glowing leaves, watching the snow pelt down outside.

18

NICKY

And now I'll get out of here, Nelson vowed, with mixed exhilaration and horror, for that could only mean, when Chris died.

His dream of travel in sight of coming true, with money in the bank and time on his hands, he sat with Chris, who seldom woke, and haunted memorial services.

The latter phenomenon *he* at least could not explain.

"Keeping in shape," Madbury quipped, "for the big one."

"Vicarious penance," Arthur sniffed, "for everything and nothing."

"In which case you are obviously ah . . . eligible to join me. There's one tomorrow, if you'd care to come," said Nelson.

"I am not a crasher of funerals," Arthur said.

"I never thought of it that way," conceded Nelson, who was open to interpretations. It was just something he felt impelled to do. He went to churches and windblown bonfires on the beach, made freezing forays into the dunes, joined pledges of spring tree plantings or memorial sails with committals at sea, was a silent presence at ceremonies of every sort—shaped to the taste of deceased or bereaved, alike only in their professed belief in an imperishable human soul.

"At my great aunt's," said Baxter, "we sat upstairs. The minister and mourners were in the living room downstairs. The closed coffin was across the hall, all by itself. We had to hear not one word of the eulogy.

"Afterward a few friends were asked to stay, and we went in the kitchen and Mother put out some sherry and a plate of saltines."

"Yours will be Irish compared," Arthur murmured.

"*My* mother," said Madbury, "was a snob and a hypocrite. All she cared about was respectability. She was never happy with anyone but herself. After my twin brother got his first promotion she always called him the Great Big Shot. She didn't even like to hear my name mentioned. At the end when she was all tangled up in oxygen tubes and stuck in her wheelchair she got the idea we were planning to put her away and tipped herself headfirst out the window. That didn't get in the obituary. Nothing real ever gets in.

"The minister preached what a good Christian she was. She hadn't been to church in years. And the organ played 'Amazing Grace.' Somebody told the minister it was her favorite hymn. She would have detested that song if she'd ever heard it."

The others smiled at this caprice of talk from one so harsh and reticent, odd too to think of Madbury as a twin.

"It bugs me that no one ever says what a bastard anyone was. All death does is make a lot of lies. We should do André. The real André. Right here!" and he grinned at Arthur sunk on his soft throne.

"André might not be amused," Arthur said wearily.

"But *we* would," said Madbury. "*That's* the point, isn't it? Why should Nelson have all the fun?"

All glowered but Baxter. Still, André's ashes in their stupendous urn on his mantlepiece were a constant remonstrance. André had given no guidance as to their disposal, nor had his friends taxed his last lucid interludes with the problem, and thus, Baxter reflected, perhaps best was let-come-what-might.

For one had no control at all. Dooley's house had gone to a couple of guys with racy tastes, who tore down walls between formal rooms, tiled the antique kitchen and baths, installed a row of urinals, got rid of all the bookshelves but one reserved for their bevy of Barbie dolls, built a tanning deck on the roof, disposed of the old cedar doors, that repaired and repainted would have lasted another hundred years, ripped out the tangle of roses, honeysuckle, and trumpet vine and replaced it with a little line of thin birches, circled with new sod, wired against wind.

"The whole herd of white elephants," i.e., what pieces remained of Dooley's exorbitant props, "had trotted off, thank you very much!" to Moontide Auctions.

Baxter had striven to outlive his nonagenarian parents, intending to comfort the last-to-die—doubtless his mother—during the desolate wait for the end. It appeared now that both might have to endure his predecession, a personal failure so deplorable that he found himself wishing for their immediate, simultaneous deliverance from existence, shying though from its mental depiction. His life now had the sole aim of seeing them into their tomb unbereaved.

Madbury was overwrought, Baxter having bought him out of the A&P on generous terms, nor was he a demanding employer, though grumpy these days, gloomy and distracted, obstinate, forgetful, evidently aging, set in his ways, fretful and hard of hearing, nearly helpless when he lost his glasses.

All were avid for Nelson's impending freedom, notwithstanding its threshold, envious, impatient for him to be off, or at least fix on a destination and give them ground for fantasy.

"Italy!" said Arthur. "Roman lunches!"

Baxter eyed him with dour regard. "Paris!" said he. "The City of Light!"

"Antigua!" Madbury crowed.

Just back, tanned and rested, Weeming and Bright had explained their unscheduled vacation. One night they had brought home a porno flick, not five minutes into which Gil had said, "I can't watch this, it's my brother."

They had been shaken. Too many friends had died, the brother included, nor had Gil known of his stint in film. They had been working too hard, fraying each other's nerves and talking about living apart for a while, edging toward a precipice, both recognized, once they found themselves upon a white beach by a sea unbelievably blue, with nothing to do but breathe easy and rediscover life.

The others were stunned—Gil and Weems were the longest lasting couple any of them knew, pillar of their commonwealth, proof of the possible. If not them, who or what *could* be counted on?

Now they confessed to a worse heresy yet: they were thinking of leaving town.

"You can't be serious," Arthur said. "Where would you go? What of the years you have invested here? You can't afford to leave."

Alas, they feared they dared not stay, as they realized the minute they got back unglad. Again they felt caught, snappish, intolerant of each other, restless, bored, dreading the future.

"Why don't you adopt?" Madbury said. "Isn't that the prescribed way to save a marriage on the rocks?"

"You might change occupations," Baxter said not quite facetiously. "Everyone in P-town has at least one restaurant in them. So I've been told. You might go in with Nicky."

Gil groaned and Weems grinned. Nicky Heldahl, whose wide culinary experience came from his habit of dining out three times a day, had been meditating an eatery since he first moved to town. Every year he added to his library of cookbooks and formed a new plan: German, French, Mexican, Thai, if he could find the right help, the right space, the right moment.

No, it was South Beach, Miami—SoBe—for Weems and Gil. The blessed sun! Warm, healing seawater year round. A new little gay community, elegant, old hotels with beautiful lobbies and restored art deco in a formerly rundown neighborhood of Jewish pensioners, genteel and safe, galleries and shops and cafés with newspapers on racks, very civilized and old-fashioned, almost European. It was like a dream!

"I thought P-town was the dream," said Nelson, who harbored itchings of his own. Why should he not go to some foreign fleshpot and plunge fearlessly into the life he had always tried to avoid imagining? Art and architecture be damned!

What a strange world! All anyone naturally cared about was sex! Everything else had to be learned. The rest of life was merely a struggle for distraction.

Ignominies beset him. He was born to be no libertine: it was museums for the likes of him. He simply couldn't do as others did. He was the son of the Judge, after all, still and forevermore, Nelson Lamont Terrence Ryder, Jr.

The son recognized suddenly with amazement that the Judge would by now be proud of him! Whatever the old man's views on sex, he would as deeply as anyone detest the disease, and laud succor of its victims.

Nelson had glimpsed nothing of his father's inner life. A worldly man, he never said anything definite about anything but the law — despite the fact that he discoursed sonorously, amusingly, brilliantly on every subject under the sun — unless perhaps it was confided to his "girlfriends," as his wife had mildly derided them.

No, Nelson Jr.'s fate was fixed, and he ought to accept it, once and for all. Amos would come to nothing, lost as he was to his own pretty sainthood. They had nothing in common, could hardly sustain a minute's conversation. In Nelson anyway Amos sought merely an uncle. And Chris, the only man who had ever wholly appealed to him, was now shrunk to the speck of his own disappearance. Why could they not have met long ago? But Chris would not have valued him then, any more than could his father.

Meanwhile he attended funerals, solace for his looming loss. He had several times tried to get through to 1075 Washington Street in Portsmouth, New Hampshire, meaning to commiserate with Selwyn — the other shoe, Madbury called him — but the phone was never answered. He noticed too that now mere word of an AIDS death, whether he knew the name or not, brought a sort of free-floating relief, not woe.

Baxter said, "I'll make up a little packet of André for you to take in case you get to Paris."

"Baked bile," said Madbury.

Nelson laughed absently.

CHRISTMAS AND New Year's passed with their kindly diversions, weighed down by the iron sky. Julian stayed in town, his mother having gone to Tucson — her purpose a little vague — and thus he suffered with the others through Nicky Heldahl's holiday disasters.

No one had seen him for some time. This was not odd, as he often visited Mutti in Magnolia, where only Baxter had ever been, returning with tales of a baroque castle with vast glass cabinets of rare crystal. They ate frozen dinners off cracked crockery, itself antique. The house was filled with artificial flowers, the first of such invention, greyish petals and splayed leaves thick with dust.

Nicky himself was odd, or seemed odd to his friends, in the first place because, apparently having lots of money, yet he seemed always in a swivet of financial distress, and secondly, because he himself insisted so upon his own uniqueness.

"Nobody knows the first thing about anyone else," he once declared. "Some people think I'm a blundering idiot."

When no one managed to dissent, a sweet, sly smile appeared on his face, and he said, "I am of course a blundering idiot."

A further silence ensued before he amended firmly, "But not of the sort that people think."

Perhaps he spent too much time alone, having a varied hoard of tranquillizers and mood elevators, in addition to his regular regimen of Prozac and a taste for Rhine wines, also fortunately an indomitable constitution and a certain optimism about life, based on the irrefutable fact that so far nothing really bad had ever happened to him, apart from this present, ongoing, quite familiar if barely perceptible, in the circumstances perfectly comprehensible, five—or was it perhaps ten?—year decline.

Lately he felt himself fragmenting into unrelated parts. Walking home one early dusk from the Little Bar at the A-House— perhaps he was a trifle unsteady on his feet, or had allowed his eyes a too-swooning salute to those of the man he tilted past on the narrow sidewalk—he observed an evident distaste accentuate the stranger's already sternly compressed lips.

Nicky staggered. What right had anyone to feel such superiority? Was he straight? Was that all it was? He shivered with grief at the old, appalling mystery. Why should healthy, warm-hearted feelings beget viciousness? Not to mention mayhem, et cetera.

Without taking off his coat he paced in front of his living room window. All was now obscured but a blurred sheen of Wellfleet across the bay. The condo spotlights trained on the beach below showed a half-sunk shell of fiberglass dinghy that had washed up the week before and would one day be gone. Nothing was ahead but dead winter.

He went out without bothering to freshen up and drove toward town, mortally bored by the dining alternatives, dreading chitchat with cheeky waiters.

He idled through town, revolted by thought of every place still open, then conceived of the clatter and bustle of the Land Ho in Orleans, a couple of burgers and fries at the bar, a few beers, the romance of real people, oblivious, proletarian types, a well-deserved respite from this hellhole of would-be celebrities.

Commending his own resourcefulness, hope bloomed and he spied a-gleaming in his headlights a most beautiful ass, an ass sweetly jeaned, perfectly formed, and perambulating ostentatiously, wantonly.

Letting up on the accelerator, he loosed a profound sigh as he coasted past, then peered into his side mirror, which was not rightly aligned. To compensate, he rested his temple against the window, veered the car a little to the left to get a better view, but when he saw that it was a high-booted, long-striding dyke possessed of one gorgeous, lean, man's ass, he felt mocked, indignant at women, especially lesbians, who, thanks to AIDS, were taking over the town, snapping up businesses gays had built.

Next he glimpsed a section of telephone pole approaching so ghostly slow he braked with gradual languor of unconcern, saw it loom in rude detail, in its immediate presence verge sudden on his left fender, knowing it would make but a scrape, an hour at the garage—heard, tremendously close, felt, shattered glass, crumpling metal, forehead windshield-thumped, knee dashboard-crunched, all, he marveled, at less than no miles an hour.

Engine roaring he backed up, producing a shower of tinkles and creak of released metal, shifted into low and resumed course, little the worse, but slowly, cautiously, down the precise middle of the street, molding with thumb and bunched fingertips a lump above his left eye the size, it felt, of a kiwi fruit, his right knee so stiff he could hardly shift.

He was beginning to think his day was jinxed when he became aware of a pulsating, blue aura around the interior of the car. He puzzled at the faintly familiar, ominous phenomenon. Then red intermittently alternated, then mixed with the blue. Both mirrors having been knocked askew, he had to look over his shoulder to confirm that it was of course the police.

He hit the brakes, neglecting the clutch. The car stopped, the engine bucked and stalled, the sprung hood heaved up, and there he sat.

Graham the cop—new, young, not yet acclimated—got out and looked in at Nicky, who rolled the window down, handed over his license and long-suffering sighed, "Not my day, I guess."

Graham could hardly demur. He slammed the hood, glanced at the damage—$1,200 was an optimistic estimate. Then, having got them both pulled over to the curb, he bent and gazed in again at Nicky, who looked forlorn, prepared to plead, already a bit smitten. He reeked, but seemed sober. And it was Christmastime.

Graham hated these situations. He knew Nicky was gay: it took one to know one, he allowed with small regret. He was a closet case himself; he just didn't want anyone to know; whose business was it but his own? And he came from a family of cops in Haverhill.

"Provincetown?" his uncle had said. "That's full of fags."

"I like the beaches," Graham had said. "I love boats."

There being an ongoing effort to get some gay policemen on the force, and not a little nasty defiance within the station, he had to be careful of how he treated gays.

Nicky was relieved. Obviously this fresh-faced guy was not going to be a bastard. What a darling, really! And for the second time of the evening all his gloom vanished, as if it had never been.

"You were going to report this, of course," Graham said.

"No, no," Nicky said. "Not at all."

"You *were* going to report this," Graham said in a more definite tone.

"It never would have occurred to me," Nicky said.

"You intended to report this," Graham said. "I am sure."

"Not in a million years," Nicky insisted, wishing to be understood in all his vulnerability vis-à-vis the incomprehensible, uncomprehending world.

"I *know*," said Graham, unhappily trying to sound severe. "I know you meant to report this. It's a mere formality. Tomorrow morning will be soon enough. You're on your way home now. No stops. Straight home."

"Oh, sure. Of course," Nicky promised, catching on at last, suppressing a request for alternate routes. "And thank you, Officer," he trilled, unable to keep a certain presumption out of his voice.

He drove straight to the Lobster Pot, ecstatic to be back in this cozy haunt, drank some beer to level off, ate some fried squid, then had a cognac and coffee, smoking with voluptuous aplomb, his lungs nicely numbed, as well as his injuries. He even felt a bit raffish, his fantasies enhanced by packing the policeman's pants with the lesbian's ass.

One moment marred his mellowest evening in months. For the busboy was Reef the bleak, the scowling scarecrow he'd passed on the street. Nicky gave a start of frightened repugnance. The dishes disappeared in a trice, along with the unsightly apparition himself, whom Nicky never glanced at again, disdainfully, patiently shaping his cigarette ash into a perfect cone against the ashtray rim.

Reef, too fierce and unaccommodating for social contact, relegated by mutual consent to kitchen work out of the public purview, had this night nonetheless been pressed into service due to illness among the help.

Flaying his failures, lost in the satisfactions of hard thoughts amid the steam and the slops, he loved to drink boilermakers at the end of his shift, hated hedonism, dismissed those not passionately engaged in some intellectual pursuit, gnawed the desperate brevity of life, the injustice of every social relation, found it nearly impossible to eat, had no impression of Nicky whatsoever.

Forgetting he had found Reef's stark features intriguing at first sight, Nicky mulled the irremediable luck of one's fated place in life, pitied this ugly drudge's skeletal pallor and rank-looking clothes, and had another triumphal cognac. Sailed home on a cloud of well-being, thinking to change his clothes and sally forth in search of further entertainment. Drove into his driveway, turned off his ignition, heard a second crunch of tires and slam of door, got out with ripe anticipation, found himself face to face with the cute cop.

Graham said sadly, "I thought you were going home."

"I was," Nicky said with sly jollity. "I just did. I *am* home. I live here."

"It took you two hours?" Graham said.

"I had to stop off," Nicky said. "I was on my way to see a sick friend."

"I see," said Graham queasily. The guy was plastered; he should have booked him in the first place, at least have made him leave his car parked where it was; maybe he was in the wrong profession; he did love Provincetown though.

"Terribly sick," Nicky said. "That's why I was so upset I skinned that pole."

"You didn't mention any sick friend," Graham said.

"It wouldn't have occurred to me . . . to burden you," Nicky said. "These things . . . exist."

"It appears your friend was serving refreshments," Graham said.

Nicky lurched against the car door. "I'm at the breaking point," he said. "I was saying good-bye."

"I'm very sorry, sir," Graham said.

At the sound of sympathy Nicky dissolved. He felt how miserable he was, how terrified and alone.

Graham knitted his brows and said, "I didn't notice it till now, but your inspection sticker is six months out of date. I'll have to write you up. You get that done tomorrow, and file that accident report. If you don't it can get pretty expensive."

Hands in pockets, one shirttail loose from his last trip to the men's room, Nicky gaped blankly at him, swaying, arching back against the door, leveraging up, collapsing back.

"You go to bed now," Graham said, "and get some sleep."

"Sleep?" Nicky wailed with indignant entreaty. "How can I sleep? What if you knew if you killed yourself everyone else would die?"

Graham felt the quicksand. Notwithstanding the leeway of community policing, he had already made nil of numerous guidelines, and now gazed at the subject with hardening eye.

Sagely rocking, knowing he had uttered some fundamental truth and feeling vindicated, Nicky awaited an answer, confident of exoneration.

Alarmed, Graham was wondering, *Is this a cry for help? A*

threat? Had I better haul him in? I don't want a corpse on my hands.

"Maybe you should call someone," he suggested finally. "Have you got a priest? Or minister? Some support group?"

Nicky snorted. "I've got more shrinks than God. What good are they? They can't change anything. Not even me."

A little reassured, Graham said, "Maybe you'd better skip the fast lane for a while, give things a rest. And lay off the sauce!"

"Death goes on," Nicky belied with jaunty nonchalance, lifting his shoulders in a prolonged shrug, ending in their sudden droop, like the fall of all things, followed by a humbly bowed head and total tilt, with intent, it appeared, of nestling upon Graham's blue-coated bosom.

The cop held him off. "Sir! Sir!" he cried, "You need to get some sleep."

Nicky mumbled accord, and tried to nuzzle, which got him thrust brusquely back against the car. If only the guy would understand—he had such curly hair, such cherubic cheeks, such wise eyes—why couldn't he give him a hug and put him to bed, then stay a while and talk? There was so much to say, so few to listen! No one!

Nicky felt himself propelled gently toward his door, helped across the threshold, released to reel between the walls of his picture-crowded hallway, heard, "Sir, you take care now."

"What for?" Nicky demanded. "I'm not going to be around much longer anyway."

Graham fled, dispirited by his pity, his failure to deal with a clear case of DUI, the chance that Nicholas Heldahl might harm himself. What should he have done? How treat the doomed taking leave of the dying? How even presume to advise? Already this job was getting impossible.

DITHERING IN HIS kitchen, trying to marshal the ingredients for a brandy Alexander, Nicky felt like crud scraped off a shoe. Guilt and humiliation wrecked his concentration. He needed something, someone, people! He thought. *Well, I will, I'll go see Chad.*

He had been promising himself this visit for months, but had yet to find the right mood, the right moment. He was simply too filled with horrified revulsion at the mere idea of AIDS, to be able to bear the ravages in some friend's face. Bad enough to be forced to see men fading before one's eyes day by day on the street, his distress suddenly overflowed with fear that Chad might die before he got to see him.

Fortunately it was still early. Nelson might likely be there. Nelson put him to shame in these matters, but Nelson liked to drink, Nelson was no AAer like so many in these arid times. And Adam could certainly have no objection to a valedictory toast.

Feeling ready once more for whatever the night might bring, he took the bottle of brandy and a quart of vodka, in case brandy did not suit everyone's taste—he had begun to envision an exalted little assembly gathered around the bed, with Chad delighted, grateful for his astutely well-provisioned arrival—got himself into the car, located his keys, sat back in the dimness to pick out the right one, then tackle the feat of fitting it into the lock, woke at first light with a back so bad it took him ten minutes of groaning to get out of the car and due to his bruised knee yet another extended ordeal to climb his steps and discover that, having left his door ajar, a cat had skunked his hallway rug and his whole house stank.

Now depression gripped him as never before. He spent the day in bed, hardly able to move or think a thought, form a plan, embrace a hope, that did not instantly collapse. All was black anguish so great it felt physical, a block of granite crushing his chest, each acrid cigarette adding, adding, adding to it. A glass of vodka only made his stomach flare.

The next day, his injuries on the mend, he went home, to borrow one of his mother's cars, had a row with his older brother, who was deathly afraid he would squander more than his share of their inheritance, quit the house in sick disgust.

In the late afternoon, on the empty Pilgrim Highway after the Sagamore Bridge, in ever greater haste to get back to the only place in the world he could stand, with Bach's dauntless exactions loud in his ears, fed by the hope of seeing the handsome cop again, who had been so kind to him it must mean something was in store, he simply sailed in the capsule of the powerful Daimler—at 95 emitting not a hint of vibration or strain—and then the infernal blue pulsing, then, at concerto's decisive finale, the siren.

Pulled over, Nicky rolled his window down, and the state cop thrust his furious face almost nose to nose with him, and shouted, "What's your hurry? Afraid you'll miss your funeral?"

Nicky recoiled into the passenger's seat, while the cop roared the questionnaire of terms for organ donations, without ever pausing to let Nicky answer, had Nicky been able.

He had never known such a chewing out, having missed military service through forthright declaration of his homosexuality, but in retrospect, once back on the road, the fear of physical assault gone, the thing that struck him most was that it seemed to have been completely genuine, not at all put on.

"I actually believe he was quite mad," Nicky in due course opined to Arthur.

Arthur made a face of humpf, without sign of empathy.

What Nicky did not relate was, upon getting home he went on a week's bender, methodically trying all hours in every bar in town, hoping to come across his cop off duty, eventually had taken home God knows whom, waked up sprawled on his bedroom rug at dawn, head ringing, guts heaving, raw in his privy parts.

THE OTHERS might laugh, might wince, at such of these follies as he divulged, but Julian met him on the post office steps one day looking more unkempt than usual, his shabby overcoat wildly misbuttoned. Nicky confided with evident trepidation, "Listen, no one knows, but how did you get the parking place next to the Pelligrino?"

Julian thought he was joking and said, "No problem."

Nicky whistled with relief. "Then it's all right," he concluded earnestly, "to shoot the Tylenol with the cribbage?"

"Why not?" Julian said.

Nicky's eyes were wet; he had two days' growth of beard; he looked sick. He said, "Even if I bought them they wouldn't stay anyway, I couldn't save the pins. The other's all right, I guess. The standarounds never leave unless something bad happens. Is yours okay?"

While Julian gaped, Nicky accosted a man coming up the steps, who stopped politely. His face went from alert to alarmed, then aped apology for possible observers, and turned away. Nicky advanced on another man, with more or less similar result, except the man laughed outright. Yet a third gravely suffered himself to be engaged, and Julian hurried back to The Maid and asked Arthur what should be done.

"By you, nothing. There are Nelsons galore to tend to the Nicky Heldahls of this world," said Arthur with magisterial complaisance. "Your studio awaits."

Julian unhappily, thankfully went back to work.

19

NELSON RYDER DEPARTS

CHRIS WHITMAN never lifted a hand again, entered his body bag while Nelson dreamed at home.

Nelson had not quite believed this death would come. His love had been so thinly expressed that Chris's death meant little more to his friends than the latest in his endless chain of volunteer bereavements. Even Chris could not have gauged the depth of his unspoken feelings, nor perhaps have much cared. The last two days Nelson had tended him like a baby. Despite every sign that Chris was fading, Nelson had not seen the end as near.

Lost, he haunted Arthur's living room or sat on the floor in Julian's studio and watched him paint, stayed on, chin in hand, long after Julian had gone in to dinner. Sometimes when the sun came out he walked about with Nicky Heldahl. Two wrecks they looked, Nicky talking, Nelson with eyes upon his feet.

"Did Nelson ever figure out what that hand waving was all about?" Madbury demanded one day when he was out of earshot.

Arthur said, "Absolutions, according to Nelson."

"Dismissals," Madbury said. "General disgust."

"Lost Battles," Arthur said.

"Good-byes, the warding off of evil," Baxter added. "Whatever you like."

Julian said. "Nelson does it himself now."

"That's right! He does!" Madbury yelled. "Only it's like: *Keep Back!*"

Nelson himself wandered in vaguely and sat down. Less grey today, he even seemed to listen.

"The sound of one hand clapping!" Madbury burst out suddenly. Nelson sat forward, hands on knees.

"What d'you think, Bax?" cried Madbury with his new, loony exuberance. No one had ever shrunk Baxter to that, even as a kid.

Baxter merely gazed obliquely at nothing in particular.

Madbury lifted his chin, projected quietly to Arthur across the room, "I've been trying to convince him to get a hearing aid."

Arthur's eyes bugged out. "Nothing's wrong with Baxter's ears," he said, "that removal of the tongue from a certain mouth would not cure."

Baxter's slight shake of the head was meant only for Arthur.

Madbury said to Nelson, "Do you know you do it yourself now? Only frontward. Like you're telling people to back off."

"Perhaps presumptuous persons like yourself, Miss Mouth," said Arthur.

Nelson wondered why others always knew more about him than he did himself. Lately he seemed to have lost his identity, too, and dreamed other people's dreams, as if his own psyche had been invaded by souls of the dead, which, expelled from their fallen flesh, sought refuge in some defenseless, living citadel.

"The sound of one hand clapping," Madbury crowed. "That's it! How many other explanations can there be?"

"That's the Dancing Angels Conundrum," said Baxter, "to which there is no answer."

"How so?" said Nelson, coming alive a little.

"As many as there are—and more—may dance on the head of a pin," Baxter said.

Nelson snorted softly. He enjoyed Baxter's scholastic bent, so rarely seen these days.

Julian saw a silver mushroom of a dance floor with bopping throngs of golden, penile angels.

Nelson said to Madbury, "That doesn't sound like Chris. I don't think he was given to jokes."

"Dementia," Madbury said.

Nelson said, "I never knew a saner man in my life," and then his whole being seemed to fall inward at remembrance of Chris's burial in Cranston.

Julian began to wonder what the AIDS virus looked like.

Rent by Baxter's impassive regard of his tremulous hands, as if they belonged to someone else, Arthur understood that he might not accept a slow end, began to feel a sharp apprehension at Nelson's impending departure.

Madbury said, "I ran into Sean Costello just looking out at the bay. Everything was dripping fog, you couldn't see the breakwater, absolutely bone-chilling. He says, 'What a wonderful place to die!'"

"I mean," Madbury said. "Tell *me* he hasn't flipped his wig!"

"Who would dream?" Arthur inquired.

"I mean," Madbury said, "he doesn't have a hair on his head. He's got tumors on his kidney. He just finished ten days of chemo. He looked hideous, but he was completely cheerful. 'What a wonderful place to die,' he says."

"He loves it here," Nelson said.

"This sleazy little burg?" Madbury railed.

"You're not chained here," Arthur said.

"Nooo," Madbury said. "But I'm not dying."

"Where would you prefer to die?" Baxter asked with rare interest.

The question had never entered Madbury's head: it sounded like a trick or a trap of some sort, and he dropped his eyes and said nothing.

Nelson said, "Sean's just doing what he wants to do."

"But it's not real," Madbury protested. "It's just denial."

"For that matter," Nelson said, "it's all denial."

"HIV brings out the best in people," Arthur said.

"One may hope," said Baxter.

"A brave death is a precious gift to the living," Nelson said.

"That's true," Madbury said, wanting to agree. "And truth is all that matters really."

Julian remembered Dr. Merckers telling him to develop a philosophy of life. But how when death was all there was? "What's this Black Dick Inn in Wellfleet?" he suddenly thought to ask.

"It's the Black *Duck*, dear," Arthur said, and everybody laughed to high heaven, all but Madbury, who sensed some secret joke and looked so baffled they laughed even more, while he ground his teeth and Julian looked blank, amazed and lonely that no one knew — had ever known — a thing about Jessica Jordan.

Baxter murmured something.

"Mmmm?" said Madbury. "Say what?" he called, raising his voice.

Rising unsteadily, Baxter said, "Orang utangs have all the fun."

They waited to be edified, but he did not oblige, and Arthur accompanied him to the door, followed by Madbury, feeling expelled.

NELSON THAT DAY began to rejoin the living, and next time he came brought Nicky Heldahl. Nicky was ruddy with the cold and all spruced up. No one would have guessed he had lately suffered a mental break, nor did he dwell on it himself. He had decided to become a dealer in contemporary art. With a view to borrowing $25,000 from his mother as a startup, he had undertaken to visit every studio in town, Julian's of course being first on his list.

Arthur's scorn could not keep Julian from getting excited. Some money would be great. He was just finishing God's Ringtoss, a work eye-catching even by his standards — a splendid member standing amid swirling mists with a swarm of quoits like anuses, like flying saucers, sailing dilatingly toward it, the parts composed with precision — he had consulted *Gray's Anatomy* and a mirror, head upside down between his legs — painted in startling hues, implacable answer to Otto Jahrling's overheard aspersions — and when Nicky saw it his praise knew no bounds, capped with a casual aside to Nelson: "He's starting to look a bit like late Guston."

Julian had never heard of Guston, set off for the library the minute they left, satisfactions deferred, possibly canceled.

NELSON RENEWED his routine with a vengeance, sitting with the sick, going to funerals, refusing to name a date of departure, nor even a destination.

"He's another André," Madbury said. "He'll never cross the bridge again."

But Nelson appeared at The Maid one day, possessed of a one-way ticket to London. "And then I'll . . . ahh . . . see," he said. "London, Paris, Rome, Athens. Istanbul if my stamina holds!"

"What brought this on?" Baxter said, frankly impressed.

"Ah . . ." Nelson waggled a nervous finger in front of his heart.

"Guilt," said Arthur, glad in spite of his dread, "is the only thing that moves Nelson."

"There's that sound again," said Madbury, with one hand mimicking Nelson's new tic. "Can you hear it?"

Nelson folded his hands together so tightly the knuckles went white. "Two funerals in one day," he explained, "did me in, I don't know why. The first was a VIP in the gay rights movement, charismatic character, brave as a lion, cheerful, absolutely charming on his deathbed, couldn't have been more seductive. Everyone revered him. When it came time for people to speak the most amazing number of them said exactly the same thing—how they met, when they became his lover, how exacting he was about every aspect of sex, woe betide one who failed his expectations. He was like a despot of love, and they were his disciples, like graduates giving their bona fides, like they were his main accomplishments in life.

"The other one was a suicide. The guy's partner said he did it because he was so afraid of dying. There were a lot of people there, a huge number! By the time I got home I almost couldn't remember a one."

"You can't *not* hear it!" Madbury insisted. "Listen!" And he cocked his head and held up a traffic cop's hand.

"He thinks he's Hitler," Arthur said.

"All these funerals," Nelson went on, "they're all mixed up in my mind. I lay in bed and tried to sift them out, and I couldn't do it. It was just one big, simultaneous funeral. The dead I could visualize perfectly well, I had no trouble distinguishing *them*, but the mourners were just a mass of faces like moons with shadowy holes for nose, mouth, and eyes. None of them had any hair, not a strand in the whole crowd, they looked the way extraterrestrials are always portrayed, big heads like drops, and they were all nodding at me from some sort of nowhere, no walls, no roof, no floor, no earth, no sky, nothing. It was very upsetting."

"Most intriguing," said Baxter.

"It must have been a dream," Nelson said. "Next I knew I was standing at the back of this huge throng of these faceless ah . . . aliens. All looking at some sort of altar way off in the distance, or maybe it was just a speck of light. I thought, *We must be waiting for something.*

"And then they all turned around and looked at me, and they were me, every one of them. It was horrifying to see so many mes, and then I had to wonder who *I* was."

"You've finally OD'd," Madbury said. "You've been quite the party-goer."

"I hadn't looked at it that way," Nelson said without heat.

Julian saw a vast assembly of penises, bending beseechingly toward some distant point he could not quite make out.

"You're just ditching Sean Costello?" Madbury said. "I thought you were going to help him learn the ropes."

Nelson hung his head. "Shop's closed," he said.

"That had a long run," Madbury sneered, but he sounded leaden.

"He got his taste," Nelson said. "I hope. He said he only feels bad for Priscilla."

"Can't she keep it open?" Baxter asked.

"Oh," Nelson admitted, and his voice sank, "her emphysema's got much worse. She's hitched to an oxygen tank. She can hardly move around the house. Her one lung just collapsed overnight."

"How disgusting!" Arthur cried.

"What?" Madbury cried, looking around. "What?"

Arthur thought a bit. "That people should die of anything but AIDS, I guess," he essayed at last.

"Enough is enough," Baxter agreed.

"She's very stoical," Nelson said. "She says, 'Well, we'll see,' even though everyone knows it's irreversible. The doctor said the whole architecture of her lung is destroyed. COPD."

"What's that?" Arthur asked with distaste.

"Chronic obstructive pulmonary disease," Baxter pronounced with gratified vigor.

"So much to learn," Nelson muttered.

"What on earth for?" Arthur demanded. "You were born morbid. Self-improvement in your case is no virtue."

"Progressive multifocal leukoencephalopathy," Nelson enunciated as if possessed.

Arthur gave him the eye of an elder defied.

Nelson said apologetically, "That's what Chris died of, if you want a name for it."

Arthur dropped his chin an inch and shook his head.

"So who's going to get the shop?" Madbury said at last.

"I don't know," Nelson said, and hung his head again.

"You're dumping everybody left and right," Madbury said. "Somebody's going to sneak in there."

Nelson said. "What I feel worst about are Chad and Adam. Julian, you might go over once in a while."

Arthur looked his displeasure.

"I will," Julian said.

"Summer is coming," Arthur admonished.

To Julian summer was still over the horizon. Time to paint stretched far away, electric, dense with grandeur, springtide a raft of desire, return of the sea of men. Summer meant sun, sun-menace, sun-need. Meanwhile the days flowed slow and the work piled up, he marveled to count how much.

"I don't know whether I'm running away or toward," Nelson said.

"Toward," said Arthur firmly.

"All those funerals," Madbury mused. "You couldn't miss even one. Remember? You were addicted."

"Well, you learn, I guess," Nelson said half to himself.

"What do you learn?" Baxter asked curiously.

"I don't know," Nelson was quick to admit.

Madbury pursued, "So what are you not saying?"

"Nothing," Nelson said, shrinking into himself.

"I'll make you up a little packet of André," Baxter said, "so you'll at least have to cross the Channel."

"All I know is," said Nelson, "I'm not going to any more funerals for a while."

Walking home, light-headed in the cold, he thought, *It's true:*

the more we know the less we know. Knowledge is only conscious igno-
rance. I must have learned something this past year, but I can't say
what it is, beyond memory, which fades. Experience is all we have,
and we can't even hang on to that.

He walked on toward London, Paris, Rome, half dead with the
wish that Chris was going with him.

20

MORE ASHES

THE DAY AFTER Nelson's departure, as Julian and Arthur were sitting down to dinner, the phone rang. Arthur answered. A confiding voice identified itself as that of Gregory Gibbons of Portsmouth, New Hampshire.

Arthur went to the living-room phone, sat down, wound the cord around one finger, eyed the talisman. Julian listened in the kitchen door, while the chowder skimmed over.

For half a minute Arthur listened, at first grave-faced, then with brows knit, then with mystified patience, till finally he began to make his fish face at Julian.

At last he interjected, "But he *is* dead?"

Arthur listened again, while his operatic visage parodied conniptions Julian could not interpret, finally said, "They were both very dear to us, yes, though they were only here a little while. Selwyn was terribly fond of you."

Another silence. In neutral tones, "Of course." Then a protracted series of stares and squints. "But what are your plans?"

More listening by Arthur, then, "We would be delighted."

Then sharply, "When?"

Eye-rolling by Arthur. Then with restrained incredulity, "But when exactly?"

Arthur gaped at Julian. "Now? Where are you?" He arose. "Here?" He covered the mouthpiece. "He's here."

"Where?" Julian said. "In Provincetown?"

"Of course," Arthur said into the phone, nodding vehemently at Julian. "Well, let me . . . You have? Good. Well, it will be nice . . . No. Yes. No, no, you're quite . . . not at all."

Arthur hung up. "He's on the way. He must have a car phone. He has, I believe, already cased the joint."

A third place was set at the kitchen table, the living room tidied a bit. A car drove in, the door opened, after six seconds clicked unclosed, clicked again, and again, then slammed, and slammed again and again, each time very, very slightly harder. Eventually silence came and Gregory himself appeared at the front door. Sat down to sup, he gave praise for the chowder, apologies for the intrusion, thanks for the hospitality, accolades for the charming accommodations, a never-ending stream.

"Only a Yankee knows the simple secrets of this delectable dish," he declared. "Debased of late. Last time I was on Nantucket I went into a most authentic-looking café way out on a wharf and got a lobster roll with ginger and capers in it."

"Actually," said Arthur, "I'm from Arkansas."

Touristic interests led one to another—descriptions, critiques, local lore. In due course they moved to the living room and ruminated, till finally Gregory said, as if it were the cud of all past conversation, "I think they both had relatively happy deaths."

Outright mention of their late friends made Julian's stomach yaw.

With soft fingers Arthur patted his chin, his mien unchanging. He felt a fondness for this circumlocutor with relentless lilt, a feeling not without wariness thanks to Selwyn's awed animadversions.

Gregory in person, despite his aplomb, looked bright-eyed and pale, hardly the impregnable paragon Selwyn had portrayed, and indeed how could he be still inviolate, after his year of deaths?

Withal his incredible bent of expression caused Julian's eyes to stray and Arthur, under his breath, to mutter, "An lil lam see divey."

By Gregory's lights their late friends had found rewards in every phase of their well-favored demises, briefly intermitted—it went without saying—by their unfortunate recourse to the mat knife, understandable but ill advised.

"And . . . ah . . . what," Arthur asked, taking refuge in Nelson's tic, "became of the . . . ah . . . their . . . ah . . ."

"Ashes," Gregory supplied with diffident definiteness. "I've brought them."

"Both?" said Arthur with a glance at Julian, who seemed to be holding his breath.

"It was Gustave's idea originally," Gregory explained. "He always loved it here. Selwyn was hoping to come down and scatter them himself, but his health never permitted, and eventually he decided to have the same done with his own."

"So," Arthur said, "you have two offices to perform while you are here."

"Nooo," said Gregory. "Just the one."

"You mean . . . ah . . ." Arthur said.

"Of course," said Gregory, "I had to locate a commodious urn. Actually it's a baked bean crock that belonged to my great aunt."

Arthur said, "You . . . ah . . . yourself . . ."

"I feel reasonably sure," said Gregory, "that if they'd had time they would have thought of it themselves. It's a perfectly reasonable inference to draw. I'm only doing what they would have done if they could. They were inseparable. And they came, of course, from the same womb."

"You . . . ah . . . combined them?" Arthur asked.

"Naturally . . ." said Gregory, sounding bemused himself, "when I poured them into the crock from their original urns, I alternated—first one, then the other—and then I stirred and shook them. Thoroughly. Gently. But thoroughly."

"What did you stir them with?" Arthur wondered.

"Just a spoon," Gregory said. "I didn't have anything else."

"No one," said Arthur, "could have dreamt this up."

Gregory nodded only slightly, the incongruous glare briefly intensified.

"We must introduce you," said Arthur, "to our friend Baxter Perkins, who has an urn of his own to dispose."

"André Evre," Gregory stated. "They were so fond of him. I have heard so much about all of you."

"And we of you," said Arthur with warm promptitude.

"There's an obvious opportunity here," Gregory said. "One that would certainly please all three of our late friends, and give us quite a lot of satisfaction too."

He placed his fingertips and points of thumbs together, bowed them out like a little mosque, and dropped his chin till it touched the dome.

Arthur looked at it blankly for a moment, then blinked.

"It makes a lot of sense," Gregory said.

As their visitor disappeared up the stairs at the stroke of ten, Julian said, "He's joking, right?"

Arthur looked at him. "I really don't know," he said.

THE VENGEANCE OF afflicting André with Selwyn and Gustave both and forevermore gave Madbury to glee, but mistrust too. Why had Gregory never called when Gustave died? Gustave had saved some money, hadn't he said so himself? What was going on here?

Gregory said, "I only wish my Rick could have gone in with them."

"And Gavin Daly too?" said Arthur.

"Why, yes," said Gregory after a hesitation. "I hadn't thought of it, but it makes perfect sense, especially from a Christian point of view. All these selfish, little discords are nothing in the face of eternity. If we are to be forgiven we must ourselves forgive."

"A little patience," said Baxter, "and we might all go in together. Last one stirs the pot."

"Chamber pot," said Madbury.

Arthur said, "I do *not* think André would be charmed."

"Oh," said Gregory, "I'm sure a *little* company would be most welcome."

Madbury had begun to conceive of Gregory's multifarious purposes. Maybe he was HIV himself. Strange those two deaths in Portsmouth—no, *four* deaths—and now he planned to contaminate the evidence with the brothers' ashes. No DNA there. He had the brothers' wills, had he not? He had. And had he not also become sole trustee of their estates? He had admitted as much, and more. Who knew who or what might not be involved? And what had actually happened to the brothers' mother Amanda? She was a bitch too. Had she somehow been disappeared herself? You never knew who to believe.

Of his dune-bound ashes, Gustave had prophesied, "The wind will know what to do with them."

"Whether it does or not," Baxter shrugged with closure. Instead of being disburdened by the approach of death, which he had looked forward to, whatever he did now felt more perilous than ever, fraught with instant remorse. "But I don't think André liked wind," he brooded. "And he certainly never set foot in the dunes."

"It doesn't really matter," said Nicky Heldahl, "does it? That's the great thing about cremation. You can end up a little bit everywhere you ever cared to be. I guess I'll stay here though."

Madbury said, "You also have to go where you're put. A little bit or a lot, or the whole pack of you. Fair's fair."

"You're not putting *me* anywhere," said Arthur.

"An unfortunate turn of ritual," said Baxter, "for those obliged to spend their lives allotting remains."

"Oh, I don't know," said Gregory. "More like a jaunt than a chore, I should think. And a good excuse to travel. Some people at least would see a bit more of the world. It certainly wouldn't harm international relations."

Baxter said, "Some of André has already gone to Paris with Nelson."

Madbury interjected. "He'll never leave London!"

"That's what I'm afraid of," Arthur said between his teeth.

Baxter went on, "André would *not* want to be left just anywhere, or thrown in with others, even friends. Everything to him was absolutely personal."

"What a laugh!" said Madbury. "When you consider what a slut he was! Where did he get off with his rules for everybody else?"

"You're a bit like André yourself," Arthur mused.

"I am not," Madbury said. "André was a snob."

"Opinionated," said Baxter.

"Bossy," Madbury said. "Now the shoe's on the other foot. André will be lucky if we don't send him to the dump." And he brandished one finger in front of his nose.

Everything Madbury did infuriated Arthur, especially his appropriation of Chris Whitman's gesture, whatever it might have meant —assuredly *not* that impossible one hand clapping.

"We'll put *you* in the dump," said he.

"The Eastham dump, would you think, Arthur?" Baxter asked.

"I'm going back to Cleveland," Madbury sniffed.

"And you?" Baxter asked Julian, to whom in a lonely moment Arthur had revealed Baxter's AIDS. Julian, with his lingering propensity to blurt, learning how much harder it was to dissemble than simply keep still, now managed only to look disdainful, seeing his hill of white tombstones under a golden sun the size of the moon, which decree he had yet to give Arthur. But he was not destined to die in Provincetown. Even so, his carcass could be shipped back. But Baxter would be dead by that time, and Arthur, and all of them, theoretically. Better settle in. Julian, for the first time, eyed such possibility leerily.

"Well, it's a *bit* early in the day for decisions of that sort," Gregory smiled at Julian. "For you at least."

Baxter's attorney had instructions for removal of his corpse to Philadelphia, with final lodgement in his family's mausoleum at Laurel Hill, there to await his forebears, unless fortune smiled and they got there first. After which none but the quick would pass those gates locked or not.

To be left on a mantelpiece for future perusal by persons unknown struck him as even more unseemly than a pauper's grave, and he chided himself to settle André's ashes promptly, or importune Arthur, who could be counted on to act with dispatch.

After a life of meditating the human fate, recent times had forced Gregory to retreat to the position that death had real significance only for the survivors—except for one's own, of course, experienced but once, dimly and without true perspective.

The Hereafter having since childhood faded from plausibility, he dwelt less upon his bereavements than upon preceding events.

The joint suicide of Rick Kendrick and Gavin Daly he treated in the light of a resolute exit from final decline, while a different principle ruled the case of Gustave and Selwyn, whose last days were richly fraternal, notwithstanding their unhappy hiatus.

The fact that Selwyn had begged him to assist in Gustave's suicide, that Gustave in the tub in water up to his neck had seemed to nod, were matters Gregory did not admit to his perorations because he had no doubt he had made the only possible choice, nor did he divulge that he and Selwyn had contrived a ceremony on Selwyn's next to last day and married each other, made a loving end.

His unctuous stardust made Arthur bilious, but revived Baxter's Egyptian suavity. His own looming death had darkened the whole human prospect. Of late he had simply lived with gritted teeth. Gregory cheered him up. For, having suffered total defeat in his quest for resistance to despair, Baxter was now facing with impaired will and inert imagination the practical problem of how to kill himself before sinking into incompetence, and deceive his parents about the cause of death. *They* would never understand self-destruction except as disgrace—or as such recourse it indeed was, knowledge he would spare them if he could.

He thanked his lucky stars for Arthur's common sense and faithful strength; for the first time in his life he felt the need of human help. A Gavin Daly would have his uses here.

Apart from the mind-crushing fear, he did not object to death at fifty. What could it matter? He had never had any hope, born without, he had always put it to himself, a little proudly. Why should he want another glass of wine or more news? Would the human race fade of radiation, the fatal meteoroid heave into view, lion with lamb lie down? Yes, Yes, No. History did not require his wary attendance, his wry mask, his savage curiosity and silly witticisms. Only his tulip bulbs gave him grief, asleep in their richly made up beds beneath the snow. How abominably selfish he was! How heartless! He loved the velvet hues of their coming spring better than anything in the world, a world for which he had long cared very little. Space, time, matter, mind—empty formulas! He knew he was wrong, knew all the reasons, like dead languages, rites of a prehistoric religion or geometric theorems learned in school, but he could not touch himself to awe, nor summon gratitude for past felicity.

His ultimate effort, lapsed at Gregory's arrival, had been to comprehend Being itself. Day after day he had sat by the window, barely breathing, alert and vacant-minded, letting objects of sight lose their names, purpose, and essence, feeling his physical borders fade, blend, flow into their surroundings, his fingertips admit kinship with whatever they met. Toward dusk a vivid sense of strangeness, of utter unfamiliarity, of mystery, almost of carefree lightheartedness seemed briefly to win out, then would come Madbury shouting.

Providential therefore to Baxter—for his specific delectation and distraction—seemed Gregory's arrival with an all-embracing synthesis. Light having been shed upon the virtues of death for others, then upon its immediate antecedents, the foregoing lives themselves all the way back to birth in retrospect acquired a happier cast, and rendered tragic interpretations perverse.

"The dead depend on us," Gregory crooned. "Belong to us, by inheritance. We should not fail them, lest we be failed in turn."

Having domesticated death, he now proposed to conquer all experience—irresistible avarice perhaps for one of his persuasion —which would infinitely fund the bank of posthumous possibilities, placing everybody's life at risk of smarmy revisions and unsought redemptions, or so it seemed to Arthur, who muttered decisively, "Rubber dub dub."

"It's only a theory, of course," Gregory blushed his smile of sheepish, humble indomitability, while the others grinned concession.

I do though, Baxter thought, care about Julian; that boy may actually achieve something.

Death was a provoking shape to Julian; what might it look like? What not?

FEBRUARY BROUGHT a letter from Nelson.

"Dear Arthur and Julian, et al., London is ducky. The sun never shines. I feel fine, and though at moments I still pine for the fabled South, I have found my place here. Who knows why these things happen?" Arthur grimly sounded the death knell of Nelson's grand tour, while Baxter stared at his fingernails, and Gregory nodded approval.

Upon arrival the first people Nelson had met ran an AIDS support system cum hospice, and in no time he was up to his ears in the Billington Trust, a complete thing in itself, with medical, counseling, and hospice facilities, and a fund-raising corps, in short, the essential enterprise writ large, and, one hardly need add, a good milieu to meet people.

"Of a certain sort," Arthur grated.

Nelson had found lodgings thoroughly uncomfortable, if cheap, so that the Trust office itself and a nearby pub, where the staff gathered, served as cordial hearth. Otherwise he walked the streets, umbrella in hand, like any tourist. At the Tate he had stepped without warning from previous centuries into a room of monumental American abstract expressionist works, and had felt an astounded pride. He had always deplored these artists and their school, but seeing them set against the long-evolved punctilios of Europe's past he was stunned by their raw vigor, flabbergasted by their beauty. He hoped Julian's paintings might some day be so nobly housed; he trusted Julian was hard at work.

Julian hoped so himself, but how know? Perhaps he should be in his studio right now; he might in the next breath, or the next, or yet the next, go and start a new canvas. He need not even ask, Arthur having grown militant in the face of summer, more avid for him than he was himself.

In general, Nelson ended, he felt better, though he meant to forego funerals. His only regret was his abandonment of Adam and Chad, whom he urged Julian to visit in his stead, and also would someone please look in on Priscilla and Sean Costello?

21

ADAM AND CHAD

NEXT MORNING, plunged in his preliminary trance, Julian was tying to conjure forms for death—canvas still untouched by brush—when Gregory appeared beaming in his studio door, rubbing his palms together so briskly they hissed.

"Shall we," said he, "convey Nelson Ryder's greetings to Adam and Chad?"

"Not right now," said Julian.

"It's all arranged," Gregory crooned. "They're expecting us."

"I haven't even got started yet," Julian said.

"Then this is perfect timing," Gregory said. "I didn't want to interrupt, but I didn't want to keep them waiting either. You can afford an hour."

Julian felt like sand in a tide. In the doorway, glancing back at his abandonment, his neck cracked and the white square for an instant swarmed with black floaters. *Sperm. Or maggots,* he thought with impatience. *I'll have to do better than that.*

THE SICK MAN and his partner lived in cramped quarters on Soper Street. Callers were met with TV din and blast of infernal heat. A humid airlessness of windows never opened, massed smells of human rot, vile meds, disinfectant, stove gas, putrid food, debris of exhaustion, exemplified a state of siege.

Every surface was covered, every niche filled with carousels of pills, plastic bottles and Tupperware, cans of Ensure, clumps of surgical gloves, jars of balm, manuals, charts, IV poles, syringes and tubing, bags of saline, rolls of tape, plastic pails, an orange sanitary disposal can the size of a beer keg, bedpans, bales of Depends, baby-wipes—mobilized, outmoded, or in reserve.

Chad by a window lay on a raised hospital bed beneath a layer of blankets—hollow eyes, a few isolated teeth like some decrepit beast's in a zoo, no eyebrows, no hair, cracked lips, lesions upon lesions, not easy to look at, though he gazed back with unabashed dispassion, while Adam made room to sit.

He and Gregory exchanged medical expertise over the TV.

The binger never left Chad's hand, and he switched channels continuously. Bursts of static went with these sometimes prolonged surfings, which hurt the ear and which Adam tried to allay by voicing Chad's contrary views or by changing the subject. And Chad, though he spoke not, seemed preternaturally alert, glancing bird-like out the window and back, out and back, while keeping watch on his visitors and three talk and game shows all at once.

Loath to sit, Julian donned some gloves and did the dishes, then cleaned the bathroom, not without shuddered auguries of summer, and upon return found Gregory and Adam, veterans well met, arced toward one another in formal, farewell embrace.

Adam embraced Julian too, adding to his thanks fervent thanks in advance for Julian's future benefactions, accompanied by a deprecatory murmur from Gregory, who kept nodding and smiling, smiling and nodding, though no expression moved Chad's face.

On the street, disarmed by the silence and fresh air, Julian grasped with a sense of helplessness that Gregory had volunteered both their services, his own as home health aide, Julian's as house cleaner, "in the capacity of reinforcements."

"Not mornings!" Julian cried.

"Noo, noo," Gregory dropped from baritone to bass. "At your convenience, of course. Of course. Only an hour or so every few days. It will be a good experience for you."

Julian wondered what he meant, then remembered the syringe

he had wanted Nelson to get him. It felt like the first thing he had ever forgotten; he knew that could not be, but he had learned a habit, a means of pure pleasure, of holding his whole past life, everything he knew, in his mind at once, a sort of fondling investigation of infinity. He knew this wasn't possible either, but loved the feeling of robust omnipotence it gave him.

THAT EVENING, at The Maid, Gregory reported. Chad Owens had lived at death's door for the twelve years since his diagnosis in March, 1976. He had fought off ceaseless diseases. Having won so many impossible battles, he and Adam did not intend to capitulate. They would never surrender, and so long as neither was vanquished in spirit death could never prevail.

To them their saga was matter for scientific inquiry, though no one as yet had been persuaded to study their pure, all-conquering will, might beyond mere science, of which both were duly proud, it being a joint command, so to speak, and especially were they gratified that Chad had been spared dementia. This too they attributed to the power of their militant spirits conjoined.

Arthur held his tongue in deference to his guest's indulgence of such vaporings, next thing to manifestos. And who could tell how much was Adam and Chad's, how much Gregory's? *A certain amount of both!* he railed to himself.

A growing worm ate in Arthur's soul. He felt crippled by the secret of Baxter's HIV—forced to own that already, while he had not known of its existence, its evil work had gone far enough to dictate the fatal name of AIDS. From his advent in Provincetown, he had relied on Baxter's comradeship; they were similars of a sort; perhaps that was why Arthur so detested Madbury's encroachments, Madbury, arraigner of every misfortune, whom Weeming had lately dubbed the Born Again Virgin.

Like a moth it bumped against the panes of Arthur's mind that Baxter should move into The Maid when . . . when . . . but he could not bring himself to think when precisely.

With Nelson gone, and Baxter having banned the subject, Arthur had no one to confide in, no one to talk to at all but Julian, who was too self-engrossed to succor him. Arthur bore the fear that Baxter might need his help to die. With Dover not yet dead three years, Arthur felt unequal to Baxter's death in any form whatever, nor could Nelson be summoned from London to superintend this—of all contemporary obligations the one true friends should be prepared to meet. Poor Nelson, a pro in a world of amateurs, had long since done his share.

Baxter himself, ever sicker, more frail, felt sunk beneath the one thing that must get done—the disposal of André's ashes—before he could take up the first and last, inescapable challenge of his life.

What to do, what to do, what to do do do with the troublous ashes? True, André had left no instructions; true, he was a most exclusive, reclusive, prickly queen; equally true that he had repented his solitary life; true, there did seem to be some genuine sentiment for mingling him with Gustave and Selwyn, of whom he had been indubitably fond; also true, democratic preference had its fair claims; but chiefly was it true that Baxter himself must choose André's terminus, and soon.

ARTHUR'S SLIDE steepened. Everywhere was only emptiness; everyone had gone the way of Uncle Noddy and Dover, or soon would. He did not mean to demoralize Julian, but his listless pallor, snappish scoldings, deepening seclusion, and slapdash dinners were insidious. Baxter's hollow eyes, Gregory's haunted machinations, Nicky Heldahl's disarray, Nelson's absence, all seemed harbingers. Julian lived on cold coffee, tossed all night, aching however he lay.

His new painting exacted superhuman efforts, half the time seemed not doable, the other half not worth doing.

Composed of a Tower of Babel in limbless human form, suggestive of a sky-scraping penis with head above the clouds, it wore a tank top of pendant penises, through gaps in which could be seen in spiral ascent a tableau of penile figures building the edifice.

One morning his eyes rebelled at sight of his colossal folly. Not only the insuperable technical problems, the crowded specifics of the scene, the sheer inertia and mute stupidity of paint, the whole project of obsession sickened him. Nothing worthwhile could come of this manic homage to Brueghel and Bosch.

He hit a new depth of despondence. Heretofore, when he had the temerity to confess discouragement or doubt, Baxter was quick to interject, "Erasmus says, 'In the great things, it is enough to have tried.'"

How that rankled! And goaded! Julian was afraid to fail on any terms whatsoever; nor able to retreat. No hope could be but in total triumph! In lieu of Jessica Jordan he would make himself the best of his age. Why not? Someone had to be. And who was Erasmus? Another name on Baxter's list. Julian was swept for a moment with nostalgia for the cozy corner, warmth of green lamp, the calming transport of a book.

He went into the bone-chilling, grey morning, and found a dead raccoon in the gutter, a full-grown, luxuriantly furred beast the size of the tire that had flattened its head, elongating its quizzical mask into a porcine snout.

Julian looked down at it. It was surely the same that lived in the chimney of the vacant house around the block, the one he had come upon calmly curled, sound asleep in the bottom of a garbage can. He had stood a long time in indecision, before going on.

Now the indignity struck him. It should be buried before putrefaction set in. But he was loath to bend near it, lest he breathe dissolution in.

Absolved that such chores fell to the DPW, he turned back with firm tread, reentered his studio, took down the slightly larger than usual, blank canvas earmarked for the portrait of death, put up a new one and painted the exotic corpse, with a line of curb stretching away into perpetuity, a great maple shedding a shroud of red and yellow leaves on it like a Klimt gown, but nothing could keep the crushed head from taking the shape of a penis, and he saw his doom anew.

By noon the memorial impetus failed, he remembered his appalling investment in his Tower of Babel, and more downcast yet he went out again, skirting the corpse, intending to try to eat something, anything; but when he reached Commercial Street he could not face the tables of eyes, the thought of food revolted him, and he walked on to the Art Association, hoping to lose himself for an hour—and there, in the Hawthorne Gallery, he met with a retrospective exhibition of the works of Otto Jahrling's students—fifty years worth—all about the same size, fifteen by twenty, crowded in three tiers on all four walls, hardly six inches apart, all depicting more or less the same scene: bay, clouds, sky, and light in various weathers, at various hours and tides, never at night, with a thin line of Long Point forming half the horizon.

It was stupefying, like several hundred windows on a single view of summer, and Julian did not at once see—nor quite believe when he did—the Master himself, bald pate, white shirt, gold eyeglasses glinting beneath the merciless lights, in perfect stillness inspecting the fruits of his school.

Julian had gone too far to turn back. They exchanged nods, and Julian, acting absorbed, started around the gallery, half blind with resentful vexation, mistook Jarhling's direction, too late realized they must shortly meet. And Jahrling was quick to seize Julian's ear—any ear perhaps—obviously brimming with zeal to edify.

It was clear he assumed Julian knew who *he* was, equally clear that if he knew who Julian was he did not care, nor hesitate to count him one come to pay homage.

Round they went together, Jahrling pointing out better or worse facsimiles of his renowned method, assessing his students' gifts and attainments, noting nuances. It grew into a grand exposition—inviting no questions, offering no justifications, magisterial, strangely magnanimous—the recapitulation of a life's work.

Julian nodded as the ringing voice and rhythmic finger went from point to point of seascape to seascape, like the indulgent survey of a self-designed, mostly reliable, assembly line. It seemed the antithesis of art, originality the only anathema. A single idea, a rigorous system of composition and color, a certain treatment of the reverence of light for water and sky, and a fanatic force of character, had wrought this hall of monomaniacal similitude, spread by now all across the North American continent, hung on walls the world over perhaps, immortality through quantity, by unmistakable parentage, an Egypt of one that would survive long after the first, last, and only Pharaoh's apotheosis, posterity too fecund for extinction.

Reaching the door to the Moffett Gallery, Julian bowed his thanks and started to step through into a still smaller room. Jahrling inquired pleasantly, sincerely, without audible irony, "Not your cup of tea?"

While Julian sought fair reply his eyes shied round the room, where glowed, at even intervals, a single row of the Master's own works, like a planetary ring, breathtaking and final. With a wince at Jahrling's bland visage, Julian lurched forward and hurried side-wise around, and around again, both ways, clown-clumsy, able neither to remain in one spot, nor go back, nor decisively move on, while a well of tears built, dammed, and spilled.

Jahrling had returned to the bosom of his disciples; Julian could hear him whistling softly. There was nothing to do but come back tomorrow and take full measure of the man's achievement, now muster grace to depart casually, without making his usual ass of himself, but how?

Resolutely emerging from resplendent luminosity into fractured dimness, he drew breath and waited. When the old man accommodatingly swung his ample belly in Julian's direction, he blurted, "*That's* champagne!"

The old man smiled vaguely, as if deaf, said nothing.

Julian walked home in shock. Passing the raccoon he kicked some leaves over it, increasing its chances of being run over again. After a hopeless glance at his Tower of Babel, he got gloves and trash bag, and transported the heavy corpse to The Maid's garbage bin.

That night he climbed and slid amid black, plastic mounds that split and spilled putrescence, fought suffocation till daybreak when, with the thrill of having outslept nightmare—better far than wak-ing—he drew a saving breath of disinfectant, woke to the dismal recognition that it was merely turps and paint.

He did a quick study of the raccoon snout in five overlapping repetitions like a partly spread fan, with black, grey, and white binding stripes, the eyes like those of peacock feathers, albeit puckered, but the effort gave him no ease, the maimed beast could not be restored nor recompensed in paint, perfected past its fate, nor survived inviolate, and thereafter Julian's nostrils met decay everywhere, even on the wind outdoors, and his unmanage-able gorge rose like a pregnant woman's.

Especially at Chad and Adam's did Julian's sense of smell afflict him. When next he went to clean and found the rescue squad van blinking at the door, he felt guilty ambivalence, stood aside shame-faced while the men in orange jackets, mobile phones in hand, conferred with Adam.

Chad had made many a trip to Hyannis. This time he had merely without warning ceased to breathe, died again another minor death. Brought back by the defibrillator, he was reviving, his pulse approaching its own faint echo of normal, his eyes clear with understanding—a common crisis, a routine rescue.

Judd, his constrained, good-humored face red with cold, said "Hullo, Esmeralda!" and bobbed his head with bluff cordiality.

Julian sidled closer. "He okay?"

"Yup!" said Judd, and shut up for a moment, gauging Julian's profile. The kid seemed to be lost in thought. Judd was lonely for some layman to talk to, to relieve his own exhilaration. There was nothing like it, this godlike sense of power, of effective mercy, of virtual salvation.

"You never get over it," he finally tried. "There's nothing like it."

Julian turned his head an inch, as if he had half heard, stared off, little wisps of frozen breath fleeting in the sun.

"When you get somebody back like that, somebody, say, in a diabetic coma," Judd veered from the case at hand. "They're technically dead. They'd be gone for good if you didn't show up pretty quick. Quick is everything. You get the monitor on, you get the paddles on, you give them a blast. You get a pulse, they start to breathe. You can actually see them coming back. For a while they don't even know where they are. You're standing around, feeling like a million bucks.

"Then they see you, they say, 'What happened?' "

Judd grinned, drew out a long, casual drawl, incarnating an insider's pride, "Ohhhhh, nothing.'"

Julian nodded, larger breaths billowing.

Judd was never sure that anyone else quite understood how it felt, how it seemed to justify his life, fill his place in the world, not even his wife, who naturally had her own notions of what his main purpose was. As so often now, the satisfaction was minimized. Chad had betrayed no trace of surprise, much less gratitude, and Adam took the whole thing in stride, joking with their frequent saviors, not, to be sure, without many thanks.

Chad *did*, it occurred to Julian, look like some kind of soldier, grizzled and lean in his white t-shirt and sockless feet in unlaced shoes, indifferent to the cold.

Judd glanced again at Julian, wondering how much candor to risk. This was the kid who painted pricks, after all. How naive could he be? Judd knew that in Chad's place he would not have wanted to live on. Of course no one knew for sure how one would feel till that time came and life was all one had—and pain—and the imminence of death. As an old-line Southern Baptist, Judd could well comprehend unreadiness for the dawn of Judgment Day.

"Some of these poor devils," he essayed at last, "you don't know what to hope for. Kind of takes the edge off."

He paused, cautious and contrite, but the kid seemed not to take it amiss, only looked young, blurred somehow. "Friend of yours?" he inquired.

"Sort of," Julian said, remembering the wild night he had sat with Chad. Adam had planned to dine with some friends; at the last moment Gregory had come down with flu, and Julian had gone to do the seven to eleven shift.

"He'll probably sleep straight through," Adam yelled above the loud TV, at moments out-howled by the storm. Rain gusts stampeded across the roof. Concussive gales shook the walls and flung floods at the windows that sounded glass-cracking. Under the eaves a slack phone line rattled and whacked. "Wouldn't you know! My one night out in months!"

A faint horn repeated in the street. "Make yourself at home," Adam called, turning the knob. The door hurtled open, wrenched him against the wall. Eerie lightning whitened the murk, disclosed low-bowed, bare-stripped branches thrashing. Horizontal rain riddled the car's headlights. The wind like a monstrous, many-handed vandal wrought havoc in the hall till between them—Julian pushing, Adam pulling—they got the door shut.

In the undisturbed living room Chad lay like a fallen Giacometti in the flickering din of the TV, conscious or not Julian could not tell.

He sat down in Adam's chair, and began hoping nothing would happen.

"If he wakes up just remind him who you are," Adam had said. "Don't be alarmed if you have to remind him who *he* is."

The storm shrieked. The house shuddered and shook. The words *Here today, gone tomorrow* trespassed jauntily through Julian's fenceless mind, he heard Madbury's caustic bray, "How's Methusela doing these days?" then André's voice recalling Adam and Chad's wedding in Beech Forest in 1968, back when it was not easy to find a minister to consecrate a gay marriage.

One had worn a white tuxedo and a yarmulke, the other a black bikini, top hat and cape. Julian couldn't remember which wore what, only that the renegade man of God had said, "I pronounce you spouse and spouse," and hard upon a sanctified kiss the couple popped a bottle of champagne, and toasted each other while everyone cheered. "That was the main event of *that* season," André had droned.

Julian glanced at the clock. Less than five minutes had passed and already he felt stretched to his limit. Had not Cahill and Dooley Jones died during his vigils, almost, it had come to seem, *because* of them, and had he not since detected redress therein, as if they were preconditions of his own flourishing?

But suppose Adam came home and found Chad dead! Everything was different here. How know what to hope for—except miracles? Best to effect a cure before Adam returned! Julian pictured the amazed couple's rejoicings and his own modest admission that even he could not say how he had done it, beyond the practice of a sort of boundless and concentrated goodwill toward the human project, for an instant triumphant here.

His reverie was too brief for the clock to describe, but the raw need to help did not fade with it, but grew large, then larger and more despairing, and suddenly shriveled away to an irreducible desire simply to get through his shift with as little trauma as possible.

Ashamed, Julian felt his title to life slipping away. Why should Chad be lying there and not him? Because he was an artist! Why else? For whom else did the world exist? Who else had any real use for it?

Now storm and TV seemed a hellish cacophony—the barometric no one could subdue, the human Julian dared not adjust. Suddenly he sprang to his feet in a confused panic—Chad had stirred!

Was even now trying with excruciating effort to change his position, his whole being focused it seemed on moving one leg one inch—from agony perhaps to peace, however brief.

Julian watched in horror while Chad half lifted his head to watch, to direct, the travail taking place beyond his waist, where beneath the blanket a little tremor could at intervals be seen to persist for whole moments and then cease, to begin again, but last less long, till finally Chad's head fell back, and he gave up or forgot or rested or slept.

Julian tiptoed to the bed and looked down; the face like an ax looked back at him.

In a providential lull of TV and wind, Julian said, "Can I do anything for you?"

"No," said a perfectly controlled voice he had never heard before.

All Julian could manage was, "I'm sorry you have to go through this."

"That's all right," Chad said.

Julian went back and sat down again in Adam's chair. The sweetness, the kind understanding in the voice, the conscious absolution of it, shrived him of every anguish. A huge gratitude swelled him, then admiration for the wreck that lay there ill in every cell, and still took pains to spare another.

On the TV a car chase skidded around corners and crashed through garbage cans and venders' stalls, then somehow the drivers were climbing a crane at a construction site, shooting at each other from behind stanchions, dodging bullets, edging their heads out and shooting again, the shrieking ricochets loud above the clangorous score and the howling storm. Next glance they had run out of bullets, but the chase continued among the girders of the skeletal skyscraper—like tailless monkeys, Julian thought. Next he knew the protagonists were grappling on the dizzy top with tiny ants moving about far below while they knocked each other down with roundhouse blows, picked each other up and knocked each other down again, did somersaults of escape, kicking one another in the solar plexus with both feet, finally rolled at the edge, choking each other, one on top, now the other, and the distant ants revolved.

Julian suddenly noticed that Chad's lips were moving, had been

How Many Die

moving perhaps for some time. With trepidation, but also with nascent confidence, he stepped close to the bed and bent to hear. The storm howled. The TV roared. The lips kept moving; Julian bent closer and tried to read them: were they asking the same thing over and over? A sip of water? The time of day? A benediction?

He felt the growing urgency, turned down the TV, whereupon the storm abated, so that Chad's voice had a particular distinctness of Sisyphusian exasperation, "What do I have to do to get you out of my face?"

And the volume shot back up higher than ever, the channel changed and kept changing, gales shuddered the house like a foundering ship, and the hands of the clock declared that a half hour had passed.

Julian admitted to Judd, "I only sat with him once. We never got to talk."

"Well," Judd said, "looks like you've got a reprieve. He's a feisty cuss. You got to give him credit. We've been here umpteen times."

Assessing the tenacity, the grim insouciance of some of these guys, Judd realized that he had ceased to think of gays as different. No doubt that was progress, he conceded, and grinned to remember the two six-foot-four Fellows from the Fine Arts Work Center, studs from out West in cowboy boots and jeans, at the laundromat one night, where Judd, who moonlighted as a carpenter, happened to be fixing a rotted floorboard.

The place was full of queens, inspired to competitive heights by their spooked audience. The Fellows had been doing their few socks and underwear, their one chamois shirt apiece and second pair of jeans, bundling the whole lot unfolded into one duffel bag in their haste to depart; and just as they were crowding together through the door the lead heckler said with derision enough to blister the last of the paint off the walls, "A bit thick in the hips!"

After that, Judd heard later, the newcomers had done their laundry up in Orleans. He longed to regale Julian with his own hilarity, but the boy had sidled away.

RELIEVED OF HIS house-cleaning duties, Julian had run back to his studio, and his still untouched canvas. He had yet to evoke a vision of death itself; meanwhile peripheral forms practically sucked paint from his brush, at the rate of three or four a week.

His Tower of Babel was done, nor was it the fiasco he had feared. On impulse he pulled it out of his crowded racks and painted Chad's face on one of the most prominent figures. Quick remorse killed his little satisfaction, and to atone he painted a picture of a wilted prick with a skull for glans with a worm snaking out of each eye-socket, themselves decaying pricks with skull heads, each with two tiny pricks emerging, with filament prick-worm-skulls emerging from them.

The background was painted the joyous blue of a sky that had banished his disappointment at a dawn cloudburst seen from his childhood bedroom window. Even Arthur raised eyebrows at this one.

22

PAST AND FUTURE MEET

BAXTER WAS CONFOUNDED by André's ashes. Endless the objections his brain raised to every idea. André was not fond of bay or sea or sand, gardens, woods, bogs, or breakwater. He was not fond of anything or anywhere except the abstract Provincetown. He might give Madbury a zing, drop them off the Monument and let the wind, et cetera, but where might they not blow? The logic of scattering them at some peaceful site was no logic for André.

Baxter was stuck, paralyzed it seemed—as if they bound him to precedence, held hostage the accomplishment of his own demise, which grew more urgent by the hour it felt. Added to his predicament was the nattering of his friends—as though, with Nelson gone, they too had nothing left on their minds.

Till now prudence had curbed Madbury's tongue somewhat, but these days he seemed over the edge, wheedling and badgering Baxter to accede to Gregory's suspicious wish to mix André with Gustave and Selwyn, and make a big occasion of their joint scattering—a mock occasion it sounded to some ears, based apparently upon the single, iron-clad indictment that all three had died.

Gregory caught nothing of Madbury's tone. Despite his conventional veneer he welcomed any innovative ritual that might strengthen communal solidarity, prompt improving remembrance of mortality—here providential in its threefold force—and promote a salutary humility and rededication to whatever principles one might profess.

Anticipation of a novel piece of performance art briefly solaced Nicky Heldahl's lack-love with the image of a genial gathering of atoms, but then he despaired of ever finding anyone willing to share bed—much less end with him as ashes anywhere.

"For pity's sake, let him rest in peace!" Arthur protested.

"At least let him out of that awful urn," demanded Weeming, who now burned with cabin fever in the sweet little saltbox he had once delighted to cohabit with Bright. They hardly spoke to each other now, recoiled when they bumped in kitchen or bathroom, slept on bed edges, got through the work day by one always being out of the office. Both felt some breaking point was near; both dreaded, waited, wanted it to come.

ONE DIM TWILIGHT, while Baxter browsed among his shelves of authors, mulling which titles should be most urgently bequeathed to Julian, André's rightful resting place appeared to him.

Madbury was gone with the car. Baxter draped the urn with a sweater, called a cab, and had himself let out near André's old apartment. Profoundly gratified to find it still unoccupied, he went around back to the privet-enclosed yard with the dilapidated split-rail fence and cracked- brick patio, where in good weather André had sat drinking, and smoking tobacco and hashish—though in historic times perfectly abstinent—and there, with a sense of firm correctness, he strewed his ashes, hurried back to the waiting cab, and when he got home poured himself a tall, weak Scotch.

He had not had felt such well-being in months, and he resolved to prolong it. What to do with the urn? Certainly it could not serve as his own; his parents would *not* enjoy its rococo hilarity. Wrong to consign it to the dump; its utility would never be outworn. Distaste for waste of wit gave him his second inspiration of the hour, simplicity itself, and he acted upon it.

Returned to the middle of the mantelpiece, it would hold undisputed sway, preside weirdly over the stark decor of his Puritanically barren dining room. It really did, he was pleased to see, a bit recall the Taj Mahal.

He committed himself to silence, the Mona Lisa smile of the Sphinx. Some day someone would take the top off, and then what a stir there would or would not be, a world well lost.

As he sat at the head of his table faintly smiling, deciding to indulge himself and skip dinner, he could feel André's approbation warming him against the dark cold outdoors and—perhaps it was the Scotch—doubter though he was of every postulate of spirit the ages had engendered, from animism to philosophic inference from human incredulity at cosmic accident, yet for the moment he felt close to all those he had loved among the dead. He felt ready.

THAT DAY IN stymied haste Julian wrenched his seized-up shower head. It broke and sprayed crazily, so he went down the hall to a bathroom with angled, facing mirrors. High on his back, between right shoulder blade and spinal column, in a spot hitherto concealed from himself, nor ever exposed to other eyes, where fingers never touched, was a black, raised, rough, irregular patch.

He tried to hope it was a dream, but the longer he looked the less did it seem unreal. What could it be? What had it been the first time? He took his shower finally for lack of anything else, his stomach hollow and fallen, and then he began to think again. With a tip of thumb at its utmost reach he felt how slab-like it was beneath the suppurating crust. Palpating it gently, lest its cells slough away in blood or lymph, he took flight in distant disappointment that it had no heart shape, then felt that this at least was a good omen, though equally a bad, or neither, or both. In his room, in a hand mirror, he saw it had no shape at all, a formless splotch like a reddish, bluish, yellowish splutter of mud.

Unremitting was the pavement to Julian's feet, his eyes fixed upon the cracked and broken surfaces and grimy grit, the patternless attractions of terrestrial minutiae. All thoughts tore at him —censorial doctors, oncological complications, biopsies, tests, X rays, the horde of intrusions upon his precarious, precious privacy, with summer suddenly sprung upon him.

Despite its impossible resurgence, against which at times he had felt immunized by faithful fear, it was still so small a phenomenon, so slight a plaint amid the universal calamity, that he was loath to indulge it. He did not like to admit to being ill, even to himself, liked less to be examined, less yet to submit to the knife again, face convalescence, disruption of work. He had almost thought all that was behind him, almost, not quite: it was really no surprise.

Still, it must be dealt with, the sooner the better—for the terrors would haunt his studio. *The use of time is fate*, he heard Baxter say. He knew he only had a few days of peace left, could barely afford them, could absolutely not not afford them, felt himself approaching a great vision. He would not yet make the sacrifice, for a few days by sheer will ignored, and then for a few more days of fierce work and deferred fear almost entirely put from mind the stupefying chance, likelihood, fact that his melanoma had returned, or at least that something rotten was going on back there where he could not see, that did not seem to be a part of him.

He had meant to deal with it. It had only been a few days, he could not remember how many, very few. Soon, very soon, tomorrow or the next day, the problem would be under care, his inaction at an end, if he could just see a little further, a little beyond the visible, mind out of time. And then fall would come.

23

A PARTY

NICKY HELDAHL'S HOARSENESS had begun to frighten him, which made him smoke more, increasing the pain in his chest. Then he got a sore throat, which wouldn't go away, no matter how medicated, but only got worse, until one day he coughed a fleck of blood.

Toward the ills the flesh is said to be heir to, his stance had been that of the ostrich: know naught, and they would pass one by. His next line of defense was the faith that modern medicine could cure anything but AIDS and old age. Now he began to weigh odds and lose sleep.

A year ago—was it only a year?—Arthur had said, "You smoke too much."

"I know," Nicky had said unhappily. "What's funny is—I don't mean funny—what I can't understand is, I don't even know anyone who ever died of cigarette cancer, and everyone I ever knew was a chain-smoker."

Two days of intermittent experiment now enabled him to cough up red-tinged phlegm almost at will, and this on cancer-dread piled fear of TB, contracted possibly, he speculated, from some PWA, though so far as he knew he had not been in proximity to any, unless maybe Nelson had passed it to him. He remembered now moping around with his head on Nelson's shoulder, after Chris Whitman's death, coincident with his own mental disturbance, whatever that had been, for all it mattered.

If the invariable price of life were death, birth now seemed no bargain. Nor could he tell his fears for fear of ridicule, nor quit smoking long enough to see if that particular remedy might help, for, if he were truly dying, what would be the use? No rousing of courage, but only dire desperation, borne upon a solid footing of vodka, let him make an appointment in Magnolia with his family doctor, who glanced at his raw throat, handed him a pack of his own favorite lozenges, not easily procured nowadays, sent him to the hospital for chest X rays, and next noon phoned to exonerate his lungs of all but their chronic ache of protest.

"You know the risks," the old man's dry, mildly affectionate voice concluded. Nicky hung up with heartfelt thanks, shocked at how shrunken and frail was this strangely dear, little man in the threadbare, tweed vest and unclean shirt-sleeves, unseen, unthought of in fifteen years.

Since Madbury's idea for a memorial mingling of the three departeds looked sadly in doubt, Nicky decided to celebrate by throwing a bash for himself, billing it as an End of February Party, good riddance to the year's worst month.

DRESSING FOR the occasion, exhausted, overwrought after another hallucinatory day on the verge, constantly blocked by a vision of the amoeba-like shape of his lesion, and stunned by its seemingly tangible growth, Julian stammered out his trouble to Arthur, who, after a shocked inspection of it—while hearing for the first time of Julian's medical past—called his doctor at home and made an appointment for Julian first thing in the morning.

In Baxter's car, with Madbury at the wheel, Arthur, sitting in back beside Julian, anguished by Baxter's bony shoulders and squamous neck, leaned forward and said with distinct displeasure, "You don't have to do this."

"I *want* to go," said Baxter.

"It's a free country," Arthur acceded.

"Good to hear," said Baxter.

Arthur said no more, after a moment slipped a hand lightly beneath Julian's collar and began to massage his nape. "I'll give you a haircut," he murmured. "Tomorrow night."

Julian released his breath, began to breathe deeply and audibly, trying to hold fast.

"You could use a trim," Arthur added in a casual tone.

"Okay," Julian said.

"Worry is useless," Arthur murmured.

Julian nodded, eager for the morrow's start on his problem.

Inside they found themselves amid a cheerful din of familiar strangers, drinking buddies, chance acquaintances, casuals from Nicky's bar life and after-hours breakfasts with mimosas for the road.

Resplendent in a blue velvet smoking jacket and tasseled harlequin's cap, Nicky was buzzed with the delights of hospitality. At sight of Julian, his proudest star of the evening, he hastened to display obeisance. "Now what may I get you?" he asked after thoroughly discomfiting his guest.

"Nothing, thanks," said Julian, wishing he were invisible.

"Oh, I can't hear that!" cried Nicky gaily. "You've got to have *something*. This is a serious celebration."

"Oh, maybe some . . . mineral water?" Julian tried.

"No, no," Nicky said, beaming and beaming. "This once you've got to have a real drink. I'm counting on you to help me celebrate. Otherwise you'll hurt my feelings. How about a beer? For starters."

Julian hated beer. Casing the bar, seeing no sign of the vivid, gold label, he said, "Tequila!"

"Tequila!" said Nicky with bemusement.

"That's all I ever drink," Julian said, attempting airiness.

"Tequila! Just the thing! A touch of the worm! The promise of spring! I never would have thought of it. That's the artist in him," Nicky expanded to a swarthy, silvery-haired man standing nearby, then rummaged in the cabinet below, produced a brand-new bottle of Cuervo Especial. "I'll make you one of my famous margaritas."

"Oh, no," Julian said. "Just straight, please. And just a little."

"Oh, I can't allow that," Nicky said, busy with the makings. He bent again, arose, held up and scrutized a glass the size of a small birdbath.

"Please," said Julian.

"No, no, it's no trouble," Nicky assured him. "It's an honor." He turned to the silvery-haired man, whose eyes perused Julian's features, as fingertips do braille. "Julian Esmeralda, founder of the School of Dixistentialism, meet Vince Vincenzo, author of *The Macabre and the Morbid*."

"*Morbid and Macabre*," said Vince.

"Oop!" said Nicky cordially. "I'm awful with names. I could never tell Tweedledum from dee, Freud from Jung. What do you think of Nabokov, by the way?"

Julian stood transfixed, hands hanging, half-conscious, while the author took his measure, still as a lizard on a window ledge. The question went unanswered, just as well no doubt.

"It's a gay murder mystery," Nicky got back on track. "Everybody has a motive, and everybody gets murdered. In the most grisly ways. Even the detective in the end, and he's slept with them all, trying to get at the truth, till he's the last one left. It's the only time he ever goes to bed alone. And then the lights go out, the door slams shut, and he begins to writhe. The last scene takes place in the mirror, very dim, as if you might be the poisoner yourself. It's very clever. It's never solved. The book ends in the middle of a sentence. When you turn the page there's nothing there but a number. Right in the middle. Vertical. Like a tombstone."

"Two twenty-two," said Vince. "Suspense cubed."

"Is that a clue?" Nicky wondered.

"The only real one," Vince said. "The rest are decoys."

"I'll have to think about that. Two, two, two, six. Sex. Well, there's no lack of that. You'll love it, Julian. He's writing a new one right now, set in P-town. He's here getting material. Perhaps he'll give you a role in it. Not as a corpse, I trust. Voilà!" Nicky presented the brimming goblet, with salt encrusted rim. "Is that the most beautiful margarita ever built?"

Julian held the glass in both hands and stared as if he were thinking of jumping in.

Nicky's roving eye kept coming back to the boy, who stood

unmoving, now returning Vincenzo's regard, his own for once unabashed. Finally he said, "So who was the murderer?"

"Don't know," murmured Vincenzo with gravelly quiet. "Unnecessary complication. It saved me a lot of trouble, not having to work that out. Couples and clues is easy. So long as nothing need fit. People love the farfetched."

Julian put down the top-heavy tequila that spilled at every tilt.

"You don't like it!" Nicky moaned with self-reproach. He picked it up, sipped, narrowed his eyes. "You're right," he said. "Too sour. I knew it was. I had a feeling."

"No, no," Julian said. "It's fine, it's great."

Nicky started another. "Hurts my pride," he said. "I have my reputation to uphold."

"Let's have a second opinion," said Vince, saved the glass from its destined end in the sink, drank half of it, puckered with obscure suavity. "Perfect!" he said.

"No, No," Nicky said. "Julian's right. It *was* a tad sour."

Another goblet soon encumbered Julian's hand. His mouth dry with fear, he drank, and choked.

"Why are *you* so glad February's gone?" Madbury quickly insinuated, pulling a fresh beer from the ice.

"I'm just celebrating," Nicky said, "and I want everybody to join me."

Madbury eyed him with veiled disbelief. That morning, after a week of uneasy inklings had turned to conviction that the Taj Mahal's position was slightly changed, he had raised its top, then glanced around in the expanding silence.

He had said nothing to anyone, never let on he knew, never would, felt robbed, mocked, threatened, the object of a plot, concocted presumably by his inscrutable employer, though others must be in on it too. These days everybody seemed devious, weaving sinister secrets or snubbing him.

"What have *you* got to celebrate?" he pursued.

"My good luck," said Nicky with cryptic emphasis.

"If you've come into more money," Vince said, "I want my share."

"Money," said Nicky a bit sententiously, "is not the most important thing in the world."

All eyes fixed upon him with dire accord.

Julian used the distraction to pour half his margarita into a parched-looking jade plant, but Nicky caught him.

"Too sweet!" he cried, crestfallen.

"No, no, just too much. Too much," Julian muttered.

Nicky tasted it. "No," he conceded, "I see what you mean. Juuu-st a tad too sweet."

"Allow me," said Vince with gallant hand, and quaffed it off. "More perfect!" he said, all the more bizarre as he was drinking wine himself.

As Nicky bent to another attempt to accommodate his premier guest—he did not really think much of Vincenzo's liberties—Julian yelped in exasperation, "Please!" seized the neck of the bottle and diverted it toward a water glass.

Nicky acquiesced with a sweet smile, but held it steady till the glass filled to a fat four fingers. "Lemon?" said he. "Or lime? Salt!"

"No!" Julian shouted, turning more heads, and to be quit of it swilled it down, where it spread to every nerve end like a night tree of lightning, beneath which a Christmas bulb blinked on and swung like a pendulum. Stark as a star in cracked ice, Jessica Jordan tap-danced within, obliterating silvery Vince.

Julian's outburst had made him the party's focal point. Arthur with withered heart watched Baxter watching Julian. Baxter seemed genuinely to be enjoying himself, an unfamiliar, pleased delight on his lips. Arthur sorrowed with rage; everything, every gesture, every expression on every face except for these two, lacerated him with their gross inanity and monstrous ignorance.

Nicky was in his element. He had finally drunk enough to numb his lungs enough to smoke without chest ache. Ah, smoke! Nostalgic smoke! Disturbed only by dulled pangs of fear, appeased by the inexhaustible vow of quitting tomorrow—or at least of cutting back to a pack a day, then half a pack, then, in no time, only the occasional one or two with coffee after meals—he felt able at last to enjoy his party. Surveying his guests, several of whom were veteran topers sure to stay to honor the dawn, he realized how wrong he was to have lost his confidence in life.

Patting his pockets for a light, the hollow filter of a fresh True Blue bit between his yellowish teeth, he found a white pack of matches presented to his gaze between two manicured fingers of Vince Vincenzo. It said in red script, *You are cordially invited to*

Julian glanced, Madbury craned. Nicky raised inquiring eyes at Vince, who opened the pack. On the inside cover it said, *fuck the shit out of me.*

To the flame Vince with a flourish struck, Nicky quickly bent, puffed and sucked a gulf of deep, narcotic completion and relief. "That's cute!" he said, coughing a geyser of smoke.

Julian snorted with aversion, caught a glimpse of his mother, wondered, suddenly, what had become of his father, that thief, and how much did he resemble *him*?

Pocketing the matchbook, Vince blandly expressed nothing at all. Madbury looked deflated and careworn amid the chortles and grins. Arthur guessed he had learned of Baxter's AIDs, which meant, one supposed, more dark comedy.

The rest of the party extended around the three great wings of windows. Nicky had a luxurious apartment; paintings covered every wall space. He was getting higher by the moment, with only a niggling guilt that he had yet to acquire anything of Julian's, partly because he had been unable to pick among his favorites but mostly because he felt so poor. It was a long time since he had spent a dime on art. Somehow he could not hold onto money any more; it seemed the less he had at his discretion the more he felt impelled to squander it on clothes he didn't want, didn't like when he got them home, never wore and found it too embarrassing to give away, not to mention his noblesse oblige in the bars.

But he could certainly save a bundle on cigarettes, and on shrinks too—an easy $25,000 per annum there. The prospect of revived fortunes made him recognize that in the last few moments he had miraculously bobbed up from a bottomless abyss, his eyes wide open, now clairvoyantly clear. He held up his glass and said quietly to those nearby, "Drink to me, my friends, I'm free!"

Julian poured another two inches of tequila and blindly drank them down. The others lifted their glasses, somewhat cursorily, knowing Nicky in his cups.

"Free of what?" said Vince.

"Death," said Nicky without needing to think. His mind was working effortlessly, like a smoothly running, first-rate engine.

Solve one problem, all others follow, links in a chain, pieces in a puzzle, teeth in a gear. He could perfectly well bear, he would even resolve with grand welcome to greet, death in its proper time and place in the natural scheme of things, where he now finally felt at home, and why not? It was his birthright and liberating in itself merely to have got that simple truth settled, once and for all.

"My condolences!" said Vince.

Nicky raised the eyebrow of one asked to accept a collect call from a stranger.

"Too bad to miss it," said Vince. "Of all things in life to celebrate, death is the best. It feels best of anything there ever was, better than Seventh Heaven, than all the orgasms you ever had rolled into one, better than any victory you ever could hope for, better than finding some lost, cherished thing, better than winning the lottery or a life supply of opium, better than being born again with perfect beauty. The people to pity are the ones who don't get to enjoy it."

"How would you know?" said Madbury.

Vince wanly smiled. "Trust me," he said.

"You might be right at that," Nicky smirked. "My ex always said his ideal was to go out playing the xylophone with his heels on God's spine."

"The big prick," Madbury said. "Custom made for Julian."

Julian invincibly saw a phallic Pilgrim Monument with a tiny figure sitting on top, looking over the edge apprehensively. He shook his head with despair at the thought of a twenty-foot-tall canvas.

Vince said," Julie Ann, Czar man. If he can, you can."

"You're a poet too," said Nicky.

"Light verse. Like my mysteries," Vince said to Julian. "All form, no content."

Madbury declared, "I'm not big on poetry, I'm no fan of Corso and Kuriac, I'm not even crazy about everything Allen Ginsberg ever wrote, but that 'Scream' is a great poem."

Such mirth broke out that Arthur's grim regard was drawn from Baxter's face to the scene it registered with such uncommon tenderness, but when he glanced back again something else, something incongruous was beginning to find expression increasingly in Baxter's narrowed eyes and compressed lips, some struggle or strain, and then with a sudden, overt grimace he lurched headlong across the room, veered not very steadily around an end table, setting down his unsipped drink on the polished surface with a heedless splash, and disappeared into the hallway, where fortunately the bathroom was unoccupied.

He got inside and shut the door at least before the awful lava flow filled his underpants and slid down his legs, in an instant making the small room stink revoltingly, chemically, like nothing human. He did what he could, but left a mortifying mess, drew breath, stepped into the hall, feeling dizzy, and made palsied haste for the front door. Arthur joined him.

"I'm going home," Baxter said, forging on.

"I'll get Mad," said Arthur, keeping up.

"Don't!" said Baxter.

"I'll drive," said Arthur.

"No, thank you," said Baxter, and Arthur, with an intimation, opened the door for him, watched him descend, one tread at a time, the seemingly endless stairs, then went to the window and watched him walk like a lame, old man to his car, inch out of his parking space, and drive slowly away.

Then Arthur cleaned up the bathroom. Short of breath from the exertions of bending in a cramped space, he glanced in the mirror and saw a flushed and mottled, old queen with a crooked wig, the lines sharpening around his pale, powdered dewlaps, and thought with dismal unsurprise, Our lives are done.

HAVING SHOWERED, Baxter lay shivering beneath a pile of covers. Against this latest nadir he held his daily catechism—Q: How are you today? A: Better than tomorrow. Then he thought of the empty urn, shut his eyes upon hot tears.

NICKY WAS FLYING. He loved bartending, his true calling, he often said, a pity to have missed. He had not once left his fortress of bottles, but he did not fear to neglect his guests, for irresistibly they came to him, with ever-happier mien, felicity he himself had wrought and constantly augmented. This now seemed to him the most worthwhile, the most momentous party, he had ever thrown, though he could not at just this tick recall the occasion. But, good God, what excuse was needed for festivities? Were they not what life was all about! And his lighthearted mood was confirmed, fear put in its place by a sign he had lately seen on a house under lavish renovation: What if the hokeypokey *is* what it's all about?

Henceforth he realized he would be able to smoke and drink with impunity. This, after all, was what he did best, what he was born for, how he invariably saw himself in dream, drink in one hand, cigarette in the other, a boyish smile upon his face. This true image proved that the morrow would bring no shadow of hangover, that sleep, as in former times, would restore both body and soul, that every puff and nip he now took would bring only greater, closer connection to the vital core of all things happy and benevolent.

Julian, having kept on with the tequila, stood blank-faced, staring across the room through the windows at the lights coming on in Truro and Wellfleet. He did not answer when spoken to, nor could he be got to attend.

Vince Vincenzo, unable to hold the strange youth's eye or ear, had slipped into tipsy inconsequence, retailing the scandals upon which his books were based, dropping names, divulging trade secrets to empty air, hardly moving his lips, looking more and more suave and relentlessly alert, like a stuffed bird with moving lips.

"It is the essential nature," Arthur was saying with harsh exasperation, "of good to be defeated."

"AIDS *is* nature," someone said.

"They were innocents, not martyrs," another said.

Gil Bright, as always happened when he drank, brooded on Charles Cahill. Weeming, dimly irritated, decided that his lover and Julian were two of a kind. There they stood, like parodies of one another, gawking like amnesiacs in cloud cuckoo land.

"Look, it's snowing!" someone cried. All turned toward the windows.

"I hate this fucking shit," Madbury said with fierce emphasis.

"It's still February," someone else protested.

"Only for another few hours," Nicky said.

"For the last five years," Adam was saying, "I've been nothing but a nurse."

"C'est magnifique," Vince pounced with sharp accent, "mais ce n'est pas la vie."

Adam smiled bleary accord, replied sadly to Nicky, "All the same, I must go."

A drop of regret seeped into Nicky's well of pleasure. "Where's Gregory?" he asked. "Didn't he come?"

"Can anyone say enough good about that man? What a life saver he's been!" Adam said. "I know he had something to do today, though he planned to be back for your party."

Nicky's stomach pitched and fell as if after all everything were irreparable. He remembered that he had yet to visit Chad, nor had he made mention of his intentions to Adam, now past recall on his way out the door.

24

THE DUNES

SHIVERING VIOLENTLY, feet numb, hands, face, arms, and legs beaded with blood, Gregory, the party forgone, stepped into his shower at The Maid, his wet sneakers and torn and tattered pants and ski jacket heaped on the floor.

The day had been a jewel. After an early-morning veil of warm rain had diminished to mist and lifted, a brilliant sun suffused the atmosphere, banished every shadow, and the temperature sharpened refreshingly.

About noon, in strange elation, he had parked at Snail Road, and set forth into the dunes, toting a beach bag containing Selwyn's and Gustave's ashes in his great-aunt's baked bean crock.

The unperformed rite had begun to oppress him. Recognizing that Baxter could never be persuaded to commit André's relics to his grand plan for communal closure, he had, without telling anyone, simply resolved to fulfill his own obligations and needs, heave the weight off his heart, return to Portsmouth, and do what exactly remained unclear, if suddenly rife with possibilities.

He also — practical soul — meant to make this little venture both pleasant and worthwhile, the first steps of a new start on the rest of his life.

He had pored over the topography of the tip of Cape Cod, shaped to his fancy like a striking viper's skull—Long Point its curving fangs, its gaping gullet the central green of forest pitted with blue kettle ponds, Hatches Harbor its glassy eye, its flat head the parabolic dunes capped by the high marine scarp.

A geological infant, dropped by ice sheets ten thousand years ago, it was all so small and benign—maybe five square miles—that it looked walkable, explorable, the whole of it, in a single day, two days, every last nook of it in three day's time at most. He felt suddenly, on his own account, laggard and remiss; this was his first real outing since he had arrived, his first, in fact, since Rick and Gavin's suicide.

The terrific, exhilarating light brought home to him how captive of grief his last two years had been. Emerging from the cool, leaf-floored corridor of oaks, climbing steeply in the sand, with nothing in sight but blue sky, he reached the peak of the first dune, panting, sweating, his face burning in the windless flood of sun.

He tied his jacket round his waist, and trudged up a further slope till he could see far and near—the glittering ocean before, the glowing bay behind. Outline and detail of minor things, pitch pine cones and perfect circles of compass grass, grains of sand in his own footprints, rabbit tracks in the vale below, all seemed equally visible, as if the rain had cleansed the air or distance condensed in the eye.

Exalted, he climbed with remembered pleasure in his legs. This was Gustave's and Selwyn's gift to him, as it was his to them. Had they lived, this moment would not be. In truth, unspeakable though it seemed, there were no ill winds.

He nearly moon-floated in leap-like strides down the frozen, northern slope. Deep in the vale below he met with the first low barrier of pines, and threaded through, following a path that skirted cranberry bogs, and came out at the foot of another dune. He toiled up, drenched with sweat. From the top he looked out over a white-shining desert of dunes rolling away in all directions, crevassed here and there with green woods. He plunged down again and up, then traveled a sort of meandering track around patches of gleaming poison ivy and immense beach rose hummocks, till it faded into a small sand bowl. He climbed to the opposite rim, descended into a similar bowl, then up again and down again, till he met with a larger, denser copse of pitch pine, softly needled underfoot, light-dappled and redolent of boyhood hideaways. Nondescript little birds hopped ahead of him in the thicket, with never a cheep of concern. Where ocean, where bay was, he no longer knew. *Nor need know,* he chided himself to jubilation.

By guess and happenstance he made a way, circumventing bogs and walls of vegetation, toiling up knobs, jogging easily down again, following openings, sometimes crawling, dragging the aggravating bean crock, wishing he had brought his gloves, edging through ever-thicker webs of spiky bush, close-grown bayberry, beach plum, black cherry, Virginia creeper, and interminable, entangling ramifications of bright greenbrier with formidable thorns.

Then sand prevailed again. He climbed another pristine dune, startled to find that the sparse shrubs crowning the height were in fact wind-tattered tops of buried oaks. Down he slid in haste, down into another, lesser swale, from which debouched a wet deer track that wound through a sweet, grassy little span, ending at another stand of lusher, taller pines, with gleams of blue beyond. He forged through, stood breathless with wonder by the edge of a small, still pond like a piece of fallen sky.

A crow flapped up, shaking the air, from a carcass on the shore, cawed twice, raucous in the silence, sailed away behind the treeline, then cawed again, staccato, uncountable, fading. Then came a faint, fast chorus like echoes, or many affirming the one. It was like a portent; he did not believe in such things except as they altered mind, but it recalled the solemn purpose of his trek, and he set the bean crock down, to rest and look around, choose where and how to perform his funereal function, noticed a red toy skiff in the weeds with a pole beside it.

He thought no further. Here was a magic glade, a fated place, wrong to deny. His friends had decreed the dunes, but neither had ever set foot in this lonely waste, knew it only from hearsay or postcard, plane or car window, had no real grasp of what was out here or what they were asking for. This would be a kinder, finer eternity than blank sand, less desolate, more contained, shapely, condensed, mystic, more . . . like Mother Ocean, if smaller, perhaps brackish, certainly brackish, salt and fresh water both, a bonus

of wholeness, which all appealed to Gregory, one of whose ancestors had been buried at sea, so honored, to be sure, by necessity,
having died there, a hundred years ago, with no ice aboard; but
still, Gregory felt certain that Gustave and Selwyn would approve
this providential change of their designated resting site, for there
was no end of sand all around—if sand was what they really
thought they wanted—sand in abundance on the bottom too, no
doubt, where they would unite finally, forever.

He hauled the skiff into the water, embarked, and pushed out
toward the middle, away from the brown lily pads and crystal ice.
He squatted, crock on knees, for a moment in the stern—there
was no seat—and pulled the stubborn duct tape off; then, trying
to purify his soul, he held his breath and waited for clear sentiment, for prayer, for their essence in him, to possess him.

But he was too exhilarated to concentrate, nor was there reason
left to mourn. All was now somehow part of the past. It had happened unawares. The mystery of the world, the peace of the day
were monumental. Touching fingertips to the ashes, he bade his
star-crossed friends farewell, and endless renewal in this right and
lovely place, stood to a sort of attention, suddenly graced with
tears, emptied out the ashes all around, wiped his eyes and looked
about with an unexpected sense of personal triumph.

The yellow and grey debris rode lightly, brightly flecked as mica,
the bone bits bobbing, saluting slowly, wonderfully into stillness.
Some of it settled like sediment, some of it swirled and spread like
galaxies in the sun, and he breathed a brave sigh of release, marveling at how easily, how naturally his ordeal had ended. Any day
these last few weeks would have done as well. Freed by time itself,
his life would now resume. He blessed the universe. He would
find a new lover and be happy; he would not find anyone and be
happy. But he would be happy; so life commanded.

When he finally leaned upon his pole to push shoreward, a
floorboard broke and the skiff with a gurgle sank. The water was
only thigh deep, but it was cold. Holding the crock above his head
—needlessly it proved—he waded through the sucking mud to
dry land, and wrung out his pants as best he could.

Astounded when his watch beeped four o'clock, he started
back, suddenly let down and weary. It had been a long way out;

it would be a long way home, and miserably cold and clammy too, and he had a party to attend, and many useful things to do—a whole new life in fact had just been born—so he hiked on, his sneakers squishing, the bean crock in the beach bag banging now one kneecap, now the other, as he kept changing hands.

An avenue of sand led straight on more or less toward where he conceived Snail Road to be, given the dimming daylight and startling shadows, and he followed it, till it branched and disappeared in some dense undergrowth. He hurried back and took the other path, which went on hopefully, a little way, skirted a bog, then narrowed, and ended at a scattering of round droppings, where a tall thicket rose, laced with bright greenbrier.

Trying to retrace his steps, he found not the pond, but another, strange glade, and stopped to take thought.

In the northeast a mountain of purple clouds dwarfed the sky, appeared, even as he watched with awe, majestically to loom, moment by measurable moment, nearer, darker, larger.

Quite a sight, he said to himself, and set out, on the double, up a gentle rise, and down into a perfect sand bowl, across its bottom, up its furthest rim, and down again, into another cavity exactly like it. On he went, panting, more and more incredulous and apprehensive. Over every crest, whichever way he turned, a new hollow appeared, like all the others, each with its complete, close horizon, silhouettes blurring, fewer and fewer features of anything distinguishable. The shadows reached eye level, and overhead the circle of pale sky faded and shrank.

He came upon footprints in the strange landscape, and followed them in bewildered suspension between gladness and fear, till amid an interval of panicky inattention he lost them—perhaps they weren't even his—and, after doubling back and making several zigzags of search, met with a pond, though not his pond, not the pond hallowed by Gustave's and Selwyn's sympathetic cinders, but a pond impassably black in the burgeoning gloom. He tried to get around it, but it kept expanding, almost maliciously it seemed, until it began to reveal itself as more like a lake, and he turned back.

The wind was coming up and it was stinging cold. Gregory was a strong, well-kept sixty years of age, with a calm, physical confidence, and did not fear for his safety, but neither did he relish a night huddled in some pitch pine grove—not wet as he was below the waist, sweat-soaked above.

He trudged on, and presently to his huge relief mounted a rise and found a sizeable plateau of sand from which he could spy a more distant horizon, fast darkening. At right angles to where he had judged town must be, the top of the Pilgrim Monument floated like an loose buoy against the turbulent sky, looking quite near, or at least not far.

As he jogged toward it, it sank from sight. The slowly sloping dune steepened till it spilled down a sharp defile and disappeared beneath a carpet of needles and leaves, and he beheld a dark gulf of forest stretching left and right before him without visible boundaries.

Apparently he could not rely on finding paths around obstacles. Till now he had followed sand, but sand had led only to dead ends. He knew where town lay, generally—straight ahead. He couldn't miss it, unless he first struck ocean, and wherever met, ocean would lead him home. Difficulties of the dark would yield to resourceful reason. He need not care where he came out, so long as he came out; he could take a taxi back to his car. He would make Nicky's party yet. *As the crow flies*, he exhorted himself, and plunged into the terrible gully.

He had not gone a yard before the first greenbriers stopped him. With ominous pains he freed the more or less unscathed sleeves of his ski jacket—but his corduroy pant legs were more securely seized, and he kicked impatiently, felt thorns rake his freezing shanks and heard cloth tear, stood still in shock to reconnoiter.

His natural assurance urged him on; to turn back would be demoralizing, with the long night in view, the wind rising. All around the dry scrub oak leaves were rattling, pine boughs bending and soughing, the whole mass of vegetation eerily agitated and astir, shapes flickering in the twilight.

He abandoned the bean crock, though it hurt his family pride, but he kept the beach bag, dear from childhood summers at Lake Winnipesaukee, and with trepidation edged on, one step at a time, deeper into the thicket, which briefly opened out, then closed behind.

Another few feet of hard-won progress and he had to confess—twisting one way, then another—that he was enmeshed, virtually a prisoner in the thorn-thick web, further advance dependent on his readiness to shred flesh, as well as garb, for the briers pierced whatever they touched, had hideously multiplied and interwoven, acting in concert now clutched at his scalp and cheeks, jabbed at eyes and ears, laid siege to his shrunken cock and wrinkled scrotum, punctured his fingertips, made him gasp piteously, with only himself to hear and be appalled in the gruesome solitude.

Back he would not, could not go—even if he knew which way back lay—refused to repeat what he had just gone through. The unknown ahead, though it be worse, seemed vastly preferable.

Unable in the gloom to tell which wetness was blood, which sweat—or both combined—maddened to extremity, he thrashed forward by brute force a foot, two feet perhaps, heard some stranger screaming with fury, stopped, fought to hold his ground, not be pulled back.

Nothing in the dreadful web broke, no strand let go: only more thorns gripped and punctured him. The whole relentless weave with utmost effort could be stretched—a little at first, then less and less, but the moment he tried to rest and merely hold his ground, it began with resistless force to resume its natural state, and incorporate him into it.

He realized the danger was real. After some thought he pulled the bag over his head, taking infinitesimal care made space with elbows and shoulders first to kneel, then to straighten out on his belly—facing which way he was too confused, too tired to guess—and little by little with frozen fingers clawed his way along miraculously appearing tunnels to open dunes. Weak with surprise and relief he climbed to his feet and started across.

Wind filled the portals of his ears with quiet roar and deafened him. No matter how he turned his head he could not hear his footsteps, even if he stamped. His shout was muffled in his mouth. He felt a looming at his heels, in fright jerked left, then right, but it was too dark to be sure nothing was there, and he whirled and whirled about. He knew—thought he knew—no beasts lived here, no abominable snowmen or Loch Ness monsters, but he kept turning, could not keep himself every few steps from wrenching his head to look back, unable to blink from his eyes' periphery a figment of menace, of vengeance it now began to seem, unfamiliar yet known, as if this day were a reckoning, proof that error could never be undone, nor recompensed, nor rightly fled.

He pushed sinister superstition aside, still felt more and more fearful—not since childhood had he felt such sheer, blind menace—and then the savage air swarmed with pelting snow and he could see nothing anywhere, nor hear a sound, and all around was only cold.

At the next summit he met an unnavigable gale of mixed sand and snow that bit at his raw face, forced him to turn back-to, then knocked him to his knees. Pummeled from every side, bearings lost, senses useless, he pulled the bag over his head again and crawled on tortured hands and knees he knew not where, except his spirits failed.

The dune sloped away. The wind abated. He rose to a crouch and ran for his life, pitched headlong down a steep bank into another snarl of vegetation, took the bag off his head, put it on one hand, burrowed in and scooped a nest of moldered leaves walled and roofed with brier, lay at strength's end, knees pulled up beneath his chin, shivering toward numb indifference.

How long before hypothermia brought drowsiness he knew not, nor in his dispassion did he care. Rick was dead; why should he care?

He caught a distant glimpse of an effigy, monarchal in will, in manner bland, inflexible of means. The windblown figure shed clothes like leaves till it was naked, then flesh till it was bones held gently as a baby by green barbed wire, last was gradually swaddled from sight by white clematis blooms, while across the towering sky clouds like seasons hurtled and the enigma of his defection faded in the memory of his new friends, only a little less long gave wonderment to his old set in Portsmouth, eventually went with each one by one into nothingness, themselves enigmas soon forgotten, and time passed on with no tomb.

Rest roused and drove him mole-like on without hope. At once, as if it had all been an aptitude test, with no consequences, a gleam of sand appeared, then another, and then a faint but widening path, along which he stumbled in the beautiful, white-filling woods, half not believing that it led anywhere but into a new maze, till his numb toe sent tumbling a pile of frozen horse droppings, and he understood with humbled heart that survival was not, had never been, the main question.

HE WAS DRINKING hot tea with whiskey, his face red-scarred and swollen, when Arthur came in, a bit slow on the uptake. "Where've you been?" said he. "It was an appalling party. We missed you. For Heaven's sake!" he cried at second glance. "What has happened to you?"

"Well . . ." Gregory began, and laughed with sheepish rue. "What was appalling?"

Arthur groaned and shook his head. "Everything," he said.

"Oh, well, now, I'm sure it couldn't have been *all* bad," Gregory said with a wince of his usual deprecating smile.

The phone rang. "Yes," Arthur answered, eyes starting at Gregory. "Yes. Yes. Yes, he is," and held out the phone. "It's Miles," he said.

UNDER A BRIGHT, still sky, Julian was veering unsteadily home from Nicky Heldahl's exhilarated party. The rogue low had passed with such suddenness that its regaling powers had increased in its wake. By now the snow had blown from sidewalk and street, and the constellations of the Northern Hemisphere again could be seen limning their myths in the ever-receding eons.

Julian was taken by the sight of Baxter's hands and face, grateful for the conversation's adhesion to the vastly distracting subject of Miles. He poured himself a glass of milk and sat down, got up at once, put some bourbon in it, and sat down again, eyes wandering about, mouth open.

Gregory said, "All in all he sounded in reasonably good spirits. He said he'd been around the world, more or less. He's staying with friends in New York. Of course he was devastated to hear of Selwyn's death, but naturally I started with his reunion with Gustave, so perhaps the news was buffered a bit. He promised us a visit in the near future."

"Old home week," Arthur said.

25

MAKE BELIEVE

JULIAN'S TUMOR REQUIRED extensive cutting—a messy, troublous procedure—but brought no surprises, no complications, only pain and stiffness afterward. He could hardly lift his right arm, but his wrist and fingers were still mobile. He thought, *I'll raise the canvas. Or I'll sit.* At moments he admired his calm acceptance of whatever might come. For every apple a worm, for every worm an apple, he mocked himself, with parallel and paradox fought fear and rested, hoarding his strength, thinking day and night of his great painting of death.

Lab work confirmed the worst, that malignant cells had entered his lymph and blood. In the nick of time, his name was added to a just-starting, experimental protocol with IL-2. Arthur made him a fine dinner, hiding his fears behind his most majestic courtliness, and Gregory discoursed practically without pause on recent medical advances on all fronts.

Julian drank a lot of wine and that night ecstatically dreamed he had found a love, just his own age, wondrous of beauty, mind and heart—perfect happiness, joy of limitless possibility flooded his psyche like a green sea—then unbelievably at once somehow Julian began to lose him, why, or to whom or what he could not conceive, nor would the fading phantom explain itself, no matter how Julian stretched out his arms and begged, nor speak one last word of benediction to him across their misty, widening abyss, nor lift a hand in farewell, but only stared with the hollow eyes of a marble bust. Desolation worse than death attended their sundering till Julian was briefly bewildered into appeasement by recognition of his love's bitter grief of betrayal. Then, with a terrible, slow sweep of his black-draped arm the young god hid his face away, and in the blank of memory Julian saw that it was himself.

As he had feared, the business of cure took from his work, collapsed his time of fantasy. What could death look like? What could he make it look like? In fury one day he wanted to squeeze out all his paint tubes on his palate in one high-piled coil, mix it, knead it like dough, shut his eyes, bow and paint with his forehead pure what? "One for the post posts," he thought. By dint of brute labor and desperate endurance of pain, he did at least a black and white canvas of a ghostly graveyard of penile tombstones all alike, signed *Why Why?*

"You're getting into words," Nicky observed. He was stunned by Julian's cancer, so like a nightmare, so inconceivable. Even before the terrible news, he had already faced the fact that he was in his worst plunge yet toward bottomless disintegration, the joyous tidings of his party having vanished in the hangover that had never quite abated, but seemed to worsen in recurrence, whether he drank or not—and now *this*.

Gregory was greyed and casual, provided rides to Boston, talked nonstop, expressed confidence in every avenue of escape, every possibility of hope, grew more certain of remission as the chances narrowed toward nil, obstinate earnestness Julian took heart from, not caring to wonder whether Gregory believed himself.

Julian's initial incredulity that exactly what he had striven to avoid had actually occurred, and so soon—was it soon? he could not tell—faded before the nauseating knowledge that death commonly proceeded from melanoma once metastasized. Assailed in his gorge, he tried to fix his mind on his one exit from agony, but terror exhausted him to sleep, and then he had to wake again, older, sicker.

Baxter could not rise from his chair, gazing at his useless books with blurred vision. He had begun to think of his library as a bequest to Julian, as well as the house to contain it—the light-filled upstairs with walls demolished would make a beautiful studio, with its view of Long Point, and just down the grassy lane a line of three huge oaks, last of the original trees of the place—and might not Julian have become in time a faithful gardener and guardian of his tulips?

Of Gregory's misadventure in the dunes Baxter thought—had it been him—he would have preferred to become bones among greenbriers than live this final futility. Steeped in the highest art, familiar of the noblest thought or felt throughout the ages, his scaffold of imagination peopled with valor, calm, and wisdom, he was powerless to seek more than an outward grace. Life was the only truth, the only value—and too little or too much of that.

Arthur raged all night at inhuman unmeaning, by day put off calling Nelson Ryder in London, unwilling to speak of Julian and Baxter in one breath, wondering if The Maid should act as hospice, not an easy project in economics, but not impossible. He had saved plenty of money. What was he going to do with it? There was nothing he wanted, nowhere he wanted to go.

The news like a hammer smashed Madbury's carapace of suspicion, which splintered like icicle glitters on a infinite vista of portentousness, unmasking Julian—who had hardly spoken a word to him lately, never!—as party to some common league to keep him in the dark about what had been going on all along. Each accomplice of each accomplice of all. Every snatch of coded talk left its fossil tracks. Gregory's incrimination lay in his secret disposal of the half-brothers' ashes—DNA forever gone—but the red evidence that persisted on his hands and face was guilt exemplified, sly, disingenuous, unwitting at best, and he sat and stared, lips one tight line, eyes darting like a cornered rodent's, pressing now one, now another, numb fingertip to his chin, theories exfoliating as he conceived them, more and more complex and estranging.

Nicky put an arm around him with concern one day, but Madbury shook him off.

Bright had an awful foreboding that Julian would slip away like Charles Cahill before he could ever make real contact with him, learn what it was that made some people indifferent to the world, and thereby free.

Recuperating, Julian tried to think, but his concentration failed except for exalting flashes of his painting, Death, which came and went, leaving not a trace. No Prick of the World could suffice. He must paint something completely else, something beyond the human. He must paint death, but death did not exist, as a girl had stopped to tell him on the street. Death was a negative of adverse conditions, she said, and proposed a course of healing through creativity. Of all people, she said severely, he ought to be aware of such resources.

He broke his silence to tell her that prophecy was his métier, medicine was for mere doctors, but she backed away shaking her head. Another day when Arthur was out a busybody came, and gave Julian words on diet, urine drinking, the need to love his cancer, which belonged to the larger tissue of things, with rights and interests of its own, and no more wanted to die than he did. He must guide and give it something else to eat, spiritual sustenance of some sort it seemed, something to tide it over a long hibernation, though the man could not say very precisely how to proceed with that.

Another person told him that God never gives anyone more than he or she can bear.

This is fame, he thought, *people coming to your door.* He sat in his studio, eyes fixed on the big, blank, white square, upon which to his amazement dust could be detected. The week before his first chemo treatment in Boston a swelling appeared in his right armpit. Quick surgery added another work-impeding wound to the one he had yet to overcome. *If need be,* he thought, *I will learn the left hand,* but his heart for the first time quailed.

The chemo, started a week behind schedule, in itself was not so bad as he had feared, not at first, but circumstance began to crowd and harry him. He felt sick and weak, and the general concern of friends that had always fostered him in Provincetown, suddenly gave their claims on him, till now kept at bay by his own casual disregard of them, a gravity less and less to be resisted.

Retrospects ravaged him. To lose his life—all possibilities made null—to have nothing to repent or regret, made him wish for what? At times he did not know; he could not even be sorry; amid the billions it didn't matter; it could only matter to him, who must always be surmounted. This roll of canvas, this particular square perhaps, was his end, unless the interleukin worked, stimulated the proliferation of lymphokine activated killer cells (LAK) that spurred the growth of tumor infiltrating lymphocytes (TIL).

Isolated, treated with IL-2, then returned to the patient, TIL are much more deadly to melanoma than LAK cells.

Greek to Julian. This rot spread like fungi in rain, ate like piranhas, killed host, died thereby.

"Like the human race on the planet earth," Madbury said, for the first time linking God with death, the churches His cover, their sermonizers His double agents and apologists.

Julian's mother phoned to say she was back from Tucson and now unexpectedly—he did not quite catch why—was off to Hong Kong. "While it lasts," she said.

Summoned from his studio, loath to speak, he wished her bon voyage, went back, sat on his stool, and re-submerged himself in astonished pride at his paintings, till now—in light of their sequels never to come—so casually disesteemed in his own eyes, done without forethought, intention or knowledge. But what had felt like travail at the time now seemed to have occurred without effort, simply something that had happened to him, beyond his control.

Now he must paint with purposeful totality, and paint fast. Now, Now, Now, throbbed like heartbeats in his ear.

"Did you know you have a disciple?" breathless Nicky asked one day. "Have you seen Alden Allen's show? He's painting pricks. Whole palisades of them. Even more garish than yours. A bit minimalist though. They don't have your je ne sais quoi."

Julian's fleeting head-shake of awe dislodged a cough. At night he had trouble breathing. He did little these days but rest and be driven to Boston and back by Gregory, and submit to x-rays and blood tests, with more and more discouraging results. The megadoses of interleukin demolished his strength, despair sapped his will.

A new tumor on his coccyx made it hard to sit. Hope was almost certain that it could be shrunk through radiation, even destroyed, treatment, he inferred, solely palliative. At Beth Israel, in a white johnnie, indistinguishable from others, he retained no personal qualities nor repute—no longer his small world's pampered favorite—became a nobody and an everybody both, a name and face to medicoes hardly older than himself, finely shaven, gravely heedful, faint breaths sweet, voices upbeat and matter-of-fact, adepts of a vernacular that sequestered, until he shut his eyes in bed, its unspeakable night-blooms.

None of them, however pressed, would estimate how long he might live, nor even how long keep on his feet. These things could not be foreseen; there were too many variables, first among them his will to live, next remission. Ultimate prognostications bore an aura of wrong, of blasphemy in their profession. The disease might at least be staved off, who knew for how long? There were cases, reversals that doctors could not explain, nor claim credit for. The important thing was never to give up, never forget the infinite preciousness of existence. He might yet live to get his embolism or lightning bolt. Like sleepless sentinels they never lost sight of this indivisible span of eternity, and he hated to be their defeat.

But he knew no help would come, or half knew, had always known. Here was the fate he had feared—heralded by his father's defection—from which he must not shrink, good luck he now recognized, so early to have glimpsed the human transience. Ever since that first lesion with its witness of mortality he had with growing concentration tried, by vigilance and care, by projection of his paintings into the future, to keep himself safe, but he had missed the one affected of the two little sites beyond reach of his eyes in the exactly facing mirrors of his solitude. It was all simply bad luck, lacking even the solace of self-blame.

His boyhood intuition, that in extremity matter was subject to mind, had never lapsed, and he resolved to kill his cancer by force of will, though he did not voice this last, strongest of hopes.

"Whatever the outcome," his youngest oncologist said, "you can take satisfaction in having been of use. Others will benefit. You are doing your part for the human future. Progress is made of a million small steps, endless sacrifice, age built on age."

"I didn't know you were a painter," another said. "My wife does watercolors, when she has the chance. It must be nice down in P-town right now."

Exhausted by loathsome combat with his armies of enemies, the voracious cancer cells in their brainless frenzy of increase, he would take refuge in the featureless image of forever. There he could rest but briefly. Sometimes his redoubled efforts seemed to carry him beyond his body entirely, compact to a diamond point of light slaughtering the ever massing malignancies, which still proliferated so fast at moments he heard their hideous yells. The struggle battered his heart, melted his flesh, knotted his muscles from head to toe, aged his psyche, so far as he could tell to no avail. All the same, at intervals, he realized that he was not going to die for a long, long time yet, a time perfectly adequate to his needs, if only barely.

April blew in with sudden warmth and distended length of day. One week the blackened sunflower heads still bowed above the winter stalks in Mrs. Silva's garden, next the year's debris was raked, the earth manured and tilled, its borders gay with crocuses and daffodils. Fat robins, harsh mockingbird and jay, paired cardinals flew, sparrows hopped about the stolid pigeons. The wind and sky, the jostling grackles in the eaves, thrilled the eye, and the weekend streets teemed with glad cries, embraces of renewal.

"To have no personal hope is one thing," Baxter had said . . . when? a year ago? "But to have no hope at all is another. And anyway," he had gone on, "if you think how exceedingly good everything can be, which no one will deny," he swept his hand about, "then think how bad they are elsewhere or even here tomorrow. There are no certainties. One may be glad or sorry, but not surprised."

Gregory had quoted Adam as saying—when? Julian could not remember that either—"When all hope is lost is when you must hope the most."

Arthur had glumly coughed aside at that.

Julian's irreligious nature could not distinguish. From agony of loss, from hatred of the ruin now spread to his liver, lungs, and spleen, from changeless news of doom, from intimations of nothingness, he turned to thought of beauty—what is it?—that most important question of all, the only question he now realized, and merely sat, breathing in and breathing out, looking at his blank canvas. Could this possibly be all he had lived for, merely to ask?

Oral morphine was losing its force. He wore indoors and out an oil company baseball cap with the bill cut off and sunglasses to spare and hide his eyes. Dizzy fevers burned and froze him, nausea clogged his esophagus. Headaches hammered, foul phlegm congested breath, legs no longer served at his behest, a dropped cane could be catastrophic, and the swelling of his brain brought visions of insects the size of the gigantic, short-faced bear, *Arctodus simus* —five feet high at shoulder, a ton in weight, with a vertical reach of fourteen feet—that kept humans off the North American continent for millennia till their kind died out, cause unknown. Only such-like marvels on TV and lime Life Savers gave him respite now.

He went for a walk one gorgeous day, and sat on Mrs. Silva's wall. He was not sure he could ever get up. Still, for a moment the sun was very pleasant. He thought, *This is what it feels like to be old —nothing to do and everything so stately.*

From her sink window, Mrs. Silva saw him sag sideways, then struggle like an old drunk to right himself. She dried her hands and went out. He had lost his hair but kept some flesh, thanks to steroids. Her repugnance at AIDS had turned in ten years to appalled pity as so many young tenants of hers and her neighbors withered and died.

"Are you all right, dear?" she said. She wore a kerchief to cover her thin hair, slippers with flattened heels and an old shift faded past pattern or color.

Julian nodded, mouth too dry to speak.

"Do you want me to call the rescue squad?" she said, and added to assure, "They'll come in a jif."

With slow effort Julian shook his head, then put out his white tongue and brought one finger near it with the air of an explorer hunting a way home from the North Pole.

Mrs. Silva hurriedly got him a glass of water. "Where do you live, dear?" she said.

"Here," he whispered. "I live here. At The Madam's Maid."

"Oh, I know, dear," she said. "You came two years ago. I remember when you moved in with Ida Gurley. I mean, where do you come from?"

Only a little while ago Julian would have been irked at the implied question of where he would be going back to; now he only wished she knew he was a painter, or least some day would hear of him, and recall this moment, and tell people she had met him.

"I don't come from anywhere," he said. "The place doesn't even have a name."

She could hardly hear him. "Don't talk," she said. "It's too nice of a day."

She leaned against the wall and companionably gazed off down the street with him, not seeing his face lit with sad beatitude, having never expected to feel at home anywhere.

Meditating God's mysterious ways, Mrs. Silva wanted to weep. No one knew why her husband had dropped dead at fifty-five twenty years ago any more than why these poor boys had to get sick and die. Why did God give most people to suffer, and some few to live high, good or bad no matter, no reason for either?

Julian made his aching, precarious way home, his unexpected diversion over. The next day he decided no more trips to Boston, no more anything but painkillers, remorseful at abandoning the doctors, especially as the protocol was not going well. He made the phone call before he told anyone.

Once done, he felt an instant inner relief and soon—absent chemo and radiation, car-cramp, nausea, days in bed—a physical resurgence. He felt almost well, had nothing more to fear, nothing to measure or weigh. He had now only to focus wholly on how to paint—if he could not defeat or escape—death. If he could do it, would that assuage? No matter, he knew. Only pride of act, of now.

Baxter took heart. He was feeling slightly better himself, with call now to remain strong and help Arthur through. His own affairs must wait.

Arthur finally phoned Nelson, who came at once, though Arthur insisted there was no immediate danger. Julian might yet get well, they agreed to agree in hanging up. Arthur answered the question of whether to tell him about Baxter's AIDs by forgetting it. The secret belonged to some future day, incumbent to ignore.

Nelson had left the film cannister of André's ashes out of his suitcase, and at the last moment in London had simply pocketed it, remembered it only when he got to The Maid, arriving by taxi in a fierce blaze of sun. Julian was out with Gregory.

"They went down to the wharf to look at fishing boats," Arthur said.

"What . . . ah," said Nelson, displaying the cannister, "did you do with the rest of André? I never got to Paris, of course."

Baxter suppressed his wish to tell, said. "He seems quite at home in his Taj Mahal. I suggest we scatter this little bit of him right here."

"Where?" said Nelson, startled.

Baxter pointed his nose at his toes. They were standing on Arthur's neglected back lawn; with a dry spring everything had lapsed here. Straw-like shafts of grass stuck up at crossed angles from little sand anthills, and strange weeds towered.

"Here," Baxter said. "Where better?"

"I don't want to step on him," Arthur said.

"No, no," said Baxter, "here," and taking an arm of each, drew them to the herb garden, no less withered than the lawn.

"I shall never eat again," said Arthur.

"In the name of this, that, and the other," Baxter intoned, guiding Nelson's hand, making Arthur at least affect to reach for the cannister, and the three together bent and spilled André's ashes on the ground. "You will eat wonderfully," he assured them.

"We will eat for André," Nelson said.

Arthur grimaced like a gargoyle.

Nelson seemed quite well, despite the occasion of his return. He was leaner than they had ever seen him, than he had ever been in all his life. He was very well dressed and looked contained, his last little fringe of hair around his ears shaved clean.

NICKY THOUGHT to get up a big show, a retrospective in truth, for though Julian had less than two years of work behind him, still he had done astoundingly many paintings.

But when Nicky broached the subject to him, he hardly seemed to hear, could be got only to shrug and shake his head, meaning what who could tell? Nicky went away baffled but determined to try again in a few days. He began to feel the weight of it, an obligation he almost felt.

Arthur worried that Julian ought to call his mother; he did not know how much she knew. Where was she? Had she even come home before sailing for Hong Kong? On what line? He had never met Edith Pelham, nor seen a photo, had only her cool, polite, brisk voice to sink him.

Arthur at least brought himself to ask if there were any paintings Julian wanted destroyed.

Julian thought briefly, shook his head.

Arthur was profoundly relieved, thankful, proud. After a moment he asked, "What would you like done with them?"

Seeming to marvel, Julian laughed.

"I'll keep them," Arthur said, "and do my best."

"Sell," Julian whispered. "Travel."

Arthur could not bring himself to mention remains.

Julian had forgotten his hill of white stones and golden moon.

HUMBER OVERHEARD talk of celebrity on the post office steps, lingered, pretended interest in his mail, hoping to hear his own name.

"He's great, eh?" a young man said. "Wouldn't you say he was great?"

"Perhaps not great," another answered thoughtfully. "I would say he was . . . perhaps . . . greatish."

"How old is he?" a third young man said.

"Seventy-five going on nineteen," said a fourth.

"He used to be quite the pretty boy," the third said.

"He didn't take care of himself," said the fourth, and they parted with somber good-byes, two east and two west.

Humber sustained the recognition that whatever Julian's stuff was, it was more than mere corny porn, and then he thought of a genial variant of his own, a way to mute the boy's brute frontality and moderate his exclusive, all-inclusive genital obsession. Awed, exalted by the tragic injustice of chance, he strolled slowly homeward to tell his wife, shocked and grieved—if gratified—that his first impression of the boy had so soon proved true.

REEF, WHO HATED fashion and false art, and despised those who were taken in by them, wittingly or not, was greatly vexed— and pained, having met the man—for he had felt no need to assess Esmeralda's accomplishment, if any, at such an early stage of his career. He was of several minds about these pricks, and had put the matter into his wait and see pudding, along with Ashingham's inexhaustible tome. On that conundrum he was still awaiting Coughlan Dice's thoughts, but Coffee had been slow, even to turn the first page, and now had gone back to cooking at Franco's. He seemed to read at the rate he wrote his never finished book, and required ponderous ruminations before voicing judgment on anything connected with the arts or life itself or—come to think —anything at all! What *was* it with him?

BRIGHT CAME TO SEE Julian at the Maid, fearfully. He did not know what to say. He could only think that Charles Cahill would have made some saving joke. Finally, after miserable evasions of his one question, *How do you feel?* he blurted, "Sean Costello died."

Julian met his terrorized eyes, and seemed briefly to take stock.

"And Wilfred Nome," Gil added, helpless with anguish.

Julian lowered his eyelids like an idol. The name meant nothing to him. Then he remembered something about someone named Wiffy who had spent all his money on a cat that died anyway. Julian looked better than he had of late, unmoved, untouched in soul, unafraid, absent as always. Bright went away amazed and relieved, eager to come again.

GREGORY PRIED from Arthur the state of Baxter's health, and put off his departure. He said to Arthur, "I think it would be best if I rented The Maid for the duration. Without hoping that it will be long or short," he added.

Arthur was amenable, though he had misgivings, felt the world tilting, things slipping out of his control. "General Gibbons," he muttered, but gratefully.

MILES ARRIVED UNANNOUNCED. Julian thought him no less handsome than described, but there was no one he could say this to. Selwyn had been alive only a little while ago, and Gustave too: now they were not. He only wished Miles would go to the Gnu Gallery and see his paintings, but he was too proud and diffident to speak. Miles wonderingly swept his eyes once across the purple and gold Imperial Penis above Arthur's mantlepiece, then turned his attention to Julian's personal well-being.

Late Friday afternoon of Memorial Day weekend, Miles and Nelson took Julian out for a spin in his wheelchair. It was another beautiful day. They rolled him down the middle of Commercial Street with miraculously few run-ins with cars. People were sitting shirtless on the post office steps, Marine Specialties was open. The Back Room was empty but getting ready. They rolled him across the dance floor and out to the swimming pool, unused since fall. The water was placid as glass. The awnings were new, the deck chair cushions refurbished.

A young man in shorts on a ladder was stringing lights around the balconies and balustrades. A paint-streaked radio on the bar blared pop music. He climbed down with welcomes and got bottles of beer for Miles and Nelson, and a Coke for Julian in a large plastic cup, no ice, which he sipped, looking through the chain-link fence to Long Point, grateful for physical stillness.

Song segued into traffic. "It's on the way," cried a gleeful disk-jockey, dire voice rising. "We have reports of cars all the way back to the Plymouth turnoff. They're just reaching the bridge. It's solid cars all the way back, they're on the way."

The young man put down his paint brush and grinned. "Don't you just love it!" he said.

Nelson and Miles, on their second beer, could not subdue their exuberance, their eager accord of praise for the weather, though notes of constraint at moments struck through. How splendid they were! Julian thought. Why could he not have lived long enough to be like them?

Julian had never gone in the water, or walked in the dunes. He had never done anything. He had gone from acrylics to oils early on, and that was all. He had never tried watercolors. Never touched clay. Nor bothered with pencil or pen. Nor known love, never mind all the men who had made him shake. He pushed the notion impatiently aside, like some fable of a primitive country he had sailed past without anchoring to go ashore.

"Look!" Nelson pointed.

Across Long Point, on the ocean side, the top of an inbound

sail ran parallel to the spit, the white triangle moving like a play-thing on a set.

"Must have been a common sight," the young man said, "a hundred years ago."

"Like a million moths," Nelson said to Julian, who saw a forest of furled sails useless to paint.

ARTHUR ET AL. were sitting on the steps when they got back. Everyone made much of Julian, got him settled like an Indian in a blanket, accepting of his silence.

Gregory spied a dandelion gone to seed in the middle of the awful lawn. Belatedly all registered that he had put down his drink and stood up, paused like a statue to outwait notice, then stepped silently forth, and using both hands dead-headed it with meticulous, almost furtive care, was now bearing it on tiptoe before him, shielding it with the other hand, like an imperiled flame.

"Don't bother yourself," Arthur said sharply.

Gregory grinned, rueful and abashed, but kept on making toward the trash bin.

"He really thinks it matters! What a joke!" Madbury crowed. "This is all make-believe."

"It is in perfect earnest," Baxter retorted.

Gregory turned, reasonable and benign. "Every ounce of prevention helps. I wasn't doing anything terribly important at the moment, and I just thought I'd take care of this before . . ." His distraction caused the ripe globe of seeds with their sails of fluff to disintegrate and drop in fragments or float off as he hurried faster, bent at knees and waist to reduce the shock of his locomotion.

Madbury said, "This is the weirdest thing I ever saw."

Arthur shook his head to himself. "Thank you," he said with dry remove when Gregory, grinning with impenitence, returned and retrieved his glass, possessed at least of partial success, some of the seeds having been diverted to driveway or neighboring properties.

Wearing only a pair of soccer shorts, taking no towel, Miles went and came back from a swim—one plunge, one fast lap and out. He was tanned, graceful, and strong. For all the others but Gregory the water hardly existed, and Miles was duly marveled at and admired. When he came down from his shower, Gregory resumed his assiduous, encyclopedic quizzing of everywhere his travels had led, everything he had done and seen, everyone he had met, everything he had heard, thought and felt.

Sunk in his blanket, full of the day's events, Julian bit bitter remorse.

26

REST IN THE MYSTERY

BAXTER WENT to see him three days later—a little way, a long walk for him now. They sat on the porch beneath the talisman and looked out at the radiant spring. Ecstatic birds flittered and swooped. White cat kept low, eyes cast up like a flounder.

Julian had the advantage of unformed thoughts and no knowledge beyond the little Baxter and Arthur had been able to instill. "What do you think happens?" he asked. "Afterward."

Whether Julian knew Baxter was dying Baxter didn't ask, nor mention his intended bequest. He said, "I'm a materialist, though there are phenomena we still don't understand, ghosts for instance, telepathy, divining, lost abilities of the primitive. What do we know about the universe? Ours may be a speck in a speck too much larger to notice ours in a larger speck yet ad infinitum. It is said one would get bored with immortality. Some say there are other lives, past and future both. Perhaps so. I am a bit done with it all myself, but I know you are not. You had much to do. It grieves me more than I can say."

Julian's eyes met his for a moment, shied away.

"Why should we live on? Who needs us? God?" Baxter said.

"What has death to do with you? Or you with death? There is nothing to fear."

Julian lowered his eyelids, sat in the red vacancy of his level voice.

Baxter mused to himself, "Science is not a science. Nothing is what it needs to be, not even nature." With unstaunched tears, caressing Julian's hand, which squeezed back once and lay still, he meditated aloud a while, and went home, sickened with himself before he had gone halfway, too feeble to turn back and somehow rise to high esprit.

Julian ate no more, too weak for anything but water. The dreadful shrill of the juicer came no more. He sank to salvage of the lost. Blank canvases in his studio leaned together, staggered against one wall, gessoed bright. They shone in his mind's eye like mirrors behind mirrors.

He rarely looked out the windows. It was in his lungs and liver. He was left with self-mockery—Michaelangelo, Leonardo, Donatello, Picasso, Esmeraldo!—and unbearable bowel miseries, stabs that made him jerk and squeak, humiliation of helplessness, foulness of dissolution.

"I can't even stand up," he said to Bright, breaking him from his day's dream of Charles Cahill, whom Bright had never had to see at a loss.

Arthur continued remiss; a mother after all was a son's responsibility, and who knew what Julian wanted? He had said little about his life before Provincetown, only that his mother was mad, his father probably dead, having never communicated with them.

"Nobody knows anything about anybody around here," Nicky lamented.

"That's why people come," Weeming said. "Half the people here are on the run."

"From what?" Madbury muttered.

"From up there," Gil said, jerking a thumb at the ceiling, at everything up beyond the bridge.

"I know I am," Nicky said. "Who wouldn't if they could?"

"Believe it or not . . ." Arthur began, but didn't bother to finish.

IN BED THAT NIGHT, Baxter dreamed of suffocation, woke to find he could not move his left arm, knew at once he had had a stroke. Otherwise he felt not much harmed, only heavy and inert. He thought of Dr. Johnson, waking in a similar state, testing his faculties by making a prayer in Latin verses. Baxter's mind seemed clear as well, though he had no Latin, no verses, nor prayer. Indeed he had a sense of relinquishment, summons to indifference. Perhaps he would be absolved after all, his problem solve itself. His parents would have to cope; they were old enough; he himself was old enough to have passed some saving mark. After his life of deference, he would have to come first. All he need do was outlive Julian, for Arthur's sake. Then, if nature failed to provide a timely coup de grace, he would call his parents, admit that he had not been feeling quite himself lately, mention his gratitude for their grand examples of gallantry, send Madbury to Boston on some errand, in his heart beg pardon of his ancestors for amounting to nothing and letting their line lapse, take Scotch and sleeping pills, let cause of death show what it might. At last he was old enough for everything.

The next morning Madbury on his way to the A&P left him at The Maid. Once sat down with unfamiliar awkwardness, he received from Arthur a cup of coffee, but had trouble managing the cup with one hand.

"What is the matter with you?" Arthur said.

Baxter told him that it was nothing to speak of.

"My dear man," Arthur said. After a moment he said, "Perhaps you should stay here for a few days where . . ."

"That won't be necessary," Baxter said. He had come to make amends to Julian for his disgraceful visit, but Julian was asleep, and Madbury returned before he woke.

Baxter came again the next day, his speech impeded. Madbury in silence sat with Arthur in the kitchen, returning Arthur's pure disdain. He felt coldly detached from the fall of the old ultimatum. Julian was always so vague about everything. All he was was questions, and not even them any more. He did not care much for Julian, or anyone. Julian was a hypocrite, a schemer, and a sham.

Baxter said, "I am going to read you Shakespeare's last play, *The Tempest*. Scene One. On Board a Ship at Sea. Thunder and Lightning."

He skipped at once to Prospero's first speeches to Miranda.

Julian listened with apparent interest, soon closed his eyes. Baxter called for Madbury to help him up, but Arthur fiercely crowded him aside and walked Baxter down the steps and lifted him into the car, light as a child.

THE COMPATRIOTS of The Maid first sought to disguise— then avoid conceding—start of the deathwatch.

In an oxygen mask, Julian dismissed death, banished regret, held his ground, strove to conceive the paintings he might have done, climb the heights, breathe the pure air, experience the ecstasy of making masterpieces, reach in mind at least his utmost consummation of possibility, but he was too tired, too weak, and to his amazement merely dreamed of things forsworn.

One day he had an episode of some sort, followed by loud irregularity of breathing, wandered when he spoke, or made faces of revulsion. "Will you get that thing away from me!" he cried in anger at the unmovable, invasive mass pressing against his right thigh.

Arthur finally realized it was Julian's hand that he meant. In fright he succeeded in getting in touch with Mrs. Pelham's attorney, who sounded old, a family friend otherwise long retired. He would try, he piped with imperturbable precision—as if it were an uncertain undertaking, and he took a dim view of outcomes in general—to locate her. She might be on the high seas. Should the boy be brought home to die? Should Mrs. Pelham go straight there?

"Have her call," Arthur said. "At once."

JULIAN LAY ON a hospital bed where the couch had been, where the talisman had been hung when Arthur first moved in. Feebly he still fought upward, marveled at the wealth of sight, fell back blind, struggled without hope, without hope of hope, to hold all that he ever was for one whole moment, rose and fell back, rose again and fell back, rose and fell, till up and down were gone.

His friends attended in sleepless limbo, intermittently watching with indifferent incomprehension the gathering crowds in Tiananmen Square; the muted commentators never smiled.

In agony Julian could not understand why, now that he was in

Rest in the Mystery

need, no one would do anything for him, cared no more than blurred words, wet cloths, drops of ice.

Physical sensation failed. He felt too light to die.

He asked, "What time is it?"

Arthur told him it was noon.

Julian seemed confirmed.

Arthur was alone with him when he died.

He sat with bowed head. On the silent TV a ponderous column of tanks was trying to get by a young man in a white shirt, who kept moving to stand in its way.

Outside was a beautiful day.

ON ANOTHER beautiful day they gathered again.

Julian was at the mortuary. His mother was expected momentarily. She had called from Hyannis.

Nelson sat upright in his new tweed jacket, hands on his knees, determined to be worthy of the occasion.

Gregory's smile blazed with unflagging, tragic joy that transfigured each as long as he could bear to look, and each clandestine glance back still seemed to re-illumine the room.

"The Immaculate Infection," Madbury muttered. He realized that Julian, a trick playing angel, of course had died of AIDS, the truth concealed by the others for reasons of their united front against him. The one time he had broached the notion of HIV— to an unbiased observer, unless they had got to him first—the squinting nurse had simply given him a macht nichts tilt of the head, and gone about his ministry. Thereafter Madbury had held his tongue, swearing never again to forget that he was alone.

"He belongs to the ages now," Nicky said. "I mean we won't." Too grieved to drink since Julian's death, he had begun to resolve to climb out of his abyss, once and for all, before it was too late, which made him feel clear, strong, and generous. He vowed to visit Chad as soon as chance offered. In its lack of urgency he saw the karma of right. Julian had died overnight practically, but Chad at his rate would probably go on forever: there would be time for everything.

All glanced at him except Baxter who gazed at the floor.

"I mean art lives on," Nicky explained, seeing in Julian's death his own birth as a writer. Otherwise he would never have dreamt of such a thing, much less have been motivated and brave enough to try. Without alcohol he could do anything. He never could draw, had no patience for paint, and only a bit more for postcard collage, but he could and would write a monograph, a close friend's bird's-eye view of Julian's short life and many works to prove that all is understood too late, that lessons learned have no use, their relevance never repeated.

"He was a fad unto himself, I'll say that," Madbury said. "Was that stuff really art? I don't mean to be . . . you know . . . But I mean, if you call something art does that make it art?"

"In its time perhaps," Baxter said.

"He belongs to us at least," Nelson said.

"And that's enough," Gregory said.

Miles, who had more or less assumed Julian's place at The Maid, suddenly noticed that Nelson Ryder looked like a Buddhist monk, felt all the more guilt-sick at having abandoned Selwyn, forgiving of Rick and Gavin Daly.

"He belongs to his mother," Arthur stated with pity piled on dread. Might she not say, *You lost me my son. How could you?*

"That's right," Madbury said. "You can never get away from your ma."

"What's going to happen to the paintings?" Gil asked. He had come alone, Weems having decided to forgo all variations of wakes and celebrate people's lives in his own way. They were back together again, extravagantly thankful and pleased with each other, frightened by what had almost happened to them. How had that all come about?

"They're mine," Arthur said. "He gave them to me."

"He made a will?" Madbury said, dumfounded. "They're his mother's, aren't they?"

Arthur looked resolute, said nothing.

"What do you plan to do with them?" Gregory inquired.

"I'm going to sell them," Arthur said.

All looked at him in disbelief, except Baxter whose eyes wandered the floor.

"Yard sale," said Madbury.

"He told me to," Arthur said. "Explicitly."

"I want one," Nicky said. "Actually I want several." He was exalted by thought of what he would write, after which he might do a whole book on some larger, general theme. For once he was in the catbird seat. And it occurred to him now, with amazed exhilaration, that his youth was really over, and his follies and pains with it. Well, good riddance. It was time—past time—to move on. And then he almost gasped at a terrible stab of loss, and his tears rained down for Julian, for all good and happy things gone.

"We must be patient," Arthur said, "and get all we can."

"We?" said Madbury. "Who's that?"

"It is going to AIDS," Arthur said.

"Didn't I tell you!" Madbury muttered to the self he called his partner in crime. "His mother may want them destroyed," he said aloud, "or think melanoma research is a better idea."

"AIDS would please him more," Gregory said, "very much more, I am sure," evoking hesitant murmurs and nods from all, even Madbury, who smirked with validation.

"He loved everybody," Nicky said. He meant not people exactly—for Julian had never showed anyone the slightest consideration—but a world of wide goodwill, just what he himself had always tried to promote, but he didn't explain, for fear of being laughed at.

Madbury suddenly understood what Julian had meant the time he had said that the only people he loved were dead. "Really!" he said with heavy sarcasm.

Gaunt Baxter glanced up at Arthur.

"Who knows," Arthur said, "what he might have done?"

Heels sounded on the walk, stopped for a moment. Then steps resumed, mounted to the porch and a woman's face appeared at the screen door.

All rose in haste, in woe, awkwardly—lopsided Baxter, who would have toppled had not Madbury, anxious-eyed, steadied him; Nelson Ryder, hands clasped before his groin, amazed that he had never told Chris he loved him; Nicky, backing back, hunched a little, hands in pockets, his corkscrew of hair alight with sun; Gil Bright, his half smile fleeting like Charles Cahill's; Miles, eyes unable to leave Nelson's profile; incandescent Gregory, trying to stand aside.

She peered within, saw looming obelisks, raised knuckles to knock.

Arthur stepped forward. "Mrs. Esmeralda?" he said. "Come in."

She heard the door click shut behind her, and seeing so many kindly, stricken, middle-aged and almost old men's faces, burst into tears.

Author's Note

Like so much of life the genesis of this book was unpremeditated, but once underway its trajectory was inevitable, its impetus omnipotent, its muse pitiless.

In my notebooks three random inklings had long languished, glimpses of stories about young men in Provincetown—a mother watches her teen-age son disappear in the summer crowds like a baby rabbit she had nursed as a child, then set free in the tall grass; a renegade sexual act begets the instant sale of a house; and a suicide attempt is countermanded by a domineering friend—mere particles, without plots, theme, or gravity.

Walking the street, thinking how desperately brief life is, how I would never get a chance to flesh out these poignancies, I said to myself, rather blithely, "Well, I'll string them together and reduce my numberless unwritten works by three." When I got home I sat down to give a week or a month to Julian Esmeralda's close race with time.

I thought it might run twenty pages, or thirty, but unknown persons, veterans, were waiting for Julian in Provincetown. Tenuous when met, figments of mock satire, they one by one grew whole, entombed in themselves, my kinsmen, for whom I weep, vital to me, if not to Julian, whose painter's blind eye was fixed on fame and something else, both more and less than human: The Prick of the World.

Each day, when I sat down to write, I never knew what would happen next, nor where it might lead, much less end, a mode opaque, at the mercy of instinct, contingency, and the kind of surprise that soon dies of its own innocence.

A sort of orphan and monomaniacal naif, Julian was soon wrested from me and adopted by the habitués of a guesthouse cum refuge from the plague, becomes its houseboy, pampered pet and remote idol, while he paints his phallic emblems of everything linear, his doting elders' edifying effect upon him far less than his upon them. His story finally is theirs.

In terrible times, when the absolute seems to rule, resolute character is all. At the mercy of unfledged imagination an artist may have small freedom, less power. But as George Kennan says, "If humanity is to have a hopeful future, there is no escape from the pre-eminent involvement and responsibility of the single human soul, in all its loneliness and frailty."